'Looking for breakneck pace and a relentless hero?
Alex Shaw has you covered'
James Swallow

'Alex Shaw is one of the best thriller writers around!
Fast paced, *Total Blackout* gripped from page one and
didn't let go … as fast as a Hollywood movie'
Stephen Leather

'Compelling and authentic. An explosive new series
with an uncompromising hero'
Tom Wood

'A perfect mix of hi-tech, high-concept modern action
thriller and old school, Cold War espionage where evil
Russians are still plotting the downfall of the West
and only one man can stop them'
Simon Toyne

'Jack Tate is a powerful character, a true Brit hero.
A cracking start to a new series!'
Alan McDermott

'Alex Shaw is a master of the action thriller.
Grabbed me from the first page and never let go'
Michael Ridpath

'Riveting thriller with an original plot and surprising twists.
Tate is totally convincing as a classic Brit operative.

D0186130

ALEX SHAW has lived and worked in Ukraine, the former USSR, the Middle East, and Africa. He is the author of the number one international Kindle bestselling Aidan Snow SAS thrillers. His writing has also been published in several thriller anthologies alongside international bestselling authors Stephen Leather and Matt Hilton. Alex, his wife and their two sons divide their time between Ukraine, England and Qatar.

🐦 @alexshawhetman
❑ /alex.shaw.982292
www.alexwshaw.co.uk

Also by Alex Shaw

Cold Blood
Cold Black
Cold East
Total Blackout

Total Fallout

ALEX SHAW

ONE PLACE. MANY STORIES

HQ
An imprint of HarperCollins*Publishers* Ltd
1 London Bridge Street
London SE1 9GF

www.harpercollins.co.uk

HarperCollins*Publishers*
1st Floor, Watermarque Building, Ringsend Road
Dublin 4, Ireland

This paperback edition 2021

This edition published in Great Britain by
HQ, an imprint of HarperCollins*Publishers* Ltd 2021

ISBN: 9780008412289

MIX
Paper from
responsible sources
FSC˚ C007454

This book is produced from independently certified FSC™ paper
to ensure responsible forest management.

For more information visit: www.harpercollins.co.uk/green

Printed and bound in Great Britain by
CPI Group (UK) Ltd, Melksham, SN12 6TR

*For my wife Galia, my sons Alexander and Jonathan,
and our family in England and Ukraine.*

Prologue

One year ago

Riyadh, Kingdom of Saudi Arabia

Outside the high marble walls, the desert was flat and featureless. An immaculate access road shimmered in the heat before it vanished into the far distance. Inside the walls, verdant green grass sparkled in the desert sun. Ornamental trees and flowers lined winding paths. In the heart of the compound was the main house, a three-floored modern interpretation of an Arabian palace. Chen Yan didn't like it.

She sat respectfully on the terrace, wearing a long, gold skirt and sipping black tea. By her side Kirill Vetrov, dressed in a light business suit, seemed totally unaffected by the stifling heat. Opposite, across a table laden with fresh fruit, sat the man they had come to see and his nephew.

'Maksim and I have known each other for many years,' their host said, a slight smile playing on his lips, 'and we have always conducted business face to face.'

Chen smiled. Men were the same the world over; they needed to be praised, honoured, coerced and tempted. 'Maksim offers his sincere apologies. Were it not for ill health he would be here, as he holds his friendship with you in the highest regard. That is why, as his trusted business partner, I am here on behalf of Blackline to discuss our proposal. What I am about to share with you has not and will not be shared with any other clients.'

The prince nodded his head for her to continue.

'The situation with your neighbour is obviously close to your heart. To have a family member not only turn their back on you but embrace a mutual enemy ...' The prince's eyes narrowed slightly. Yan continued. 'They have risen above their station. Their relationship with the Persians is a security and moral threat to the entire Arab brotherhood.'

'For a foreigner, you are well briefed, madame,' the prince said reaching for a sliver of pear in an attempt, Yan thought, to hide his annoyance.

This was shaky ground, and this was why Vetrov sat next to her as both her personal bodyguard and the focus of what she was about to expose. 'I understand certain measures have been taken to rein in the wayward ruler of your neighbouring state, but I would like to show you an example of the assistance we can provide to bring them to heel.'

The smile returned and the prince spread his palms. 'By all means.'

Vetrov reached into his attaché case, withdrew an iPad Pro and handed it to Yan. She brought up a video.

'Simply press the play icon.' The prince clicked his fingers and Salman Al Nayef, who had been sitting slightly behind his uncle, approached and took the device. He held it in front of the older royal, who retrieved a pair of frameless reading glasses from a pocket in his thobe and poked at the glass display screen with his finger.

His face took on a perplexed expression as he viewed the footage. 'This video I have seen. I am aware it was found on a mobile phone years after the bombing, and broadcast across all the world media a week ago. It is sad that a once great city was targeted but I am thankful that the noble *shahid* ended the immoral lives of so many non-believers.'

Yan nodded. 'He was indeed a noble *shahid*, and now he will be at peace in paradise.'

The prince took another sliver of fruit.

'Please be so kind as to swipe left and press play. If you could focus on the other individual in the footage, the figure who did not explode.'

Al Nayef set up the second video and pressed play. The elderly Saudi squinted, despite his glasses, and leant forward.

'Is this you I am seeing here, Mr Kirill?'

'Yes, Your Highness,' Vetrov replied, his tone emotionless. 'You are one of only a handful of people in the entire world to see the original footage.'

'Original?'

'Your Highness,' Yan now took over, 'this new footage, which the world has seen, and which the British authorities are now using to chase down the second bomber, is fake. It has been manipulated.'

The prince looked up at Al Nayef. 'Play it again.'

Yan kept a thin smile on her face as they watched the video. The old man looked up and spoke. 'They are absolutely identical with the exception of the man's face.'

'Quite so. We have used our unique technology to remove all trace of Mr Kirill and replace his face with that of a rogue operative, who will, once identified, become the sole focus of the British investigation into the bombing.'

'Uncle,' Al Nayef said, 'may I ask a question?'

'You may.'

'Ms Yan, how is it that your technology is so advanced it has not been detected?'

Yan was encouraged by his question because she believed the older royal did not fully understand the complexity and sophistication of this technology. 'That is the salient question, Your

Highness, and one that can be answered with a simple statement. We are the only people in the world who can achieve this.'

Al Nayef continued, 'This is a process and technology you have pioneered?'

'It is. We believe it will be at least five years until anyone else can achieve anything remotely rivalling this, and by that time we will be two generations ahead.'

'A powerful tool.'

'Nephew, it is not a tool,' the older Saudi said, suddenly understanding, 'it is a weapon.'

Chen nodded. 'It is, Your Royal Highness.'

'We would like to use this technology to aid our cause,' the older royal stated. 'Now let us discuss how.'

4

Chapter 1

Port Hercule, Monaco

Jack Tate's hair was long; so was his beard, and both itched. Wraparound sunglasses and a dark baseball cap obscured his face. The beard, shades and hat gave off the impression of someone attempting to not be seen, which was at odds with his loud Hawaiian shirt, red slacks and green Adidas trainers. Tate wasn't attempting to be hip, he was trying to look like someone else – Egor Blok – a Russian assassin held in a black site, at an undisclosed location in Eastern Europe. Blok had a lousy fashion sense, and on the circuit he was well known for it, as well as his recent spiralling gambling debts. Tate just knew he felt daft, but here in Monaco even the most outrageously dressed specimens blended in with the principality's gaudy, glitzy, glamorous *mise-en-scène*. Tate scratched his neck. The Mediterranean sun was starting to make him sweat.

In Monaco only the rich mattered, and to the rich only the super-rich mattered. Tate's target was one of the super-rich. To these people he was invisible and that was why he was hiding in plain sight, on a boat. Tate liked the water and he liked boats, but didn't know much about them. The one he was lounging in was a Tullio Abbate Soleil 35'. Which meant it had been made by

5

the Tullio Abbate shipyard and was 35 feet in length, but he only knew this from reading the sales advert for the vessel. When dressed as Blok, but using a different Russian ID, he'd bought it a week before, over the border in Italy. With its muscular lines, and a top speed of thirty-five knots, in most marinas it would be a flashy item. In Monaco it was a plaything.

Tate sipped water, not champagne, as he observed the procession of rich residents and bewildered tourists meandering along the promenade. To his right, the expanse of Port Hercule stretched into the bay. Powerboats, many larger than his, and small yachts, gave way to super-yachts bobbing gently in the sparkling Mediterranean waters on the sea-end pontoons. Further out, vessels too large to enter the port sat at anchor. These were the mega-yachts of the truly wealthy. In among all of this, regal-looking polished wooden tenders ferried their guests to and from the jetties.

Some, Tate imagined, found the principality the pinnacle of sophistication, but it didn't float his boat. He'd much rather be halfway up a mountain. Instead, he was team leader of a four-man E Squadron unit. One member of his team was dressed in scuba gear on a small launch out in the bay, another was parked up in a people carrier across the French border and the last was guarding the safe house in Nice.

Tate's mission was classified at the highest level because E Squadron's existence was an official state secret. Run by the Secret Intelligence Service, it was formed on an ad hoc mission basis from serving members of the Special Air Service, Special Boat Service, and the Special Reconnaissance Regiments of the British Army. But Tate was an anomaly. A new initiative had seen him transferred from the SAS and made the only permanent member of E Squadron. Two years later he was still alive and kicking in doors, which to him was a relief.

Tate sipped his water and kept "eyes on" his target, or the target's boat at least. But his weren't the only eyes scanning the marina. With approximately one policeman for every hundred residents and a CCTV system among the most extensive in the world, Monaco was friendly soil. But the target was also from a friendly nation and the attack would upset both of them. What would be completely unfriendly would be the response once the target's uncle realised his nephew, and aide-de-camp, had been murdered by a desperate Russian hitman. This was in addition to the loss of the sixteen million euro in diamonds he'd been transporting.

Due to the clandestine nature of the operation, Tate had decided against standard communication equipment, which if recovered could possibly imply the involvement of a nation state. Instead, each man had been issued with a Bluetooth earpiece and burner iPhone loaded with WhatsApp, for its "end-to-end encryption" ability and a VPN to add an extra onion skin of security.

Touching the button on his earpiece, Tate connected to Chris Salter, the SBS commando in the distant boat, as he moved to the helm. He spoke with a Russian accent, his words vague enough to hide his intention and his true nationality if overheard. 'Have you seen our friend yet?'

'I have eyes on. He's on deck, on schedule. They're preparing to come ashore. I count five. The target, two BGs and two crewmen. Target is dressed in cream slacks and a navy-blue shirt. They are lowering the tender.'

'Understood,' Tate stated. He turned the key in the boat's ignition and started the Soleil 35's twin Volvo Penta D4/300 engines. He cast off both the bow and stern lines, before pushing the throttle forward. With a mild whiff of diesel fumes he moved away from the mooring and started to navigate the route out into the bay.

'The tender is in the water,' Salter stated, over the open line. 'Stand by, stand by. They are in the tender. Moving ...'

Tate pulled off his Oakleys and raised a pair of field glasses to

7

his eyes. He focused on the mega-yacht's tender. One crew member was at the helm whilst the other made sure that the passengers were seated. Tate noted with relief that none of them were wearing life preservers. Moving his field glasses, Tate pulled focus and just made out the splash as Salter rolled backwards from his launch into the sea. He was ready.

As he cleared the port, Tate pushed the throttle forward and the prow of the Soleil 35' sat up. He leant down and pulled a black kit bag from under the table in the seating area next to him. It was open and from it he gingerly retrieved a stubby H&K G36c assault rifle and held it ready below the line of the gunwale. He took an inadvertent sidestep as the boat was momentarily buffeted by the waves when it left the port for the bay itself. Ahead Tate saw the tender bobbing gently by the giant stern of the mega-yacht.

Tate had rehearsed and refined the plan, and each of the E Squadron operators knew exactly what to do. As the tender moved away from the Saudi-owned mega-yacht, Tate approached it on a parallel course – still not a threat, just a plaything going out for a cruise. The distance between the two vessels closed. Tate could now make out the facial expressions of each man on board, the two crewmen in white polo shirts looking professionally relaxed; the two bodyguards in their tight-fitting suits, looking hot and uncomfortable; and the target who had now turned his head and was looking directly at him.

Tate waited until the last possible moment and then swung the Soleil 35' directly into the path of the oncoming tender and put the engines in full reverse. It was the nautical equivalent of an emergency stop and Tate's boat was now broadside on to the tender. He put the throttle back to idle.

The tender started to turn, taking evasive action, and then Tate swung the H&K up and sprayed the bow with 5.56mm rounds. The crew member at the helm ducked, but one of the two bodyguards was now on his feet, a pistol in his hands. Tate cursed as the last two rounds of his magazine hit the body-guard, catapulting him back into his seat. Tate changed magazines and acquired his target, the Saudi. The one remaining bodyguard was trying to shield the royal but he'd pushed him aside and bounded to his feet, as though he was outraged and demanding an explanation. The Saudi's left hand held the handle of an attaché case, which was chained to his wrist, whilst his right hand had formed a fist, which he was shaking. Tate sent a burst of rounds into the Saudi. The target cried out, stumbled to his left, toppled over the port side of the tender and plunged into the Mediterranean Sea.

'*Suka! Chort!*' Tate hollered in anger, in Russian, as he saw both man and case disappear below the surface of the water. Using his left hand, he opened up the throttles to full. The Soleil 35' reared up and powered away from the tender. Tate turned and, one-handed, emptied the rest of his magazine above the stern of the tender, to keep their heads down.

He now had to concentrate on his own exfiltration. He passed Salter's abandoned launch and headed south-west, the speed making the boat buck rhythmically as waves broke against it. He needed to put as much distance between him and the hit as possible. The entire attack had been so swift Tate's planning had calculated the local authorities would not have started to react yet.

But he was wrong.

A siren sounded behind him and Tate turned his head to see a patrol boat belonging to the Monaco Maritime and Heliport Police Division rounding the stern of the Saudi mega-yacht and ploughing after him. Tate swore again, this time in English. Where the boat had come from he didn't know, but he knew he had to get it to focus on him. Tate tapped his earpiece in the forlorn hope of speaking to Salter but when the call wasn't answered, it confirmed what he already knew: the SBS man was still under-water. He needed to buy Salter time to get back on his boat and away with his cargo. The cargo was the most important part of the mission; even Tate himself was expendable.

Tate could outrun the patrol boat, but much like a car chase it was what was further down the road he may run into that worried him. He assessed his options. If need be, he'd use the pair of grenades in his bag to scuttle the boat, and then he'd swim ashore – but he didn't want to risk being hunted like a drowned rat. Tate let the patrol boat inch closer, then he throttled back and came to an almost standstill, reached into his bag, and then in his best hackneyed acting gesticulated with his right arm to show his frustration with the engines. All the while, however, the engines were still running and his H&K was ready on his seat.

The larger vessel approached him, riding high on a bow wave. He could make out a man at the helm and a further two with automatic weapons slung across their chests. The military of Monaco was the third smallest in the world after those of Antigua and Barbuda, and Iceland, but that did not mean its men and women were untrained. Nevertheless, he imagined this was the most excitement they'd had for years, and he didn't trust their trigger fingers. A loudhailer blasted orders at him in clipped French: 'Turn off your engine! Raise your arms above your head!'

Tate had run out of time. He brought his two hands together, transferred what he was holding in his left to his right and pulled the pin. He counted, one … two … and then he hurled the grenade at the bow of the oncoming patrol boat.

As he'd calculated, the crew were too slow to react, and the grenade exploded ten feet ahead of the vessel, showering the rising bow with shrapnel. Immediately after the explosion he whipped up his H&K and poured rounds at the vessel.

Tate turned, grabbed hold of the wheel and pushed the throttle full ahead. The bow of the Soleil 35' shot skywards as it lurched forward. At the same time the police patrol boat veered to port.

The two vessels shot away from each other, as though Poseidon himself was separating them. There was a moment of silence, a moment of indecision from the police and then a barrage of shots rang out. Tate ducked, knowing that a lucky bullet was all that was needed, but also that the shots were being fired in an attempt to keep face rather than with any hope of stopping the fast-retreating target. Tate kept his focus forward as he ran parallel to the coast in a straight line. At maximum speed, within a minute he had left the police launch behind and a minute later had left Monaco and was off the coast of France.

He passed Cap d'Ail and headed directly for the marina at Beaulieu-sur-Mer. To the west the coastline alternated between jagged cliffs and sandy beaches. With the exception of a high-powered motorbike, which could cut through the traffic on the undulating, winding coast road, the Soleil 35' would beat any land-based vehicle to their destination, police included. Tate just hoped that there wasn't already a reception waiting for him.

Over the roar of the engine and the cadenced crashing of the waves against the hull, Tate now heard another pulsing sound, one that he didn't want to hear. He had company, uninvited company.

He looked back and studied the sky. A smudge of colour, coming from the direction of Monaco. A helicopter was on his tail. Tate couldn't yet make out what type it was, but he was no stranger to either abseiling out of one or being hunted by the same. His mind flicked back to the events of a year before in the US, when a Spetsnaz team in a modified GlobalRanger had forced him out of the sky. He slammed a fresh mag in the H&K, but defending himself on a bucking boat from a swooping chopper would be no easy thing; spray and pray would be the order of the day and he could not and would not lose any more time by slowing down to engage. He just hoped that if it came to it the pilot would care more about losing his life than losing his target.

Tate held the short assault rifle against his right leg to minimise its profile, and continued to motor. The helo was moving fast; it grew larger and then Tate relaxed. It was a civilian Eurocopter EC130. It swished past the boat, just above the height of the cliffs. His iPhone rang.

'I have the package,' Salter stated over the crashing of the waves.

'We have company. Monégasque patrol boat.'

'Have that. Am proceeding as planned.'

Tate ended the call.

He slowed the Soleil 35' as he started to approach Beaulieu-sur-Mer. The faster he motored the quicker he would be able to get ashore, but a slower approach would raise fewer French eyebrows. Tate scanned the shoreline with his binoculars. Apart from general pleasure craft he could see no official-looking vessels or watchers on the shore. Only now did he repack the H&K into the kit bag and zip it up. He woke up his iPhone and called the team driver. 'How are we?'

'All clear, Guvnor,' the SAS man growled back in deadpan Glaswegian.

'Police?'

'None.'

'ETA seven zero minutes.'

'Have that.'

Tate throttled back the twin Volvo engines further as he followed the channel to enter the marina. Unlike its counterpart in Monaco, which was protected from the sea by the curvature of the bay, the Beaulieu-sur-Mer marina and yacht club was fronted by a man-made breakwater. Eyes darting in every direction from behind his dark Oakleys, he entered the marina proper and immediately made a turn to starboard and motored past the pontoon-mounted *Total* petrol station to the first row of berths. This was where the largest of the vessels were moored, serious powerboats and cruisers.

Four berths in, there was a gap between two imposing vessels.

Tate took in the name of the largest. It had *"Princess 72"* printed on the side. The other was shrouded in a large cover and looked as though it hadn't been moved in a while. Both towered above his own boat and would provide some cover. He slowly backed the Soleil 35' into the berth, and cut the engine. Tate secured the boat and cast his eyes around the marina. This end was quiet, and there was no one obviously watching him, but that probably wouldn't last for long. Tate quickly scanned the boat's interior for spent shell cases. He found a handful, the rest having been ejected and whipped away into the sea, and put them back into his kit bag. He then removed a packet of alcohol wipes and started to rub down all the surfaces. After thrusting the used wipes into his kit bag, Tate then hefted it onto his shoulder and stepped off the Soleil 35' for the last time, making sure to leave the boat's keys in the ignition as an open invitation to any light-fingered passers-by. If it got stolen it would muddy the waters even further, and if not, the police would confirm that the boat had been bought and used by the known Russian hitman Egor Blok, or someone who looked very much like him.

Without pausing he leisurely followed the perimeter walkway towards the main entrance. In front of him the sun glinted off the white-walled villas of the town, and behind them rose mountainous hills like the jagged spine of some ancient beast.

Tate reached the main car park as a gunmetal grey Renault *Trafic SpaceClass* executive people carrier turned in from the coast road. Without looking at the office or the security box, Tate pulled back the sliding door and climbed inside.

'Crap here, isn't it?' James "Paddy" Fox's voice was gruff, guttural, Glaswegian and laced with sarcasm. 'Neither a stick of rock, nor a donkey to be seen.'

Tate rolled his eyes; he was used to the Glaswegian's dour humour. 'Any issues?'

'None.'

They left the marina complex and joined the one-way system,

which would enable them to drive out of town in the direction of their second rendezvous point. Both men had memorised the local area and knew the streets as well as any local taxi driver.

Tate opened his line again with Salter. 'ETA?'

'Five minutes,' Salter reported over the thundering of waves in the background.

The interior of the Renault fell silent for the next few minutes. The veteran SAS operative continuously scanned the road and his mirrors, whilst Tate sat by the door with his H&K at the ready. Stuck behind a slow-moving local bus on the narrow roads, their progress was slower than envisaged and by the time Fox pulled the Renault in next to the scooter parking area, overlooking Plage la Calanque, eight minutes had elapsed. Unwilling to leave the vehicle and visually tie himself with it, Tate sat with his eyes fixed on the path leading down to the beach. Another minute rolled past and despite the air con, Tate felt a wetness at his temples. He absentmindedly scratched his face with his left hand. Motorists passed them and such was the ubiquity of the vehicle's use as a taxi that even though it was illegally parked, no one paid them a second glance.

And then someone did.

'Plod,' Fox said.

'I see them.'

'It's bloody Laurel and Hardy!'

To their left a pair of police officers were strolling towards them. The first was shortish and rotund whilst his partner was gangly. At that exact same moment there was movement from the opposite direction, from the beach path. The broad-shouldered figure of Chris Salter appeared. He was wearing a cut-off scuba outfit, carrying a black holdall and ushering a thinner man towards the road. Tate impatiently watched them approach. The road was too narrow for the Renault to turn and they couldn't reverse against the oncoming traffic, not with a pair of advancing gendarmes. The only option Tate could see was to draw the policemen's attention away from the van and towards him. For the second time that afternoon he knew the mission was more important than he was.

'Change of plan,' Tate said. 'I'm going walkabout.'

Fox turned in his seat, a quizzical look on his craggy face. 'You sure?'

'No other option. You get to the safe house and I'll see you there.'

Minus his H&K and bag, Tate opened the sliding door of the executive Renault and stepped out. He'd know immediately if his description had been circulated. For the gendarmes to link him to the attack in Monaco was acceptable but Salter and the man he was accompanying had to get into the van. Tate shut the door, and swaying like a drunk, ambled in the direction of the policemen. After several steps he let himself slip off the kerb and stumble into the road. An oncoming car sounded its horn. Tate shouted in angry Russian and raised his middle finger. He stepped back onto the pavement and then pretended that he'd just registered the presence of the gendarmes.

'Good afternoon, gentlemen! Could you help me? I'm looking for an exciting place to drink!' Tate said, in Russian-accented English.

Both Frenchmen had scowls on their faces, disgust at dealing with a belligerent, drunk foreigner rather than fear or apprehension at confronting a violent suspect. So far so good.

The nearest of the two, the gangly one, spoke in French.

Tate shrugged.

The second officer took over, switching to English. 'Show me your ID.'

'ID?' Tate frowned, swayed.

'Passport. Papers. Documents.'

'Ah, I understand.' Tate slowly reached his right hand into the back pocket of his trousers. As he did so he turned his head just enough to see the door on the opposite side of the Renault open and the two men get in. Tate casually retrieved a wallet as the Renault drove past. 'I have these papers.'

The second officer grabbed the wallet and examined its contents. 'You have broken several laws: drunk in public, jaywalking and using obscene language.'

'Have I?' Tate shrugged, innocently. Perhaps he had, or perhaps this was a shakedown; either way it gave the rest of the team time to make good their escape.

'Yes, you have! There is a penalty for each of these offences.' The officer now had Tate's euros in one hand and the leather wallet in the other.

A wide smile formed under Tate's beard, and he nodded. 'Surely there is some financial accommodation that could be made? Could I pay a, how do you say it, "on-the-spot fine"?'

Laurel spoke in French to Hardy who nodded then addressed Tate. 'My colleague has informed me of the required fine. You have here enough to cover it.'

'That is good news.'

'It is.' Hardy handed him back the empty wallet.

There was a crackle of a radio transmission. Laurel frowned. He unclipped his radio with his left hand and spoke into it, in at first slow then progressively faster French. The fatter officer's eyes widened. A vehicle passed them, a seagull squawked overhead but other than this the only sound was the muffled voice on the other end of the radio, at police dispatch. Tate swayed slightly on the spot. As Laurel listened, his eyes narrowed and he took a step forward, shortening the distance between them. The man's right hand traversed towards his baton. He said something to his colleague.

With his left hand still full of euros, Hardy started to reach with his right for his baton. The time for talking was over. The two batons meant that this wasn't going to be a fair fight, and it couldn't be, because Tate would win that with ease. He had to be quick and he had to be fast and the two officers, who had suddenly been reminded of their real jobs, had to go down. Hard. Tate threw his empty wallet at the face of the first gendarme, stepped sideways and drove his elbow into the face of the second. Tate followed the elbow with a fist and the officer collapsed into the road. Turning on the spot, Tate kicked the first officer, who was still gawping at him, in the groin. A fist to the side of the head landed him next to his colleague. Tate booted the pair of them again, just to stop them from getting up, grabbed his wallet and his money, and sprinted away in the opposite direction to the van.

There were shocked faces and a yell of outrage from another pedestrian and a few cars beeped their horns as they went past, but no one attempted to stop him or to give chase. An elderly couple moved aside, both cringing as he ran by.

'That's another fine mess you've gotten me into,' Tate muttered to himself as he left the scene.

He knew the road layout and had agreed the route with Fox. Unless the van wasted time negotiating the one-way system again it would take the mini-roundabout and drive back past the two police officers. Tate ran up the street, towards the salmon-pink-walled Royal Riviera hotel on the corner. Now out of sight of the two gendarmes and anyone who had seen the altercation, he slowed to a walk. He pulled off his baggy shirt, exposing the white muscle vest he was wearing underneath, and balled it into his left hand.

Tate carried on up the Avenue Jean Monnet and paused at the access road for the Hotel Delcloy complex. A taxi entered with two passengers in the rear. He allowed himself now to glance back down the avenue before and saw the Renault round the corner. He let it pass him and carry on up the hill. His phone vibrated in his pocket.

'Last chance for a lift. There's a junction up ahead; I'll meet you after it on the left,' Fox stated.

'Negative,' Tate replied. 'Get to the safe house.'

'Aye.' He heard Fox audibly sigh. 'Have that.'

Tate ended the call.

Tate knew he wasn't going to blend in anywhere, and as long as the van wasn't linked to him, that was all that mattered. Confronting the gendarmes had been a dumb decision but his only play: it made him the sole target. He stayed where he was, hidden from direct view of the passing traffic, and waited for the taxi to re-emerge. He heard sirens scream down the hill. The now empty taxi reappeared.

Tate flagged it down and asked the driver to take him to the Hotel Negresco on Nice's Promenade des Anglais. The driver started to complain but a fifty-euro note made him change his mind.

Tate sat low in the back. The traffic become heavier as the taxi passed through the centre of Villefranche-sur-Mer and then entered the outskirts of Nice.

Forty minutes later Tate arrived back at the safe house. He'd covered his tracks by ducking in and out of the Hotel Negresco via different doors, and then taking a second taxi that dropped him two roads away from the safe house. He went through the large gates and up the gravel drive that led towards the villa.

The exterior walls were painted a pastel yellow and it was surrounded by a bright green lawn and palm trees.

Salter, now dressed in jeans and a dark T-shirt, secured the gates behind him. 'Fancied a bit of shopping, did we? Our guest is in the living room with Paddy.'

'Cheers.' Tate walked up the steps to the entrance of the villa. Inside the temperature was several degrees cooler, due in part to the high ceilings, white walls and white marble floor. Tate crossed the voluminous entrance hall and entered the living room. The space was sparsely furnished. One figure sat at a table whilst another stood at the far end, framed by the window.

'You're alive then?' Fox noted with mock surprise.

Tate shut the door and walked farther into the room. 'Just.'

The other man now stood and faced Tate. He was equally as tall as Fox but a lot narrower, and thirty years younger. 'This is the man who shot me!'

'It is,' Fox said, a slim smile forming on his face. The veteran SAS man had most recently been operating as a security adviser to several royal houses in the Middle East, whilst in fact being on the SIS payroll. It had been Fox who had recruited their guest as an SIS asset, suggested that he defect and set Tate's mission in progress.

'Paddy, you personally guaranteed my safety.' The man's accent was Oxbridge; in fact Tate thought he sounded more English than he did. 'Without your assurances I would not have agreed to this, but it is this man who made my escape possible.'

Tate took in the figure of His Royal Highness Salman bin Mohammad Al Nayef, the man they had been sent to extract, the man who had made a deal to pass on detailed information regarding his uncle's business and personal links to an alleged new terrorist threat. Al Nayef may well have been a member of Saudi Arabia's extended royal family, but he wasn't getting anything more than a "sir" from Tate. It was something the man needed to get used to. 'I'm happy you made it here in one piece.'

A broad smile appeared on Al Nayef's face. 'Did you see how I stood up, and waved my fist at you?'

'I did,' Tate said.

'It was something I saw in a film. It felt like the right thing to do.'

Tate humoured him. 'It was. You looked brave.'

Al Nayef shrugged and dipped his head, abashed like a teenager. 'Was I convincing?'

'Totally.'

'I practised.'

Tate frowned, concerned. 'Where was this? Did anyone see you?'

'No. No one saw me. I was on my own, in my cabin. I watched several Hollywood action films to study their technique.'

'Armchair warriors are the most dangerous,' Fox said.

Tate coughed back a laugh.

Al Nayef went on, 'And like a Hollywood film you used blanks in your gun, but it was highly realistic.'

'Extremely,' Tate agreed. In fact, his first and third magazines had been loaded with standard rounds; it was only the second that he had "shot" Al Nayef with that had contained blanks.

Al Nayef extended his hand to shake Tate's. 'All because of you I am here. You are a good man.'

'But his fashion sense is a bit shite,' Fox said.

Tate shook Al Nayef's hand. 'I'll leave you both to it.'

'Cheers, sonny,' Fox said, and winked.

Unlike everyone else, Tate still looked like an extra from *Miami Vice*. He shut the door and took the stairs to the first floor. Stage one of the mission was over, but it was far too soon to relax. The authorities in Monaco, France and neighbouring Italy would all by now be aware that an attack had taken place. Rescue boats would be searching for Al Nayef, or his body, and Tate's description of course had been circulated. Tate thought about Al Nayef. He'd seemed more excited than scared, as though it was an adventure and he wasn't running for his life, as though he'd not quite comprehended the seriousness of his situation.

Perhaps if he saw what Tate was about to do now, the true precariousness of the situation would hit him? But Tate knew Al Nayef must not see what was in the room he was about to enter.

Tate walked into the master bedroom and shut the door behind him. Plastic sheeting covered the room and reminded Tate of an episode of *Dexter*. A pile of crumpled, damp clothes lay on the floor. A naked male body was positioned squarely on a plastic sheet next to this. The corpse was intact with the exception of a missing lower jaw, but the face had been mutilated. Deep lacerations cut right across it; the nose was missing and the cheekbones broken. The dead man's unrecognisable face looked as though it had got in the way of a heavy ship's propeller.

A supply of surgical masks, gloves and white protective coveralls lay on the bed. Tate donned a set then moved to the corpse and dressed it with difficulty in Al Nayef's clothes.

Ten minutes later Tate stood back to admire his grotesque creation. This had once been someone's son, perhaps someone's brother, husband or father. An abrupt sense of remorse tightened his chest. He had once also been someone's son, and so had his brother but unlike the corpse before him they both lived whilst their parents did not. And the man who had murdered their parents – Ruslan Akulov – was still free. Tate felt his remorse turn to anger.

'Do we know who he was?' Fox said, as he appeared behind Tate, a cup of coffee in his hand.

Tate answered without looking up. 'No idea. All I know is that he was delivered here and is fresh enough to pass for our friend downstairs.'

'Dental records?'

'That's probably why the lower jaw is missing, too tricky to copy.'

'Poor bastard.'

'Yeah.'

'I didn't mean laughing boy here, I meant Al Nayef. Today he's royalty, tomorrow he's just Joe Public.'

Tate stretched his back. 'That's the name SIS should have put on his new passport.'

A smile split Fox's craggy face. 'I haven't given you yours yet, have I?'

'No.' Tate frowned.

Fox let his smile turn into a grin. 'I wouldn't shave until you've checked it out.'

Tate removed the coveralls, gloves and mask. 'So can I have it?'

Fox reached inside the pocket of his denim jacket. 'Here.'

It was a genuine United Kingdom passport, and had been aged in order to not rouse suspicion. Tate looked at the photograph page. He closed his eyes and sighed. It was a real photo of himself, with a sensible haircut but it had a Hulk Hogan, horseshoe-style moustache that drooped around either side of his mouth.

Chapter 2

Topeka, Kansas, USA

It was June the 12th – Russia Day – and Ruslan Akulov sat at a booth in the back of a diner in Kansas, almost the geographical centre of the continental United States. Physically he was very far from Russia but gastronomically, much nearer. The diner in Topeka's Little Russia neighbourhood had been open for over seventy years serving Russo-German food. Akulov bit into a pickle, which reminded him of those his grandmother made in her village on the outskirts of Moscow. It was a little after eleven in the morning and although the place had just opened, more than half of its thirty-five covers were full. A half-dozen booths lined one side of the diner and six bar stools faced the full-length bar on the other; a couple of tables had also been squeezed in near the back wall to accommodate latecomers.

A police officer wandered in and took one of the remaining bar stools. He greeted the old guy serving and within a minute a large plate of ham salad appeared in front of him. Akulov took a piece of his own ham; it was the best he'd had in a while. There was a comfort here that Akulov missed. He was a citizen of nowhere and belonged to no community. He was Russian, yet the passport he carried was American and the language he used now was Boston-accented English. He ate another pickle. Akulov didn't think of himself as a sentimental person and had no strong attachment to anything or anyone; in fact, the only family he still had were those men he'd served with in the Russian Army. Yet even his old classified Spetsnaz unit, known only as the Werewolves, was disbanded and its surviving members scattered. Some he knew were dead, a few worked for private military companies, and others had simply vanished.

To the world Akulov had vanished too, disappearing into the American heartland. But to do what he still did not know. To start again, to be reborn or to sit and grow old in obscurity? Regardless, he was no longer Ruslan Akulov; he had become Russel Cross, a thirty-six-year-old independent insurance broker, a job so dull-sounding that when asked what he did for a living, he was never probed further.

Akulov knew a little about the brokerage business, but not insurance brokerage. It had been his broker who, for a thick fee, had facilitated his past contracts. When he'd dropped out of the circuit, his broker had lost a sizeable meal ticket and, he imagined, was less than happy. As a habit Akulov occasionally checked the "draft folder" of an internet-based email account. There his broker left messages for him, unsent therefore untraceable as emails, and deleted by the reader once read. Only he and the broker knew the password to the account and the name in itself was a random mixture of numbers and letters that meant nothing to either of them. This was also where his broker would leave a link to a dedicated page on the dark web where details of each new contract were posted for a specified time before being deleted. Randomly the broker would leave details of the next account to be used.

It was a simple, secure and trusted system. Each time Akulov accessed the email account he used a one-time burner phone, and given both the illegality of their actions and the sums of money involved, he was as certain as he could be that his broker had done the same.

Broker. Akulov let the smallest of smirks appear on his lips. The broker was actually his agent.

Akulov pulled a new burner phone from his pocket and powered it up. As he waited for it to log on to the cellular network – he didn't trust Wi-Fi – he continued to eat his early lunch. Any moment now he expected to have company at his table, and when that happened he would either need to leave or close down the phone.

He logged in to the email account. He had read but not deleted the messages his broker had sent him since his disappearance. The first had appeared a month afterwards. It had been simple, one line, direct to the point: *'Where are you?'* It was followed two weeks later by *'Are you alive?'* There had been several more in between and the last he'd received had been two months previously. It simply stated, *'If you have read this you are in danger.'* He'd ignored it. The words were nonspecific, meaningless and could have been a ploy.

Akulov blinked as he saw the new message appear in the folder. He couldn't understand it. *'British Intelligence have conformation you survived your last contract. They are actively searching for you. Kill/capture.'*

Akulov frowned. The last contract, the assassinations, the hit list given to him. It had included three British diplomats, two he had liquidated. But it had also listed high-ranking American targets, and he had killed all three of those. Why was it the British who sought him, and not the Americans? Why was it not a joint mission? It was a riddle, and he hated those. If he replied it was confirmation he was alive, but if he didn't …

The door opened. A middle-aged couple stepped inside and looked about. They saw his table and started to approach. Decision made, he deleted the message and tapped a two-word reply: *'Why? Explain.'*

Akulov stood, approached the counter and with a nod handed two notes, a $20 and a $10 to the old guy serving.

Outside dark storm clouds now dominated the sky and a light wind blew spots of rain into his face as he walked to his hire car. The Challenger was parked between an old pick-up and a Ford Explorer in police livery. He got in and turned the ignition. Instantly the 5.7-litre Hemi V8 engine rumbled to life. American muscle, it put the faintest of smiles on Akulov's face. He slowly reversed, looked back at the single-storey, red-fronted diner and then sped off down Porubsky Drive.

More rain now started to hit his windshield and the clouds had become darker still. And then rain started to hammer on the windows of the car like stormy fists as he carried on along the road. He was leaving yet another place his nomadic existence prevented him from knowing. Guessing and second-guessing the opposition, those who had hunted him, who had sought to kill him, had made for a life of continual movement, one that he had tried to escape but one that now was reaching for him once again. Wipers frantically pushed the rain away from his screen. The lives he had taken, the dreams he had destroyed were now preventing him from living his own.

He passed a couple on foot, hand in hand, without an umbrella between them. Hair was plastered to their faces, clothes were clinging to their bodies, their eyes were locked on each other. Loneliness gnawed at Akulov. He had been in a crowded diner but was a man forever alone. This was not the life he had been forced to choose; this was the life he had been created for. Forged out of Mother Russia's strongest materials and tempered by experience, Akulov was no longer a man. He was a weapon.

Wichita, Kansas, USA

Akulov had chosen the town because he'd liked the name and the hotel because it was anonymous, part of a mid-level chain and incorporating a conference centre. A dozen near-identical domestic sedans sat in the parking lot. He found a space for his Challenger around the side of the building where it was less likely to draw attention. He entered the hotel reception and took a room for two nights – it gave him options – and showed his driving licence and credit card issued in the name of "Russel Cross". A middle-aged man with a fixed smile and dull eyes handed him his key card and explained there was a free hotel shuttle service to and from Dwight D. Eisenhower Airport, just 0.9 miles away, should he need it, and then wished him a "pleasant evening".

Akulov found his room, which was as requested on the end of the block. Once inside he locked the door and placed a rubber wedge underneath it for added security. The room had a red feature wall. He was glad it was behind the bed so he wouldn't have to look at it. A card boasting "free Wi-Fi" was on the credenza in front of a large flat-screen TV. Akulov sat on the bed and powered up a new burner smartphone using the cellular network. He logged in to the email account he shared with his broker.

And there in the draft folder was a new message.

'British intelligence have confirmed your identity as the Camden bomber. One week before the EMP attack on the US last year, a smartphone was discovered during the renovation of a commercial property overlooking the site of the Camden bombing. It contained video footage taken of the attack. In this video you are seen abandoning a van at the entrance to Camden Market, then walking away to detonate both the IED and the vest worn by your accomplice. The UK believe you masterminded the attack and recruited the Chechen. The final death toll was thirty-one. This included the parents of the brothers Simon Hunter and Jack Tate – both employees of SIS.'

Akulov sat back and closed his eyes. This was why it was the British and not the Americans who were after him. Assassinating key individuals was one thing but committing an unprovoked act of terror in London was something completely different. He remembered vaguely the news stories at the time. Two devices had been detonated together: a huge car bomb in a panel van and a suicide vest worn by an illegal immigrant from Chechnya. Camden Market had been instantly transformed from a vibrant sea of shoppers into a scene of carnage. Akulov reread the message, willing it to have changed.

Akulov dropped the phone on the bed and sat in silence for several long minutes before raising his hands to rub his face. His hands were shaking. He clenched and unclenched his fists. The shaking subsided, reduced to a quiver, but did not disappear completely.

Images of the dead, those he had killed, and there were many, played in his head, passing in front of his eyes like an internal cinema screen, a grotesque trailer. He saw their faces, the moment of their deaths, and the waxy pallor as they became lifeless shells. But what he did not see were any innocents. What he did not see were any targets liquidated in London.

Akulov followed the link his broker had left and accessed a page on the dark web. Here he saw the footage the British authorities had been using to investigate the attack. It wasn't just one video, it was a collection of videos. Two from interconnecting Camden Council CCTV cameras and one from a Transport for London camera affixed to a bridge. These three did not show his face. The most damning of all footage was from a tourist's smartphone. The smartphone that had been lost. It clearly showed Akulov in the background exiting a panel van, walking away, turning before the next corner to look back and then pressing a button on a mobile device to trigger the explosions.

There was a problem.

It wasn't him.

He was never there.

He was being framed.

Akulov's face was now an emotionless mask as he watched

and rewatched the footage, each time trying to see where it had been manipulated, how his image had been inserted into the scene. But there were no tell-tales, no distortion or image pixilation. Although he had had some training, he was by no stretch of the imagination a computer specialist. What they had done couldn't be possible.

As far as he saw it there were three ways to prove he was not the man in the footage. Firstly to establish that the footage had been doctored, secondly to establish the identity of the real perpetrator and thirdly to confirm that he had been somewhere else at the exact same time.

He memorised the address, closed the page and then tapped in a Google search for the Camden bombing and confirmed the date. He knew where he had been, but he also knew that getting confirmation of that was an all but impossible task. In fact, the only person who knew for sure that he had not been in London on that date was the broker who had sent him on another contract on the other side of the world.

He had no idea how the footage had been manipulated. He did, however, have an idea of who the real bomb-maker may have been. The bombing had taken out the Hunters, and the fact that his broker had mentioned them was a sign. He knew from the attack on the US the previous year that Maksim Oleniuk – his last employer – had ordered the hit on them. And Oleniuk's private military company "Blackline" had sourced its specialists exclusively from his broker.

He needed to think. Akulov slipped off the bed and onto the floor. He snapped off thirty hard, fast press-ups, then changed the position of his hands, bringing them together to work on the inside of his chest. He sat up, his chest warm, and thought about his broker. A fellow Russian, who before the implosion of the mighty Soviet Union had been a KGB intelligence officer. The broker's identity was a secret but Akulov had refused to work for someone whose name he did not know. Knowing each other's identity was a failsafe and like the Cold War status quo, mutually assured destruction was guaranteed if either talked. And neither had. His broker had grown richer from Akulov's completed contracts and the halo effect of controlling Russia's most feared assassin continuously brought in both new contracts and clients.

Akulov turned, and started to do sit-ups. He knew his broker had handled this contract and chosen the contractor from a small pool of talent. And that talent pool contained many operators personally known to Akulov. He continued to train his stomach until it burned before he got up, moved to the bathroom and showered.

Towel-dry he sat on the bed and was back in the email draft folder. Now a myriad of questions swirled in his head, but he deleted the broker's message and tapped in only the most important: *'Give me his name.'*

Rising from the bed, he was about to power off the handset, remove its SIM card and flush it down the toilet but he had a better idea. He checked his watch: it was still early. He decided he would take the free shuttle to the airport.

A half-hour later, with dark blue baseball cap and a pair of thick-rimmed, low-power reading glasses worn to obscure his face, Akulov walked into the steel-and-glass construction that according to a sign was the "*USA Today* Readers' Choice Best Small Airport 2020". It had been a year since the EMP attack on the US had knocked out most electronic circuitry. This included CCTV networks. The majority had been replaced. Some in smaller out-of-the-way places had not, and Akulov had used this absence to his advantage. As a matter of national security, all airport surveillance systems had been among the first to be replaced.

Akulov had not stepped foot inside an airport for well over a year. It was a risk, if his gut instinct was right, and he had learnt to listen to it. He studied a large display map, and then made for the Aviators Café, the only eatery serving booze that was located pre-security screening. He ordered a beer and a couple of sandwiches and took a seat at the back. He'd left the burner phone on, deliberately so. It was early evening and trade was still brisk at the terminal. He ate, drank and pretended to check his phone for the next hour – getting up once to get a second overpriced domestic beer, all the while carrying out counter surveillance. Finally satisfied that his phone was not being traced, and that his current identity was not on any watch list, he checked the email account. Once again he was surprised to see a new message so soon.

'The intelligence came from a reliable source within British Intelligence. The contract was not meant to conclude by way of bombing. I cannot give you a name.'

Akulov glared at the phone screen, willing the words to impart more information than they already had. He deleted the message and wrote his own: 'Give me his name or I give up yours.'

He started to put away the phone then had a better idea. He added a second line to the message: 'I demand a face-to-face. Tomorrow.'

He knew this was a break point. His broker either accepted a meet or all contact would be terminated. Akulov didn't like to gamble; it made no sense to take chances by making decisions based on incomplete intelligence, but on this occasion he gambled on receiving a reply, and a fast one. He finished his beer. It wasn't great but it was better than his native *Baltika*, which he'd been forced to drink in the Red Army. He had a thirst now and would happily have sat in the bar, had it been more comfortable, and drunk several more. There was something about the dark, dank Russian beer bars. They had a heart; they had a soul.

Akulov sighed. A soul was something he had lost years ago when he took his first life. He blinked and snapped out of his introspection and refreshed the email account. There was a new draft message: 'Miami. Tomorrow. 3 p.m. It is safe to take a plane – the Americans are not looking for you.'

Could he believe the broker? Could he trust what his broker was saying? Could he really catch a commercial flight without being stopped? If the British wanted him and didn't want the Americans to learn of his identity, surely he wouldn't be stopped? Akulov wet his lips. Yes, the Brits could ping him on the CCTV system and that would work in his favour. He sat for a moment more as he attempted to weigh up his options. What if the messages were not from the broker at all? Akulov looked at the iPhone's screen, willing it to give him the answer. He tapped out a new draft message: 'Prove this is you?'

He went to the American Airlines desk to ask. There were no direct flights to Miami, but the desk clerk told him he could take a flight via Dallas/Fort Worth. There were several leaving the next day. Akulov decided he'd take the first, getting him into Miami a little after eleven in the morning. He took the free shuttle back to his hotel.

In his room, door locked and rubber wedge under the bottom edge, he once more logged in to the email account. There was a reply. It confirmed without doubt the person he was communicating with was his broker, and that their operational status was "normal". It was one word, written in Russian.

Канадец.

Akulov felt the hand of a ghost squeeze his chest. "*Канадец*" – *Kanadets* – the Canadian. Only he and his broker knew the significance of this name to him. He wiped away the word, replacing it with three of his own: 'See you tomorrow.'

Akulov undressed and lay on his bed. He'd get four hours' sleep in before he needed to be back at the airport to return his hire car and catch his flight.

Chapter 3

Fifteen years ago

Russian Army Spetsnaz Training Camp, undisclosed location, Northern Russia

Heavy-footed, Ruslan Akulov trudged into the frozen camp, one man in a line of exhausted, numb conscripts wading through fresh, knee-high snow. The light of the Russian winter moon reflected off a world covered in a bright, white coat. The sharp outlines of the training facility were softened, all sound dampened. Akulov could hear only the quiet crunch of his boots as they flattened the soft snow, and his ragged breath escaping through the threads of his balaclava. His group had marched through a blizzard that would have sent sane men scrambling for cover; the wind swirling snow like needles into their faces, penetrating every layer. Too numb to shake, the men had continued on knowing that to stop was to risk death. Each of the weary, frozen figures around him had been plucked from the most recent intake of conscripts and put through specialist training designed to make them falter. And already a third of them had.

Brutal exercises had forced them together, forming friendships and creating allegiances. Akulov, near the back of the line, had just two men behind him – a recruit from Volgograd named Vetrov and a monstrously muscled Buryat from Russia's Far East christened Dorzhiev. An order shouted through the icy air caused the men at the front to stop and those at the rear to concertina into one another.

'Welcome to your new home!' their training sergeant, a grey-haired, glacial-hard soldier yelled at them before he disappeared through the doorway of a squat barrack building.

Still wary of making mistakes, it was a few frosty seconds before the men followed. In the gloom of the barrack's interior, lit with dull flickering bulbs, Akulov noted the rows of two-tiered bunks and the men who inhabited them. Their eager eyes assessing him. These were troops from the previous training cycle. Called up during the summer intake, Akulov's arrival meant that they had now become the "*Stariki*" – old men. This was their domain, and they were ready to "officially" welcome the little fish – the "*Salagi*" – to their world.

The imposing figure of Dorzhiev was the last of Akulov's group to push through the doorway. He glowered at the Stariki, jutted his chin up and stamped the snow from his boots.

Jumping down from his top bunk, a dark-haired man, whose size rivalled that of Dorzhiev, moved towards him and held out his hand. 'Welcome, brother. Let me take your pack.'

'Thank you, brother.' Dorzhiev grunted and shrugged out of it.

A wide smile split the Starik's face. He hefted the sodden pack into the air, then turned his attention to the remaining new arrivals. He pointed at their feet. 'You dogs can sleep on the floor in your own filth. Were you not taught to wipe your boots when entering someone's home?'

Dorzhiev made eye contact with Akulov. There was a long moment of silence.

'If you wish to be dogs,' the Starik said, 'we will teach you to behave like dogs. Remove your packs and get on your hands and knees!'

Vetrov dropped his pack, and got on all fours. Hesitantly the others, including Akulov, did the same. Shielded by his backpack, Vetrov stealthily reached under his coat and removed his belt. He wrapped it around his right fist. Before Akulov had the chance to think or ask why, the Stariki got down from their bunks and attacked. Feet and fists connected with the legs, backs, stomachs and heads of the unsuspecting eighteen-year-old conscripts. Muffled cries and shouts filled the room. Akulov tensed, preparing for the beasting as they neared him.

Vetrov rose in a blur of movement. His belted fist connected with the jaw of one Stariki and then the stomach of another. He continued to fight, seemingly slithering and gliding from one contact to another. Within seconds two men lay bleeding whilst two more stumbled back holding their faces. Akulov and the others were now on their feet, ready to join the fight. The older soldiers edged away, unsure what to do, wary of the newcomers.

Vetrov met Akulov's eyes; his face was relaxed. He nodded and then he addressed the leader of the Stariki. 'You can have the bottom bunks. We shall take the top.'

The Starik laughed. 'You'll learn soon enough. What's your name?'

'Vetrov.'

At a nod from Vetrov, Dorzhiev barged forward into the Starik, grappling him to the ground. Yells of anger filled the air as the ranks of the Stariki advanced again. For Akulov it was an epiphany; he knew he could run or march the longest but now was his chance to prove he could fight. Why should he accept a beating from these boys who were no more than a year his senior? Who were they to him? He slammed his fist into the face of the Starik nearest him. A second man swung an ill-advised foot at him. Akulov sidestepped and drove his boot into the soldier's groin. Around him the interior of the tent had become a moving

35

mass of arms, legs and screams. The older recruits had not been ready for a battle and their stockinged and plimsolled feet were no match for the heavy, sodden boots of the greener conscripts. Yet their more advanced training prevailed and gradually the younger, wearier soldiers in their cumbersome greatcoats started to falter, to fall.

'Enough!' The gravelly voice of the training sergeant, who had been watching impassively from the sidelines, froze the action quicker than any Siberian wind.

Akulov was panting heavily, but it was with a controlled fury not exertion. Standing either side of him were Vetrov and Dorzhiev, the last of their platoon on their feet. The only three who had not succumbed to the Stariki. Akulov's limbs felt like lead and his chest burned yet he knew he would yield to no man.

'This is the true Spetsnaz! The Wolves have arrived!' The men parted like a sea as the sergeant moved into the centre of the impromptu arena. 'Stariki, you shall retain your top bunks, and Salagi you shall have the bottom. You three: Vetrov, Dorzhiev, Akulov. Grab your packs. Come with me. This tent is no place for Wolves!'

Present day

Nice, France

Jack Tate towel-dried his hair and studied himself in the mirror. The quick, rough haircut Paddy Fox had given him wasn't the best but if he used enough wax it would look acceptable. What he was less sure about was the Hulk Hogan style moustache he'd had to adopt to mirror his new passport photo. The quality of the passport image was remarkable. Neill Plato, the technical officer responsible for support to several SIS desks and E Squadron operations, had once explained to him that any manipulated passport photo would stand up to the highest level of scrutiny and only lose enough definition to seem fake when blown up to well over A3 poster size. He flexed his biceps in the mirror and smirked.

'Mr Jack?'

'In here.'

His Royal Highness Salman bin Mohammad Al Nayef entered the bathroom hesitantly. Even though he'd been up till the small hours undergoing questioning from Paddy Fox, he didn't seem tired. He looked excited. He ran his hand through his raven-black hair. 'What do you think?'

Tate studied Al Nayef. Fox had given him a makeover too, but Jack suspected that his fellow SAS man had taken more time and care with the royal than he had with Tate. Al Nayef's immaculate beard had been shaved off and his hair cut shorter on the sides and back. He was wearing faded black skinny jeans, a grey T-shirt with some type of logo on it and a pair of Converse boots.

'Do I look more Australian?' Al Nayef asked.

'Like a young Hugh Jackman,' Tate said, with a straight face.

'Wolverine?' Al Nayef smiled. 'Then I should thank your colleague. I like your moustache. It makes you look very noble, Mr Jack.'

'Looks can be deceiving.' Tate picked up his Rolex from the shelf above the sink. It was the only piece of technology he would be travelling with, and although encrypted phones were common-place, he'd rather travel without one than risk possible compromise. Within the next half-hour he and Al Nayef would leave the safe house in the Renault for Nice Côte d'Azur Airport where they'd take a short flight to Milan before boarding a Qatar Airways flight to Doha. At Hamad International Airport Tate would hand Al Nayef over to an officer of the Australian Secret Intelligence Service, who would then accompany the royal on to Sydney.

In Sydney it was another short hop to Canberra where he

would be debriefed and questioned again by a representative of the SIS and the ASIS. As members of the "five eyes" intelligence alliance – known as FVEY, the UK and Australia were obligated to share all pertinent intel they garnered from Al Nayef with the other three members – Canada, New Zealand and the US; however, the fact that the royal was alive and about to be given a new identity in Australia was a secret neither the SIS or the ASIS were going to share.

'Are you ready to leave?' Tate asked.

'Yes, I think so, Mr Jack.'

'Just Jack. I'm not going to call you "Your Royal Highness" or "sir" and neither is anyone else from now on. You need to get used to being one of the common people now.'

'I shall try my best, Jack.'

'Good.'

Tate moved past Al Nayef and back into the bedroom where he started to dress in casual business attire. Al Nayef followed him in and stood awkwardly by the door.

Tate scanned the room. All trace of their presence in the house had to leave with them. The SIS employed a team of "cleaners" to "sanitise" operational spaces but E Squadron missions, which were above classified, had to do without. In short, Tate's team had to pack up their own kit and clean their rooms.

'Have you ever been to Qatar?' Al Nayef asked.

'No.'

'I was there several years ago. Before the recent troubles, when we Gulf State nationals – Saudis, Bahrainis, Omanis, Emiratis and Qataris – moved freely and associated like brothers. My uncle had several meetings with the emir.'

'Did you meet the emir?'

'No. I wanted to; however, my uncle said it was best that I did not.' Al Nayef shrugged. 'Perhaps he was jealous of his youth or his freedom to rule his country as he deemed fit, something we do not have in the kingdom.'

'I see.' Tate had grown out of politics.

'And that would account for his actions and intentions.'

Tate shot Al Nayef a quizzical look but said nothing.

'Morning,' the gruff, Glaswegian voice of Paddy Fox boomed as he entered the room. 'I just wanted to bid you both safe travels and say goodbye.'

Al Nayef shook the older man's hand with vigour. 'Thank you, Paddy. I will never forget you and all you have done.'

A smile creased Fox's face. 'It's better that you do forget, as officially none of this ever happened and I wasn't here, Your Royal Highness.'

Al Nayef smiled.

'Good luck, Salman,' Fox said.

'You too, Paddy.'

Fox turned to Tate. 'Jack, I need a word. If you'll excuse us?'

'Of course,' Al Nayef said.

Tate followed Fox out of the bedroom and onto the landing.

The older, red-haired intelligence operative walked to the far end away from the room and leant against a bannister. He looked back the way they had come to make sure Al Nayef wasn't in sight before he started to speak in a quiet tone. 'The name of the ASIS guy you'll be meeting in Doha is Liam Saville. He's a top bloke, former military and Old Bill. He's got a photo of you – with the tash.'

'Thanks.'

Fox pulled out a photo from his pocket. 'Memorise his face.'

Tate took the photo and studied it for ten seconds before handing it back. 'Done.'

Fox nodded. 'Al Nayef's doppelganger should wash up some-where today but there's still every chance the Saudis have seen through it. The kid in there hasn't got a clue. He means well but he's naive. If he gets snatched by anyone he'll talk and then we're all in the shite.'

Tate was puzzled. 'Why not just use his intel and leave him in?'

'For the same reason. If he'd stayed, he'd have been found out. His intel was too good to risk losing him. Sending him "down under" is much better than the alternative, even if it does mean eventually sharing his intel with the Aussies.'

'I see.'

'Time to go. Enjoy your free holiday.' Fox slapped Tate on the shoulder. 'Right, I'm off to collect me pension.'

Chapter 4

South Beach, Miami, Florida, USA
Smith & Wollensky was on Miami Beach and the place to be to enjoy the sunset. The lunchtime crowd had thinned and the sundowners had not yet started to arrive in force. Akulov took a table inside the all but deserted interior; the covers outside seemed far more popular. He ordered a bottle of overpriced imported spring water and waited. He had scoped out the place an hour before, and as far as he could tell there was no reception party waiting for him. As a location for a clandestine meeting it had its advantages. With a narrow path immediately in front that gave way to the ocean, the only place to conceal an observation post was one of the windows of the high-rise apartment buildings on the neighbouring Fisher Island. And he had defeated any line of sight listening or optical devices by choosing to sit inside.

Around him the rich went about their daily routines on the walkway. Couples in conversation strolled leisurely, parents promenaded their young in pushchairs, and joggers in brightly coloured designer sportswear pounded the pavement.

A light breeze drifted in from the ocean. It brought with it a note of brine and seaweed. Akulov appeared relaxed but he wasn't.

41

Like the sea there was something lurking beneath the surface. Meeting in Miami was not wise. A decade before, each member of his unit, the Werewolves, had been ordered by the GRU to memorise and familiarise themselves with a list of global cities, to become experts on the places. Of the US population centres his had included New York and Washington. He had not been assigned Miami, and that put a crease in his operational map. It exposed him. It made him an easier target for a snatch squad or a well-placed round.

Akulov studied the pedestrians heading his way. An elderly man – with a large, black poodle trotting by his side – power-walked on the edge of the promenade, and further back, an ash-blonde-haired woman – wearing a fitted, maroon suit – walked her small dog. With perfect etiquette, she nodded formally at everyone she passed. He noted no one who appeared out of place. Eventually the woman with the small dog drew level with the restaurant and nodded warmly at the waiter. There was a sparkle in her emerald green eyes as she removed her sunglasses and looked at him. She was twenty years his senior yet he found her stunning. He nodded back and watched as she came inside. She clicked her fingers and asked for a water bowl for the dog, ignoring a sign that said "Strictly No Pets" then bent down to tie him by the lead to the steel leg of Akulov's table. The dog yawned and curled up on the floor.

'I must say it's a lovely afternoon.' The language was English, and so was the clear-cut, cultivated accent.

Akulov didn't reply. He continued to scan the other restaurant patrons and passers-by.

She looked past him. 'This a favourite place of mine, to sit and watch the world go by. Although what one sees here on Miami Beach is hardly real. Outside these few square miles the world is a dangerous place.' Her eyes fell upon a speedboat as it powered past leaving a wide, white wake.

'For me it has become more dangerous,' Akulov stated.

'Quite so.'

The waiter appeared with a bowl for her dog. She ordered a large glass of Sancerre. 'I'm glad you are here, in the land of the living. I had hoped to see you again.'

'This isn't a social visit.'

'What we do has purpose; it has meaning.'

'For me, or your clients?'

Her eyes locked on to his and he remembered her past, what little he knew of it and how Valentina Tishina had been one of the KGB's most effective female agents. She lowered her voice. 'I made you aware of the situation because I do not want to lose you.'

'You don't want to lose your commission.'

She paused as the waiter brought her wine. She took a sip and smiled as her palate approved. 'Voluntary retirement is one thing; compulsory retirement is something completely different. The British were given your name by a credible source, and a friend of mine then passed the information on to me. But you and I know it is a lie, and the man who gave the information to the SIS knew this too. The SIS, however, do not.'

'So tell them they have the wrong man.' Akulov drank his water.

'If only it were so simple. For me to admit any involvement would be a career-ending event.'

'Me being framed is not?'

'I must say I was hurt by your threat. I have always been fair with you, even treated you like a—'

'Son?'

Anger momentarily flared in her eyes. 'A younger brother.'

'Thank you.'

She drank, regained her composure. 'One simply cannot surpass French wine.'

'Give me a name.'

'I have certain safeguards in place; however, regardless of this

43

I would prefer to live out the remainder of my life as a free woman.'

'Who was it? Tell me who the real bomber was.'

Tishina sighed heavily. 'One of the twelve.'

Akulov's eyes narrowed. Were his suspicions about to be confirmed? 'Are you going to say his name?'

'Vetrov.'

Akulov felt a sudden chill wash over him, and the cool ocean air wasn't responsible. The twelve Werewolves had been a brotherhood. Selected from various Spetsnaz units of the Russian Army and Navy, each chosen for their individual abilities. Akulov had been their top sniper, whilst Kirill Vetrov had been the demolitions expert, and the team leader.

'The contract called for the liquidation of two targets. The contract did not call for two explosive devices. The contract certainly did not call for civilian casualties.'

'Why give him the contract?'

'Oleniuk.'

'Who gave my name to the SIS?'

'No one. The SIS were handed the iPhone found during renovation work. It's the only footage that shows the face of the Camden bomber. Once they studied the footage they had a match to you. I don't know from where.'

'Tell me about the footage. How was is altered?'

'I have no idea, and as far as the SIS are concerned the footage is real, beyond all reasonable doubt.'

'Someone has fabricated it.'

'You are wanted for an act Vetrov has committed. An act I know you find, as I do, abhorrent. We are not monsters, we are not lunatics but Oleniuk was and Vetrov continues to be so.'

'He is also one of your specialists.'

She drank more wine before replying. 'He cannot be trusted. He's now working for the men I sent him to kill. He has gone rogue.'

44

Akulov turned his head, faced her square on. 'So this is about your survival now? Mine is secondary?'

Tishina shrugged. 'You cannot blame a girl for looking after number one. Besides, you are the one being targeted first. The British do not want this to become public; even the Americans remain uninformed. That is why you were nether challenged nor stopped at the airport – the Americans have no idea you are on their soil and the British certainly aren't going to risk them finding out by asking for their assistance in apprehending you. If the SIS find you, you'll either rot in a cell in a black site or rot in a hole. You have a choice: clear your name or forever be a target.'

'Or vanish again.'

'As you wish. But I know you better than that. This is eating away at you, the thought that those who matter believe you have committed this atrocity. What of your code then? What of your humanity, your soul?'

Now it was Akulov's eyes that showed anger. 'And what of yours?'

'My soul died decades ago but my conscience is clear on this. There were two targets, and that is that.'

Akulov finished his water and wanted something stronger. 'So I need to locate Vetrov, get a confession, send it to London and wait for my name to be cleared?'

'Something like that.'

'Why would the British believe me?'

'They wouldn't, but they'd believe Jack Tate.'

'I see. After I get the confession, I give it to Tate, the man who thinks I murdered his parents?'

'Persuade him and London will follow.'

'Where is Vetrov?'

'He was last seen in Texas.'

'Where?'

'Check your email.' She untied her dog's lead and stood. 'Thank you for the wine; it was good but you need to work on your conversation skills.'

Akulov said nothing and watched her sashay out of Smith & Wollensky and disappear in the direction of the beach. He too had to go. He left a fifty-dollar note on the table, got up and walked in the opposite direction, not knowing if he would ever see her again.

Headquarters of the Secret Intelligence Service, Vauxhall Cross, London, UK

Neill Plato sat in his overwarm, cramped office and munched on a fig roll. He ignored the biscuit crumbs falling onto his maroon shirt and tie as he reread the alert he'd just received from GCHQ – the UK government's intelligence and security organisation responsible for signals intelligence.

'Golly,' Plato said, and reached for another biscuit from the quickly emptying packet.

Plato was a technical officer, a computer and electronic surveillance expert who was shared between several departments including the Russian Desk. Although this bit of intel had also been sent to his sister organisation, the Security Service – commonly known as MI5 – because the bombing took place in the UK, Plato knew it was the Secret Intelligence Service who would be acting upon it. The official reason for this was because the perpetrators were overseas and from a foreign organisation. The unofficial reason was that the parents of one of their own had been among the victims. He played the attached video file: footage from three different airport security systems in the US. He studied them in full. He played the footage a second time, but now running it through his own facial recognition system. His program confirmed what GCHQ had said: there was a 92.4 per cent match between the face on all three pieces of US footage and the same face that appeared on the smartphone footage of the Camden Market bombing.

Too excited to sit, Plato nimbly got to his feet and brushed the accumulated biscuit crumbs from his torso. Leaning forward over his keyboard, he now played the US footage on three screens and brought the Camden footage up on another. He paused each screen when the face was full on to the camera. He crossed his arms and studied the wall of monitors that faced him. The Camden image was clearer than the US ones, but in his opinion, they were identical.

'We've found him!' Plato croaked, his throat inexplicably becoming dry.

Plato tapped a few buttons and made a footage comparison video, which he then copied on to his iPad. He reached for his desk phone, but thought better of it. He'd take this immediately to Pamela Newman.

Plato left his office and took the lift up to Newman's floor. He reached his boss's door and knocked, rocking slightly on the balls of his feet as he waited for a reply.

'Come in.'

Plato bounded into the room, his cherry-red Dr Martens propelling him forward. 'I've got something for you.'

'Tell me.'

'We've had a hit on the facial recognition program.' He moved towards her large desk and handed her the iPad.

Newman looked at the device and pressed the play icon. Her eyes narrowed as she concentrated. 'Is this who I think it is?'

'Yes.' Plato smiled broadly. 'GCHQ believe it is the same person, and so do I. There is no doubt. We've found Ruslan Akulov.'

Newman nodded, seemingly agreeing. 'How old is this footage?'

'It was captured twenty hours ago at Dwight D. Eisenhower National Airport in Wichita. He caught a flight via Dallas/Fort Worth to Miami International.'

Newman frowned. 'What's he doing in Miami? And why has he popped up now after a year?'

Newman continued to look at the iPad and watched the screen once more. 'You can't take a flight in the US without getting scanned so why do this now?'

'He's ready to turn himself in?'

'Perhaps.' Newman's reply was non-committal and Plato could sense there was something she wasn't letting on, but she was his boss and privy to secrets that he was not. 'Can we track him at the other end?'

'Yes we can. Now that he's been pinged, if he's captured on any other system I'll get an instant alert.'

'Good.'

'So what would you like me to do now?'

'Just keep doing what you do best and let me know if you find anything else.'

'Will do.' Plato left her office to return to his.

Newman sat back in her chair and let her gaze wander to the ceiling as she traced the last of the evening rays dancing on the grubby plaster. What she hadn't told Plato was that the Americans did not know Akulov's identity. It had been her decision, and hers alone, to keep the UK's largest ally in the dark. Akulov had killed American citizens a year ago, the Russian had murdered British subjects in cold blood both in the UK and in the US and, what was more, she personally knew several of them. The Americans couldn't have him.

She glanced at her wall clock, at this time of year eight thirty in the evening in London made it ten thirty at night in Doha and half past three in the afternoon in Washington, DC, and Miami. Tate would still be in the air and as he was travelling clean, not contactable until he was at his hotel.

It was at times like this that she wished the old spy films were accurate, that she did in fact have an emergency bottle of malt in her desk drawer to celebrate victories and drown the sorrows of defeat. The strongest stimulant she had, however, was black coffee, and now her cup was cold. She drank it anyway, savouring the bitter taste as it slipped down her throat. She tapped in a US number and called the SIS station chief in Washington: Simon Hunter. He needed to know what she now did.

Chapter 5

Miami, Florida, USA

Akulov had shelled out for a room at the Holiday Inn, Port of Miami, not due to the place's location or even that he intended to spend the night but because he'd wanted something corporate, large and anonymous. In front of him on the glass-topped desk he had a new burner smartphone, laptop and printer. The last two items he'd bought that afternoon from a tech store in a mall. He didn't trust hotel business centres or copy shops with a USB. Commercial ventures had a tendency to save jobs on shadow memories or drives for legal or insurance reasons and the Russian was not going to run the risk.

Using the smartphone as a hotspot, he connected the laptop to the internet and accessed his email. There was a message in the drafts folder from Tishina and a link. He followed the link to the intel she had left him on the dark web and downloaded it as a zip file. He opened the file and printed the photos and documents off. The whole process took him a little under five minutes.

He studied the photographs, seeing the face of Kirill Vetrov for the first time in five years. Pushing aside a wave of memories he continued to study the images with a professional detachment.

They had been taken on three different occasions. The first set showed Kirill Vetrov with a pair of Hispanic men. As Vetrov was the same height and build as him – exactly six foot – Akulov could estimate the height of the other two men. They were extremely short, but had gym-wide chests and shoulders. The photographs had some lowlight pixilation because they had been taken covertly inside a Houston bar, but the faces were clear enough. The three men seemed to be celebrating – their table was littered with shot glasses and tequila bottles.

The next set of photographs revealed Vetrov in discussion with a man whose jet-black hair was tied back in a ponytail; but it wasn't his hair that struck Akulov, it was his height. He was not just tall but gigantic. He was over seven foot tall, with a bodybuilder's physique that bulged through his T-shirt. The image showed the pair standing outside an apartment block beside a white Cadillac Escalade. The location too was noted as Houston.

The last set presented Vetrov at what appeared to be an open-air rifle range. In each photograph he was training armed Hispanic men. In one he was prone and aiming an assault rifle and in another he was watching over a row of men who were doing the same. The location of the range was noted as La Tijerita, Mexico.

And then Akulov read the documents. There was a profile on each of the two short men. They were twin brothers – Angel and Caesar Mendez – who ran the Mendez drug cartel, based around the Mexican border town of Matamoros. Caesar Mendez was primarily based in Houston, Texas, to ensure the smooth distribution of their product. This was after a turf war with the rival Arellano Cartel had followed them from Mexico. It gave a list of his favoured hangouts, which included the club in which one of the sets of photographs had been taken. Caesar Mendez's enforcer was a man nicknamed "the Giant" – real name Luis Bravo. The Mendez brothers were the targets Vetrov had been sent to liquidate, who had persuaded him to work for them. Nowhere in the briefing notes did it state who had ordered the contract on the Mendez brothers.

Neither Akulov, Vetrov nor any of the other specialists Tishina had on her books were bound to her, indebted perhaps due to the lucrative contracts she attracted but nothing more. They could walk away. However, Vetrov's actions had undermined her professional standing and that of the business as a whole. Akulov sighed. He was in the business of murder for money, pain for profit. Profit. The world swirled around in his head. There was something else in Houston, something Vetrov could leverage for profit. A list of addresses he had memorised many years ago flashed back through his mind. Akulov frowned. Could this somehow be interlinked?

Akulov picked up one of the photographs and studied the face of his former team leader. He now did not fight the memories and let them engulf him like a tidal wave. Akulov had a choice to make. There had been a time when the twelve Werewolves had been brothers. They ate together, drank together, trained together and finally fought together. Each took an oath above and beyond that of allegiance to Mother Russia, that they would defend each other to their last breath. But all that stopped in Syria. Two Werewolves were killed by a kid with a lucky shot from an RPG, as they moved from the apparent safety of the Russian command base to their forward operating base. It was the lack of training of their attacker that had shocked them the most. That some child could kill a Werewolf went against everything they had been taught.

The deaths damaged group morale and cohesion like nothing ever before. There was an almost physical change in several of their brotherhood, but most of all in Vetrov. He no longer saw the local civilians as non-combatants; it had been a malnourished teenager who had taken out one of their Kamaz trucks and murdered two of their brothers, and not a hardened ISIS fighter. Akulov became uneasy, and his unease increased with each day they spent in theatre. It was not that he doubted their orders or their missions but that their methods had started to become increasingly like ISIS themselves.

The remaining ten Werewolves had started to splinter, with Vetrov leading a smaller group in an assault role and ordering the others to act as a rearguard or overwatch. Time and again families were terrified as the Werewolves invaded their homes, destroying what few possessions they had, beating their men and shooting anyone who got in their way. Vetrov's new mantra was results over everything else. But then came the day that Akulov could stand it no more.

Chapter 6

Six years ago

Aleppo, Syria

It was the hottest day yet, a debilitating forty-nine degrees Celsius in the shade, or one hundred and twenty Fahrenheit, as the Americans would say, but there were no Americans in the vicinity, only Russian Spetsnaz. Akulov lay covered in a mixture of sweat, grit and dust as he looked down the optics of his VSS Vintorez silenced sniper rifle. Intelligence had located the Emir of the Inghimassiyeen, the elite shock troops loosely affiliated to al-Qaeda. Abu Al-Muthanna, arguably the most significant of the high-ranking jihadist commanders, was in South Aleppo with a detachment of battle-hardened men. Their job was to defend the city by launching guerrilla attacks on the lines of Syrian Government forces who surrounded it.

In Akulov's mind "city" was now too grand a name for the extended pile of rubble and rubbish that stretched in front of him towards the horizon. It may well have been a city once but now it was no more than a man-made wasteland. But civilians still lived there. He had watched in wonder for the last two days, seeing them moving among the rubble, walking along the shattered concrete of the once proud boulevard, and refusing to give up on Aleppo. Life as they knew it had been blown apart, literally, but still they stayed. Some of his fellow Spetsnaz surmised it was a sort of post-traumatic stress that kept them there, a mental switch flicked in their heads that prevented them from accepting the crushed concrete was all that was left of the place they once called home.

There was movement in the glassless, second-storey window a block away. A bearded figure wearing a dark green jacket peered out. It was one of the target's men. Akulov'd seen the fighter before, one of half a dozen who occupied the shattered apartment building's second floor. The top three storeys of the building, which stood on the corner of a crossroads, had been lost to mortar bombardment by ISIL when they took the city. Heavy shells had torn away whole floors and the lives contained within them.

There was a low crunch of concrete from his left. Akulov rolled away from his rifle and brought his Makarov pistol to bear on the source. A moment later he relaxed. It was Kirill Vetrov – team leader of the Werewolves.

'Easy.' Vetrov held up his hands. A large bottle of water was in his right. He handed it to Akulov. 'Anything new?'

'Nothing.'

'We're going in at nightfall. Command has received intel that Al-Muthanna is planning to launch a raid at daybreak tomorrow.'

'Understood.' Akulov drank.

'You are to remain here and provide overwatch.'

There was a long silence. Beneath the grit and dirt, Akulov's brow furrowed. 'You need me on the assault team.'

Vetrov smiled at him. 'I need your rifle here.' He slapped him on the back. 'Who else can shoot as well as you? Stay sharp and keep your eyes on. Understood?'

'Understood.'

Akulov turned his focus back to the target building as he heard Vetrov make his way out of the room and negotiate the steps leading down to the ground floor.

The sun set fast in Syria. From his hide, Akulov watched it go down. Shadows lengthened, expanded and then the town about him was plunged into darkness. He switched his scope to night vision and the street below became a world of greens.

Vetrov spoke in his ear: 'Wolf 1 to Wolf 6, you have overwatch.'

Akulov clicked the pressel switch on his jacket to acknowledge the update.

Vetrov spoke again: 'Stand by ... stand by ... GO!'

Akulov kept his focus fixed on the unnatural world a block away. He scanned the floor used by the target. He could detect no movement from within but sensed it to his left on the street below. He removed his eye from the scope and saw the snake of five men tactically advance towards the building, weapons up. They were now under his protection; he alone would be responsible for taking out any threat, any shooter or sniper before they could get a shot off against the rest of his team. Eye back on the scope, Akulov surveyed their path and the numerous rooftops and battered balconies that offered nests for gunmen. Nothing. He continued to scan, alternating between the narrow aperture of his rifle's scope and the wider view offered by his IR-enabled field glasses. What he was doing was a two-man job – shooter and spotter – but Akulov was accustomed to working alone and that was just another ability that separated the Werewolves from any other Russian military unit.

There was a sudden movement in the target building, on a lower level. A face in the window, then another two behind the first. The clarity was not great but Akulov could see that none of them had beards. They were wearing hijabs. The woman nearest the window attempted to climb out of the window, whilst the others helped. Akulov moved the scope away and up, back to the target room. Now a face in the window peered out, but this one had a beard, and he was manoeuvring a long rifle. The outline was recognisable. It was a Dragunov – the most popular Russian sniping rifle of all time. The head turned and looked back into the dark green of the room behind before once again facing front and then dropping behind the scope. Akulov did not hesitate. A single, suppressed round silently soared from his VSS Vintorez. It hit the fighter in the forehead and blew out the back of his skull. The Dragunov fell forward and out of the window whilst the fighter fell backwards.

'Wolf 6 to Wolf 1, shot taken. Sniper in target window neutralised,' Akulov whispered into his throat mic.

'Copy that, Wolf 6.'

Scanning the other windows on the same floor, Akulov became aware of multiple shadows moving, too nebulous to target with certainty. Below the Werewolves had reached the cover of a building on the opposite corner of the crossroads. They remained unseen by the members of the Inghimassiyeen above.

'Wolf 6 to Wolf 1, be aware of multiple x-rays mobile in target building. Will target all opportunities.'

'Wolf 1 to Wolf 6. Understood.'

Now that first blood had been taken, Akulov felt as though he was inhabiting another plane of existence. The world around him had slowed yet his cognition had remained at a higher level, a faster speed.

The drop from the first-floor window where the women had been was less than two metres. High enough to inflict injury on the unlucky or infirm, but low enough to be fully survivable. A figure in a black abaya dropped out, hit the ground and crumpled. Akulov willed the woman to rise. Long seconds later she did and held up her hands to the window and a figure above. And then she suddenly folded in half and fell sideways, as though hit by an invisible force …

She had been shot by suppressed rounds. Akulov struggled to subdue his anger, his outrage as he saw the Werewolves advance towards the building. The point man, Wolf 1, paused, targeted the window and sent a burst of rounds into the second woman who was already hanging out. The woman dropped and landed by his feet.

The booming sound now of unsuppressed rounds, the barking of Kalashnikovs, forced Akulov to channel his anger and use it. He acquired targets in the windows and further inside and fired, taking one out at a time.

'Cease fire, Wolf 6.' The command came from Wolf 1, as he led the assault group inside.

Akulov pulled his eyes away from the scope and wiped his brow with his sleeve. He picked up his field glasses and scanned the building. Flashes erupted from the second floor as the assault team engaged the remaining ISIL fighters, but his concern was now the women – the two who had been shot and the one who had remained inside. He saw a woman run out of the main entrance to the building. She reached the first body and dropped to her knees. Even from a block away Akulov could hear the sound of her keening – and it cut through him like a lethal Spetsnaz knife.

Present day

Hamad International Airport, Doha, Qatar

Tate's professionalism had triumphed over his urge for a drink, he'd stuck to soft drinks but eaten his fill from the "on demand dining" menu. Al Nayef, however, looked wobbly as he stood and reached for his cabin luggage, which was now all he or rather Ali Karim – the name on the passport he was using – possessed. This made Tate extra cautious as they joined the other four passengers from their cabin, two of whom were Qataris in impossibly white guthras and thobes, and alighted from the airbus. The flight had landed twenty minutes ahead of schedule but time was still tight for Al Nayef's Sydney connection.

58

Tate had studied the layout of Hamad International and knew both arrivals and transit passengers followed the same route until arrivals took an escalator down to immigration but there was nothing to prevent him from chaperoning Al Nayef until the Australian ASIS man met him.

Tate let Al Nayef continue down the air sleeve and into the terminal proper. He was walking slower than the other business class passengers and Tate caught him up as they turned a corner.

'Do I still have to pretend I don't know you, Mr Jack?'

'No, you can talk to me now, but my name is Mike, and remember you are Ali.'

'Ali Karim.'

'Correct.' Tate wasn't worried about Al Nayef forgetting the specifics of his new legend – the name he was travelling under – because on his arrival in Australia he would have the choice of a new one. All record of Ali Karim having entered Australia was to be wiped from the database and he would cease to exist.

As they continued on towards the end of the long hallway, foot traffic became busier as the economy class passengers caught them up and arrivals from other flights filtered in.

As they got to the end of the hallway Tate spotted a traveller sitting on a steel bench at the bottom of the escalator, casually checking his phone. He looked up directly at Tate and held his gaze. Tate recognised him from the photograph Paddy had shown him. The man stood and slowly slipped his phone into the right pocket of his jeans then dropped his arms to his sides with his fingers splayed out and he subtly patted the air.

Tate closed the distance and then stopped two metres away from the traveller but Al Nayef continued on a step, unaware. He stopped abruptly and turned. 'Are you the man from ASIS?'

Tate saw the man visibly wince. Tate rolled his eyes. 'Yeah, I know.'

'Seeing as we're on camera anyhow …' the Australian held out his hand '… Liam Saville.'

'Mike Stotter.' Tate shook Saville's hand.

'Ali Karim.' Al Nayef repeated the gesture.

'Any issues?'

'None,' replied Tate, as he continued to keep a trained eye on the passing passengers.

'Listen, guys, we've got just under fifty minutes until the flight leaves. They normally hold it for business class passengers but I don't want to push it.'

'Agreed,' Tate said. 'In that case, hello and goodbye.'

'Goodbye, Stotter.'

Tate turned to Al Nayef. 'Good luck.'

Al Nayef gave a hesitant smile. 'Thank you, Mr Jack.'

Tate shook his head, looked at Saville. 'Enjoy, he's all yours.'

'Fantastic,' Saville replied.

Chapter 7

Houston, Texas, USA

Ruslan Akulov stood at the end of the bar, a bottle of cold beer in his hand. Oddly enough for him, he felt at home. The music was what the Russian would have described as "hard rock", and the bar reminded him of rowdy nights out in his hometown. This bar, however, was not a garish, pricy imitation run by the Moscow mafia, this was the real deal. Akulov took a sip of his drink, and observed the crowd mingling. He gazed out across the burgundy-walled room at the happy hordes, the drinking flotsam and jetsam. Old denims and dull leathers mixed with high-end designer labels. He tapped his booted foot to the beat and allowed the smallest of smiles to appear on his lips. He was enjoying himself.

Before he'd given in to answering the cryptic messages from his broker, his past year in the US had been spent roaming, never staying too long in one place and living off the sizeable amount of cash he'd liberated from a criminal gang in Maine. The remainder of the cash, with the exception of the ten thousand he kept about his person, lay hidden under the floorboards of a barn in rural Nebraska. In an emergency he'd use funds transferred into Russel Cross's chequing account, but he preferred cash. He'd visited all the places that as a kid growing up in Russia he'd only ever seen on TV and in movies. Akulov had another swig of beer and tried to let himself relax. What better way to seem like a guy having a good time than to be a guy having a good time.

In Miami he had destroyed his burner phone, laptop and printer and put them in several trash bags in two different commercial dumpsters at the rear of his hotel. The flight from Miami had been uneventful. His genuine US passport and driving licence, bought from a trusted supplier, still remained unflagged by the American authorities and enabled one of Russia's most feared assassins to travel with ease. He'd got a room at a chain hotel near the city centre where he'd taken a taxi directly to the club, the place he had identified from his broker's intel. He needed to understand the layout if this was to be the place where he made his move.

It was eleven, and the bar had yet to fill up. Akulov nodded at the barmaid. She smiled back at him. With her long, raven hair, black singlet and tattoo sleeves, she looked like she was part of a rock band and he imagined she probably was. She turned to serve her next customers and his gaze now fell upon the pair of women who'd appeared at the bar. They were speaking hurriedly, excitedly in Spanish, a language he too spoke. The bartender leant forward to take their order and then moved away to complete their complicated requests.

The woman nearest to Akulov looked up at him, a wide smile on her face. She looked too young to be out drinking. Her friend said something in her ear and she turned away. They carried on speaking animatedly to each other until their drinks arrived and the woman nearest to Akulov passed over a black-coloured credit card. An *Amex Centurion* card, the card of millionaires. The barmaid placed the PIN machine on the bar and took payment. Once the card was returned the women started to drink greedily, as though the drinks may at any moment be snatched away. Akulov guessed the pair were out on an illicit night out, possibly using someone else's card. They didn't look like thieves, so a parent perhaps? Again, it made no difference to him. He finished his beer, turned and made his way to the restrooms.

He walked along the dark corridor. The volume of the music faded. Straight ahead was a fire door leading out to the alleyway at the side of the building, but he turned right and entered the bathroom, its stark strip lights making him squint. He used the urinal. Before he had finished a group of three men entered.

He instantly recognised one of them.

Akulov immediately felt his body tense. He slowed his breathing and forced himself to relax, something that was counterintuitive but necessary if he needed to suddenly take evasive action or attack. Muscles moved faster when reacting from a relaxed state. Two of the men were bulky and flanked the third who was smaller, and shorter, but moved with the easy swagger of supreme confidence. His chest and shoulders were gym-wide. The two heavies checked the cubicles before nodding to the much shorter man and opened a door for him. He closed it and they took sentry positions, one guarding the cubicle and the other the main door to the bathroom.

Akulov buttoned up his Levi's, stepped to the basin and washed his hands. There were two loud sniffs from the cubicle. In the mirror, his eyes met those of the nearest heavy.

The man's complexion was dark, his hair was slicked back and a weighty moustache drooped over his top lip. 'You want something, *cabrón*?'

Akulov said nothing. It would be easy to take both men out now then turn his attention on their boss, but the bathroom was not a controlled environment – anyone could enter, anyone could overhear and then of course the hallway was probably being filmed. He moved towards the hand dryer. The man by the door now glared at him. Akulov took a deep breath, to oxygenate his muscles before he made for the door, but as he did so the cubicle door opened.

63

'We got a problem?' the smaller man said, his accent Mexican, the tone confrontational.

Akulov continued to the door but the second heavy now blocked it. 'Don Caesar asked you a question, *puto*!'

Akulov turned, so that he could see all three men. Caesar Mendez, dressed in black jeans, black shirt and a black leather waistcoat, had his chin jutted up and forward. Akulov nodded, slowly, respectfully. 'No problem at all.'

'Then keep it that way, my friend,' Don Caesar replied, a wide, thin-lipped smile splitting his face. He addressed his men in Spanish: 'Let him go.'

'Thank you,' Akulov said, and exited the room at an easy pace.

For most of his adult life Akulov had been around powerful and dangerous men. The truly powerful had no reason to pretend to be dangerous, and the truly dangerous had no reason to display their power. Unless they were afraid they were about to lose it. There had been no glimmer of recognition in Caesar's eyes, no hesitation when he had spoken. Akulov was still unknown by the man, for the moment at least.

Back at the bar his half-empty bottle was where he had left it, but the two women had moved away, their place taken now by a couple dressed in dirty jeans and faded T-shirts. In his dark Levi's and black polo shirt he didn't stand out, which was what he had hoped for. The bar was busier now but he managed to get the barmaid's attention and ordered a new beer. He wasn't going to drink from a bottle he had left unattended. The three cartel men came back into the room. The heavies looked each way. The one with the moustache glared at him again, before they made for an occupied table halfway down the room and against the wall. The trio stood briefly before the table's occupants got up, and moved away. Then they sat.

The new beer arrived, so cold the bottle sweated, and he drank it thankfully. Outside the Texan air was hot and dry; inside the AC struggled to repel it. Houston seemed an enjoyable place but he wasn't there to enjoy it, he was there to find Vetrov. And he'd just found his new employer. The party people now had started to arrive.

Akulov sipped his beer and let himself relax, a fraction, just enough to blend in and just enough to look normal. At thirty-six he was by no means the oldest person in the place but he'd noticed that the clientele were a younger demographic – twenty-somethings dancing, drinking and swaggering. And the three cartel men observed it all from their table. Akulov had eyes on Caesar and the question was, what would he do now? He had meant this evening to be reconnaissance, an initial assessment of the place and not as an immediate strike point, but the man was here. Akulov had no illusions about getting him to talk. He knew Caesar would not willingly give up Vetrov and his exact location. But the man had seen him, as had his two goons, which meant if they saw him again, given their line of work, he doubted it would be put down to coincidence. Akulov internally cursed; he'd messed up, which was not something he did, ever. He sipped his beer, but it now tasted bitter.

The two Spanish-speaking women he'd seen earlier made another trip to the bar. Akulov noted the reaction of Caesar and his men as the pair passed their table. It seemed to be more than leering, as if they were discussing something. He noted that the women paid them no attention. The two groups certainly weren't together. Akulov leant against the bar, his tolerance to booze in the Spetsnaz had once been much higher, but he knew it was time to call it a night. The beers were small and he'd had, what, three, four? Nothing in the real sense of drinking. Two or three pints as the British would say, perhaps a litre and a half in Russian terms, but any more and he'd risk his tactical awareness. His bottle was empty. He caught the barmaid's eye and shook his head. He decided he'd leave the place now. From his intel he knew that Don Caesar was in most nights and he now knew the layout and feel of the both the place and the man much better.

Yes, Akulov decided, tomorrow he would come for the Mexican cartel boss and the man wouldn't see him coming.

Something bumped his arm at the bar and he looked sideways. A pair of large brown eyes set in a fresh but flushed face looked back at him.

'Sorry,' she said.

'No worries,' Akulov replied, automatically switching to Spanish.

'I'm Sofia.'

'Russ.' If he'd not been working, her attention would have been welcomed. A decade and a half of death had changed him, but on the outside his full head of dark hair still got him noticed.

'This is Juana.' Her friend appeared at her side, and linked arms with her.

'Hello, Juana.'

The second woman smiled but said nothing.

Akulov made a show of looking at his watch. 'Ladies, it's late and I need to go. Enjoy the rest of your evening.'

Sofia pouted and placed her hand on his arm. 'But everyone here is so boring. Can't you stay?'

'Did your mother put a stop on her credit card?'

There was a frown then a flash of anger. 'How did you know? Did she send you to spy on us?'

'No, I just saw earlier that you had a black Amex card, which obviously wasn't yours.'

'Why? Because I'm Mexican?' Her eyes narrowed.

'No, because you looked too young to have one of your own.'

'I'm twenty-two!'

'My apologies. I am an old man and my eyesight isn't what it once was.'

'She stopped it,' Juana said. 'We've run out of money.'

Akulov reached into his jeans pocket, retrieved a handful of bills and handed her a hundred. 'Here, have a drink on me. And sorry again.'

66

'No strings?' Sofia asked, slowly taking the note.

'None.'

'Thank you.' Sofia touched his face with her hand, pulled him down and planted a kiss on his mouth.

It was the first time in a long while he'd been kissed. He looked past Sofia and saw Don Caesar giving him daggers. Something odd was happening here. 'Did you two come on your own?'

'Why do you want to know?'

'No reason.' Akulov shrugged. 'Enjoy.' He placed a couple of notes on the bar for his drinks and made towards the exit, purposefully walking directly past the Mexicans and watching them from the corner of his eye. Their glares followed him. He looked back as he pulled open the door, and watched Caesar head directly to the bar. His two men tailed their diminutive boss. The girls were still waiting to be served. A moment of indecision hit Akulov, which was unusual and unnerving, but he shook it off – they were nothing to do with him – and let the heavy door swing shut.

This part of town was the former industrial district. It was quiet but the wide streets were well lit. Akulov glanced up and noted the security cameras on the front of the building facing the bar. Lights and cameras. He imagined that police patrols were also not too far away. Several taxis waited on the opposite side of the street, ready to turn and swoop back to collect fares. Akulov raised his arm and hailed one. But what drew Akulov's attention was the nose of the large white Cadillac Escalade that protruded from the side street to his right. It glowed as the streetlights reflected from its pristine paintwork. He imagined it was what J. R. Ewing would drive if he was alive today. The driver's window was open and a trail of cigar smoke drifted out, carried on the warm night air. The engine wasn't on, but it didn't look as though the vehicle would be parked up there for long.

A shrill electronic note sounded and the driver flicked his cigar out of the window and picked up his phone, the screen illuminating his face. And then he switched on the engine. Someone's driver, someone who didn't need to or want to use a taxi. And that someone, Akulov knew, was Caesar Mendez.

In the stillness of the heavy night air Akulov heard a door open, and the muffled sound of the music from the club. But it wasn't the entrance he had just stepped out of; it was the side door, the fire exit near the bar. The driver's gaze now seemed to be focused on his rear-view mirror and as if to confirm Akulov's observation, he leant out of the SUV and looked back.

The taxi pulled up in front of Akulov. The cliché of following the car popped into his head, but he already knew where Mendez lived and from the assessment in his briefing pack he knew the residence had multiple layers of security. Again he decided that the club was the best strike point but not now, not tonight. He opened the door, got in and was in the process of closing it when he heard a scream … His eyes met the taxi driver's in the mirror.

The cabby shrugged, as though he'd seen and heard it all before, and then asked in a Texan drawl, 'Where to?'

Akulov turned in his seat and saw the huge frame of the Cadillac driver make a hasty exit from the equally oversized SUV and head into the alley. There was another scream, high-pitched, female.

He heard a woman shout, in Spanish, 'Juana, run!'

Akulov frowned. Juana – one of the two girls from the club. Without saying a word to the taxi driver, he exited and jogged to the corner of the building. He stepped around into the alley and Juana all but slammed into him. Her eyes were wide with fear, and the Cadillac driver was a couple of steps behind. What he saw, further down the alley and illuminated by a lamp above the fire exit, was shocking, but not surprising to him. Sofia was being held by the two heavies he'd had the encounter with inside. And in the middle of all this, Don Caesar was standing with a phone to his ear, seemingly without a care in the world.

68

Juana raised her hands, desperately trying to grab Akulov. 'Help us!'

Akulov pulled the woman behind him, and pushed her around the corner. He blocked the SUV driver's path. The man was monstrously large and the speed he was moving meant that he couldn't stop his huge frame in time to avoid Akulov's foot. The leg-sweep collided with his shins, the closing speed enough to make him instantly airborne. Luis Bravo "the Giant", Caesar's enforcer, crashed onto the tarmac hands first then chest. He grunted, winded, and then pulled himself to his knees. His jacket fell open to reveal a large, silver revolver squeezed into a pancake holster. Instinctively, Akulov lunged for the Giant's gun and heaved it out of the holster with one hand whilst delivering a punch to the side of the man's skull with the other.

Eyes wide with anger, the Giant swung a long arm at Akulov, but Akulov stepped around the arm and hit the Giant across the head with the revolver. The huge man lurched back against the wall, dazed.

There was another scream. A gunshot rang out followed by a second, two quick rounds fired from a handgun. Chips of concrete flew up by Akulov's foot. He dived towards the opposite side of the alley and came back up with the silver revolver pointed towards the men and the woman. Three guns, one held against the side of Sofia's stomach, one pointed at him by the second heavy; and the third was being pulled, jerkily, from its concealed-carry holster by the hand of Caesar. In the corner of his eye, Akulov saw the Giant try to stand and fall back against the wall.

They were quick, very quick; these were men Vetrov had trained well. Speed came from an understanding of the tactical situation and that came from training or experience. And men this fast, this experienced, were not amateurs. What he had found himself witness to was not a random act. The cartel soldiers on one side and the black Amex card on the other … It was an abduction.

And an abduction meant that Sofia was valuable to the cartel, and that meant the man holding her, and pushing the gun into her, would not shoot her unless he was ordered to, and those orders would come from Don Caesar. These observations and calculations came to Akulov in a matter of milliseconds, but he was slower than he should have been, would have been if he hadn't been drinking and hadn't been retired for the past year.

Akulov acquired the second gunman, the heavy who had already fired at him. He was the salient threat. The heavy fired again and started to run at him, to rush him. Akulov felt a sudden gust of air as the round whipped past his head before burying itself in the rear of the Cadillac. Akulov returned fire, pulling the weighty trigger, twice, in quick succession, as fast as he could be with a revolver. It bucked as each round left the barrel. Unused to the balance of the .357 magnum six-shooter, his first round was wide but the second obliterated the heavy's face.

Even before the goon had hit the ground, Akulov had the pistol trained on the second, the one who was holding Sofia. But the gunman was moving, his gun up and pulling the woman in front of himself as a shield. Akulov ignored her and fired. His round found the man's exposed left shin. He spun, sideways; his arms flew up and an animal-like yell erupted from his maw. It was silenced a second later when the next round from Akulov's pistol eviscerated his heart, instantly reducing him to nothing more than a bag of meat and bones.

Akulov reversed direction and reacquired Don Caesar. The man's gun was up and now pointing at him, and a sneer was visible on his dimly lit face. There were two rounds left in the six-shooter. Akulov pulled the trigger but as he did so there was movement and a roar to his right. What felt like a tidal wave hit him and threw him into the air to come crashing down on the far side of the alley, against the brick wall of the neighbouring building. The revolver flew from his hands and skittered away into the shadows. Seconds later a crushing weight fell upon him, pinning him to the ground, and huge hands clamped around his throat. The Giant leant in, pressing him back into the trash-covered tarmac and brick.

He tried to buck, to move, but the massive man was too heavy. There was a popping sound and then a crack and needles of pain pierced the skin of his spine. The Giant grinned down at him through the gloom. From somewhere within, Akulov found something, a fury he had been taught to harness. He managed to turn his left shoulder and slammed his open palm against the Giant's ear. The huge man grunted and squeezed harder. Akulov's vision started to grey out and he began to lose consciousness. The lights of the alley flickered and blurred. He tried to strike the man again, but his arm didn't move.

A voice – male, Mexican and pained – yelled from seemingly a long way off, 'Get me out of here!'

Without warning, Akulov felt himself being lifted into the air and then swung against the wall like a rag doll. The back of his head hit the bricks and what vision he had disappeared.

In the darkness he could hear words and the scraping of feet and then a high-pitched scream. Akulov's eyes snapped open. He was lying face down in the alley, his left cheek flat against the warm tarmac. With blurred vision he watched the Giant trying to help his boss. Caesar was standing, leaning against the man who was two foot taller than he was. His right arm was limp, while his left hand clamped his shoulder. Akulov's round had winged him.

Akulov's head felt as though a giant hand was squeezing it from behind, which he noted was ironic. Ignoring the throbbing pain, he managed to push up to his hands and knees. There was a glint to his left – broken glass, the bottle that had smashed and cut into his back as the Giant had forced him into the ground. His eyes searched desperately for the revolver, one round left, two targets, one-armed, probably a full magazine. He saw it lying against the wall, equal distance between him and the two remaining Mexicans. Akulov knew that if he continued playing dead he'd soon be exactly that. He had to move. The alley was silent again now save for Sofia whimpering by the closed fire exit. Rooted to the spot, splattered with the blood of the man who had held her, she was like a weeping statue.

Akulov took a deep, calming breath, filling his lungs till bursting point, and closed his mind to the pain. Now he had to act. The Giant was supporting his boss, with his back to Akulov. Like a sprinter exploding out of the blocks, Akulov sprang forward towards the revolver. His legs felt rubbery and his gait was uneven, but he was still fast enough. Caesar saw Akulov and started to shout instructions at his enforcer. But it was too late. Akulov reached the revolver, snatched it up and carried on moving. He barrelled into the Giant, left shoulder first, jarring his whole body, pain now streaking down his spine, but making the monster stumble forward and trip over Caesar. Both men were down and Akulov scrambled backwards to his feet with the large revolver trained on Caesar's centre mass. One round left, two targets.

'Don't move,' Akulov panted, in Spanish.

The Giant lay face down, but Caesar was on his back.

'You know who I am, *pendejo*?' The cartel boss's voice was incredulous.

Akulov listened to distant sirens and watched the Giant's right hand slowly moving in the gloom.

'Hey! *Pinche estúpido!*' Caesar said, in a louder voice. 'I'm talking to you!'

And then the huge man shot his right hand out to reach for something. Two targets, one round. Akulov darted forward and struck the Giant on the back of his head with the heavy revolver. The Giant became limp.

One target, one round.

How long did he have before the police arrived? And how long did he have before he was unable to escape? He fixed his eyes on Caesar's. In the dim sodium lighting he saw outrage, and anger but not fear. Was this a result of the drugs the cartel boss had snorted?

'Where is the Russian?'

'What?' Caesar's eyes twitched.

'Where is Vetrov?'

'You're here for him?'

'Yes.'

A sneer now formed on Caesar's face. 'He is in Matamoros.'

'Gracias,' Akulov said, and fired his last .357 magnum round into the cartel boss's heart.

Akulov focused on Juana and Sofia.

He checked they were OK, collected Juana's bag from the ground, and then led them towards the idling SUV.

'Get in the back, both of you, and stay down.'

Numb with shock and fear, both women complied.

The whine of sirens grew louder in his ears. Akulov jogged back to Caesar, each step making him wince. But pain was good; it kept him sharp. He took the man's wallet, and then he saw his gun – a sub-compact Glock – lying on the ground just past the prone form of the Giant. Akulov collected the Glock and ran back to the SUV. He leant against the vehicle, sucked in a deep breath, and blinked several times until the world stopped spinning.

He got in the Cadillac, dropped his bounty on the passenger seat, and pulled away. It was only now that he saw his taxi hadn't moved, and that its driver was standing on the road filming with a smartphone. Akulov cursed. He didn't know how much the man had seen or recorded but he was a witness nonetheless. At that moment a pair of cruisers appeared at the next junction, on his left. Resisting the urge to floor the gas pedal, Akulov pulled the conspicuous Cadillac out into the road and at a leisurely pace headed in the opposite direction.

Akulov drove in silence and took a moment to adjust his seat. Luis Bravo was easily a foot taller than him. He had no idea why the cartel men had attempted the abduction, so instead focused on getting both himself and the two women away from the scene.

Akulov stuck to the posted speed limit and headed in a general south-easterly direction. As his adrenalin started to ebb away, various parts of his body began to ache, each sending in a "damage report" to his brain. He pressed the lump on the back of his head and the pain increased, but nothing moved and it wasn't wet. He'd received a mild concussion for sure but there was little he could do about that. He took in a deep breath and let it out slowly: no warning signs from his lungs or ribs. His shoulders and thighs were stiff, but that was expected. He worked his jaw, his ears still ringing from the thunderous retort of the silver pistol. He let his eyes dart to the passenger seat and the two handguns lying on it. He now recognised the pistol as the six-inch barrel version of the Colt Python. The six-shooter was an expensive, well-made piece but not the best choice for a modern gunfight. The other pistol, the sub-compact Glock, was the unusual G33 version which, like the Python, chambered the serious .357 magnum round. A much more sensible, if snappy weapon. Both had a recoil that had to be accounted for.

He continued to drive through Houston. Every few seconds he glanced back at the two women and at the road behind him. They were huddled together. Sofia looked straight ahead with a blank expression on her face whilst Juana's head lolled against her friend's shoulder. The women would start to react soon, and he knew that he needed to control that when it happened.

Stomach churning, due to the booze and adrenalin dump, he left the sprawl of Houston and took the I-69 south. An interstate was the fastest route away from the city; however, it also carried the highest risk of being tracked by surveillance and law enforcement cameras.

As the lights and traffic of the city faded behind them, he decided it was time to talk to them, to control both the situation and their response to it. 'You're safe now.'

Sofia met his gaze in the mirror. 'Safe?'

'Yes. Safe.' He could see she was still trying to understand what had happened. 'Those men tried to kidnap you. I stopped them.'

She blinked, looked out of the window on either side, as though awaking from a daydream, or more likely a nightmare. 'This isn't the way to our hotel! Where are we?'

'Where are you staying?' He didn't want to answer the question head on.

'The Four Seasons.'

'OK.'

Sofia suddenly became panicked. 'Where are you taking us?'

'I'm taking you somewhere safe.'

'What do you mean? Our hotel is safe. It's a five star; it has security guards and cameras and everything.'

'I understand but the men who attacked you may know where you were staying. Perhaps they had someone at the hotel who was watching you?'

'That's creepy.'

Akulov had a sudden thought. 'Why did you choose that bar?'

'I asked a guy at the hotel; he recommended it.'

'A random guy?'

'No. The bellboy.'

'Then he was probably the guy paid to watch you.'

'Who are you?' she asked.

'My name's Russ. We met at the bar. I gave you money for some drinks – remember?'

'That's not what I meant,' Sofia snapped, suddenly alert.

Juana looked up now and asked, 'Are you a cop?'

'No, I'm just someone who helped you. I'm not a cop.'

'I'm going to call my uncle,' Sofia said, reaching for her handbag.

Akulov realised his error. Both women had phones, everyone did, and he had Don Caesar's phone. All three of them could be traced, and then there was the SUV too – did that have a tracker?

75

He was on a highway doing fifty-five and there was no way he could safely stop her from making the call. And besides, how would he explain to them that he was a good guy, yet didn't want them to call for help? He decided to let them make the call and concentrated on the road.

'Uncle? Uncle! Yes, it's me Sofia!' She started talking in quick-fire Spanish. Her tone was just short of panic.

Akulov listened as she gave a full account of what happened. He heard her apologise for leaving home without saying where she was going.

'Miguel wants to talk to you.' She shuffled forward and handed him the phone.

Akulov glanced at the screen. The call was being placed by WhatsApp. He said, in Spanish, 'Hello?'

Miguel replied in the same. 'Who is this?'

'My name's Russel. I was at the bar when your niece and her friend were attacked.'

'Who are you?' The same question as his niece. To which Akulov gave the same answer. There was a grunt and then Miguel asked, 'Can I trust you?'

'I just shot three men to save your niece.'

There was a pause at the other end, only the sound of the man's laboured breathing, as if he was trying to suppress some emotion. Then the voice became calm, the tone even. 'Listen to me, Mr Russel, what you have done is a very brave act. I need you to remain very brave until I can meet you to collect my Sofia and her friend Juana. Can you do that?'

In the darkness of the SUV's interior, Akulov's eyes narrowed. Bravery didn't come into it. There was training and there was action. Nothing else. 'I can do that.'

'Do not take them to their hotel; take them somewhere else.'

'I understand.'

'WhatsApp me a pin of your location, when you arrive, and I will be with you by tomorrow morning.'

76

'Understood,' Akulov said again.

'Goodbye, Mr Russel.'

The call ended. Akulov placed the phone in the cubbyhole between the front seats.

'Can I have my phone back?' Sofia asked.

'When we arrive at our destination.'

'Where is that?'

'It's another hotel – your uncle told me to take you there.'

'So why can't I have my phone now?'

'Miguel said so. It's best that you don't use it, because we can be traced.'

'Miguel is always so paranoid!'

'And this time his paranoia is justified. You were almost kidnapped!'

'And what are you doing, if not kidnapping us too?'

'Evacuating you to safety. Juana, please give me your phone too.'

There was a loud sigh and she passed her iPhone forward, in a pink fluffy case. 'Nice.'

'Thank you.'

The Cadillac became silent as Akulov concentrated on the road. It was so empty that the large white SUV looked conspicuous. The I-69 became the US-69 and the road narrowed and the traffic decreased even more. Akulov read the road signs. He had never been here before but knew what he was searching for. Somewhere big enough to have several hotels and motels, but small enough to be overlooked. They passed Beasley and Kendleton before he decided to take the off-ramp at Wharton.

He drove through the main drag, past economy chains including Holiday Inn Express and Motel 6. He turned onto a smaller road and saw a more promising place. The Countryside Inn was set back from the road and bordered on three sides by ploughed fields. It was made up of two conjoined orange-tiled buildings, a single-storey restaurant and a two-storey accommodation block.

Half a dozen vehicles, a mixture of SUVs and pick-up trucks, sat outside. Akulov took the access road around the entire complex. The restaurant was closed but there was a light on in the reception area adjoining it. He manoeuvred the large Cadillac back into the shadows at the rear of the complex.

'I need you both to stay in the car.' Akulov cracked open the two front windows an inch then switched off the ignition. He glanced at Don Caesar's phone, and was on the verge of turning it off when he decided against it. He hid it and the large silver revolver under the passenger seat. If both the SUV and the phone could be traced, it made sense to leave them together. But he did pop the man's wallet into his pocket. He took the car key, the women's two phones, and the small Glock and stepped out. 'Stay here, OK?'

'Sí,' Sofia said.

'I'll get us a room and then get us inside.'

'Us?'

'Yes. One twin room. You two can take the beds and I'll keep watch on the door.'

He left the SUV and headed towards the reception entrance. The fresh night air revived him as he slowly walked towards the car porch in front of the reception entrance. He stopped and then stared back at the Cadillac. He'd taken the phones but hadn't locked it. He mentally shrugged to himself. If the women ran, they ran – at least then his part in their ordeal would be over. The reception door unsurprisingly was locked. He pressed a bell and heard a distant trill. Nothing happened. He rang again and peered through the glass. A reception desk and a couple of soft chairs had been arranged in what seemed like an orange interior. A faint light shone from behind the reception desk. This time he rapped on the glass and rang the bell again.

Abruptly light spilled into the room and a figure stepped out, silhouetted by the light, his shape chillingly familiar. Akulov automatically reached for the Glock until he realised that the silhouette was not a shooter in a ballistic helmet and NVGs, rather a kid in his late teens with a large set of green camouflaged gaming headphones with a boom mic. He switched on the lights to reveal his shaggy blond hair, baggy red-checked shirt and faded blue jeans. He crossed the room and opened the door. Too trusting, Akulov thought but perhaps that would be to his advantage.

'May I help you?' the gamer asked, with overt politeness.

'What are you playing?'

'Fortnite. You play?'

'I prefer Minecraft.'

The kid smirked. 'You want a room?'

'Yeah.'

'Just you?'

Akulov could lie, he knew he could but given the kid's age a version of the truth would work better. 'Me and a lady friend, if you understand me?'

'Yeah?' The kid's eyes widened momentarily before he tried to act cool. 'I do.'

'How much for a twin room?'

'Twin?'

'I like my space.'

'Ah. Eighty bucks, but you know, double occupancy et cetera.' He shrugged.

Akulov reached into his jeans and pulled out several notes. 'Here's a hundred if we can keep this off the register? My friend has an ex-boyfriend who doesn't know he's an ex yet.'

'No can do. It's the regulations.' The kid folded his arms. 'I'm going to need to see some ID.'

'You sure?'

He pursed his lips and then his eyes darted up and left. 'How about I give you that twin room, but just say its single occupancy? I mean I only saw you here, didn't I?'

'Deal.'

'But I'll still have to charge you for double occupancy.'

Akulov smirked and handed him the cash. 'Have you got a top-floor room on the rear corner?'

'Come inside. I'll check.'

Akulov followed the kid inside, where he tapped away at a cream-coloured desktop computer. 'So, ID?'

'Here.' Akulov handed over his Boston driving licence. It listed an address he'd visited once, an apartment block with thirty flats, as his home address. He had no idea if the exact flat was currently rented out.

'Ha, thought you weren't local – with that Boston accent an'all.'

Normally Akulov wouldn't make conversation, but being friendly with the kid would make him less likely to tell the police or anyone else who asked more about him, so he made some idle chitchat.

The kid tapped a few keys, then gave Akulov back his ID and a key attached to a large piece of thick plastic. 'There you go. Enjoy, the room I mean. Breakfast starts at seven, ends at ten. Not included in the price. Sorry.'

'Thanks.' Akulov nodded, and winced as he felt a sharp twinge of pain.

'You OK?'

'Just a headache.'

The kid jutted his chin up at Akulov. 'What happened?'

In the light of the lobby Akulov noticed the dirt on his shirt. 'I fell off a damn kerb; the streetlight was out. Can you believe it? I don't suppose you have any ice or a packet of Advil?'

The kid gestured to the drinks dispenser. 'No to the ice – the machine is out of order – but I've got tablets.'

'How much?'

'No charge, they're not mine.' He reached under the desk and handed over a blister pack.

'Thanks.'

Akulov walked at a brisk but not overtly fast pace, the pace of a man who had somewhere to be, and someone to be with. He took the exterior stairs up to the second floor and scouted the entire exterior once. The town was quiet, save for the distant tail lights of passing cars on the interstate and the air was now still, but heavy with the promise of distant thunder. He took the steps back down, approached the car and opened the rear doors.

'Time to get out, ladies.'

'You got a room?' Sofia asked.

'No, they were full, but he said we could use the stable.'

Her eyes narrowed.

'It's up the stairs and turn left. First door.' He looked at the women. They didn't move. 'Go.'

Akulov followed them up the stairs, then let them inside. The pungent fragrance of floral air freshener fought to mask a musty odour. Small-town USA, Akulov thought to himself as he switched on the light and shut the door. The floor was covered by a hard-wearing brown carpet and the walls were an inoffensive shade of cream. A large flat-screen TV was affixed to one wall opposite a pair of queen beds. Two armchairs stood at the corner facing the door. The bathroom was at the rear. Akulov decided it needed some positive spin.

'Two beds, one for each of you. I'll take the chairs.'

Juana went into the bathroom and shut the door. Sofia stayed in the middle of the room, her arms folded across her chest, defensively. Akulov sat in one of the armchairs, knowing he'd look less threatening if he wasn't standing or blocking the room's only exit. He popped three of the Advils and dry-swallowed them.

'You're hurt?'

He took Sofia's phone from his pocket, tried to open it up and realised it needed a passcode to unlock it. 'What's the code?'

'Why?'

'I need to send your uncle our location by WhatsApp.'

'It's my date of birth.'

'Which is?'

81

She paused, embarrassed, and then told him. She wasn't twenty-two. Akulov felt old – he was twice her age. He opened the app and sent their location. Then he took Don Caesar's wallet from his pocket and inspected the contents: $900 in cash, a photograph of the dead man holding an alligator by the jaws, credit cards and a Texas driving licence in the name of Caesar Mendez. He took the cash, added it to his own and dropped the wallet on the coffee table.

'Who are you?' The shower started up in the bathroom. Sofia took this as a sign to move and sat tentatively on the edge of the bed farthest away from him. 'You shot three men, but you don't even look worried. Aren't you afraid?'

Akulov decided a little bit of truth would go a long way. 'They weren't the first men I've had to kill. I used to be a soldier. I've been shot at before; you get used to it.'

'So what are you now? A *sicario*?' She folded her arms, hugging herself.

'No.' Akulov smiled. The Spanish word for hitman sounded good as it rolled from the lips that had kissed him an hour earlier. 'I'm just a guy who was out for a drink.'

She stared at him, as though trying to read his mind. 'Where are you from?'

'Boston. You?'

'Matamoros.'

Which was interesting, as it was where Caesar had said Vetrov was, but Akulov didn't let it show. 'On the border.'

'Do you know it?'

'I've never been to Mexico.'

'You should.' She frowned. 'Where did you learn Spanish?'

'Spain,' he lied.

She nodded. 'That's where the accent is from – you sound Spanish.'

'When I speak English?'

She rolled her eyes. 'When you speak Spanish.'

'Ah.' He switched to Spanish. 'It is late and you both have been through an upsetting experience. You need to rest. Why don't you go and freshen up then try to get some sleep. I'm going to turn the light off and wait over here for your uncle to arrive.'

'No.' Her voice was resolute. 'I'm fine. I'll stay up.'

'Fine. Do what you want, but there is a rule in the Army. Sleep when you can and eat when you can. We don't have food but you both have beds.'

'Can I have my phone back now?'

'No. Not until your uncle arrives.'

'You said I could have it!'

'I promised to keep you both safe.'

He stood, flicked off the light switch, and then retook his seat. Akulov sat in the dark, in silence, barely able to pick out the woman on the bed. There were no words and no movement for several minutes until, with a sigh, Sofia got up and joined Juana in the bathroom.

Akulov stifled a yawn. He was tired, dehydrated, and worst of all concussed. He berated himself for not searching the SUV for water, but he couldn't leave the room now and doubted the quality of the wet stuff dribbling from the bathroom faucet. He sat and listened, to the sound of the night outside and the women within. There was much muttering from the bathroom and the sound of the hairdryer being switched on. Twenty minutes later, with half-opened eyes he watched both women return wrapped in large hotel towels and robes. Akulov turned in his chair, to make sure he was facing in the opposite direction and pretended to be asleep. Gentle snores forty minutes later alerted him to the fact that the women were asleep, or very accomplished actors.

Akulov stood and made sure the door was locked before he quietly crossed the room to the bathroom. He shut the door before he turned on the light. He removed his polo shirt and assessed himself in the bathroom mirror. His torso felt stiff and he had the start of a few bruises on his neck and chest. He turned and angled his side to see his back. It was grazed from the wall and cut from the broken bottle. He wet a wad of toilet paper and dabbed at the abrasions and tears. He splashed his face with water and dried it on the last clean towel in the small bathroom before he shook out and cleaned his shirt as best he could. It wasn't much of a bandage but now he wound the remainder of the toilet paper around himself to give his back a little protection. When he went back through the door, the women were still snoring.

He was drowsy, but knew he had to stay awake a while longer. If they had been followed, they'd be receiving visitors soon. He retrieved Sofia's iPhone from where he'd placed it on the floor and tapped in her date of birth. Now was the time to understand why the Mendez Cartel were after her. He needed to learn more about her; she was no normal young woman. But what he immediately found on the phone was exactly what a normal young woman would have. An Instagram account, a Facebook account and a couple of other platforms he hadn't heard of. He opened Instagram and scrolled through her posts, mainly finding photographs of her with friends, including Juana, at restaurants, shops or at pool parties. There were a few of her with a dark-haired muscular boy, and one of her sitting on his lap. The picture was surrounded by a heart-shaped frame.

He read the messages below it. The boy's name was Daniel Arellano. The surname of Mendez Cartel's greatest rival. He doubted it was a coincidence. Facebook said her full name was Sofia Becerra and, as she had told him, she was from the border town of Matamoros. She seemed to be an only child. As he scrolled he saw posts about and photographs of her house, a large villa with verdant grounds and a pool. And then in among all the happy snaps of friends and parents there was one of her with her arm around a serious-looking, barrel-chested man with the largest moustache he had even seen. The post read: 'Happy Fiftieth Uncle Miguel!' Akulov studied the face, consigned it to memory.

He blinked, fighting the drowsiness that was threatening to

engulf him. Continuing to use her phone he searched for more information on Daniel Arellano. Tellingly he found no social media accounts under that name so he switched to a wider internet search. It brought up a newspaper article from a Mexican publication, about an outreach project started by Arellano senior to improve local child literacy. Maybe Uncle Miguel was a cartel man. Akulov felt a sense of satisfaction, because his assassination of Caesar Mendez would provoke a reaction from his brother, Angel Mendez. And if Akulov could be certain of anything it was that his old team leader Vetrov would protect his own interests. And that meant safeguarding his new boss, and travelling with Angel Mendez when he came to Texas to find his brother's killer and avenge his death.

Akulov battled to keep his eyelids open, but had one last thing he wanted do to before he gave in to sleep. He opened the email account he used to communicate with his broker and typed a message in the draft folder: 'One Mendez down.' And then Akulov closed his eyes.

Chapter 8

InterContinental West Bay, Doha, Qatar

Even though Qatar was two hours ahead of France, Tate was awake before the sun came up, a can of Coke from the minibar in hand, and gazing out of his high-floor window at the skyline of Doha's West Bay area in the distance. A myriad of architectural styles had been placed side by side and back to back on a piece of land that just twenty years before was sand rolling and billowing into the sea. The man-made vista reminded him of Hong Kong with each tower and skyscraper illuminated with pulsating lights. His flight to Heathrow was late in the evening, which gave Tate time to unwind. And after the planning, and the mental and physical stress of the mission, he needed it. There were city tours and sights to see, and shopping he imagined too, but all he really wanted to do was eat, drink, swim and bask in the Gulf sunshine.

He moved away from the window and caught his reflection in a large mirror. The moustache had started to grow on him, literally, but now he could see that his Paddy Fox special haircut needed work. It was uneven, blocky and made him look like Oddbod – from *Carry On Screaming*. A smile creased his face as he remembered watching it as a kid with his brother Simon and their dad. He hadn't spoken to Simon for a couple of weeks. He checked his Rolex: 4.45 a.m. in Doha made it 21.45 in Washington the day before, a bit late for a social call.

Tate was travelling clean and with the exception of his own mechanical Rolex had nothing with him. This included a complete lack of any electronic device of any kind. He wondered how Al Nayef would feel without his status, trappings of wealth and of course Twitter, Instagram and Facebook accounts. Tate had never used any type of social media platform; they hadn't existed when he'd joined the British Army and by the time they had he was already in the SAS and prohibited from creating one.

Tate lay back down on his bed and closed his eyes. And then the room phone rang. He sat up and reached for it. 'Yes?'

'The name's Adrian Potkins, and I've got a message for you. I'll be up there in five.'

The call ended and Tate hurriedly threw his travelling clothes back on. His clean set lay still unpacked in his hand luggage. He went to the door and opened it, letting it stay ajar. The room was darker than the hallway, so he'd be hidden in the shadows. And then he waited.

He heard the lift arrive at the end of the hall, the doors open and the footfall of a single person on the thick hotel carpet. There was a knock, before the door swung open. A slight man stood there, illuminated by the hallway lights. He was in his mid-forties with shaggy brown hair, and wearing scruffy khaki cargo shorts and a creased, cream linen shirt. Tate noted that he kept his hands on display by his sides.

'Can I come in?' It was the same voice from the phone, and Tate now detected the trace of an accent that hinted at Australia or New Zealand.

'Make yourself at home.'

'Thanks, dude.' The man sat.

Tate pressed a wall-mounted switch and the full room lights flicked on. 'I imagine we have some mutual friends?'

'You imagine right,' said the man.

Tate shut the door.

'As I said on the phone, I'm Adrian Potkins.'

'Good for you.'

'I just need to retrieve my phone?' Potkins kept eye contact with Tate, retrieved a phone, dialled a number then held it up to his ear. 'I'm with him now. OK, will do.' Potkins held out his handset. 'She wants to speak to you.'

'Put it on speaker,' Tate ordered.

The unmistakable voice of Pamela Newman, Tate's SIS handler, filled his ears. 'Jack, Mr Potkins is with us.'

Tate took the phone and noticed that it was an encrypted handset. He turned off the speakerphone function. 'What's happening?'

'Jack, this is a fastball. I need you to go to Texas. Immediately.'

'Why?'

'We've found Akulov.'

All thoughts of his last mission and Al Nayef vanished from his mind. The walls seemed to shift and his chest felt suddenly tight. Tate tried to control his expression but felt his jaw clench. Through this he managed to say, 'Explain?'

'He was pinged taking a flight to Miami yesterday morning from Wichita and then a second flight a matter of hours ago from Miami to Houston.'

'Why expose himself now?'

'I think it was intentional. He looked directly at the cameras before he took both flights.'

Tate was puzzled. 'So he wanted to be seen? Again, why now?'

'Perhaps because he knows we are looking for him and the Americans are not?'

'How?'

'I don't know, and that worries me.'

'I'll have to ask him that personally.'

'Do so. You'll get a full briefing pack when you're stateside.'

'Understood.'

'Jack, I want him alive.'

Tate paused but again said, 'Understood.'

'I sincerely hope you do.'

The line went dead and Tate handed the phone back to Potkins. 'Tell me how I can get to Texas.'

'You're booked on the QR flight to Texas leaving at 07.50. We have to leave now, so I need you to pack.'

'OK.' Tate slipped on his shoes and zipped up his Samsonite cabin bag. 'Done.'

Outside, they got into a 4×4, passed through the ornate arched entrance of the hotel complex and followed the signs for Doha. Tate felt giddy and his stomach churned as his mind drifted back to the last time he had seen Ruslan Akulov, the man who killed his foster parents. Back then, in Washington, Tate had not known Akulov was the bomber. Akulov had not been identified as the suspect on the Camden footage. That had only happened afterwards, when the lost smartphone had been found and Tate's world had been turned upside down.

For a year Tate had shouldered the burden of Akulov's escape from justice. Now he had a chance to avenge the death of the couple who had raised him as their own. But it wasn't just the Hunters who had perished in the Camden bombing. The relatives of the other victims needed justice too, and that was not going to happen if Akulov was allowed to live. He was an animal and Tate was going to put him down. He closed his eyes and forcefully took several long, deep breaths. Did his brother know the news? Had Newman consulted with him?

Wharton, Texas, USA

Akulov's eyes snapped open. He saw the pre-dawn light seeping in under the door and around the curtains, and then he turned his head and registered the two beds. He remembered. He was in a hotel room with two women and his head ached.

Akulov checked his watch. It was after five a.m. he'd slept longer than he intended, but the first light of day was still an hour away. He'd butted the second armchair up against the first to make a makeshift bed. He lifted his legs from the chair and swung to his feet. Wincing as his back and chest complained at the sudden movement, he reached under his shirt and pulled off his impromptu dressing. He stepped into his Timberlands, retrieved the Glock from under his chair and slowly made for the window. Raising the curtain delicately, he peered around it. There was no one waiting for him, no team of *sicarios* preparing to take his life.

He deliberately moved to the door. It had been cut slightly too short for the gap it filled and he could feel an almost imperceptible breeze waft in. He opened the door silently and stepped outside. It was Saturday morning. Wharton was still, the air fresh and scented with earth from the fields that bordered the hotel. In the near-dawn he was satisfied with his choice of hotel. The flat fields gave little cover to any approaching threats. He walked a full circuit of the exterior walkway, taking care not to make a sound as he passed each room.

He was thirsty and hungry, but the restaurant wouldn't be open for several hours. He needed to search the Cadillac. Scanning the fields once more, he took the steps down to the car park. The Cadillac's paintwork glowed. It was some fancy finish, a custom colour and that meant it was unique and memorable. He had to ditch it. He blipped the fob, cursed as the lights flashed once and there was a dull, melodic ping – the sound seemingly magnified a million times in the stillness. He opened the passenger door and took the large silver revolver and phone from under the seat. There were a series of missed calls on the phone but when he tried to unlock it the operating system demanded a code. He put the phone and the revolver back under the seat.

On impulse he opened the glove compartment. An interior light illuminated a metal hip flask, and what he had been hoping for: a small bottle of water. He took the water, confirmed that the seal was intact before taking a sip to wet his mouth and then popping three more pills. Once these were swallowed, he greedily emptied the rest of the water down his throat. He locked the car. It blipped and flashed again … and then he heard the sound of a vehicle approaching. His view was obstructed by the hotel buildings, but the sound grew louder, a rumbling, burbling lazy V8, the type tuned for torque not top speed and that meant it was a heavy vehicle, a pick-up or an SUV. Something told him to take cover because another of his kind, a predator was approaching. He heard doors open and close and then he saw the nose of a vehicle creep around the edge of the hotel building. Akulov dropped to the ground and shuffled beneath the Cadillac, lost – he hoped – into a world of shadows.

He now saw that the approaching SUV was a black Cadillac Escalade, the negative of the vehicle above him. It continued to creep nearer, its headlights off, its running lights off, as though it were a gigantic black panther stealthily stalking its prey. To his right he heard the but silent slapping of rubber-soled boots on concrete. Two dark figures, holding assault rifles, edged around the corner of the building – one crouched and low and the other higher. They were professional, trained, and ready to take different arcs of fire. Akulov stayed immobile, pinned in the gloom. The black Cadillac stopped several car lengths away from his own. A door opened and he saw brown cowboy boots, with shiny steel accents, scrunch onto the dirt. There was a scraping of small stones as the boots approached his SUV and halted within inches of his nose.

'Go up the stairs,' the owner of the boots ordered the two gunmen, in Spanish.

Akulov watched them start to move, tactically and with awareness. The cowboy boots moved away too. Akulov pulled the sub-compact Glock from his back pocket and leopard-crawled out from under the Cadillac. Soundlessly he stood behind the

91

owner of the cowboy boots, at arm's length, the Glock pointed at his head.

'Hands up,' Akulov said, the phrase in Spanish reminding him of an old John Wayne movie. 'Turn around slowly.'

'Are you Mr Russel?' the cowboy boots' owner asked in English.

'Turn around slowly and you'll find out.'

'OK.' The man turned. Akulov recognised the serious expression on his face, the barrel chest and the largest moustache he had even seen. 'I am Miguel Becerra. Please lower your little gun.'

'Tell your men to lower theirs.'

Miguel whistled. Akulov saw the movement from above and then heard footfall on the metal stairs as the men advanced. 'Stand down.'

Akulov raised his right hand to his side and then slowly returned the Glock to his back pocket.

'I trust my niece is still safe?'

'Safe and sleeping.'

'Mr Russel, you are an interesting man. I recognise a fellow professional when I see one. My first question to you is who do you work for?'

'No one.'

'I see, and before that?'

'A select clientele.'

'Why were you in Houston?'

'I was looking for someone.'

'And did you find them?'

'Not yet.'

Miguel gestured to the white Cadillac. 'Do you know who that belongs to?'

'Caesar Mendez.'

'Correct. And do you know who Caesar Mendez is?'

'He's dead.'

Miguel's eyebrows arched skywards. 'Because of you?'

'Yes.'

'That is good news for me but deadly news for you, Mr Russel. Caesar Mendez was a Don of the Mendez Cartel. His twin brother Angel Mendez is the other. They are ruthless, violent, remorseless animals, and they never forget. I am afraid that you have signed your own death warrant.'

'They'll have to take a ticket and wait in line.'

Miguel let out an onerous laugh. 'You are either insane or very confident of your own abilities.'

Akulov didn't need to reply.

'So, shall we get my niece?'

'I'll give you the key.' Akulov slowly reached with his left hand into his pocket and handed Miguel the room key.

'Thank you.' Miguel took a step towards the hotel then abruptly paused, turned and pointed at the white Cadillac. 'Tell me, who was with Caesar?'

'Two heavies with guns – they were reasonably competent. They're also dead. And a giant. I took his gun and left him in the gutter.'

Miguel's moustache quivered. 'You took the Giant's gun?'

'A silver Colt Python. It's what I shot the others with. It's not a great weapon.'

'Then, Mr Russel, you are most definitely insane.' Miguel carried on walking towards the hotel and after Akulov confirmed the room was indeed on the second floor, took the steps up. He rapped heavily on the door with his thick knuckles. 'Room service.'

Inside there was audible mumbling but no one came to the door.

Akulov understood what was going through Miguel's mind. The Mexican would not enter unless he knew it was not a trap. 'I'll open the door and go in first.'

'Agreed,' Miguel said, handing the key back.

Akulov entered the room. Both beds were empty, but the covers had gone. He could hear low voices in the bathroom. 'Stop hiding, ladies, your uncle is here.'

Tentatively, a head peered out from behind the bathroom door.

'I did not drive all the way from Matamoros because I wanted to play hide-and-seek,' Miguel said, his voice aggravated but the tone playful.

'Uncle Miguel?' Sofia's head peeked out further.

'Yes, it is me. Now get dressed. I need to take you home. I'll be waiting outside.' He led Akulov back onto the walkway and shut the door. 'She had an argument with her mother – did she tell you? I love her like a daughter but she is extremely spirited. She fights with my sister like cat and dog. She was always in too much of a hurry to grow up, and now she has.'

'I understand,' Akulov replied. 'But tell me, why did Mendez try to abduct her?'

The Mexican nodded. 'It is a long story. He had a business disagreement with Francisco Arellano, who is a close family friend. His son Daniel was Sofia's boyfriend. And that is all I can say.'

They fell silent. Miguel was a talker and Akulov wanted to give him the chance to do so. They watched the start of the sunrise. In a couple of hours the morning freshness would be replaced by the dry dust of the day.

Miguel continued, 'I owe you a debt, Mr Russel. Sofia's parents owe you a debt.' He reached into his jacket and retrieved an envelope. 'In here you will find $5000. It is yours. Please accept it as a token of our gratitude. My card is also in here. I am personally indebted to you. You can call me anytime.'

'Thank you.' Akulov didn't need the cash, but money was money, and turning it down would have constituted an insult.

'One word of warning, Mr Russel. Walk away from this place. Now. Leave Texas. Do not come back. Never on any account visit Matamoros or the surrounding area. If Angel Mendez or any of his men see you they will kill you. I suggest you book a flight to a Caribbean island, drink rum and kiss women.'

Akulov nodded. Miguel had said his piece and now it was his turn. 'I can't walk away. I still have to find someone.'

Miguel's eyes tightened and a micro-expression of doubt flashed across his face. 'Who?'

'A Russian.'

Miguel visibly relaxed. 'I do not know many Russians in Houston.'

'I believe he is in Matamoros, but I think he will be in Houston soon, with his boss.'

'I am guessing his boss is Angel Mendez?'

'Yes.'

'You are playing a most lethal game, Mr Russel.'

There was no other way to get the information so Akulov was blunt. 'Are you with the Arellano Cartel?'

'You think any Mexican businessmen who has armed bodyguards must be a member of a cartel?'

'You arrived here with highly trained armed guards, and I do not believe they travelled across the border with their assault rifles. That means you have ready access to both men and arms in the US.' Akulov paused for a moment, then decided he had nothing to lose. 'The man I am looking for is called Vetrov. He was paid to assassinate the Mendez brothers yet now he is working for them.'

'I see. And what, Mr Russel, are you here to do? Complete his contract and then terminate him also?'

'No. He has information I need, intelligence I need.'

'So let me ask you, did you kill Caesar to draw this Russian across the border or to save my niece?'

'They were trying to kidnap your niece. I stopped them.'

'An interesting answer. You had no ulterior motive in rescuing a girl associated with the Arellano Cartel?'

'I didn't know who she was.'

'That was noble, if a little convenient for your operation.' Miguel beckoned him further away from the door, towards the end of the walkway where it was less likely they could be overheard. He leant against the railings. 'Francisco Arellano is dead.

His son is missing. My sister forbid my niece from calling him, hence the argument, hence her running away to Houston. It makes no sense, but then young love rarely does. Yes I work … worked for Francisco Arellano … but I warned him against taking such action against the Mendez Cartel.'

'What action?'

'It was his contract the Russian accepted, and the Mendez brothers discovered this. What is the Russian to you?'

'We once worked together.'

'Mr Russel, your spoken Spanish is too Spanish for you to be an American. So you are European, Spanish or perhaps even another Russian?'

Akulov shrugged. 'What does it matter?'

'Tell me again, what is it you want from the Russian?'

'Information.'

'Regarding?'

'A personal matter.'

'Will you complete his contract for me? Will you eliminate Angel Mendez? The cartel will pay you the same.'

'If your offer of help is real, I will.'

'You call my number on that card, and tell me what you need.'

'That's reasonable. Send the payment to the same account you used for Vetrov.'

'Mr Russel, I think you are crazy, but I like you.'

'Gracias,' Akulov said before he turned, took the steps down, and got into the Cadillac.

In the almost light of day he knew it was a stupid move to make, but it was the fastest move. There would be no reasoning with the cartel unless he took out its leadership, and if he did that, he expected that whoever was second in command would be more worried about establishing it as their own than coming after him, even if they wanted to. He was unretired, at least for the moment.

He thought about Sofia and her family and wondered if her

parents were involved too. They were wealthy and the easiest assumption to make was that this too came from the cocaine business. He started the SUV, pulled out of the parking lot and continued to make the worst possible tactical move by starting the drive back to Houston.

He threaded his way towards the highway and then Caesar's phone rang. Akulov fumbled for it under the seat, causing him to swerve on the near-empty road, but he managed to retrieve it. He answered the call and waited in silence. The words came in Spanish, fast and angry. He used the same language to reply. 'This is not Caesar. This is the man who killed Caesar.'

There was a pause and all he could hear was breathing, so he ended the call. If they didn't know Don Caesar was dead, he wanted to give them time to check it out.

Akulov carried on towards Houston, retracing his route in reverse. The phone rang. He ignored it. It rang out to voicemail. A minute later it rang again. He ignored it again. On the third ring he answered. It was a different number, which he memorised and then answered, 'Hola.'

'Who is this?' A different voice this time, harder, older perhaps, more senior, but definitely Mexican.

'I am the one who killed Don Caesar.'

'Do you know who this is, *cabrón*?'

'Are you his mother?'

There was a moment of silence, just heavy breathing and static. 'Oh you're a dead man! This is Angel Mendez, *pinche estúpido*! Do you have any idea who I am, *puto*?'

The phone went quiet once more as Akulov imagined the man at the other end had become apoplectic. When the voice spoke again it was no more than a whisper. 'I'm going to find you, and when I do I'm gonna make sure that you die in the slowest, most painful way I know how.'

'I am easy to find,' Akulov replied calmly. 'I'm driving your brother's Cadillac back to Houston.'

'Oh, you're one dead man!'

Akulov had never enjoyed using profanity but decided now was a good time to do so. *'Chinga tu madre.'*

He'd started a war, and in war the generals used their best men. And the Mendez Cartel's best man was Vetrov. All Akulov had to do now was to work out where he wanted to be when Vetrov eventually found him. But by the time that happened he hoped he'd have backup, and he hoped that backup would be someone just as deadly, just as lethal as he was. If his looking at the airport cameras trick had worked, that backup would be Jack Tate.

Chapter 9

International airspace

During his SAS career Tate had grown used to sleeping on aeroplanes. They were usually uncomfortable military transports filled to the brim with cargo, kit, weapons and farting soldiers, which made sleeping in the Qatar Airways business class cabin easy, or it should have done. As soon as they levelled out Tate turned his Q Suite seat into a bed, closed his door and shut his eyes. He was tired but his body was also ready to face the Russian again, if he could find him. Eyes closed but mind wide awake Tate lay and willed himself to sleep.

He gave up after half an hour and his bed became a seat once more. He ordered a large whisky from the "dine on demand" drinks menu, then ate breakfast and watched a film. An hour into possibly the most unrealistic action thriller he had ever seen, and a second whisky later, Tate made the bed up and drifted off to sleep.

And then the dream started. His unconscious mind told him it wasn't real, that what he was experiencing had indeed once been real but the way it was happening now, the replay was just an illusion created by his brain's need to work out solutions to problems.

He was in Eastern Ukraine to support The Shadows, a pro-Ukraine partisan unit who were trying to prevent the Russians' imminent attack on Mariupol. It was a hot August evening and he was on the upper floor of a bomb-shattered farmhouse overlooking a municipal building being used as a headquarters by members of a Baltic Fleet Spetsnaz unit. A pair of BMP-2 – light-armoured vehicles, faster than a tank and suited to urban warfare – sat outside the base alongside an APC – armoured personnel carrier.

As he continued to observe through his field glasses, a distinctive whoosh came from behind and to the south of him, and then an all but inaudible keening as the first grenade of The Shadows' attack whistled on its arc through the darkening Ukrainian evening. There was a thunderous explosion and the APC was hurled upwards and crashed against the wall of the base. A moment of unnatural silence followed before flames engulfed the heavy troop transporter and leached up the walls.

A second RPG landed next to the side wall, ripping a gaping hole in the concrete. Figures ran out of the building into the dying daylight in time to see more grenades turn the remaining two armoured vehicles into expensive pieces of scrap metal. The Russians furiously tried to resist the surprise attack by returning fire or escaping into the fields out of the kill zone, but it was futile as RPGs tore into everything around them.

Grabbing the AK he'd been given for personal protection, Tate carefully crabbed from the broken window at the front of the house to the collapsed rear wall and the open field. He froze. Movement. In the field, but in the wrong direction. He dropped to the floor. Russians. A group who had not been hit by the attack, had not been in the target building, and had been unsighted by either him or The Shadows were now flanking his side's firing positions.

He was in danger of being cut off from the three two-man fire teams in the field behind. And then he saw the Russians were being led by the man he was there to personally target, the intelligence officer from Moscow – Maksim Oleniuk. Tate estimated there were twelve men, spaced out, weapons up, advancing on The Shadows. More than enough to launch their own assault.

Tate flattened himself on the bare wooden boards of the first floor. He had an elevated view of the field and the Russians moving within it. Unseen like tigers in a forest they stealthily traversed the chest-high crops of old sunflowers that had grown, never to be picked. And past the Russians he could see the men he was there to help – The Shadows. Tate tried to switch the fire selector on the Kalashnikov to single shot, but it was as though the selector had been welded in the wrong position against the stock of the rifle. But he knew this wasn't so. He had tested it himself, toggled its position several times. It had been fluid and easily switched between modes. He finally managed to move it and cursed. He looked down the iron sights.

Maksim Oleniuk was easy to pick out; he was broader and slower than his men. He was an easy target even with the AK, which was generally used for short bursts or spray-and-pray attacks. He breathed out slowly and squeezed the trigger. It didn't move. He squeezed again; nothing happened. Tate cursed and squeezed with all his strength and finally a single 7.62mm round left the end of the assault rifle. It traversed the distance to the Russian officer in what seemed to Tate to be slow motion. It missed him and blew away the head of a sunflower to his right. Tate swore.

Oleniuk turned, eyes searching for an attacker, but at his own eye level. Tate sighted again, acquired Oleniuk's head and squeezed the trigger hard, harder than ever, and he kept on squeezing as nothing happened and the target moved away. And then a second round left the Kalashnikov, flying in a slow line … and at the very same moment, Oleniuk stopped dead, his face upwards. His eyes met Tate's and then the 7.62mm round struck the Russian intelligence officer square in the face, ripping it away in an implosion of skin, blood, bone and brain. Oleniuk spun around, but did not fall and when the body had finished spinning it was facing Tate again, but now it was no longer Oleniuk glaring back at him.

It was Ruslan Akulov and he was raising his own Kalashnikov.
An entire magazine emptied on full auto tore up the distance
between the two men.

Tate scrambled backwards on his haunches, but could not move
out of the way as each and every round the Russian assassin fired
struck him. His body convulsed as daggers of pain tore through him.
His vision turned red as blood poured into his eyes. Tate tried to
open his mouth to scream, but no words came out, and then he
tasted the familiar metallic tang of blood. He couldn't breathe and
then he couldn't see as his vision darkened and became black.

Tate reached for his face and pulled the blanket away from his
head. He opened his eyes and found himself back in his business
class cabin. Tate raised his seat, opened his personal door and
headed in the direction of the toilet. After locking himself in, he
splashed water on his face to wake up and wash away the vestiges
of his nightmare. During the course of his career he'd occasionally have flashbacks, night terrors, but they were unusual. And
he had never relived the scene he just had. The SIS shrink brought
up dreams at their bi-yearly assessments, always asked him to
talk about those he had had recently. But Tate could rarely
remember them, and those he could generally involved groups
of naked women in hot tubs. He doubted Dr Grzegorzek would
appreciate hearing about those.

He combed his hair with his hands and adjusted his moustache.
He moved back to his seat, sighed when he saw that he still had
five hours of flying time left and ordered a tomato juice. Akulov
had gotten into his head, and Tate knew exactly how he was going
to remove him, permanently.

Mexican airspace

In a smaller and more exclusive aeroplane, Kirill Vetrov observed
his boss, Angel Mendez. The Mexican drugs baron was seething.
The rest of the men on the cartel's private jet were overly busy

inspecting their feet or looking out of the windows; Vetrov was the only man to meet his gaze.

'What are you looking at?'

'This is a foolhardy move.'

'Are you calling me a fool?' His eyes were wide with anger.

'Only fools rush in where angels fear to tread.'

'You making fun of me?' Angel jumped from his seat, Glock G33 in his hand. 'You saying I'm a fool, or a coward?'

'I'm making you angry, off balance, is what I am doing. Look, you cannot control your actions. You're seconds away from firing your handgun and making the jet depressurise.'

Angel frowned, and sat. He leant forward, his face like thunder. 'What is your point?'

Vetrov wet his lips, his tongue momentarily flicking out serpent-like. 'This is a trap. Caesar's killer wants you to go to Houston so he can take you out too.'

Angel thumped his chest with his hand, still clutching the small Glock. 'Let him try. He is one man; we are the Mendez Cartel!'

'Is he?'

'What?'

'Is he one man?'

'Of course.'

'What if he has a team, an army?'

Angel looked down. Put his Glock on the table next to him. 'What are you telling me? You think this is, what, another crew? The DEA?'

'I have no idea, and neither do you. That is the issue. We do not know who did this, yet we react like this, like he or they want us to.'

'What if this is your broker?' Angel sighed and leant back in his seat. 'What if he has sent another *sicario* to complete the contract you did not?'

'My broker is a wise man.' Vetrov saw no reason to correct the

103

gender. 'He now knows that I work for you. It is better for him to lose one contract and one client rather than his life if he sanctions further action against you. It is business after all. As a businessman I am sure you understand this?'

'Sure.' Angel held up his hand and clicked his fingers. Within seconds a flight attendant appeared carrying a crystal decanter filled with tequila and a matching tumbler. She poured a double measure. Angel made no move to avert his eyes from her cleavage as he took the glass, downed the entire contents and gestured for her to repeat the process.

Vetrov had remained silent as he'd watched the pair of them; it was what he was good at. He imagined how easy it would be to kill them both before anyone else on the plane could stop him. It was what had marked him out even from the rest of the Werewolves: his ability to watch, assess and to analyse before making the correct decision with decisive, deadly action. That a man as capricious as Angel Mendez headed a billion-dollar cartel was dangerously absurd but the man had his uses and that was why Vetrov had orchestrated his enlistment as a cartel soldier.

'My brother did not deserve this,' Angel said, his eyes now moist, as the woman retreated. 'To be gunned down in an alley like a dog.'

Vetrov nodded, but he believed that was exactly what a genetic half-scoop like Caesar had deserved. 'It is bad indeed.'

'These men of mine, who you have trained and selected, they are the best?' Angel gestured expansively around the cabin at the five other men.

'They are,' Vetrov lied.

'In your opinion how would they fare against real Spetsnaz?'

Vetrov lied again: 'They would be a good match for them. Your team may not be real Spetsnaz but they are true Wolves.'

'Wolves? I see, not Werewolves?'

Vetrov's eyes narrowed slightly. Hearing Angel Mendez utter

104

the name of his unit was akin to blasphemy. 'Werewolves do not exist. Wolves are real and so are their teeth.'

Angel knocked back the rest of his drink. 'That I like.'

Vetrov made no comment. Werewolves were real and there had once been twelve of them. He knew that at least half of those still existed on this earth.

Beasley, Texas, USA

Akulov ditched the Cadillac in Beasley, a small place that was home to both a large red-brick church built in honour of St Wenceslaus, and the 786 truck stop. However, he thought ironically, there was no snow. It was still early and the only people out and about were the truckers and the staff at the diner and gas station. He had no doubt the police would now be trying to trace the SUV and that unless Mendez had someone very senior on his payroll at the Houston PD, the Giant – if he was neither dead nor in a coma – would be held for questioning.

Akulov parked the garish SUV around the side of a sleepy-looking house whose plot backed onto seemingly never-ending fields. He killed the engine, stepped out and listened, waiting for any noise or movement. When none came he clambered back into the Cadillac and set about wiping every surface he had touched with a half-depleted packet of wet wipes he'd found in a storage cubby on the driver's side, which had also contained a well-thumbed copy of *Juggs* magazine. As he cleaned, he searched the SUV and found a small leather holdall in the trunk, like an old-fashioned doctor's bag. In it was a roll of duct tape, a packet of condoms and two autoinjectors: stab and press pens designed to deliver a single, preloaded dose of a specific drug.

Akulov felt himself getting angry. He'd seen such kits before, and had no doubt the cartel men had planned to use it on Sofia and Juana. He took the bag back to the driver's seat and placed the two handguns and Caesar Mendez's wallet inside before he locked the Cadillac, tossed the key and Angel's phone into the field and walked away.

It took him ten minutes to get to the truck stop, eight more to find a trucker driving in the direction of Houston and $100 to persuade the guy to let him ride along.

An hour later the trucker dropped Akulov off near to the address he had given. Akulov started to walk through the outskirts of Houston. It was warmer now the sun was up, and the city was awake and busy with people. He found a coffee shop, sat and ordered a large breakfast of pancakes, bacon and sausage. He hadn't eaten properly since a mall sandwich in Miami and realised that he was ravenous. The bag he had brought from Miami was in a left-luggage locker at the airport, but he mentally went back over the details of the report it contained.

He finished and paid for his breakfast and left the coffee shop. Looking up he spotted a CCTV camera and made sure that it had a full shot of his face as he pretended to look past it and into the sky as though marvelling at the towering Houston architecture.

Houston, Texas, USA

Tate sat in the back of the large, black executive minivan facing his brother, Simon Hunter, as the van sped away from the airport.

'I'm surprised Newman let you come?'

'She tried to stop me,' Hunter replied.

'Who's the driver?'

'Local talent.'

'I see.' Local talent was a phrase used to describe the loose network of contractors the SIS used as and when needed. They were all British expats and all former servicemen.

'Don't worry, the back is soundproofed.'

'You hope.'

'I know.'

Tate pointed to his moustache. 'Have I got you to thank for this?'

'No, I think it was random, brotha!'

'Ha-ha.' Tate stretched out across the leather seats. 'OK. What do we know?'

Hunter was immediately serious. 'Akulov has been pinged in Houston. Most recently two hours ago.'

Tate sat up straighter, the fatigue from over twenty hours of air travel within thirty-six hours instantly vanishing. 'He's still here?'

'But that's not the odd part.' Hunter paused wearily. 'He was standing directly under a camera. It's as though he wanted to get pinged.'

Tate flattened down his moustache, a tic he'd developed since Nice. 'Then he wants us to find him. Akulov wouldn't make such a basic mistake.'

'No, he wouldn't.'

Tate looked at his brother. In the last year he seemed to have aged as the obsession with finding Ruslan Akulov had driven him, haunted him and ultimately controlled him. When they'd encountered the Russian assassin a year before, they had not known what he had been part of. The Werewolves had been well known by E Squadron. Tate had read the file many times and knew all about Akulov's particular skill set. Tate glanced up at the full-length panoramic sunroom and the skyscrapers of Houston that now encroached upon the sky.

'He wants us to come. He wants us to know he's here. It's a trap. High ground everywhere, we'll be easy targets.'

'You think he's after us?'

'Sure.'

'Why?'

'We haven't forgotten about him. The dead can't speak, and they can't pull triggers.'

'But we can.' Hunter folded his arms and Tate saw the slightest shiver. 'What a happy thought.'

'You still having the dreams?'

Hunter nodded, said nothing.

Tate thought back to a year before when his brother had been abducted and held captive by Akulov's boss – Oleniuk. And then in front of him, Oleniuk had executed the woman Simon loved.

'What do you want me to do?' Tate asked his brother.

'Kill him,' Simon Hunter replied, 'without hesitation.'

Tate gave the slightest of nods. 'Tell me again how you felt when I killed Oleniuk?'

'Empty.'

'And did it bring them back?'

Anger flared in Hunter's eyes. 'You know it bloody didn't! Nothing will. Oleniuk ordered our parents' deaths and that bastard Akulov ensured they happened.'

The brothers fell silent; the only sound now was the whirring of the air conditioning.

Tate knocked his knee against his brother's. 'So, give me the intel, soppy.'

'Two hours ago Akulov was seen standing outside this diner.' He handed Tate an A4 printout. It showed a figure, gazing upwards, his focus just past the camera but his face clearly displayed. The time and location was marked in the corner of the recording. 'Neill Plato's got alerts set up. And here he is again last night arriving at George Bush Intercontinental.'

Tate took the second photo.

'Looking up again.'

'It's as though he knows that the Americans aren't looking for him but that we are.'

'Exactly,' Hunter said. 'I think so too, and I said the same to Newman.'

'So what, we wait for him to pop up again?'

'Neill is trying to see if he can be tracked, but Akulov knows what he's doing. He hasn't shown up anywhere else since.'

Tate tapped the first image with his index finger. 'Where is this place?'

'South-west Houston.'

'Then that's where we need to be.'

'Because?'

'Because we've got to start somewhere, and I'm hungry.'

'OK. I've got a full tactical kit in the boot. I just hope we don't need it.'

Chapter 10

Downtown Houston, USA

The apartment was shabby and empty except for a king-sized bed in one room and a pair of large, leather La-Z-Boys in the other. Angel Mendez sat in one of the chairs, cigar in one hand and a tumbler of tequila in the other. His chair was flanked on either side by two of the men handpicked by Vetrov. In the other chair, which had been repositioned to face the first but with a respectable distance between them, sat Detective Ken Vinyl of the Houston Police Department.

Vetrov leant against the window frame, his focus both on the street below and the room around him.

'What I like about you, Vinyl, is that you don't show off. You don't flaunt what you've got,' Angel said.

'Thank you.'

'Look at that suit, man. What was it, four hundred bucks?'

'Three oh-eight.'

'There you go, three hundred bucks – a JC Penney special. But those shoes are something else. What did they run to, two thousand eight hundred?'

'Two thousand nine.'

'Two thousand nine hundred bucks, made-to-measure gator skin loafers – am I right?'

'You are.'

'I am always right. Always right. So this is when I know I can trust a guy on my payroll. The money doesn't change him. He's not out going all *Miami Vice* on my ass and getting the flashy suits and jewellery and chick-cars. No, he invests his cash, like I'm investing in him, and he only buys quality items – and those shoes are subtle, *güey*!'

'Thank you.'

'Real nice, I may need to get myself a pair of those. Now tell me, Vinyl, off the record …' Angel smiled at his own word play, as he always did each and every time he used the same joke, before his face abruptly became serious. 'Who is this *pinche puta* who killed Caesar?'

'Russel Cross.'

'Russel Cross? Sounds like a *puto* name to me.' Angel raised his glass to his lips. Vetrov noticed there was a slight tremor in his hand. Angel drained the glass and threw it to the man on his right who deftly caught it and took it out through the door and into the kitchen.

'He was in a cab just before it happened, and then he jumped out, and then the cabby filmed it all. Here.' Vinyl got up from his seat and offered the phone to Angel.

Angel snatched the smartphone and pressed play.

The only sounds to fill the room for the next four minutes were the screams, gunfire and then sirens. Vetrov would study the footage later; he had to let his *patron* go first.

When Angel spoke next his voice sounded different. It was a fraction lower, quieter. He had just viewed the last minutes of his twin brother's life. 'Is this the only copy?'

'Yes. That's the cabby's phone.'

'What about the in-car camera?'

111

'It didn't show his face. His head was down, like he knew to hide from it.'

'*Pinche puta!* Has the cabby been taken care of?'

'He has been taken care of financially.'

'No. I want him taken care of permanently. Understand?'

'I do,' Vinyl replied, without hesitation. 'I'll do it myself.'

'What about the CCTV in the club?'

'I made a copy then wiped it. It just had him entering and leaving the establishment and going for a piss. He was standing at the only part of the bar not covered by the cameras. Cross knew what he was doing but I did get a print of his face from the camera in the hall, good enough to match his driving licence.'

'And the cameras in the street?'

'They're broken, didn't record anything that night.'

'*Bueno.*' Angel clamped his cigar between his teeth as he zoomed in on part of the film. It was the face of Russel Cross. Angel took a screen shot. 'Hey, Vetrov, put your "airdrop" on.'

Vetrov retrieved his phone and did as requested.

'Tell me about Russel Cross?' Angel continued.

'He's thirty-six, a Boston native. He's an insurance broker. No priors, no convictions, no military service.'

'What?' Angel sounded incredulous. 'It's a fake ID, got to be. Did you see how he handled himself? I know a trained professional when I see one and this guy ain't no insurance broker!'

Vinyl shrugged. 'That's all I got.'

'Home address?'

'Boston is on his licence but I made inquiries. They don't know him at that address; it's an apartment block and people move in and out all the time.'

Vetrov stared at his phone and for the first time in years he felt something bordering on fear. The footage was now over a year old and he had hoped the British would have captured the man on it by now, an eloquent way in which to rid the world of his old friend. 'This man is not named Russel Cross. This man does not have military training, he has advanced military training. This man is not a man, he is a Werewolf.'

'Wait … what you saying, Vetrov?'

Vetrov moved away from the window and into Angel's field of vision. 'I know the man on the film. His name is Ruslan Akulov. He was Wolf 6.'

Angel shot to his feet, stabbing the air in front of him with his Cuban cigar. 'See, I knew it! This *güey* is a pro! So you're telling me, Vetrov, that he's one of yours?'

Vetrov sighed wearily and wondered how much longer he would have to put up with Caesar for. If he needed to, he would liquidate everyone within the room. He would kick Caesar in the head, then roll to the table, take out first one then the other bodyguard, before shooting Vinyl, and then the men from the other room would enter, all speed and confusion, and he would gun them down. If he had to. Which he told himself he wouldn't do, just yet. 'The man is a traitor. He resigned from my team after our operations in Syria.'

'He's what, a *sicario* now?'

'Exactly.' The next words were hard for Vetrov to say because they held a truth he had never vocalised. 'He's probably the best Russia has ever produced. I believe he's been sent to collect on the contract that I did not.'

'Hey, you said that wouldn't happen! We whacked old man Arellano; he ordered it with his *puto* son Daniel. So who's ordered this?'

'Akulov has the same broker I had. I was wrong about him; it looks like the broker wants to keep face.'

'And lose his life? Call him, warn him off! Now!'

'That's not how it works.'

'No?' Angel's brow contorted. He was not used to his orders being questioned or refused. 'Then, my Russian friend, tell me how it does work?'

'I leave a message in a draft folder of an email account.'

Angel Mendez nodded. 'So write the message.'

'I can't.'

'Why?'

'I no longer know what the correct account is. The broker will have cut me off.'

'Use the old one. Try. Do it. Do it now!'

'Very well.' Akulov opened a VPN then tapped in the link for the last email account he used. It still worked. He managed to open it and get into the draft folder. 'Tell me exactly what you want to say, *patron*.'

'Tell him this: "Stop the contract. Do not target Angel Mendez or the cartel will come for you, your wife, your children and your parents!" OK, you got that?'

'Yes.'

'Show me.'

Vetrov held the iPhone in front of Angel's face. The cartel boss made a fuss of reading it. '*Bueno.*'

'But he will not stop, even if ordered to do so.'

'What?'

'Ruslan Akulov will not stop. Once he accepts a contract there is no turning back.'

'This *pinche estúpido* thinks he can come to Houston, murder Caesar then take me out too?' Angel was breathing hard and his face was red. 'You better be telling me the truth, *cabrón*, that this is nothing to do with you.'

'It is the truth.'

Vinyl got to his feet and cleared his throat. 'We've got his face, and we've got his name. If you let me release that, you'll have the entire Houston PD hunting for his ass.'

Angel cocked his head. 'You can guarantee that he's brought to me for justice?'

'I can't guarantee it.'

Angel pointed his cigar at him. '*No mames*, Vinyl!'

114

Vetrov noted that Vinyl didn't understand the Spanish statement. 'I know how he works; he's hunting you, Angel.'

'I ain't no goddam *puta* prey! Nobody ever hunted me, you got that? No no. We have options. We hunt him. We take him out when he's least expecting it.'

Vetrov relaxed slightly. The imminent danger to him had passed. 'We make him think he's hunting you, but really we are waiting for him.'

'Exactly what I was thinking. Like a trap!'

'Yes.'

Angel vigorously nodded. 'OK, OK. Tell me where you wanna do this?'

'I imagine he has the same intelligence pack on you that I did. I'd have attacked you where you least expect it, your place in River Oaks.'

Angel retook his seat and held out his hand. A fresh tumbler of tequila was placed in it. 'River Oaks, now I'm liking the sound of that.'

'I can have my men, men I trust, step up patrols on the place,' Vinyl offered, hurriedly.

'No. He's gotta think we aren't expecting him. Here's the plan. We wait, then once he's there we call in your men. *Pinche estúpido cabrón* breaks into my place – a big-ass home invasion – and attempts to off me? Sure we need the cops to take him away, and of course he resists arrest.'

'Don't circulate his photo,' Vetrov said. 'You don't want anyone thinking they can curry favour with you by trying to take him out.'

'You're right. That's very wise.' Mendez had a thin smile on his face.

Vetrov glanced at Vinyl. Although he too was nodding and smiling, the Russian could read his trepidation even if Angel could not.

'There is one more thing,' Vinyl said, his voice sounding strained. 'You need to formally identify your brother's body.'

Angel, glass in hand, made the sign of the cross then necked the tequila. He got back up to his feet tossing the tumbler over his shoulder, where it was caught once again. 'Please take me to my brother, Detective Vinyl.'

Buffalo Bayou Park, Houston, USA

Akulov guessed the British had seen him on camera, but he didn't know for sure. All he had to go on that they were targeting him, was the word of his broker. Any intel was only as good as its source, however, and he didn't know who hers was. He'd found a phone shop, bought two more burners then had a taxi take him to Buffalo Bayou Park.

The park, according to his driver who would not stop talking, had cost the city a staggering fifty-eight million dollars to create, was one hundred and sixty acres in size and built alongside ten miles of waterways.

Akulov paid the driver, with a generous tip, and headed into the park. He liked parks but unlike those he'd hung around in as a youth in Moscow, this one was clean and not dotted with trash and drug addicts. Akulov realised that since he'd stopped being a patriot the mist of propaganda had been removed from his eyes and he had started to remember things as they had been rather than how the Kremlin had insisted they were. He paused to take in the vista of the towering glass skyscrapers of downtown Houston beyond the park as they stood proud beneath the vivid blue sky. Houston was where many came to make their millions and that was why the Mendez Cartel were here to ensure they made theirs.

Akulov knew if he were being tracked by a sniper, an open space like the park made him as easy to hit as a paper target on a range, but he very much doubted anyone would have found him yet and if so that they would use that particular method to take him out. Angel Mendez seemed like a caring, up close and personal kind of psychopath; meanwhile he knew Jack Tate would also want to do it face to face.

Akulov pulled one of the two burner phones from his bag and used the internet to find the telephone number for a certain office in Washington DC. He clicked the link to dial the number.

'Good afternoon, British Embassy, Washington. How may I help you?' The voice was American, not British, which made Akulov's deception easier.

'Good afternoon,' Akulov said, using a British accent, 'could I possibly speak to Simon Hunter please?'

There was a pause before the receptionist said, 'I'm sorry, Attaché Hunter is out of the office.'

Akulov carried on, keeping up his deception as a blasé British expat. 'Listen, love, I'm a friend of his and I'm in Houston where I was meant to meet him but he's not turned up.'

'Sir, I'm sorry about that, but Simon is not here at the moment. If it's an urgent matter I can take a message?'

There was no surprise in the woman's voice that Hunter was expected in Houston, just concern that he had not made an appointment. And this told Akulov something. 'OK. Please pass this message on to Simon. 'My name is Ruslan Akulov. I'm in Houston waiting for him. He can get me on the number I'm calling from. Is it displayed on your phone?'

'Yes, sir, it is.'

'OK that's it. Please pass it on as quickly as you can. It's very important, as I'm only going to be on this number for the next hour.'

'I will do so, sir.'

'Thank you so much.' Akulov ended the call.

If that didn't get their attention, then nothing would. He continued to walk along the path and enjoyed the gentle breeze that made the tops of the trees in the lower park sway. He didn't have much of a plan, but what plan he did have involved him being able to confront Tate and persuade him that he had nothing to do with the Camden bombing. Once this was achieved the questions of who, how and why they'd framed him had to be answered, and he didn't know if he'd be doing that with or without Tate's help.

He saw a young mother pushing a stroller. One child was sitting inside and another was riding a board attached to the rear. The woman was walking briskly and wearing running gear. This was a glimpse of a life that Russia had forced him not to have. None of his former unit members had had any links with family, or any responsibilities outside the Spetsnaz. Their sole focus, their only family, had been each other. And Vetrov had gradually destroyed that family with his illogical vengeance and foolhardy leadership. Operational successes continued to happen but at the cost of more Werewolf lives.

The Werewolves had been, still could have been, the best Special Forces unit in the world, but Russia had let them be used as shock troops in a misguided military adventure. Of the twelve, merely six still lived after their operations in Syria had been concluded. And then Akulov had formally and amicably left the Russian Army. He had not kept in contact with the remainder of the twelve, but Wolf 8 had been killed last year. Now there were, as far as he knew, five Werewolves left and he was surely soon to be reunited in one way or another with Wolf 1.

The woman drew nearer to him; she was attractive and had a glow about her that shouted contentment. They made eye contact. He smiled and she turned away. Yes, this was the life he had given up, and he couldn't let himself regret it.

The phone rang.

'Yes?' Akulov held it against his ear.

'Who is this?' the voice asked, in Russian.

Akulov understood immediately who was on the other end. He decided to reply in Russian. 'Jack Tate, this is Ruslan Akulov.'

'Where are you?'

'I am in Houston. We need to talk.'

'Really, about how you murdered my foster parents?'

118

'Exactly that. If you do not want me to vanish again you will meet me at "Uncle Joe's Diner" one hour from now. Understood?'

'I understand you.'

Akulov looked at the phone. The number had been withheld. He powered it off, stopped walking, removed the SIM and let it fall to the ground. SIS knew where he'd be; he had no reason to let them track him going there.

Uncle Joe's Diner, Houston, USA

Tate pulled open the door and entered the diner. It was packed. Immediately a waitress met him. She was dressed in a traditional apron and hat that matched the colour scheme of the eatery's interior. She smiled, but her eyes seemed tired.

'Welcome to Uncle Joe's. I'm sorry but there's going to be a bit of a wait for a seat.'

Tate glanced around. The only available seats were at a booth, in the far corner, at the back of the diner. And they were directly opposite a man he recognised: Ruslan Akulov. And Akulov's eyes were burning into his. 'I'm meeting someone. He's got the booth back there.'

'In that case, follow me.'

She led the way, menu in hand. Tate now saw that more and more of the customers were in police uniform or looked like off-duty police officers.

'Here we are.' She placed the menu on the table. 'The specials are on the board.'

'Thank you,' Tate said, as he sat, his eyes fixed on the Russian.

'Wait a minute.' The waitress pointed at Tate then Akulov then back again. 'Are you two brothers?'

'Cousins,' Akulov replied, his Boston accent not betraying a single note of his true heritage.

'Yep, definitely related.' She smiled. 'I'll get you both some coffee.'

Tate eyed the Russian's hands, which were flat, palms down

on the table top. A knife was in easy reach. Neither man spoke. The coffee came and the waitress left, saying she'd give them time to look at the menu.

'I am armed, Jack. I imagine you are, and so are ninety per cent of our fellow diners. If you were to pull a gun in here it would be like "the Gunfight at the O.K. Corral"', Akulov said, quietly.

'That was Arizona, not Texas,' Tate said, his tone terse.

'You are chasing the wrong man, Jack,' Akulov continued.

'Am I?' Tate replied, switching to Russian.

Akulov nodded and switched to the same. 'The man you are looking for is called Kirill Vetrov. He designed, planted and detonated both devices in Camden.'

Tate placed his hands on the table in front of him, fingers splayed. 'We have you on tape. Walking away from the van, squeezing the detonator. Murdering my parents.'

'The tape is a fake.'

'I didn't take you for a coward. You've murdered innocent civilians, women and children ... Are you really not man enough to accept the consequences of your actions?'

'I am, and I continue to do so, but that was not me. I did not murder those people.'

'Were honour and integrity not traits the Russian Army demanded?'

'The man whose name I have given you was my team leader. He is a demolitions expert.'

Tate paused, the tiniest ray of doubt starting to pierce his black anger. 'What proof do you have?'

'I can tell you Oleniuk ordered the hit.'

'Oleniuk is dead.'

'He gave the contract to my broker and specified that it be given only to Vetrov.'

'Words mean nothing.'

'Jack, something is happening here. Fake video footage has

been created that even your own technicians believe is genuine! The creators have used this to make you look the wrong way. Think what else they could do. Who else they could target and what they could achieve.'

Tate drank his coffee, but he couldn't taste it. He looked around the room and started to feel too warm. Akulov was an assassin, but was he a murderer too or just a con man? 'Tell me why you wanted to kill Oleniuk?'

'You were there. You saw it. You understood it. He broke the code.'

'Your code.'

'The code that binds us professionals.'

'There is no us.'

'I do not target innocent civilians. And I know that you do not either.'

Tate felt his anger rise. He took a deep breath before he replied. 'I'm not an assassin.'

'We have both killed for our country. The only difference is that I get paid a rate commensurate with my level of skill. What do you get? A medal awarded in private because the noble United Kingdom finds what you do too distasteful to make public?'

'You're deluded.'

'We are all born mad, some remain so. Is that not what Samuel Beckett said? I'm telling you about the potentially biggest threat to your country's national security in decades, yet you refuse to see it.'

'You murdered a lot of innocent people.'

'I was on the other side of the world.'

'When?'

'On the day of the bombing.'

'Where?'

'Doha.'

'Doha?'

'Qatar.'

'Yeah, I know where Doha is, Akulov.'

The waitress returned. Tate ordered something, just to prevent her from asking again.

'I did not kill your parents. I have told you who did. He will be in Houston, if he is not already here, by the end of the day.'

'If any of what you are saying is true, I'll have to take you in. This has to be investigated.'

'By whom? The SIS? And what happens to me in the meantime? I get to sit in a black site in South America or perhaps nearer to home in Romania?'

'That's how justice works, the type of justice you deserve anyway.'

Akulov nodded. 'Stay here, do not try to follow me or you will not see me again.'

'I can't let you leave.'

'You cannot make me stay. Look around. Are you going to make a citizen's arrest?'

Akulov stood.

Tate stood.

Akulov held out his hand.

Eyes were on them, so Tate shook the Russian's hand. The grip was firm. He managed a strained smile, and switched back to English. 'Remind me where we're meeting up?'

Akulov pulled his hand away. 'You remind me of your number. I will send you a text.'

Tate recited the number of the handset his brother had given him.

'It was good to see you again.' Akulov turned.

Tate watched him leave the diner and sat again but this time on the side of the table the Russian had used, facing the door. He pulled out his encrypted iPhone and called Plato. There was a moment's pause before both ends connected as they performed an electronic handshake. 'Neill, he's mobile. Have you got him?'

'I have him on the street heading west. Ah, he's entering an underground car park, a block away from the diner … Bum. No "eyes on" there. Looks like their system is down.'

'Brilliant.' Tate knew the techie was trying his best, so he bit his tongue. 'OK. Keep me updated.'

'I will.'

Tate's food arrived as he ended the call. It was a massive cheeseburger with a mountain of fries.

'Your cousin left?' the waitress asked.

'He did.'

'You're British?'

Tate had to be polite, the waitress didn't deserve sullenness. 'I am.'

'And your cousin's from Boston?'

'We're the same family but two different sides, two different branches.'

Her brow wrinkled. 'Well, you enjoy your meal and try not to get too much of it in your cute moustache, honey.'

Tate had forgotten about the Hogan tash. He looked down at his food. He hadn't been hungry before but now he was. Eat when you can, sleep when you can.

He started to eat as he attempted to digest what Akulov had said. He needed to call his brother, not knowing quite how to explain the meeting, why Akulov was able to walk away, and whether he believed anything Akulov had told him. He called Plato again.

'Sorry, I've not been able to locate him yet—'

'Neill, I need you to look at something else.'

'Go ahead.'

'Check footage of all arrivals at Hamad International on the date of the Camden attack.'

'Er, right …' Plato paused. 'That shouldn't be too much of a huge hassle, providing they still have the tapes. Shall I bracket it two days either way?'

'You know best.'

'Got it. Who am I looking for?'

'Akulov.'

'Ruslan Akulov?'

'No his brother Bob,' Tate said sarcastically, and instantly regretted it.

'Um, OK. Does this mean you think he wasn't in London?'

'He says the London footage is fake.'

'It's not.'

'Either way, can you check the footage?'

'Leave it with me.'

'Thanks, Neill, I owe you one.'

'You can get me a bottle of absinthe from duty-free.'

'Will do.'

Tate finished the burger and was glad he'd ordered it. He paid the bill, left the customary tip, which Americans seemed to hold sacred, and left the diner. He turned right out of the eatery and was soon walking past the multi-storey that Akulov had entered. The Russian would be long gone by now.

Tate's mind was a mess. If the footage was fake, why was Akulov in Doha? Why hadn't anyone noticed the doctored footage? Plato had run all of the usual tests on the smartphone, even more than usual. He had been convinced it was genuine. Tate stopped at a crossing and realised that he had no idea where he was. He dialled Hunter and asked to be picked up. He would rather have the conversation about Akulov face to face.

Chapter 11

St. Regis Hotel, Houston, USA

Wearing a fresh set of clothes and rubbing his clean-shaven face Tate exited the bathroom. It felt good to be himself again. His body had no idea what time it was, but his eyes could see that night was falling outside the hotel window. He joined his brother by the full-length window.

'So what, we wait?' Hunter's voice was terse.

Tate said nothing. His brother had every reason to be angry with him. In his mind he had let the man he'd been pursuing for a year slip away. In truth Tate had started to believe there may be something in Akulov's story, but he couldn't explain it to Simon or to himself. 'We need to rest; that's what we need to do.'

'Rest? I've been bloody resting since last August. Now is the time for action!'

'OK, boss. Tell me what to do.'

'Find him and kill him.'

'You know I would if it would make things right but ...' Tate's voice faded away.

'But what?' Hunter turned, leant against the glass and looked at his younger brother. 'You don't think he did it – is that what you're trying to say?'

125

'I'm saying that given his actions—'

'Jack! This guy planted a bomb that blew our parents to pieces! And last year he assassinated, among others, two British diplomats and attempted to murder a third!'

'Something isn't right here.'

'Yeah, your head!' Hunter turned back, and gazed out at the city. 'I'm sorry.'

'Hey, if you can't shout at me, who can you shout at?' Tate put his arm around his brother's shoulders. 'Look if I had no doubts then Akulov would be nothing more than a stain on the floor and a bad memory, but it doesn't make sense.'

Hunter sighed. 'Tell me again what he said?'

Tate removed his arm and leant with his forearms against the cold, wall. 'He didn't say an awful lot – just that it wasn't him on the tape because he was on the other side of the world at the time.'

'In Doha.'

'In Doha.'

'That's a coincidence. Did anything happen in Qatar back then? Did anyone vanish loudly, or quietly?'

'You'd know more than me.'

Hunter shrugged. 'Perhaps. But I heard nothing.'

'He said we should be concerned that someone has the ability to manufacture fake footage that is indistinguishable from the real thing.'

'We know that Kirill Vetrov checks out. He was the team leader of the Werewolves, but again what of it? Where's the link?'

'He's a demolitions expert.'

'And Akulov isn't?'

'Fair point.'

'Did you ever think we'd be doing this, Jack?'

Tate was confused. 'Doing what?'

'The pair of us, standing in a suite in a luxury hotel a million miles away from Camden and trying to decide who lives and who dies?'

'Yeah, that's exactly what I told the careers adviser at school I wanted to do when I grew up.'

Hunter smirked. 'Who are we to decide?'

'Who is anyone to decide? We're a line of defence, that's all. We keep the monsters at bay.'

River Oaks, Houston, USA

The price of real estate in the central Houston community of River Oaks ranged between one point six and twenty million dollars. And because of this it was a place the Mendez Cartel liked to call home. Both Caesar and Angel owned houses there as did several of their lieutenants including Luis Bravo, aka the Giant. Of course the "dons" had the largest houses out of the group but neither had succumbed to the same greed that had led many *narcos* to want the biggest and the best. The Mendez Cartel men lived among the wealthy and successful of Houston, seemingly as equals. Houston was not a place for them to flaunt their wealth; it was a place to make it and to invest.

As natural attrition caused homeowners to move on, the cartel moved in to purchase what they could. Never paying over the odds enough to draw any attention to themselves and always through an impressive array of Caribbean-based shell companies. Each company had a different point of contact within the cartel and it was this point of contact only who would liaise with the relevant real-estate brokers. Over time they bought up entire swathes of River Oaks with dirty money, filtered through legitimate business. Some places were even rented out to young professionals or retirees for a reduced rate, just to add to the legitimacy of the operation.

The most important three homes in the cartel's portfolio – those belonging to Caesar, Angel and Bravo – were surrounded by an invisible tripwire of cartel-owned houses, whose residents were either on the payroll and enjoyed a reduced rent or were full-blown cartel men. Security cameras had been subtly angled to provide network coverage of the entire area and linked into a main control centre. And the control centre was based in a room in the home of Luis Bravo.

Vetrov mused, as he stood in the Giant's living room, that Bravo was the monster guarding the gates to the Houston underworld, a real-life, and modern incarnation of the mythical Cerberus or perhaps the giant cyclops Polyphemus. Either way the monster now sat in his mansion on River Oaks' Del Monte Drive with his tail between his legs as Angel Mendez gave him a dressing-down the likes of which even a seasoned Russian soldier like Vetrov appreciated.

'That *cabrón* beat you with one strike? One slap on the head and you were down, down for the count like a sack of shit. Shit in the gutter and he takes your pistol, and he kills MY BROTHER?!'

Even sitting taped to a dining-room chair in the centre of his living room, Bravo was taller than Angel, a fact that made the cartel leader even angrier. His mouth was taped closed and his eyes were wide. The only part of Bravo's body that could move was his head and it was twitching and jerking from side to side vigorously, shaking angrily, denying each sharpened syllable of Angel's vitriol.

'*Estás pero si bien pendejo!* Oh? You wanna speak? You wanna tell me I'm a liar? That this didn't happen like I say it did? That the film on this camera is faked?' Angel held up the iPhone, his brow furrowed for a moment as he swiped at the screen and then the footage played in full HD on Bravo's top-of-the-line 85-inch Samsung television set. On the screen, Akulov was clearly visible arriving at the corner of the bar building. Angel let the footage continue for a while and then he paused it.

He placed the iPhone delicately back into the pocket of his jet-black jeans and advanced upon the hulking form of Bravo.

'Now you wanna tell me this didn't happen? We all hallucinating here?'

Bravo continued to shake his head.

Angel ripped the duct tape away from the man's mouth making him gasp. 'What d'you wanna say, *cabrón*?'

Vetrov could see the Giant's muscles twitching. He knew military men, he knew soldiers and he could read his mind. He was nearing the point of no return, when he had nothing to lose except his life and everything to gain. Bravo could spring up, take his master off his feet and toss him around like a rag doll. Angel was pumped on a heady cocktail of anger, remorse and tequila and it could prove fatal.

The other cartel men around the room, and there were four of them, were looking down, not wanting to make eye contact with Angel, not wanting to incur his wrath.

Vetrov contemplated the best course of action. Mendez had the money he needed and the street-smart intelligence that had built the cartel, but he was as unstable as a three-legged mule. Bravo was an intimidating physical force but he lacked a business mind. In the end there was no real contest.

Vetrov stepped between the two, sensed Bravo relax a fraction, but saw Angel rise up on the balls of his feet. 'This is exactly what Akulov wants! Don't you see? He wants your cartel to implode, to eat itself from within. You have lost your brother' – Vetrov crossed his chest – a meaningless movement but one he knew the Catholic Mexican respected – 'God rest his eternal soul, and he can never be replaced, but there is no reason to lose your Giant. Akulov made a grave error when he let Luis live. He did not know that he had superhuman strength, and an iron will. I have seen this Akulov in action and I can tell you that the blow he delivered would have killed a lesser man. It would have shattered his skull and broken his neck. So while we all mourn your brother, we should rejoice that the Giant Bravo has not and cannot be defeated!'

Angel had become stock-still as he contemplated Vetrov's words, grasping how this was indeed snatching glory, and pride from the jaws of defeat.

Vetrov knew he had to press on. 'Don Caesar was too a remarkable man. One on one, hand to hand, he would have wrung the skinny neck of this Russian asshole, but Akulov used a gun – the mark of a coward. And now it is up to you, *patron*, to avenge your brother like a man and to do it with your unbeatable giant by your side.'

Angel paced the room, every eye on him. He eventually fell back into the huge, maroon leather settee with a sigh. He looked skywards and Vetrov saw his eyes were moist, and then tears erupted and flowed down his face. 'Oh, brother, I will avenge you! You have my word, *hombre*.'

Vetrov turned to look at Bravo who was sitting in shock. He addressed him, voice low but firm, 'Get up and get out.'

The big man stood, the chair splintering as he did so but bits of it still affixed to him with tape. He half waddled out of the room, and on seeing a nod from Vetrov so did the rest of the cartel men.

Angel fixed his reddened, watery eyes on Vetrov. 'What are you, Kirill? Some type of wizard, who can control the minds of men? I was ready to kill Luis, there and then. I was going to slit his throat, like a pig, and let him bleed out on his expensive *puta* carpet but you stopped me, man. You showed me I was wrong. What you said is right: we have to be strong, we have to fight together, we will continue the legacy of the Mendez Cartel in my brother's memory.'

'Then that is what we shall do.'

'So tell me, how are we going to prepare for this *pendejo*?'

'I know how he thinks, and I know how he will attack. He will not stand a chance.' Vetrov moved to the TV set and switched it off. The image of Wolf 6 faded and went black.

Vauxhall Cross, London, UK

The only item in Neill Plato's office not state of the art was his teapot, which stood in the corner of the room covered in a stripy knitted cosy – a sentimental present from his aunt. The cosy was also practical in that it prevented the heat from the pot escaping into the air-conditioned room, which had to be kept at a constant and specific temperature to ensure his systems worked at their optimum levels. Plato really couldn't really think of a better job than this. He remembered going to a networking event for programmers and being the only one without a business card, because he wasn't allowed to say what he did. The room had been divided between the mega-money flashy types either working for "big tech", or others who worked for start-ups and then a few in mundane government departments.

Plato had looked around, sipped his orange juice – these events never had absinthe – with a knowing smile. Whilst he listened to boasts about new algorithms or contracts won he remained quiet, proud that what he did effected real change, and protected everyone in the room. In his little office he was very much left to his own devices. The fact that not many of his fellow SIS officers understood exactly what he did and how he did it also helped.

He leant back in his chair and munched on a fig roll as he calculated how long it would take him to hack into the Qatari airport security network and view the footage he required. Yes the country was classified as friendly, and yes he should in theory ask for access, but he knew it would be treated with scepticism and if anything at all out of the ordinary was found, the Qataris would consider it an insult. People were funny, both in the "ha-ha" and the peculiar sense of the word. He much preferred computers, numbers and algorithms, which was why he was at his happiest when he was alone with his systems. Most people dreamt of escaping to a desert island, and whilst that would be nice he would only really enjoy it if he had a computer room to poke around in, oh and of course a reliable supply of Earl Grey. Perhaps, if he ever got bored with the SIS, he should get a job designing and upgrading IT and security systems for Caribbean hotels?

There was a ping. He swivelled his chair back around and peered at his central screen. He was in.

Plato's fingers tapped in commands and accessed files and several times had to avoid electronic tripwires but five hours later, which in Plato time had felt like five minutes, he had downloaded the files he needed, and left the system with no one any the wiser.

Plato took the footage, dropped the facial recognition program over it and let it run. There was a hundred and twenty hours of footage to search per camera. In data terms this was a huge volume. He had, however, only chosen to include footage from cameras that captured passengers as they first left their aircraft and arrived in the terminal, and a pair of cameras placed at the entrance to the terminal. This cut the total number of cameras he had to look at by two-thirds. It was still, however, a lot of footage.

Plato looked at his watch. To his dismay he realised that it was already a quarter to ten at night. He lived a forty-minute tube ride away, which meant that by the time he arrived in his street his usual fish and chip shop would be closed. Plato sighed. Oh well toast and Marmite it was for supper again. He locked his office, leaving the recognition program crunching the voluminous amount of data. If it found anything, he'd get a text alert on his encrypted iPhone. He yawned now that he was out of his realm and heading home for the night.

The Four Seasons Hotel, Houston, USA

Whoever had compiled the intel on the Mendez Cartel had performed an admirable job. The cartel owned, albeit via shell companies, three mansions on River Oaks' Del Monte Drive. These were the residences of Don Caesar, Don Angel and Luis Bravo. To augment his intel package, Akulov now also used Google

Earth and Street View to carry out an initial close-quarter recce of the three properties. They were set back from the road within their plots yet clearly visible, as were all the houses on the Drive. Many of them had attempted to provide some respite from potentially prying eyes by planting mature evergreens dotted around their plots.

Angel Mendez's place, at 3000 Del Monte Drive, was on the north side of the street. It was a long, double-fronted, two-storey, Mediterranean-style chateau and was painted in what a real-estate agent would describe as being "a tasteful mid-butter colour". A pool-table flat, wide front lawn that had been raised two feet higher than the sidewalk sat in front of it and a two-foot hedge marked the boundary. Two steps led up a dead straight path to the recessed front door adorned with a pair of columns. Around the sides and the back of the house, towering mature trees screened the rest of the property but with the magic of Google Earth, Akulov was able to fly overhead and see the long, narrow outdoor pool on one side and the summerhouse on the other. The thick tree cover prevented him from getting much of a view of the rear garden.

It was an impressive property but the front was highly exposed, which was good for security purposes as any unwanted visitor would be on display but not so good for him or anyone else attempting to gain access.

Immediately across the street, Caesar Mendez's mock-Georgian period property was on a similar-sized plot. It had a path that meandered in wide curves through large trees. This house had more tree coverage at the front. The left side and the rear were completely hidden by lush, thick trees.

The third property of interest to him was Luis Bravo's house. It was several plots away on the same side of the street at Caesar's residence. It was smaller than the other two, perhaps less desirable, which befitted someone of lower status even if he was of a much higher stature.

Akulov knew that neither Mendez brother had children, but both had women who lived in the houses, "unofficial" wives the briefing pack had said, concubines Akulov had surmised. Now that Caesar was no more, he imagined that his woman had cleared off or been paid to leave, or perhaps been "offed". But that still made him ask the question: would Caesar's house be empty? It was the perfect observation post from which to prepare for and indeed launch an attack on Angel, with a clear line of sight, and Akulov was pretty sure that where Angel went Vetrov would follow. Wolf 1 would not leave his new principal unprotected, especially when he believed he was about to be attacked.

Akulov had stopped off for supplies at a specialist electronics store and felt prepared for what he knew would come as he lay back on the five-star hotel bed. It was the same place Sofia and Juana had stayed at. One of the bellboys had been overly attentive after hearing his name upon check-in. He had insisted on walking him to his "Pool View" room and explaining the full functions of the TV remote and air-conditioning system. Akulov had given him a tip as he left, making sure to let him know that he'd be in all night.

It wouldn't take long for the cartel to spread his name around Houston among its web of informers. Akulov had no illusions: in order to find the name he was using and to keep the shootings quiet, the cartel had to have some serious influence with the local police department. Of course if they knew his name, they had matched video footage of him with his driving licence, both of which resulted in him no longer being a faceless assassin.

As the last of the Advil made the throbbing in his head recede to a mild ache, he closed his eyes for a moment in an attempt to visualise his plan of attack. The events of the previous night had pushed things forward rapidly. Vetrov would look at it the same way he had.

Vetrov would assume Akulov would launch the attack from Caesar's house. Of course to counter Akulov's skill as a sniper,

Angel would be kept indoors, away from the windows. Therefore, even if he could gain access to Caesar's house, undetected, and set up he would be prevented from getting a shot. Stalemate, or a waiting game, waiting to see which side made a move first. And in that type of game with an entire cartel behind him, Akulov knew he would lose. The cartel could flood the street with its soldiers and Akulov could calmly shoot each and every one, until either his rifle failed or he ran out of ammo and then the cartel would send in a second wave. And then he would go down fighting.

So Vetrov too would come to the same conclusion as Akulov that to snipe from Caesar's house was not tactically acceptable. So where then? Akulov imagined Vetrov poring over the same intel pack, trying to pinpoint exactly where Akulov would attack from.

So, whichever way Akulov looked at the intel he had, the only way to get to Vetrov was to undertake the hit on Angel. He had never broken a contract and had no intention of doing so. Would Angel Mendez really stay in Houston waiting to be targeted by his brother's killer? Would Angel's desire for revenge override his sense of self-preservation? From his existing interaction with the man and the intel he had, the answer was a resounding yes.

Using a new burner phone, Akulov checked the email account he shared with his broker. He logged in, went to the draft folder and saw a message. It was from her but the content was not what he expected to see:

'Message received from AM via Wolf 1: Stop the contract. Do not target Angel Mendez or the cartel will come for you, your wife, your children and your parents!'

Akulov deleted the message. There was no need to write his own. Angel Mendez obviously had no idea how the contract circuit worked and how those who ran it, namely the brokers, were considered untouchable. But it was natural for the man to want revenge on those responsible for Caesar's death – Tishina and himself. Tishina was inaccessible, unobtainable, but he was not. He checked his watch. It was time to taunt the man.

From memory he tapped into his burner the number Angel had used when he'd called Caesar's phone, in the hope that he hadn't changed it.

The number rang out without being answered. Akulov closed his eyes … and then the handset rang as the number called him back. He let it trill twice before he answered it. 'Hola!'

'Who is this?' Angel Mendez's voice was slurred and slow-sounding as though he was drunk, or drugged or both.

'You know who this is.'

There was a pause before Angel replied, incredulity in his voice. 'You're a crazy son of a bitch!'

'Correct, Angel. I'm so crazy I am standing right outside your front door.'

'You think I'm falling for that horseshit? You'd like me to come to the window, wouldn't you?'

'I'm waiting.'

'So you can use your little gun on me?'

'It's a little gun for a little man. It's Caesar's gun.'

'Oh you gonna die, *puto*, and I'm gonna be the one to pull the trigger.'

'Come and get me.'

There were more muffled voices at the other end of the call and what sounded like the start of an argument. Akulov continued to listen until the line went dead.

He lay back, satisfied. Psychological warfare at its most simplistic, and it had confirmed that at least as of a minute ago Angel Mendez was at his address on Del Monte Drive. Akulov opened the app on his burner, which showed the feed from the miniature surveillance cameras he'd stuck to the wall in the hotel landing. They were working and showed no movement. He looked at the timer on his phone. Within the next hour he was sure to have visitors.

Chapter 12

Sugar Land, Texas

Chen Yan rented a house in Sugar Land, one of the fastest growing
and most affluent of cities in Texas. As with the Mendez Cartel,
she had chosen a modest property in order to fit in with the local
community but unlike the cartel this was not because she did
not wish to flaunt her wealth, rather that her billions were
currently frozen and unavailable to her. For a billionairess to be
down to her last three million, mere pocket change, was a cata-
strophic state of events, and she put the blame for this squarely
on the now deceased shoulders of Maksim Oleniuk. If he was
still alive she would have liquidated him herself, demanding she
deliver the killing blow, but that opportunity had to been stolen
from her.

The success of the EMP but the utter failure of Oleniuk's side
of their operation the previous year had cost her everything.
Chen Yan had gone from being revered as "the Electronic
Princess", owner and founder of one of China's largest and most
respected electronics manufacturers, CY Holdings, to being
wanted by the US authorities as much as bin Laden had himself.
But the difference between her and bin Laden was that her involvement in the EMP attack and the hunt for her was classified. It

was specialised agencies with three-letter acronyms that sought her out.

The result of all this for Chen was that she had not been able to leave the US for a year and had had to use immediately accessible funds squirrelled away to purchase a new identity and continue her work. The second phase of Blackline would go ahead, and this time she would not be beholden to any feeble male mind or ego.

She lay, under the silk sheet, sated and relaxed as the Russian former soldier, who had fulfilled her needs, stood looking out of the window. He was the only staffing element of Blackline she had maintained and it was he who, following her specific instructions, would allow both her finances and power to be rebuilt.

She did not make small talk; she never had. It was a waste of mental processing and time, and time was always money.

'Losing Caesar Mendez was unfortunate.' Her English was flawless, the accent gained whilst studying her MBA at the New York Institute of Technology. 'You must not allow Angel Mendez to be killed.'

Vetrov's English had an instantly recognisable Russian intonation. 'I am aware of that, Chen.'

'Being aware of something and being able to act on it are two different things. If we lose the ability to influence the Mendez Cartel we must start again.'

'I will find and stop Akulov. I know how he works and I know his capabilities.'

'His appearance is troubling but not wholly unexpected. The SIS were not as efficient as we had hoped. Take care too of the situation in Matamoros.'

'I will. But—'

'But what?' She cut Vetrov off.

'I have left Angel unguarded. I have broken the basic rule of a bodyguard.'

Chen kept her tone flat but in the darkness her eyes narrowed with anger. 'You are not a bodyguard to anyone but me. Do you understand?'

'Yes.'

'Isn't Angel Mendez secure in his own home, sleeping off his overindulgence behind ballistic glass and protected by competent men you have trained?'

'He is.'

'Have you not trained the Mendez men in Mexico to fight?'

'I have.'

'You will use them to liquidate the entire Arellano family. Without the family to lead them the Arellano Cartel will crumble and the Mendez Cartel will expand to take control of trade.'

'I understand.'

'I hope you do, Vetrov. You still have to impress me with your performance as a soldier.'

Vetrov turned to face her. In the dim bedroom lighting she saw the wrath in his eyes. She also saw that he was again hard. She pulled the sheet aside, exposing her nakedness and let him advance. 'When I have finished with you, you may return to Mendez.'

Vauxhall Cross, London, UK

Neill Plato hadn't received any alerts during the night. The flat he shared with no one, except his vast collection of exotic teas, had been quiet but then a ping arrived disrupting his morning Alpen. It was a cryptic message, designed by him, that simply stated: "Philebus 16.2". The Philebus was a Socratic dialogue written by Neill's namesake in the fourth century BC. "Philebus" was Neill Plato's shorthand for "active search result" and the number that came afterwards was the percentage match a specific piece of footage had achieved. In this instance the probability of a match, at 16.2 per cent, did not set his pulse racing.

An hour later, Plato sat at his desk and checked the result. The results of the facial recognition program on the Hamad

International Airport footage had pulled up one hit, with a sixteen point two probability of a match. He brought up the footage and peered at the frozen image.

Plato found himself shaking his head. It had caught a traveller quickly pulling on a taupe-coloured sweatshirt. On the sweatshirt there was an image; it was a face. Plato's program had halted the footage and made the match at the exact moment when the face on the sweatshirt was covering the traveller's actual face. He didn't recognise the image and the person who was wearing it was a rather rotund, middle-aged woman. He'd have to investigate his program to prevent these types of errors from happening again. He added it to his mental to-do list.

Plato checked his watch. It was only three a.m. in Houston so he decided to send Tate a short message with the results. Less than a minute later his phone rang.

It was Tate. His voice sounded thick with sleep. 'Neill, are you sure there was no other match?'

'Yes, quite sure. The program is very effective.'

'OK. Thanks. Back to plan A then.'

'If plan B was finding him, what was plan A?'

'Losing him.'

'Erm OK, go back to sleep.' Plato frowned as he ended the call and then started to look at his emails and requests from the desks he liaised with. After the operations of the previous few days there was now a lull in workflow. His phone rang. Jack Tate again. 'This isn't room service.'

'Did the camera see everyone's face?'

'What do you mean?'

'What if an individual's face was obscured by say their hand, sunglasses, a hood or a hat?'

'As they left or boarded their plane? Highly unlikely as there are multiple cameras for security purposes. I did also look at the pair of cameras immediately before at the exterior terminal entrance.'

140

'Which capture travellers and non-travellers?'

'Exactly, belt and braces. That would have shown me everyone who entered the airport, not just those who flew.'

'OK. Thanks, Neill, and hey, sorry for telling you how to suck eggs.'

'That's fine. Now go to bed.' Plato's mind switched to eggs, pickled eggs to be precise and the best ones were sold by his local chippy. He'd make sure he got his huss, chips and pickled egg on the way home.

Still musing on his supper and with his stomach producing phantom rumbles he decided to watch a bit of the airport footage, and chose to monitor the same flight that the false hit had appeared on. He watched the procession of passengers, which had arrived from the Far East, appear at the end of the corridor and approach the camera. For the first few steps there was much obscuring of faces, Qataris wearing sunglasses and other travellers adjusting hats and hoodies, but sure enough each and every face was picked up and mapped, before passing the camera. A thought occurred to him. If sweatshirt woman had not shown her face at all, would his system have managed to have tracked her across the terminal? It was an interesting exercise, especially if she had taken off the sweatshirt or added a layer over the top.

Plato retrieved his large Thermos flask from his backpack and wandered out of his office towards the canteen, in search of his hot water. He took the lift to the correct floor and stepped out into the corridor, his gait changing slightly as his Dr-Martens-encased feet bounced ever so slightly on the linoleum that replaced the carpet in this area. The woman could hide her face but the rest of her was on display. He came to a sudden halt, closed his eyes and sighed. Why was he being so thick? She may have changed her face but she wouldn't have changed her gait. And if he ran his gait-recognition program, as he had before on operations, he'd be able to track her. In fact he'd be able to search for anyone he had a data set for. That's what he would do: belts, braces and more braces.

Plato arrived in the canteen, boiled his water, added it to his flask, carefully closed it and headed back to his office. Strictly speaking, carrying scalding liquids even in a sealed container was against health and safety, but this was generally ignored. Once he'd transferred the water to his teapot and it was quietly infusing, he got to work with his task. He brought up the footage of the Camden bombing, the smartphone footage that showed Ruslan Akulov. He brought up the new tape of Akulov from the several US airport cameras and the street CCTV systems. He started in chronological order by making a copy of the Wichita airport footage, and dropped his gait-recognition program over it. A series of green lines and dots mapped Akulov's movement, creating a biometric reference set. Plato put the software to work and got up to attend to his tea.

He returned, cup in hand, a minute later to be greeted by a prompt on the screen he had not expected to see.

'No corresponding data set found. Create new set?'

'How odd,' Plato said to himself. Was it a bug? Or were the two sets really different? He ran the program again and got the same result. Puzzled, Plato checked the footage captured of Akulov arriving at the airport in Miami. He sipped his black Earl Grey – adding milk would make it an abomination – and awaited the result. He was presented with two options. He paused.

Plato sat still for several moments, his eyes flicking as his brain tried to compute the data in front of him, the possibilities and the implications. He started to believe that it wasn't a bug. He continued the same process with each and every bit of footage he had. The gait-recognition system, his gait-recognition system he had designed himself, told him the same thing.

Plato sat back in his chair and swivelled around slowly as he started to understand what was happening. His brow was damp with a sudden sweat. His hand shook as he sipped his tea. He knew this day would come. There was even a name for it – "The Infocalypse". But before he accepted it, he still needed to check the Qatari footage.

He loaded up all the digital footage taken from Hamad International Airport, tapped in commands and left it running. It now made no difference if he was sitting in front of his computers or not; it wouldn't speed the process up.

Plato stood. He needed to think and he'd do so over lunch. He left his office.

Sugar Land, Texas

Vetrov's phone began to ring before he'd left Chen's driveway. He ignored it until it screeched at him again on the freeway.

'Your cell was off!' Angel Mendez sounded outraged.

'I was underground, checking the merchandise. There was no coverage.'

'We found Akulov!'

'Where?'

'The Four Seasons. I'm gonna go there and personally stick a shotgun up his *puto puta* ass!'

Vetrov was firm but calm. 'Do not go anywhere. It is a trap.'

'He's the one in the trap!'

'Listen to me, Angel, you are not thinking correctly!'

'Me listen to you?' Angel hissed. 'I'm your boss! I'm your *patron*! Got it?'

Vetrov's hands tightened on the SUV's steering wheel. He was no one's underling, he was a leader and he had been the leader of the most elite fighting force the modern world had ever seen. Yet he was being ordered around in turn by an emotionless narcissist and a psychotic midget. 'Got it.'

'I've gotta hit him tonight.'

Vetrov's face was set in a snarl but his words when they came showed only contrition and concern for his boss. 'Please, *patron*,

143

I know Akulov and this is a trap. The hotel is not the right strike point.'

'It is the only point to strike at him! He is cornered!'

'You cannot assault a five-star hotel in the middle of Houston!'

'I can't? Who are you to tell me what I can or cannot do?'

'Think of the fallout! Vinyl can cover up your brother's death but not a firefight in a downtown hotel!'

'We got silencers, man.'

'It will bring out the FBI. They will be all over this if you start shooting up The Four Seasons.'

'Vinyl's gonna get the cameras turned off. No one is gonna see nothing.'

The double negative wasn't encouraging. Vetrov was incredulous but kept his voice calm. 'Send some men, but not anyone who is guarding you now.'

'Why not? He's one man, one dumb *cabrón*. What can he do?'

'Kill anyone and everyone you send against him.'

'And what can he do against the Mendez Cartel?'

'He can kill it.'

'Kill the cartel?' There was a throaty laugh at the other end. 'Then perhaps he should be working for me instead of you, Vetrov? If he is so invincible!'

Vetrov's knuckles went white on the steering wheel and his foot subconsciously pushed the gas pedal making the automatic gearbox change down and the V8 growl.

'Vetrov! You still there?'

'Yes.' He felt blood rush in his ears. Perhaps he would kill Angel Mendez himself. 'Stay where you are, Angel, or you will die.'

Vetrov ended the call and concentrated on getting back to Mendez's house in River Oaks as quickly as he could.

Five years ago

Syria

Akulov tossed his helmet on the ground and poured the bottle of tepid water over his head. It ran in rivulets down his face and onto his chest, washing away the sweat and dust.

'Hey! You, soldier! Put that helmet back on. Now!'

Akulov wiped his face with his hands to see the source of the shouting. A Russian soldier wearing sergeant stripes. He was huge, the typical build for a paratrooper, and his uniform was spotless. Akulov knew the type, a parade-ground pit bull.

'Didn't you hear me? Put it back on or I'll put you on a charge!'

Akulov lifted his helmet from the ground, dusted it off and then put it under his arm. He had no intention of putting it back on; the nearest enemy fighters were ten miles away and separated from them by a strip of featureless desert tundra and deserted, destroyed compounds. Akulov turned and started to walk away; he had neither the time nor energy for a verbal fight.

'Where the hell do you think you are going?' The man advanced and placed a meaty hand on Akulov's shoulder.

On instinct, Akulov ducked, twisted and threw the senior soldier up and over his shoulder depositing him in a dusty heap on the ground. Wide-eyed the sergeant glared at Akulov, who symbolically dropped his helmet. Akulov's voice was just above a whisper when he spoke. 'Do you really want to die today?'

'Which unit are you from?' The man got to his feet, anger imprinted all over his face as his eyes scanned Akulov's debadged fatigues. 'You think you are better than me? Tell me, that's an order – which unit are you with? I'll see that you are thrown into the stockade! Or perhaps you'll be shot for this!'

Akulov advanced towards the larger man, feinted with his right then struck the man in the gut with his left fist. As the man doubled over he hit him on the side of head with a right elbow. The sergeant twisted sideways and dropped to the ground. Akulov took a step back. His pulse rate hadn't risen and his breathing hadn't altered. The man lay still for several seconds before managing to roll onto his stomach and get on his hands and knees. Using his right foot, Akulov pushed him hard. The sergeant overbalanced and fell sideways and ended up lying on his back.

'Never mistake a werewolf for a dog,' Akulov snarled and walked away.

To his left a battered Toyota Hilux truck drew to a stop among a cloud of dust. The truck was known as a "technical" and was a civilian vehicle augmented with a heavy machine gun mounted on a baseplate in the rear. This particular technical had been taken from the anti-government rebels and repurposed by Vetrov to be used on lightning-quick raids into enemy-controlled territory.

Again having been placed in the position of overwatch, among the rocks on the hillside above the target village, Akulov had seen the mission unfold before him. The others had been ruthless in their pursuit of ISIS fighters but several villagers had been caught in the crossfire as they attempted to escape. And all this had been magnified in Akulov's scope and with the magnification of the civilian casualties came the magnification of the anger he felt for his team leader, and his followers. What once had been a brotherhood, a family, was now divided by a simmering feud.

Vetrov got out of the Toyota and stretched. He was dressed as a local, but his bearing marked him out as a Russian. Without looking in Akulov's direction at all he started to wander away towards the prefabricated hut that housed the unit. He was followed by the driver and three of the other four men who had been riding on the truck bed. The fourth man, a large figure, dropped down and bounded directly to Akulov.

'That was a close thing.' Dorzhiev gestured back over his shoulder with the flick of his head. 'Each time I wonder if this will be my last day on this earth, but I would rather die for something than live for nothing.'

Akulov looked up. 'You should stop volunteering.'

'What? And give up a place at the front of all this?' He held out his huge, long arms expansively.

'Seriously, you can't agree with the way Vetrov is leading us?'

Dorzhiev shrugged. 'He is our chief. We must follow his orders. Sure, sometimes civilians get hurt, but that is the way of war.'

Akulov looked away at their hut, as the last of the others stepped inside. Had Dorzhiev changed too? Was his the only dissenting voice left? 'And what of the way of the warrior?'

Dorzhiev punched him in the shoulder. 'You forget, Ruslan, we are not warriors; we are Werewolves.'

Akulov opened his mouth to reply but never got the chance as an explosion pelted him with sand and dirt. Dorzhiev was knocked from his feet and Akulov stumbled to his knees. Akulov shook his head to clear it and looked around as troops started to run for cover, all except the sergeant who stood stock-still in the open, like a rabbit at night, caught in headlights. Akulov crabbed towards his comrade, who lay on his back, eyes closed, and slapped his face. 'Dorzhiev! Get up! Get up! Move it!'

The larger of the two men opened his eyes and sat up. A trickle of blood seeped from his temple. 'What was that?'

'Mortar fire.'

The pair scrabbled to their feet as low yet unmistakable whines filled their ears and then more shells rained down on the base. The other Werewolves were running out of their building, weapons in hands. Akulov saw Vetrov get into the cab of the Toyota. It reversed, swung around and stopped sideways on to collect two more Werewolves who were rushing forwards.

'C'mon!' Dorzhiev ran towards the technical.

Akulov hesitated for a fraction of a second and then followed. Dorzhiev got to the vehicle several strides ahead of Akulov and used his huge legs to launch himself into the back. Vetrov was at the wheel. He locked eyes with Akulov and shook his head. As Akulov prepared to jump on the back, the truck bucked away, tyres churning the dust into a thick, cloying cloud. Akulov slipped and hit the dirt, his hand stretched out in front of him. Vetrov accelerated away and glanced back over his shoulder with a sneer. He'd intentionally left Akulov behind.

At that moment, another mortar struck, so close to where the truck had been that the shock wave lifted the back wheels of the Toyota off the ground, before it continued on. All Akulov could see was sky as he was hurled backwards through the hot, heavy summer air.

Present day

Texas

In the darkness he heard thuds and voices. He tried to shake his head but it wouldn't move and then another sound he recognised made his eyes snap open. He was no longer lying in the dust and rocks in Syria; he was on a luxury bed in his hotel room. An electronic beep from his phone had woken him up, meaning one of the two motion detectors he had set up on the landing had been triggered. It was linked to a miniature surveillance camera, which was trained on the hotel room diagonally across the hall from his, the room he was officially staying in and not the empty one he was camping in now.

Akulov quietly got to his feet, fully dressed and wearing his boots. Standing on the threadbare carpet he continued to watch his iPhone screen as he dragged Caesar's Glock from under the pillow. A train of figures approached the door. Each was armed. The first in line took something from his pocket and pushed it into the slot, whilst at the same time the second man raised his pistol and trained it on the door. Akulov noted that the shape was elongated; it was suppressed. And then the first gunman opened the door and the second stormed inside followed by the rest of his team.

Akulov opened his own door and stepped out into the hall, weapon up. The last of the assault team stood in the doorway opposite, with his back to him. He was dressed in an ensemble of double denim with a red bandana and holding a suppressed Beretta. Akulov's Glock was going to be loud, and it was going to draw attention. He shot double denim in the back of the head. The single, heavy magnum round pitched him forward and into the room. Akulov entered behind the falling corpse.

The next gunman was stumbling and trying to turn. Their eyes met and he swung his own Beretta up but Akulov's Glock found him first. Two rounds obliterated his skull. Akulov continued to advance, catching the two remaining gunmen whilst they tried to react. The third fired. A snatched shot, at point-blank range but the handgun was out of position. Akulov felt the disturbance in the air as the suppressed round passed within millimetres of his right ear. He dispatched the gunman with another devastating double tap. The large corpse sprawled backwards against the last gunman, tipping him onto the large hotel bed. The final gunman sprawled on the bed, his large stomach exposed. He gripped his Beretta with a rigid hand, but his left hand was raised in the universal sign for "don't shoot me".

'Never mistake a Werewolf for a dog,' Akulov said, and shot him once, in the forehead.

The whole room was filled with the familiar stench of gunpowder and his ears rang with a tinnitus silence. Akulov popped his head around the door and glanced up and down the hall. He couldn't see any cameras and the ten other doors were closed, but behind them he imagined numerous phones, making numerous 911 calls. He glanced around at the dead men. Had these been the only men Angel could get at short notice or was this the general standard of the cartel soldiers?

He sighed. He'd used six rounds to shoot four men. The drawback of the sub-compact Glock 33 was its standard nine-round magazine. He had three rounds left. He needed more ammo. He took each man's handgun, awkwardly stuffing them into the various pockets of his jeans.

He stepped over to the fire alarm on the wall opposite, smashed the glass and set it off. Darting back into his room he put the handguns into his bag, grabbed it with his left hand and took the stairs down. In the stairwell he was instantly jostled by those from the floors above and below. He joined a surge of disorientated hotel guests in varied states of dress in the foyer and, keeping his head down, let himself be carried out onto the pavement.

His eyes darted left and right and he looked for further threats. A team of four would have come in a van or a couple of cars, and their transport and wheelmen would be waiting for them.

To his left, a figure stood under a broken streetlight, his face illuminated by his cell phone as he gesticulated wildly. And directly across the street there was another man, a tall thin guy in a suit. He was leaning against a dark-coloured, domestic sedan with his arms folded. Akulov had a feeling that he was a cop.

One of the watchers he could safely take out, without further consequences, but the other would be more problematic. Akulov turned left and headed for the guy on the phone, who was now facing the other way and talking hurriedly in Spanish.

Akulov increased his pace. He was still shielded by other guests moving in all directions. He got to within five paces of the guy on the phone and saw the nose of a minivan poking out from the corner behind him. The guy turned as Akulov raised his Glock and dug it hard into his gut.

'Don't think about it.'

The phone dropped out of his hand, hit the sidewalk and fell apart. '*No ... no comprendo.*'

Akulov stamped on the phone, crushing it into the sidewalk, to make sure the guy couldn't be called back or tracked, and switched to Spanish, 'Just get in the van nice and slowly.'

'OK ... OK.'

Akulov pushed him again with the Glock and the guy took

150

the two steps to the van. He blipped the locks and the lights flashed. Akulov cursed silently. 'No, get in. Don't do anything stupid or I'll shoot. Got that?'

'Sí.'

The guy opened the door and climbed in. By the time he was sitting Akulov was already through the door on the other side. 'Let's go.'

Pedestrians hurried past the front of the van and then one swung around the side. 'Don't move!'

The regulation Glock 22 pointed squarely at Akulov's face through the open window, and the badge in his left hand removed any doubt that the thin man, in the suit, was a police officer.

'Drop the key in the footwell,' he ordered the driver.

As the driver complied, Akulov assessed his options. He wasn't going to shoot a police officer, the man was just doing his job, but he also wasn't going to allow himself to be taken in.

The thin man backed away from the van. 'Open the door. And you, driver, you stay where you are!'

Akulov did as he was ordered but left the Glock in the shadow of his bag.

'Now get out and raise your arms above your head.'

Again Akulov complied. In the dim light Akulov locked eyes with the police officer. It was the eyes that always gave away emotion, intention and movement.

'Can I help you, officer?'

'Good God, you've got that Boston accent down like a native,' the thin man said, with a languorous Texan drawl. His left eye twitched as a strand of his long hair fell forward. 'The Kremlin must be very proud of you.'

The police officer knew who he was, which meant he worked for the cartel, which meant he was fair game. A mistake on the thin man's behalf but an error that decided Akulov's course of action. He let a smile crease his own face and jerked his right hand down a fraction. The thin man's eyes darted to the movement

151

and at the same time Akulov took a step and shot his right foot up into the police officer's groin. The thin man doubled up, his shoulder-length hair falling over his face like the head of a mop. Akulov twisted and slammed a blunt right elbow into the side of his head. The thin man dropped. This was the second man he'd rendered unconscious in an alley in as many days.

Akulov frisked him, grabbed his wallet and phone, then darted back to the van where, wide-eyed, the driver was feeling frantically in the dark footwell for the keys. Akulov retook his seat, picked up his Glock and pointed it again at the driver.

'Give me the key.'

'Please, don't shoot me.'

'Give me the key.'

'Here.' The driver handed it over.

'Put him in the back.'

'What?'

'Do it.'

Akulov kept the pistol on the smaller, younger man, as he dragged the detective to the doors and manhandled him inside. By the way the policeman's head and arms flopped it was clear that he was still unconscious, especially when his head fell against the floor. The driver shut the door.

'Get back in.' Akulov waited until the driver had retaken his seat behind the wheel before he sat again and gave the keys back.

'Drive.'

'W ... which way?' asked the driver.

'Left.'

The driver straightened up, turned his retrieved keys in the ignition and the minivan lurched away from the side of the hotel and onto the road, heading out of the city. Vehicles with sirens flashed past them on the other side of the road. Akulov saw a mall up ahead, its large parking lot empty at this time of night. 'Take us in there, drive to the far end and then kill the engine.'

'W ... why?'

'I don't want to waste gas.'

The driver said nothing more as they entered the parking lot and then came to a halt in the shadows, facing the exterior wall of the neighbouring retail building. The cabin fell silent save for the ticking of the engine as it cooled and the ragged breaths of the driver.

Akulov now looked at his face. Latino, late twenties, not some young kid but not high up the chain either. 'What's your name?'

'Pedro.'

'Listen up, Pedro. I need you to get in the back and tie up the cop. I presume you've got stuff back there that you can use?'

'Yeah, I got a bag of cable ties and duct tape.'

'What a coincidence.'

'I don't understand.'

'Go. Tie him up.'

'OK.'

'Make sure he can breathe – you would not want to be a cop killer.'

When he'd finished, Akulov ordered him back into the driver's seat. 'Pedro, I know who sent you, but I need to know where they are.'

'I don't know nothing, man.'

'You drove a team of four cartel soldiers with silenced pistols to my hotel to kill or capture me.' He dug the Glock into Pedro's side. 'And this Glock killed them, and now I've captured you.'

'Pl … please don't shoot me, man!'

'Do you know who this Glock belonged to?'

'N … no?'

'Don Caesar, and I killed him too.'

'I … I don't know anything. I'm just the driver.'

'Is that true?'

'Sí, it's true. I'm not lying to you, man.'

'So there's nothing you can help me with? Nothing you can tell me?'

'I don't know anything. I swear on my mother's life!'

'That is OK. I had to ask,' Akulov said, his voice sounding reasonable. 'So in that case, if you cannot tell me anything and if you know nothing, you are no use to me.' Akulov moved the Glock higher, placing it against Pedro's temple.

'No … please … don't!'

'But you told me you don't know anything?'

'I do! I do!'

'You were lying to me, Pedro?'

'Sí.'

'Last chance. Where is the man who sent you?'

'He's at River Oaks.'

'Don Angel is at River Oaks?'

'No, man, I mean yes, but the Giant sent me not Don Angel.'

'The Giant,' Akulov said to himself; so he hadn't killed him. Which was probably an error. 'What's the plan?'

'What plan, man?'

Akulov knew that severe stress made people forget and stumble over words and in some cases could diminish cognition enough so that simple questions and commands had to be repeated to be understood. 'What was your plan after the *sicarios* got to me?'

'The plan was to bring you back, you know – dead or alive – to the Giant's house, where you'd be kept until Don Angel could get there.'

'Where is Don Angel?'

'He's at home, but he says he's not leaving till he knows we've got you. The Russian advised him.'

Akulov felt his pulse quicken only now. 'Explain.'

'Vetrov told him not to move.'

'How do you know?'

'I was there.'

'And the men I killed – who were they? Don Angel's security detail?'

'Detail?'

154

'Bodyguard team.'

'No, they kinda float around the street.'

'So the street has less security?'

'Yeah.' Pedro closed his eyes as if realising his mistake. 'Oh, man, Don Angel is gonna kill me.'

'Doubtful.'

'Why?'

'He may not get the chance.'

'C'mon, man. I told you everything!'

'Did you?' Akulov dug again with the Glock.

'He's got four men in the house with him.'

'Who?'

'Don Angel. There's him, the four guys and Vetrov.'

'Is that all?'

'Yeah, but they're good. Came from Mexico with him. He calls them his "presidential guard".'

'What about the Giant? How many men does he have?'

'You kidding me? None – he don't need any. He's a one-man gang.'

Akulov processed what he'd learnt. The cartel had used valuable resources to attempt to snatch him, but not men who mattered.

'So, the plan was that you would just drive the van up onto the Giant's property, and ring the bell?'

'No I was gonna call him first.'

'With the phone you dropped?'

'*Sí.*'

'Who were you on the phone to?'

'My girl.'

'Is that true?'

'Yeah, she's mad at me for not being with her tonight.'

'You called your girl at three in the morning?'

'She works nights.'

'What's her name?'

'Delores.'

'Have you got a photo?'

'On my phone. And in my billfold. It's in the glove box.'

'Show me.'

Akulov retracted the Glock, let Pedro lean forward. The light came on in the glove box. Akulov saw a billfold, but he also saw an Uzi.

'Don't even think about it!'

'Hey, man, I didn't know that was there!'

'You are the world's worst liar – you know that?'

'Sorry. Please … please don't hurt me.'

'Hand me the Uzi, slowly, keep your finger away from the trigger.'

Pedro handed him the Israeli machine pistol. Akulov placed it on the seat to his right. If he collected any more guns, he could start a store, or a war. 'Now show me your billfold.'

Pedro held up the cracked leather pouch. 'Hey, man, you what, gonna rob me too?'

'Just show me her photo.'

Pedro pulled out a passport booth photo of a blonde woman with a large smile on her face. It momentarily reminded Akulov of someone he used to know, someone he saw die a year before. He snapped out of it. 'Nice.'

'What, you thought coz I'm a Mexican I had to date a Mexican *mamacita*? That's racist, man.'

'Do you live together?'

'Yeah.'

'Give me your driving licence.'

'Here.'

Keeping one eye on Pedro, Akulov quickly scanned the address. 'OK, have it back.'

'Happy?'

'Ecstatic. Do you want to see Delores again?'

Pedro nodded.

'Then don't mess me about.'

'OK.'

'Who was the cop?'

'His name's Vinyl; he works vice.'

'And he's on the cartel payroll?'

'I dunno, man.'

'I'm getting bored.' Akulov pressed the Glock harder against Pedro's skull. 'Is he on the payroll?'

'Hey, man! That hurts!'

'Not as much as a bullet. Answer my question.'

'Yeah. He runs interference. He made sure the cops never had your face.'

Akulov furrowed his brow. 'My face?'

'When you shot Don Caesar, the cops never got no tapes of that.'

'Who's his contact at the cartel?'

'What d'you mean?'

'Who does he call?'

'It was Caesar, now it's Bravo and Angel.'

'So he was watching tonight. He would have called them both?'

'I can't be sure, man.' Pedro swallowed. 'I've told you all I know. You gonna let me go now?'

'No.'

'No?'

'I need a lift. Take me to River Oaks, take me to Del Monte Drive.'

'But the Giant will kill me!'

'Not if he's dead.'

'What?'

'Just start this thing up again and take me to the Giant.'

Engine running again, the minivan swung back onto the arterial road and Pedro drove them, in silence, towards River Oaks. They passed still-sleeping streets, shops and parks, until they entered the wider, private drives and roads of the exclusive residential area. Seeing the place on Google Earth and scouting it in reality were two different things and Akulov had to rely on Pedro's sense of self-preservation to get them to the right place. The van turned the last corner and Akulov knew that Bravo's house was two ahead on the right.

'OK, stop here.'

'But the house, it's just—'

'Listen to me, Pedro, if you want to live to see Delores again.'

'OK.'

'I am going to get in the back, with my bag and my guns. You are going to drive onto Mr Giant's property and ring on his bell. Tell him I killed the team but you shot me when I tried to escape. Tell him I'm alive and you put me in the back of the van and lastly tell him you lost your phone.'

'He won't believe any of that,' Pedro protested.

'He will if you give him this.' Akulov took Bravo's heavy Colt Python out of his bag and pushed it into the driver's chest. 'You took this from me.'

'You stole his gun? You da man, man.'

'I try.' Akulov nodded. 'We need to go. Remember what you have to say. I'll be pointing the Uzi at your back and remember your girl.'

Pedro swallowed hard. When he tried to speak his voice was barely a whisper. 'OK.'

'Drive.'

Akulov clambered over the seat and into the back of the minivan. He checked Vinyl. The guy was still out cold, which was and wasn't surprising at the same time. He removed the detective's jacket, in an attempt to make him look less like a cop, and arranged him so that he lay face down on the floor, with his back to the door. Akulov then readied himself, to the right of the door, out of direct view of anyone opening it. In the dim light thrown by the passing street lamps, he exchanged his Glock for one of the silenced Berettas and took one of the autoinjectors from the bag. He knew he would definitely have to shoot the Giant with one of the two.

He felt the minivan slow and then turn as it crawled onto the drive heading up the side of Bravo's house. Akulov knew that from here even in daylight they would be hidden from prying eyes by the tall, full trees.

Pedro stopped the minivan and stayed in his seat. Almost instantaneously, as though they had been expected, a door opened and an angry male voice addressed him. Akulov took a deep breath to oxygenate his muscles and to make him relax. Beretta ready he flipped off the protective cap of the autoinjector. Footsteps approached.

'You didn't call!' the voice said in Spanish.

Akulov listened to Pedro give his story. If he deviated or attempted to warn the Giant, Akulov would simply shoot blind through the thin steel of the van. The Giant listened to the explanation in silence and then Akulov heard him approach. His whole body tense, Akulov crouched, ready to strike. There was a long pause before the sliding door started to open, slowly, cautiously. Light fell on the unconscious body lying face down on the floor.

'You got him! You got the Russian *puta*!' the giant growled as he put his gun away.

Akulov had forgotten just how huge the Giant was. Bravo ducked down and leant into the space, his arms reaching forward to grab the immobile form lying in front of him. Then he froze, half in and half out of the van, like a bear caught red-handed stealing a picnic from a group of tourists. His mouth moved, but no words escaped his lips. Using his left hand, Akulov pushed the Beretta hard into the side of the gigantic head and a fraction of a second later stabbed him in the right bicep with the auto-injector. At point-blank range there was nothing at all Bravo could do. If Akulov squeezed the trigger, a 9mm round would kill him instantly.

'Back up, step away.' Akulov's voice was low and the tone even.

The Giant started to shift his weight backwards. His lips parted as though he was about to speak but before they could form any words Akulov deftly pistol-whipped him across the side of the head, where the bone and skin was thinnest. The Giant stumbled backwards, a ribbon of blood spurting from his temple, and dropped to his knees.

Akulov followed him out of the minivan, keeping the handgun trained on his head. The Giant wobbled and then slumped backwards.

Akulov paused, waited for the Giant's form to settle before he moved the Beretta to point at Pedro who was standing, pale-faced with his eyes on Bravo. But then Bravo's eyes opened and he pulled his beloved Colt from the back of his waistband. Autoinjector still sticking out of his arm, like a spear thrown at colossus, he swung the six-shooter up, triumph in his eyes.

'That shit has no effect on me! Say goodbye!' The Giant pulled the trigger. Akulov didn't react; he didn't need to. There was a loud click as the hammer dropped but found an empty barrel.

Akulov didn't want to shoot, didn't want to turn this confrontation noisy, as even the suppressed Beretta would make a distinctive sound to trained ears, so he kicked out at Bravo, his foot catching him in the head. Bravo absorbed the blow and using his left arm's elongated reach, swatted Akulov sideways. Akulov lost balance and crashed over the low wall separating the drive from the lawn. His back hit the concrete hard and the wind was knocked out of him, but he managed to roll onto his front and then get to his knees.

'You wanna play?' Bravo's voice sounded too high for a man of his size.

Intuitively Akulov threw himself to the left and rolled again, as the huge man lunged at him. Akulov was on his feet; the Beretta lay on the sprinkler-wet grass out of reach. Whatever had been in the autoinjector was either dud or ineffective. This was going to be a fistfight.

'You got lucky in that alley. You humiliated me.'

'Yes.'

'Puta!' Bravo charged. Akulov jinked away from his first blow but again underestimated the man's reach and was hit by a second, square in the face.

An explosion of stars filled his vision. *'Chort!'* Akulov swore as he slipped on the damp grass and fell. He felt blood running down his face, his vision blurry. He recalculated: he was fighting someone forty per cent larger than average. Which meant a forty per cent longer reach and forty per cent harder strikes. He started to feel his anger rise. However good the Giant was, Akulov knew he was no match for a Werewolf.

Memories of his training flashed into his mind. Days spent fighting in rain-soaked fields with frozen hands. The face of his old trainer looking down at him as he lay in the dirt, blood running down his face. The Giant may have been taught to fight, but Akulov had been trained to kill. He paused for a moment longer, let out a groan and held his face, playing for time. The Giant looked down at him and grinned. He was beginning to relax now that the fight was almost won. But it wasn't …

Akulov sprang back to his feet and ducked under one huge haymaker. As Bravo's momentum carried him on, Akulov zeroed in on the points he had been trained to target and kicked the Giant hard in the kidney. Bravo stumbled, and grabbed his side. He stepped back, a flicker of something like fear in his eyes. He took a deep breath, turned, and came again, but this time his moves were slower. Bravo's eyes were glazing over, his limbs weak and juddery. Akulov felt a sense of relief as he realised the sedative was finally starting to work. The Giant swung his fist, but it was sluggish, and Akulov easily swiped it aside. He stepped left and swung his boot into the Giant's groin. There was a howl of pain and the huge man collapsed on the ground. Akulov stepped closer and dealt a final finishing kick to the man's jaw. His eyes rolled up into his head and his body went limp. Akulov panted for breath and, head throbbing, spat out a mouthful of blood onto the ground.

'Don't move, *cabrón*!' Pedro said, holding an Uzi.

Akulov let out an exasperated sigh. He tried to relax, but the spray-and-pray machine pistol would shred him if Pedro so much as coughed.

Pedro moved nearer. 'Put your hands up!'

Akulov knew that the boy had just made a big mistake. Keeping eye contact, Akulov raised his arms above his head and then as Pedro stepped forward again, he ducked and leapt closer, instantly decreasing the distance between them. Pedro shouted but Akulov dropped his shoulder, grabbed the Uzi, and knocked it out of Pedro's grasp. In one swift motion, he flipped the machine pistol around to deliver a savage, clubbing upper cut. Pedro's head jerked back and he dropped.

Akulov let himself fall too and went prone immediately, next to the cover of the low wall, expecting at any moment to hear voices and boots approaching. He lay there, his blood pounding in his ears but could hear no other sounds. Slowly he got to his feet and inspected first the unconscious Pedro, blood seeping from his nose and mouth, and then Bravo. The monster was sleeping like a baby, now that the sedative had kicked in. Akulov collected the Giant's Colt before he moved back into the deep shadow of the van and checked his watch. It was four a.m., the second day running he'd been up before the sun. The night was his friend, his accomplice. At the moment its dark shroud was hiding his presence at the property, but that would change as soon as dawn broke. Or as soon as either Vetrov or Angel realised their men hadn't checked in. He was in a precarious position.

Akulov looked down again at Pedro. He'd given the cartel man a choice and predictably it hadn't ended well. The former soldier, former assassin, realised he'd become soft, less ruthless than a man in his profession must be. But hadn't he decided to retire, decided to feel? Wasn't that what this last year had been all about? All he knew was he had to clear up the mess around him. But first he had to check the house.

Moving slowly and ignoring the pain, he pushed the side door open and crouched. He listened to the interior sounds, but couldn't hear anything that suggested another living human was inside. He moved into what he imagined had been built as a mud room and then entered a corridor that led left to the kitchen and right into what appeared to be a dining room. He opened his mouth slightly and listened again. Now all he could hear was a distant, rhythmic ticking and an electronic hum. As his eyes adjusted to the dark interior he saw dull, blue light leaking from beneath a door further along the hall. It seemed to be the only source of light in the sleeping house. Suppressed Beretta by his side, he approached the door and then placed his ear against it. The hum grew louder, but he could hear nothing else. He grabbed the handle, pushed it down and stepped in.

There was no one inside, just a bank of TV monitors. Most displayed views of the street and the two houses owned by the Mendez brothers, but another displayed the parking lot of an industrial unit. The equipment was top of the line and the image quality was as sharp as the night allowed. Some of the screens had a green hue to them, whilst one had infrared. Akulov noted that two of the screens were trained on the same window. As he watched first one and then the other, he could see two figures writhing rhythmically, one was very short but wide.

He retraced his steps, conscious that at any moment either of the two men outside could wake up and raise the alarm. He moved out of the door, weapon up, quartering left, right, up, down, searching for targets. At a crouch he moved to Pedro. The cartel soldier was still unconscious. He left him and checked the Giant. He was still out for the count. Akulov kicked him and there was no reaction. Akulov tucked the cumbersome suppressed Beretta into the waistband at the rear of his jeans, managed to get his arms under Bravo's armpits and heaved him backwards. After the initial tug he moved without much resistance on the damp grass. They reached the wall and Akulov managed to roll him over the top. There was a thud as he landed on the concrete path on the other side, but Akulov didn't care. He paused to listen and catch his breath before dragging the Giant into the house. Akulov left him on the floor of the mud room and went back to the van to grab the cable ties and duct tape.

When he returned, he found that the Giant had disappeared. He cursed himself and drew his handgun. Edging into the house he could see a wide, damp line on the wooden flooring that glistened in the light thrown by the open door of the CCTV room. He ran the last few steps to the room and found the big man sprawled on the floor, partly covering an overturned chair.

Akulov pushed the Beretta against his head for the second time. 'I'm almost going to be upset when I kill you.'

Bravo's eyes opened, and he spoke, his words slurred and slow. 'Y … yo … you don't understand …'

The Russian removed the pistol, moved away from Bravo and crouched in the corner. 'Then explain it to me.'

He watched Bravo manage to summon enough control of his body to make it to the opposite wall. He sat back against it, his head hanging low, chin resting on his thick, muscled chest. 'I had no choice … but … to … to work with them. They threatened my mother … my sister … if *the Giant Bravo* did not join their cartel.'

'Is that a fact?' Akulov said, flatly.

'*Sí … sí* … Look at me. I am a genetic freak, and because I was big the Mendez Cartel insisted and demanded I be their enforcer.'

Akulov noticed the man's speech was becoming clearer as the narcotic wore off at a rapid rate. 'You should be honoured.'

'What honour is there? My mother made me study at school, and at night too. I am a security expert. I designed this whole

164

system. I am in charge of communications and security; I want to fight with my mind. But no. I am seven foot two so I must fight with my fists like I did as the Giant Bravo!'

Akulov laughed.

Bravo raised his head. The cut on the side had stopped bleeding but a scarlet streak ran onto his forehead. 'Go ahead, mock me. Better still, shoot me here like a dog, because if you do not then Angel or his pet Russian will.'

'Vetrov.'

'Yes, your previous boss. I know who he is and who you were. I also know what they have done to you.'

'Explain.'

'I do not know how they did it, but I know you did not plant that bomb in London.'

Akulov started took a step forward before he stopped himself. The big man was good, almost had him believing.

'You are thinking, why should you believe me? The sedative you gave me has completely worn off. I could have attacked you when you came into the room, I could now, but then you would shoot me and one of us would die. Either way they win.'

'The Mendez Cartel.'

'Blackline.'

Akulov shivered. 'What do you know about Blackline?'

'The EMP was only their first weapon.'

Akulov stood, but kept the Beretta trained at Bravo's head. 'What is the second weapon?'

'Shoot me and you will never know, and you will also never clear your name. What is it that Vetrov told me? Ah yes, he said that you had a "code" and that was why he could not trust you. You would not do what was needed if it broke your code. I am asking you now to abide by that code. The code that makes you different from us animals. Take me from here, as your prisoner, and I will tell you everything.'

'Everything?'

'I will tell you what I know. I cannot tell you any more.'

'Why are you turning on your masters?'

'My masters?!' The Giant's fists clenched. 'They are not my masters. They are not my betters. All they have is money and the fake loyalty of the dogs it buys for them. You and I, we are above them.'

An alarm bell rang in Akulov's mind. It all felt too easy. Bravo was saying exactly what he thought he wanted to hear; he was giving up information. The only conclusion he could make was that he had been schooled by Vetrov in what to do and what to say. Even so, he had to take the chance that Bravo did know something. 'Disable your entire CCTV network.'

'I will, if we have a deal?'

Akulov nodded. 'Do it.'

Akulov tracked Bravo as he pulled himself up, righted his seat and then sat heavily. He reached under the desk and turned off several plugs. 'Done.'

'OK. Move it.'

He let the Giant go first and they exited the house. Pedro was still lying on the ground.

'If you want to shoot him, I have no objection.'

'Isn't he just a driver?'

'Pedro? No, he is in charge of drugging girls to be "used for fun" and selling them on.'

Akulov thought back to the night he had rescued the two women. Pedro had not been there, but the drugs had. 'Can you pick him up?'

'Of course.'

The Giant bent down and scooped up Pedro with his two huge hands.

'Put him in the van with Vinyl, tie him up and then get in the front, driver's side.' He threw the bag into the van.

Bravo followed Akulov's instructions but asked, 'What did you do to Vinyl?'

166

'I hit him.'

'You hit hard. He may be dead. I have wanted to hit him for a long time.'

Akulov made no reply. He waited for Bravo to sit then got in beside him, Beretta still trained at his huge mass.

'I need to adjust this seat; it is designed for dwarfs.'

'Go ahead.'

Bravo pushed the seat back as far as it would go and then tilted the seat-back too. He ended up sitting on the seat-back. There was the sound of something snapping as he shifted his bulk. 'Where to.'

'You have somewhere?'

'I do. North-west of here in Fairbanks Heights.'

'How far?'

'Twenty minutes at this time of night.'

'Drive.'

Bravo turned the ignition and pulled away. Even without Akulov's instructions he only switched on the headlights once they had turned out of Del Monte Drive. Akulov split his focus between the road ahead and Bravo. The window was open and he noticed the Giant was blinking every few seconds and taking deep breaths, but from the position he was seated in it would be impossible for him to launch an attack with any force or leverage.

Akulov decided engaging in conversation would keep the man sharp. 'Tell me about Detective Vinyl.'

'Cheap suit, expensive shoes. He runs interference for the cartel. He was watching tonight and was supposed to call me.'

'Just you or Angel too?'

'Just me. I was to then keep Angel updated.'

'Not Vetrov?'

'No. The Russian listens to the phone calls, and advises.'

'Angel is expecting a call from you?'

'Sí.'

'Call Angel. Tell him you have me. Tell him Vinyl says he must

167

stay at home because the Feds are on their way to investigate the shootout at the hotel; and because of this for security reasons you have taken me to Fairbanks Heights.'

'That is understandable, occasionally the FBI sniffs at us.'

'Tell him to only come tomorrow. No tricks, and make it sound real.' Akulov pulled his latest burner from his pocket and Bravo dictated the number. Akulov pressed "call" and it was picked up on the third ring. Akulov put it on speaker. The voice that answered sounded groggy, which made the Mexican accent even more pronounced and there was a giggle in the background.

'Who this?'

'Don Angel, it is me – Luis. I have Akulov. I am taking him to "the place". Vinyl says the FBI are coming to investigate the shooting at the hotel, so it's not safe to bring him to Del Monte.'

'Shooting? What's happened?' Angel now sounded much more alert.

'That Russian asshole tore through our men like they were nothing. Vinyl shot him and then Pedro stabbed him with some of the stuff he keeps in the van for the girls. So he's sleeping.'

'Tell me he's not gonna die?'

'It's a through and through in the leg, but Vinyl is livid. He says you need to stay home until morning, in case the FBI come to Del Monte.'

'He has a point, but Screw Vinyl; he's nothing. OK, Giant, you done good. Keep Akulov on ice for me. If he gets away, I'll have to talk to your mother again. You understand?'

Akulov saw anger momentarily flash across Bravo's face, before he said, 'Sí, Don Angel.'

Mendez ended the call. Akulov powered down the phone, in case it was a trap and in case it was being tracked.

'Was that believable enough for you?'

Akulov knew the answer but wanted Bravo to confirm it for him. 'Why did Angel mention your mother?'

'Why do you think? He likes to remind me he knows where

168

my mother and my sister live. If I fail him they would not like it. You see, I am risking their lives coming with you. You must understand, I want out. I want to be completely out of this life.'

Akulov made no comment. It sounded too coincidental to him. 'This place we are going to, you call it "the place"?'

'*Sí*, I have a mathematical mind not a creative one.'

Akulov saw a signpost for Fairbanks Heights. 'Tell me about the two girls.'

'The ones you took from us?'

'Yes.'

Bravo told Akulov what they had planned to do with the girls as revenge against the rival cartel.

'The boyfriend is alive?'

'I have no idea,' Bravo said, matter of fact. 'However, the father is dead.'

'How did Angel find out who had ordered the hit?'

'When Vetrov introduced himself to the brothers, he had a present for them. It was the head of Don Juan Arellano.' The big man smiled. 'He literally brought them the head of the Arellano Cartel.'

Akulov's mind flashed back to a different time, and a different place – it was vintage Vetrov. The minivan slowed and they took a turnpike off the highway onto an access road and then into an industrial estate. The sky was starting to turn pink as Bravo brought them to a halt in front of an industrial unit. It had both a small door for pedestrians and a large up-and-over door for delivery vehicles. 'The keys are on the keyring for the van.'

'Cut the engine, get out and open the door.'

Akulov followed the Giant out, all the time checking for any hint that it was a trap. He saw a CCTV camera covering their approach and switched his mind back to the house and the video feed of the same view. He imagined it was the same camera; he hoped for the best and planned for the worst.

The Giant opened up the main door. 'Shall I drive it inside?'

'No. Walk.'

The Giant sauntered into the vast interior of the building. Akulov darted inside and immediately moved to his left, taking him out of the doorway and any direct line of fire. He scanned the gloom for threats and saw none.

'You want lights?'

'Switch them on.'

Industrial-strength lights blinked on, flooding the interior. Akulov saw no immediate threats. The double-warehouse-sized unit was empty save for a sectioned-off area at one end, which he presumed was an office, and several vehicle-sized shapes under sheets. He stood motionless, listened. Heard nothing.

'Bring the van inside.'

'OK.'

Akulov followed the Giant, got back into the van and they drove inside.

'Shut the warehouse doors.'

The Giant said nothing and obeyed.

'Now open the van and take Pedro out.'

'*Sí.*' Bravo opened the sliding side doors, and bent down. There was a muted murmuring. 'Vinyl is awake.'

'What about Pedro?'

'I think he is dead.'

Akulov moved nearer, still with the Beretta ready. He saw Vinyl, eyes screwed up against the overhead lights, struggling with his bonds. Next to him Pedro was still. 'Pick up Pedro.'

Without any effort Bravo raised the much smaller man from the floor of the van. He held him aloft, draped over his two arms like a butler holding a long coat. 'He is dead.'

'Drop him on the floor.'

'Drop him?'

'If he's dead it won't hurt him.'

Bravo took several steps away from the van and held Pedro out in front of him.

170

'Do it.'

Akulov looked on as the body fell from a height of over a metre and a half. Pedro made no move to protect his head, as he dropped. He was a literal dead weight. There was a sickening crack as the back of his head hit the unforgiving, concrete floor, but no cry of pain, or moan or anything at all that would suggest Pedro was anything other than dead. The only sound came from Vinyl who was protesting.

Bravo kicked the corpse. 'He was a sack of shit, and now that is all he is.'

Akulov tapped Pedro's face with his booted foot. The blood leaking out of his skull and glassy fishlike eyes told him all he needed to know. 'Put him back in the van. The cartel can have him back.'

'I like your style,' Bravo said. He picked up the corpse, as if it weighed nothing, deposited it inside the vehicle, next to Vinyl and wiped his hands on Pedro's jeans. 'And Vinyl?'

'Help him out.'

Bravo pulled Vinyl out and to his feet. He hopped and stumbled like a penguin. His wrists were still cable-tied together at the front of his body, as were his ankles, and his mouth was painfully sealed with duct tape. Akulov had to admire Pedro's efficiency.

Bravo yawned. 'There are soft chairs in the office. I have not slept much, and look at this face – I need my beauty sleep. Please, can we go over there? I will tell you all I know – we can also secure Vinyl.'

'Lead the way.'

Bravo grabbed Vinyl by the scruff of his jacket and dragged him across the space and through the door. Akulov prepared for attack, but there was no one inside, just a meeting table on the left, facing leather settees and La-Z-Boys. Akulov pushed Vinyl into one of the chairs, and with a nod from Akulov, sat in a second and reclined it. He yawned again and visibly relaxed.

Akulov remained standing. His fatigue was gone as adrenalin flooded his system. Vinyl had become silent but his eyes were fiery with anger. Akulov nodded at Bravo. 'Now tell me all you know.'

Del Monte Drive, Houston

Vetrov was tired but it was nothing like the fatigue he had experienced on military operations. Dawn was breaking but he had not yet been to bed. His "boss", who'd been attempting to drive away his grief with alcohol, drugs and the services of several women, had gone quiet a quarter of an hour ago and Vetrov knew he'd not surface now for several hours. Vetrov's warning to not send men to snatch Akulov had been ignored and according to the Giant the snatch squad had been noisily liquidated. Wolf 6 had taken them out, yet much to Vetrov's incredulity had then been captured by Vinyl.

Had Vinyl just got lucky or had it been Akulov's self-righteous code that had caused him to get captured? Vetrov would bet everything he owned that Akulov's capture had not been down to Wolf 6 becoming sloppy.

Vetrov observed through the thick, ballistic glass as the sky lightened. It was a new day for the residents of Houston and he sincerely hoped the last day Akulov would see. But something was niggling at him. Could Vinyl and that lackey, whose name he didn't know, have really taken in Wolf 6? To him it seemed impossible, incredible, and yet the Giant had claimed it was so.

If Akulov was not at the facility, then what had happened? Why was the Giant insisting that they had Akulov? It came to him, like a revelation. Had the Giant placed a new contract on the Mendez brothers? Was that the reason why he was the sole survivor of the gunfight with Wolf 6 in the alley that had killed Caesar Mendez? If this was the case, Akulov was working with the Giant. He needed to check this, and one phone call would reveal the truth.

Vetrov retrieved his phone and called Vinyl. He hadn't called the vice detective ever before; he hadn't needed to. The call connected, but the phone at the other end rang out to voicemail. Vetrov removed the handset from his ear and stared at its screen, as though willing it to ring. It didn't. He now knew that the only way to disprove his suspicions would be to go to Fairbanks Heights and see for himself if Akulov was there. If for any reason he attempted to leave now, Angel would either prevent him or insist on coming too. Unless he went now, whilst his boss and the rest of the house was asleep.

Vetrov let his mind wander to the ongoing Blackline operation. He pictured the effect the cyberattack would have once his hacker's new footage was released. It would create chaos in the Middle East leading to, his Saudi client predicted, regime change. And with change came opportunity and with opportunity came wealth.

The lights of a car illuminated the street below. In the pre-dawn light, Vetrov could see it was a dark, domestic sedan, not the type driven by the residents of this upmarket part of town. Not a car that would blend in. It came to a stop on the opposite side of the street, directly outside Caesar's house. The headlights went off. Vetrov noted that the driver and passenger did not exit the vehicle. Federal agents. The vanguard, the first to arrive and take watch on both houses owned by the Mendez brothers. Vetrov now knew he would not be leaving the house until the men left the street. Or unless he was innocently driving to the airport.

There was nothing to be done. The house was secure, there were a pair of federal agents outside and if Akulov was on the loose he wouldn't attack them now. Vetrov's mind went back to the well-trusted military mantra – sleep when you can and eat when you can. He moved away from the window, lay on the bed and closed his eyes. He'd get several hours' sleep before Angel woke up and made more demands of him.

Chapter 13

Five years ago

Syria

'Any movement?' Wolf 1 said.

'*Nichego*' – nothing, Wolf 6 replied.

'Counting down.'

The world in front of Akulov was rendered a familiar, unearthly green by his night vision scope. Away from the capital and its wealth, the dust-blown deserts and barren mountains hadn't changed for a millennium. From their OP in the foothills there was no way to tell if the collection of single- and two-storey buildings that constituted the village below were eight or eighty-eight years old. The only feature perhaps linking them to the latter part of the twentieth century was the uniformity of their lines.

The "Kanadets" – the Canadian – Kevin Belanger had gone missing after entering Syria two years before. Presumed dead, he had reappeared four months previously as a prisoner held by the Jabhat al-Nusra, a Salafist jihadist group aligned to ISIL. The shaggy hair and bushy beard, as shown on al-Nusra propaganda videos, did little to hide his emaciated frame. This was a very different Belanger to the clean-shaven thirty-two-year-old former chemistry teacher who'd left Halifax, Nova Scotia, to spread his faith.

Akulov knew nothing more about the man, but he was glad to be part of the four-man team tasked with extracting him from the Jabhat al-Nusra. The Russian government were keen to succeed where others had failed. Drone intelligence had given the location of the compound in the valley below, well within the territory Russia had decided was its alone to monitor. HUMINT – human intelligence – provided by the Werewolves had now pinpointed Belanger's location: an unremarkable single-storey building on the eastern edge of the village. For two days now they had watched Belanger being led out of his makeshift prison twice each day, carrying a bucket, which he emptied. Whoever his jailer was, they were at least attempting to be humane. They had seen only three other fighters, which made that a team of four looking after one man. Equal odds, four against four, but not equal at all, never equal to four Werewolves.

'It's time,' Vetrov said.

'Have that,' Akulov replied, his voice low, his focus on the compound, on providing overwatch as Vetrov slowly slithered backwards and out of their hide.

Wolf 6 watched Wolf 1 as he and the other two descended the scree-covered hillside with practised guile. This was the moment of maximum exposure; they were in the open with just Akulov's keen eyes to intercept any threats. Complete radio silence, completely deniable, and as always their unit did not officially exist.

There was a distant glow in the sky, not the sun. An explosion. Then another. Too far off for the sound to instantly register, close enough for the flash to momentarily flare in his scope. Akulov screwed his eyes shut for a matter of a second before opening them once more, to movement …

Two bearded figures, three hundred and fifty metres away,

tracking parallel to the compound, using the exterior wall as cover. They were armed, which was de rigueur in this part of the world, but their rifles were not slung across their backs; they were being carried at port arms, ready to move and acquire targets. Akulov's team were operating under strict radio silence; even an intercepted hiss of encrypted transmission would alert the opposition that they were in the area.

Akulov's VSS Vintorez sniper rifle, like the 9mm AS Vals carried by his brothers, was suppressed, but a suppressed round still made a sound and any noise in the bowl-shaped valley below would carry. The heavy subsonic 9×39mm rounds when fired from the internally suppressed VSS were quieter than most but not as accurate for long-range shots. This didn't overly worry Akulov. He was the best there was. He followed the two gunmen with his scope. There was no mistaking their direction or their targets. They knew the Russians were there. And that meant they had spotters of their own, and that meant they too had overwatch. There was nothing to be done: either he was being targeted or he was not. Akulov had to deal in facts. He acquired the second of the two, the one who was following his partner, the one who was less tactically aware. His head filled Akulov's vision. He smoothly, slowly exhaled whilst he squeezed the trigger; there was a metallic, raspy whisper. A moment later the gunman jerked backwards as the heavy round tore through his skull. Before he had stopped falling, Akulov's next round was on its way to his colleague.

There was the gentlest of mechanical coughs from his east. Another sniper rifle firing, a different sound from his own. Instantly Akulov flattened himself into the dirt, trusting whoever was shooting at him had missed … They had. Barely. There was a ping as a round ricocheted from the rocks to his right.

The need for stealth had been ripped away. He had to escape the line of fire. With his right hand, Akulov reached back, into his pack, for a white phosphorus grenade. In what seemed like an agonisingly slow action he brought the grenade to his other hand, pulled the pin and lobbed it to his left, shut his eyes and went prone. The metallic canister arced through the fresh night air, and unseen by Akulov exploded in a thunderous, roaring, blinding white cloud. The area filled with thick white smoke, creating a wall between him and the direction of the shooter. The grenade would both obscure his retreat and ignite anything it touched.

Akulov scrabbled to his feet and moved as fast as his he could in the gloom. He had little chance of finding the shooter, but he could still lay down fire on any targets below. He angled up, further away from the valley and hopefully higher than the sniper. Hands and feet working in unison, he climbed until he pulled himself around a large rock.

There were gunshots from below, echoing around the valley floor. He peered past the rock. Where it had landed, his grenade had set fire to what little vegetation there was. It hindered the use of his night vision scope but would also do the same to any other combatant. In the lee of the rock he swept the village. He reacquired his team, pinned against the wall of the outermost building, taking fire. Two buildings over, he found a gunman on a roof. Firing wildly down at the Russians with a Kalashnikov.

Akulov squeezed his trigger and the gunman jerked sideways. The village fell silent. The Werewolves continued to prowl forwards. Akulov now found a spotter on another roof. He had a pair of field glasses raised to his eyes. A single shot sent him toppling backwards over the edge to the ground below. As his comrades moved to their target Akulov continued to scan the village.

He saw no one.

But he knew he wasn't alone.

Below, the Werewolves made entry to the target building. Meanwhile, the phosphorus from his grenade had burned itself out. The hill was dark once again. He swung his scope to his left and searched for the shooter who had targeted him. There was an imperceptible scratching of scree as loose stones were displaced under the weight of something moving. A human would make more noise, yet a human who had been bred for generations to hunt in the local mountains and foothills would not. Akulov relaxed his breathing. If the noise was caused by a human, they were moving and therefore their aim wouldn't be as good as his, especially in the dark. Akulov waited.

A pair of figures emerged from the green gloom, following what looked like a goat trail, which angled up in his direction. It was the sniper and spotter who had targeted him. The first was wearing a pair of night vision goggles and quartering the area in front of himself with an AK-47. The second was walking behind, his NVGs pushed up atop his head, and he was carrying a long rifle. His eyes were wide and his head inclined sideways in an attempt to use the more sensitive rods at the corners of his field of vision. The first jerked to a halt, as though he had just suddenly seen Akulov; the second reacted quickly and stopped too.

Akulov had five rounds remaining in his nine-round magazine. He shot the first man twice in the chest and then sent two more rounds past him towards the second. Both men fell. Pulling his sidearm, and leaving his own rifle behind, Akulov rose. Without checking for signs of life he put another round into each man's centre mass. There was no point in taking a chance he didn't need to.

Only now did he look closer at the pair. Both men's NVGs were bulky and outdated, probably first- or second-generation units, but the fact they had them at all showed a level of sophistication that Akulov had not encountered before from the insurgent fighters. The sniper's rifle was a battered Dragunov; Akulov acknowledged that to have been shot with this would have been ironic. The other fighter had a workmanlike, wooden stock AK-47 or a Chinese copy – he couldn't tell in the available light. He picked up both weapons and took them back to the rock. And now he listened again to the still air. Silence. It didn't make sense. He understood the smoke had hidden his retreat but why had they not attempted to target his three-man team below?

Akulov slowly moved back to his hide, to his ammo and his equipment. The world around him was still, silent. He clicked in a fresh magazine. He scanned the village. Anything that moved was an enemy. But nothing did. He'd killed six men, but had any of these been the original four guarding the Canadian? The best-case scenario was that the Belanger was now unguarded, and worst case was that there was an unknown number of insurgents waiting to attack them. He continued to scan the silent village and the rest of the valley. Nothing stirred. He focused on the target building and saw Wolf 1 now standing outside waving him down. Vetrov's eyes narrowed; that wasn't part of the plan. Akulov continued to watch, and Vetrov continued to wave. He scanned once more then exchanged his VSS Vintorez for a Val and slipped on a pair of NVGs.

He made his way slowly down the hill and into the village. The original inhabitants had no doubt been moved on one way or another. The sky had started to lighten but still the world around him was too dark to manoeuvre through without the sophisticated optics strapped to his head. Once on the flat of the valley he moved faster, still alert for danger. He reached the target building.

'They had men on the hill?' Wolf 1 was in the doorway.

'Two we missed.'

'Dealt with?'

'Yes.'

'That is an issue. There is a bigger one inside.'

'What is it?'

'See for yourself.' Vetrov stepped aside.

The room was furnished with nothing more than a metal-framed bed in one corner. Next to this what looked like a pile of rags lay on the floor. Akulov crossed the room and went through a door that led to the second room, where the Canadian had been held. The two other Werewolves were kneeling either side of a figure who was sitting up, ramrod straight on the floor with his hands raised above his head. The man had something attached to his torso. On his chest was a light, its colour bleached white by the NVGs. It slowly pulsated.

'Pl ... please ... I ... I don't know who you are, but you've got to help me.' The voice was low, and sounded hoarse as though its owner was not used to speaking. The language was English.

The other two Wolves remained silent. Akulov started to understand what it was they were inspecting. The Canadian was wearing an improvised explosive device, a suicide vest.

'Do you understand me?' The voice was still hoarse but the tone was now desperate.

Wolf 1, Vetrov, appeared at Akulov's shoulder. 'This is the issue.'

Akulov thought back to the sniper and his spotter on the hill, the man who had targeted him and missed, the man who had not attempted a single shot at the rest of the team. He thought about the two gunmen stalking along the perimeter, taking an unobscured route that exposed them to fire. All four of the Werewolves were now in the room with the Canadian, with the IED. It was a trap ...

'Please talk to me!' Belanger said now, his voice louder.

'Where is the trigger?' Vetrov said, in Russian-accented English.

'Th ... the what?'

'Trigger?'

'I ... I don't have a trigger.'

There was a trilling sound. Belanger flinched. The two Werewolves by his side jerked backwards ...

The vest didn't explode. The trilling continued.

'Is that a phone?' Vetrov asked, incredulously.

The Werewolf on the left of the Canadian moved back towards the mattress, lifted the corner and pulled out a large, satellite handset. Vetrov took it. He raised his NVGs then tapped a button, and a voice started to talk, in English:

'Russian soldiers. The device Mr Belanger is wearing will detonate if he leaves the room or if you attempt to remove it. We do not want to kill Mr Belanger, but we will if our demands are not met.'

'Who is this?' Vetrov asked.

'You are speaking to Abu Mohammad al-Julani!' The voice, whilst sounding tinny over the satellite phone now had an air of pride. Akulov recognised the name as that of the emir of the terror network, but it could have been anyone. It continued, 'You may take Mr Belanger if you release my men you illegally captured in Aleppo. I will message their names to this phone, and you will then use this handset to contact your superiors.'

'No,' Vetrov said. 'Those men are terrorists. They attacked our base. They killed Russian troops.'

'If you do not wish to die, you will follow my orders. I have eyes on the facility where my men are being held. I will give you one hour to secure their release, otherwise I shall detonate the device and Mr Belanger will unfortunately be no more. Do you understand me, Russian soldiers?'

'I do,' Vetrov replied.

'One hour.' The call ended.

'Please, you have to get me out of this!' In the darkness, Belanger's wide eyes glowed like alien spacecraft. 'I ... I don't want to die.'

Vetrov switched back to Russian. 'Wolf 6, 7 and 8. Go now to secure our exfil point.'

Wolves 7 and 8 left the room. Akulov stayed where he was. The sat phone pinged. Vetrov looked at the screen and swore in Russian. He then raised his hand to shoulder height and let go of the handset. It dropped onto the unforgiving concrete.

'What's happening?' Belanger asked. 'You have to get me out of here. Please call your boss!'

'I will call no one.' He turned to Akulov. 'Get out, Wolf 6. That is an order!'

'You need to defuse it.'

'Go.'

Akulov didn't move. 'Kirill, what are you doing? You and I are trained for this. We need to defuse the device!'

'Go.'

'No.'

'That is an order!'

'No.'

'Very well. I do not negotiate with terrorists.'

In a swift movement, Vetrov swung his Val up from his side and shot the Canadian in the head.

Present day

Texas

Akulov sipped his coffee. He gazed at his two "prisoners" through the bars in the door. He'd used two more autoinjectors, one on each man. He'd hoped there may be a cumulative effect on the Giant, but as he had rarely relied on narcotics to do his bidding, he was just guessing. Both men were sprawled out on the floor and snoring heavily. They were, however, no longer in the office and conference room but in another room that Bravo had neglected to tell him about. It was a room specifically designed and built as a cell. Hidden behind a false wall in a back corner, it was a reinforced concrete box with a prison regulation steel door. He was under no illusion that the room had been well used by the cartel as the floor was angled, there was a drainage hold in the centre and the air carried a strong scent of bleach.

Akulov was impressed with the construction, but the Giant had been less so when he and Vinyl had been ordered inside. If either came round and managed to escape, he'd be the first to give them a medal. He locked the outer door, which hid the cell from view, and walked across the warehouse interior. Passing the van, he gave no second thought to the corpse lying in the back. He listened at the door for any tell-tale sounds from outside that would alert him of a trap but heard only the wind. It gently pressed against the metal panelling and whispered underneath.

He opened the door and stepped through into early morning Texan sunshine. He was going to walk towards the nearest store, and on the way, he'd call Jack Tate.

Chapter 14

The St. Regis, Houston, Texas, USA

'This eggs Benedict is superb,' Tate said, mopping the side of his mouth.

'That's eggs royale; it's the salmon one.'

Tate inspected his fork. 'I thought the ham was soft.'

'And tasted like fish?'

'I hadn't noticed that – it's the Hollandaise sauce.' Tate took another bite, a puzzled expression on his face. 'There's one with spinach too. What do they call that?'

'Eggs I won't eat,' replied Hunter.

'It worked for Popeye.' Tate shook his head. It was eight a.m. and they were sitting, eating breakfast as though nothing was wrong in the world. The elephant in the room had either not woken up yet or was hiding in the bathroom. But he would appear soon enough. Tate had slept badly, and it hadn't helped that Plato's message had woken him up just when he'd drifted off. Later during the night he had started to question himself and realised that he had been an utter fool to let Akulov walk away; he should have gone after him, should have done something. What was the word of a former Spetsnaz killer worth anyway? But something inside him, perhaps it was his British sense of decency, had made him want to believe that Ruslan Akulov had not murdered his parents. The couple had actually been his long-term foster parents and perhaps that slight alienation he had always felt from them had tempered his pain, his grief, but either way he knew that Simon was hurting.

Their plates empty, the elephant appeared and nudged them both on the shoulder.

'So are we going to just sit and wait?' Hunter asked.

Tate shrugged. 'This is a black mission. We can't ask the locals to help and put out an APB, and anyway, Plato has the CCTV cameras covered.'

'Akulov is very good at not being seen.'

Tate agreed. The bombing had happened three years ago but it had only been a year since the "found footage", as the media had called it, had surfaced. It was this footage, taken on a lost iPhone discovered during renovation work, which had shown the face of the Camden bomber. That face had now been confirmed as belonging to Ruslan Akulov. Just under a year had passed since the EMP attack on the US had, among other things, destroyed all its functioning CCTV and surveillance systems. Major cities and institutions had new systems up and running but there were still considerable blind spots. Akulov, it seemed, had been exploiting these ruthlessly.

Hunter picked up the newspaper he'd discarded when breakfast had arrived. He opened it up to read the smaller stories inside, having already read the front pages. 'Death of a prince.'

Tate arched his eyebrows. 'Our prince?'

'The fake one, and he's only made page five on the international edition. It says here that French authorities found a body yesterday, which has now been confirmed as that of His Royal Highness Salman bin Mohammad Al Nayef, of Saudi Arabia. The corpse was discovered snagged on rocks off the coast of Cap d'Ail, on the French Riviera. Al Nayef was attacked two days ago, on his launch in Port Hercule by a bearded gunman ... It is believed, although not confirmed by either the Saudis or the principality authorities, that it was a robbery gone wrong … An attaché case that was chained to his wrist has not been recovered … Al Nayef was known to hold both a safety deposit box and a clearing account at a private Monaco bank … The prince died of multiple gunshot wounds to the chest … His identification was hampered by the length of time his corpse spent in the water.'

'And that fact he didn't have a face,' Tate added.

'The Saudis are demanding a full inquiry.'

'Jolly right too.'

Hunter put down the paper. 'At least that's one operation that's going well.'

Tate stood and moved to the window. From their room they could see both the Houston skyscrapers and the large houses of the expensive River Oaks area, nestled in among tall, lush trees. Downtown felt soulless to him but he had to admire the cleanliness of the city, at least compared to the grubbiness of London. An electronic ping made him turn.

'Message.' Hunter held up Tate's iPhone. 'It's Akulov. He wants another meeting.'

Tate crossed the room and sat next to his brother on the large settee. 'Where this time?'

'The Houston Police Officers' Memorial at Buffalo Bayou Park.'

'OK.'

'I want to go.' Hunter was resolute.

'Simon, that's not wise.'

'Really? You think perhaps I'll kill him with my bare hands? Or perhaps I'll just let him walk away?'

Tate said nothing.

'Do you think he'll kill me? Is that it? In the middle of a public park in broad daylight?'

'No I don't.'

'Look, Jack, remember who used to run E Squadron?'

Tate rolled his eyes. Before Newman took over and Hunter

186

accepted his current position in Washington, he had been Tate's boss. Although Tate had argued that since he was "on loan" from the SAS to the SIS, technically he didn't report to his brother. It had been Hunter who had planned the missions and carried out both tactical and intelligence assessments. But Hunter wasn't a field operative, and both men knew it.

'OK.'

'OK, what?' Hunter frowned.

'You can come along too.'

'Jack, I wasn't asking for your permission. It's a two-man job.'

Vauxhall Cross, London, UK

Plato entered his office with two fresh packets of fig rolls under his arm. He shut the door and hurriedly sat at his desk. As he'd been paying for them in a Tesco Metro store, he'd received two alerts on his footage search – both with a high probability of a match – the first of which was 86.4 and the other 89.1. His screens were black but once he'd nudged his mouse and input his password they came back to life. He clicked on the first. It showed a male passenger, white, mid-thirties walking with what appeared to be business class passengers dressed in suits or local Qatari attire. He didn't recognise the man. He hadn't seen him before and was pretty sure he wasn't on any watch list that he'd seen.

The footage ended with him passing the camera and heading towards the passport control area at immigration. Plato paused the footage. Even though it was his gait that was being analysed Plato wanted to see his face. He saved a still of it. Plato waited to see what footage had matched with the man in this video. The computer loaded and then a notification appeared. It had matched with the footage of Akulov at the airport in Wichita. The man in Qatar had, according to Plato's program, the exact same range and angle of movement in their feet, legs, hips, torso and arms through the step cycle – their gait – as Akulov. The gait in both pieces of footage was the same.

Plato's mouth dropped open. 'But ... but come on ... he's got a completely different face!'

He tapped a different command into his system and made a new copy of the footage. He then looked at the second hit. It showed what appeared to be the same passenger stepping out through the revolving doors of Hamad International Airport and walking to the official State of Qatar *'Kawa Taxi'*, taxi rank.

He opened his new packet of fig rolls and munched slowly as his mind processed what his computer system already had. Ruslan Akulov, the former Spetsnaz Russian assassin who had been identified on the Camden bombing found footage, had now also been matched in Wichita airport, by the gait-recognition software. However, on the Hamad International Airport tapes, the facial recognition software found no match but the gait recognition did. He finished his first biscuit and ate a second. And then most baffling of all on the Camden footage, Akulov's face was recognised but his gait was not. He knew gait differentiation was not completely foolproof, yet it was highly persuasive. And Plato was highly persuaded.

'Welcome to the Infocalypse, ladies and gentlemen. Please ensure that your photo ID matches your face,' Plato said and had to suppress a nervous giggle. He wiped crumbs off his top with a sweaty palm. It wasn't funny; what he had uncovered and the implications therein to both national and international security was mind-blowing.

Mouth dry, he went to his teapot, knowing that he had half a cup left of cold, stewed tea but he needed something to drink. He noticed that his legs were wobbling, but was it with fear or elation that something huge was happening, a whole new epoch for digital information and cyber war and he was the person who had discovered and prevented the first true attack? He wanted to run into Pamela Newman's office and tell her the good, bad and potentially game-changing news but his thoughts were running too fast for his mouth. No. He needed to relax, take a few minutes to compose himself and then he would go. But there was one more thing he could check, and hopefully this would, beyond all reasonable doubt, prove that somewhere, somehow, someone had used AI – artificial intelligence – to produce synthetic media that was indistinguishable from reality.

Plato sat again and started to mentally plan what he had to do in order to prove his theory. He pulled up the Hamad airport footage that had given him the second hit. On a paper pad, he made a note of the time the man he now believed to be Akulov had appeared. He studied the figure, which did not have Akulov's head but was carrying a bag. A single cabin luggage bag. Plato zoomed in and could make out a Qatar Airways Business Class tag hanging down from the bag's handle. The figure was not holding anything that would lead Plato to believe that he had spent any time in the small "on arrival" duty-free shops.

Plato then pulled up the first match, which showed the man exiting his plane and entering the terminal. He made a note of this time too. Plato cross-referenced the arrival times with the airport's historical live arrival data, which told him that the arrival was from Singapore.

Now that he had the flight number all he had to do was to break into the immigration data base and pull up all the Singapore arrivals. Once he had that then it would be a matter of copying the specific video feed for the desk that the man passed through. But breaking into one of the most secure databases Qatar had was not an easy matter.

He knew that what he was about to do was not sanctioned at all by his boss, but if he didn't do it, he would not know for sure if his theory was correct. He ate another fig roll and decided he had no other choice. He started to hack into the State of Qatar's Immigration Database.

Their driver pulled into the small parking lot at 1400 Memorial Parkway and let Hunter out before accelerating back into the flow of traffic and driving away. Hunter knew nothing about the park apart from what he'd read online and seen via Google Street View. The parking lot was on a mound directly above the monument. At this time of the day the place didn't look busy, which would make his approach much easier to see and he imagined was exactly what Akulov had wanted. He stepped onto the grass to his left and walked towards a footpath below, which took him directly to the base of the monument. Trees lined the outer edge of the path and disguised a drop to a second path below and then the Buffalo Bayou itself.

The sky above was the brightest of blues and the sun reflected from the distant skyscrapers. The mix of manicured greenery and futuristic architecture was a million miles away from Camden and reminded Hunter of sci-fi films he'd watched as kid, like *Logan's Run.* The path reached a crossroads of sorts. He paused and looked around. The only people he could see were walking on the bridge. He turned right, towards the monument.

Hunter remembered from his quick research that morning the monument was laid out in the form of a Greek cross. The stepped granite pyramid in front of him was the sole part to rise above the ground, and was topped with a reflecting pool surrounded by pink granite slabs engraved with the names of over one hundred fallen police officers. It was a brutal, tough yet moving structure. As he neared the pyramid a solitary figure appeared from around the other side. Their eyes locked and the man nodded. It was a uniformed police officer, either paying his respects or patrolling the area. They passed each other and Hunter continued on towards the granite structure.

He could see no one else so checked his watch. It was gone nine thirty. Akulov was late but Hunter knew how these things worked. The Russian would be watching from somewhere, checking that Jack Tate had come alone. Hunter suddenly started to doubt himself and his insistence to meet Akulov. Hunter continued inspecting the monument. He felt exposed, but also angry that the man who had murdered his parents was toying with him like this.

The high number of leafy trees in Buffalo Bayou Park provided a large amount of cover, except for the area devoid of trees – the Houston Police Officers' Memorial. Tate was across the bridge, standing with his back against a tree. He had a line of sight to the monument and the paths that led to it, but there were many blind spots. These were caused by the undulating ground, other trees and the granite slabs of the monument. Unlike his brother he was happy to wait for Akulov to make contact. Something told him that the former Spetsnaz operator meant them no harm. But as it stood the evidence against the man was watertight.

Tate tapped out a text message to Hunter: 'Any luck?'

'Not yet.' Hunter's reply came almost instantly.

It was now nearing ten thirty, and Tate and Hunter had been in place since nine thirty. Tate didn't mind waiting. He went into an almost trance-like state where he would constantly assess the environment around him. It was a skill and a discipline he'd had to develop in the SAS.

His mind drifted back to years before when he'd been on "Selection", trying to join the Regiment. After being captured during the escape and evasion exercise, as 99.9 per cent of all recruits were, he had been taken, hooded, and locked in a room. For eighteen hours he'd shook with cold and endured deafening and repetitive white noise. It was an effort to disorientate him, to break the hopeful applicant, but it wasn't the only tool used. Tate had been made to stand in various stress positions for hours on end; legs spread, leaning forward palms placed flat against cold, intolerant concrete, or standing with his arms outstretched at his sides like a letter T. Each time he had wobbled or moved, heavy hands and harsh words would move him back again. But he'd somehow managed to endure.

When he did it for real, in a dry, dusty irrigation ditch in Afghanistan, next to an al-Qaeda-occupied compound, the cost of moving would be his life.

Today was a lot easier than both. He was leaning against a tree, and although the temperature was rising from hot to awful, the park wasn't a bad place to be. Tate brought a bottle of complimentary St. Regis mineral water to his lips and drank.

Akulov paid the driver and exited the taxi, making a turn at the end of the block and heading towards the park entrance. The path he chose took him parallel to the meandering waterway and would eventually lead to a bridge opposite the Police Officers' Memorial.

Akulov made an exaggerated display of checking his watch and broke into a jog as though he suddenly realised he was late. He checked to see if he had attracted a tail, or if there were any watchers who moved to match his pace. But no one did. He slowed to a walk and leant against one of the many trees, again scanning the immediate area, looking for anyone who seemed out of place. He pushed away from the tree and started to walk, eventually reaching the end of the bridge and noticing a figure leaning against the railings at the other end. The man looked familiar. It wasn't Tate, but he was English.

Akulov slowed his pace and made sure that his hands were at his sides, palms open and away from his body. The man turned and did a tiny double take. Akulov imagined it was nerves, but he wanted to assure Simon Hunter that he personally meant him no ill will.

Hunter did not move, and thirty agonisingly slow seconds later Akulov extended his hand. Hunter didn't reciprocate. Hunter's jaw was clenched, his eyes boring into Akulov's so hard that the

Russian imagined two laser beams shooting out of him like in a Superman movie. But Akulov's focus was over Hunter's head at the world behind and around him, looking for the person he knew must be nearby.

'You're late,' Hunter said. 'You wanted to meet. Why? Did you want to turn yourself in?'

'For a spy, you do talk a little loud.'

Hunter said nothing.

'I know who killed your parents.'

'Do you really? The thing is, Akulov, I have incontrovertible evidence it was you. You also murdered two of my embassy colleagues.'

'The Americans don't know about your friends, do they? That is why I've been able to walk around the US for the last year.' Akulov leant sideways against the railing. 'I met a vice detective last night. His name is Vinyl and he is being paid by the Mendez Cartel to keep my face off the radar.'

'What does any of this have to do with HM Government?'

'The Camden bomber is also on the Mendez Cartel's payroll.'

'What are you trying to say? That a drugs cartel blew up my parents? That's absurd.'

'My former team leader, Kirill Vetrov, did it. At the time he was employed by Blackline.'

Hunter's face visibly paled and he repeated, 'Blackline?'

'Yes, Simon.'

'You lied to Jack. You said you were in Doha at the time of the bombing. We checked the airport footage. You were not.'

Akulov sighed. 'That is impossible. On the date of the bombing I took a Qatar Airways flight from Singapore to Doha. Do you not understand? If I am not on any of those airport tapes, this is much bigger than I realised. It means whoever did this had access to or hacked into the security footage of two different international airports in two different sovereign states.'

Hunter folded his arms and shook his head slowly. 'Your cover story is getting more and more Jackanory!'

'Jackanory?'

'It was a TV show, where stories were read out to entertain children.'

Akulov turned and pushed his back against the railings; he was tired. He took a breath and explained about the events of the previous night.

'Look, the only people after me are you and the cartel. Vetrov is working for the cartel, and he's trying to stop me from getting to him.'

'To prove your innocence.'

'And to ask why I'm being framed.'

Hunter tutted, an action Akulov found odd. 'So what, you want Jack and I to help you, is that it?'

'Your help would be greatly appreciated, but just a promise not to stand in my way would be acceptable.'

'A promise?'

'You two are English gentlemen, men of your word.'

Vauxhall Cross, London, UK

It was gone four in the afternoon before Plato had managed to hack into Hamad International Airport's security camera system and the State of Qatar's Immigration Database. The bulk of this time had been taken up cracking the firewall on the immigration database in such a way that when he left there would be no trace of his visit. It was by far one of the hardest systems to crack and once achieved a large smile creased his face. Now, as he finished downloading the relevant digital footage and immigration files, it was almost an hour later.

He brought up the tape of the traveller with Akulov's gait but not his face, as he waited in line for immigration. In what had become a well-practised execution now, Plato dropped his gait-recognition program over the source footage. Green lines and dots mapped the subject's movement and a biometric reference set was created. His prompt appeared on screen, and yet again it matched with the data set from the initial Wichita footage.

Plato repeated the entire process with the next set of footage, which showed the traveller with the wrong face standing at the immigration booth, then walking towards the camera.

Plato got up from his chair and did a lap of his cramped office, which consisted of four paces in each direction. He rolled his shoulders and swung his arms as though he was an Olympic swimmer preparing for a race. He sat back in his seat, wiggled his fingers and then opened the immigration list. He wasn't looking for names; he was checking faces. In his time window, twenty passengers had entered the State of Qatar. Using a few quick commands he extracted those twenty files from the records and scrolled to their faces. He stopped forty seconds later at the sixteenth face. He smiled at it, reached his hand out and traced its contours with his index finger, as though any moment he expected it to vanish. Plato punched the air, an action that he had never in his life remembered doing. The sixteenth passenger to enter the State of Qatar within his time window was using a passport in the name of a James Chapman, and he had the face of Ruslan Akulov.

Plato's fingers shook as he attempted to call Tate's phone. He waited for what seemed like hours, first for his phone to connect, then for the phone at the other end to ring and then for both phones to complete a digital handshake, confirm their identities and finally open a secure line.

'Neill, yes?' Tate's voice was crystal clear, as though he was standing over Plato's shoulder.

'Hi, Jack.' Plato found it hard to get the words out. He took a deep breath. 'Akulov is not the Camden bomber.'

Tate's eyes widened. 'Neill, say again.'

'Ruslan Akulov is not the Camden bomber. He cannot

physically be the Camden bomber. He was in Doha on the day of the bombing.'

'How?' Tate kept his responses short; even though he'd moved nearer to the bridge and was observing the conversation taking place on it, he was still attempting to be covert.

Plato explained the anomalies with the footage. '… I have him on film at Qatari immigration, with his gait and an unknown head, yet at exactly the same time on the immigration database a passport with Akulov's face was being scanned.'

'How would they miss the immigration records?'

'Perhaps they couldn't break into them. It was an extremely robust firewall; it took me a while and well, I'm SIS.'

'You're the best.'

'Top ten, perhaps.'

Tate smiled. 'So the film is a fake?'

'It's a deep fake. I know it is synthetic media but I can't distinguish it from reality. I can't see how it's been done. Whoever is responsible for this has access to or has designed algorithms that are way more sophisticated, in terms of artificial intelligence, than anything we've ever encountered before.'

Tate thought about the implications. 'So it's a type of weapon?'

'Yes. It could be used to topple governments, or start wars. Quite simply it would grant the ability to place people in places they were not, doing things they didn't do.'

'Like planting a bomb in Camden when they were in the Middle East?'

'Exactly. Jack, this is the world's first documented use of a synthetic human face that is indistinguishable from the source footage. This is the ultimate deep fake.'

'But hang on a moment, how is it possible that this footage was faked? It was vetted, wasn't it, after it was given to SIS?'

'Yes. Thoroughly. Especially as it was found two years after the actual event, I had to start from a position of scepticism. As you remember, I used every resource I had to interrogate the footage.

And so did GCHQ, and so did my counterpart at MI5. The answer is that I don't know how it was faked; all I know is that it was. And it was created sometime after the bombing,' Plato stated.

On the bridge, Hunter and Akulov were still talking. Tate continued to watch them as he spoke. 'So someone planted the iPhone specifically for it to be found?'

'Yes, or perhaps just gave it to us at a time that suited them. It was found by a builder.'

'Just to confirm—' Tate had to be absolutely certain '—you are stating that, without reasonable doubt, Ruslan Akulov was not in London on the day of the Camden bombing?'

'He was in Doha, or to be exact, in the air en route to Doha from Singapore.'

'Neill, this is outstanding work.'

'No it's not, Jack. I didn't spot it before.'

'No one did.' Tate visualised the face on his "wanted dead or alive poster" fade but although he had a name, he didn't have a face to replace it with. 'I think I have a new suspect for you.'

'Fire away.'

'Kirill Vetrov. He was the team leader of Akulov's Spetsnaz unit.'

'The Werewolves?'

'We need to see if he was anywhere near Camden on the date of the bombing.'

'OK, I'm on it.'

'Neill, thanks.' Tate ended the call. They'd been hunting the wrong man. He took a deep breath and dialled Hunter's number. He could see up ahead on the bridge, Hunter slowly reach into his pocket. It took several rings until he answered, but he spoke before his brother. 'I've got news. Akulov isn't the bomber.'

'Jack, what?'

'Akulov didn't do it.'

'I don't understand.'

'Plato just confirmed, Akulov did not kill our parents. Stay there with him. I've got visual on you both. Tell him to turn around; he'll see me approaching.'

'What?' Hunter replied after a pause, but Tate was already moving.

Tate walked out of the trees and towards the bridge. The bright Houston sunlight made him squint even though he was wearing shades. Akulov's eyes were on him. He stopped three paces away, forming a V shape with the other two men. 'Hello, Ruslan.'

'Hello, Jack.'

Tate wasted no more time. 'We know it wasn't you.'

'Jack what's going—' Hunter started to say but Tate cut him off.

'Our in-house tech expert has confirmed the footage had been altered, but he has no idea how.'

'Really? Neill has no idea?' Hunter's eyebrows rose.

'Nope.'

'It's a deep fake,' Hunter said.

'Yes,' Tate replied.

'This changes nothing,' Hunter snapped. 'What about the two British diplomats you murdered?'

Akulov sighed heavily. 'They were legitimate targets. One was the military attaché and the other had ordered military attacks that resulted in civilian deaths.'

'Right,' Hunter said, with no attempt to hide his sarcasm.

'Your parents and the others murdered in Camden were not legitimate targets. And as you now know, that was not me.'

'OK.' Tate wanted the real killer, who was out there somewhere with this new weapon. 'We're not coming after you. It's a truce. Agreed?'

'Jack!' Hunter protested.

'You two were never my enemies,' Akulov said.

'Where is Vetrov?' Tate asked.

'Kirill Vetrov is with his paymaster, Angel Mendez, in River Oaks.'

'How do you know this?' Hunter folded his arms.

Akulov explained. 'I have a place and I have someone there. The cartel's head of communications. He knew Blackline was responsible for the EMP and he says they are behind this new weapon.'

'He used the name "Blackline"?' Hunter gave Tate a sideways glance.

'He did.'

'Then this is what, part of another planned attack by them?' Hunter continued.

'Yes. He knows where to find the guy who might be able tell us how the weapon works, the computer person who created the deep fake.'

'Where is he?'

'He would not tell me until I gave him some sort of guarantee of safe passage away from the cartel.'

'What can you offer him?' Hunter asked, with sarcasm.

'I said the British Secret Intelligence Service would protect him.'

'You did bloody what?' Hunter was incensed. 'You first of all told him who we were and then made assurances on our behalf?'

'I did.'

'Enough.' Tate shot his brother a look. They were wasting time. 'We need to leave.'

'And go where?'

'His place.'

Hunter sighed and nodded. 'Agreed. I'm calling our driver.'

Tate waited for Hunter to move away and make the call before he spoke. 'Let's get something clear here; this is a temporary arrangement. We need Vetrov, and that is the only reason you are still standing there and not being taken away by a team.'

'Jack, I'm not your enemy, but I'm not your friend. When this is all over you plan to detain me. Do I have that right?'

'You do.' Tate had four years of anger, resentment and grief, and a year of that focused on Ruslan Akulov but now it had to be directed somewhere else. He felt an emptiness, but more than that a resurgence of his grief. Previously he had felt impotent, now he felt a building sense of empowerment and anticipation.

Hunter put his phone away and rejoined them. 'ETA five minutes.'

Chapter 15

Vauxhall Cross, London, UK

Dread, that's what Neill Plato felt. Dread and excitement in equal measure. In uncovering the deep fake, he had broken both national and international laws. He ate the last of his fig rolls as he tried to make sense of what he knew and how to present it to Pamela Newman.

The discovery of the faked footage, in Plato's view, suggested they had entered the "infocalypse", a time when misinformation and disinformation defeated society's ability to differentiate between what was and what was not genuine. Starting with double-exposed Victorian photographic frames creating fairies at the bottom of the garden, it had now ended with moving, talking images almost indistinguishable from real life. But this deep fake had surpassed even that.

Plato knew that he could lose his job, or his actions could lead to criminal prosecution, yet his duty, his oath to protect the interests of Her Majesty's Government took precedence over his own liberty.

He stood, brushed the crumbs from his shirt and left his office.

Working for the Secret Intelligence Service was not a nine-to-five job. This was more the case the more senior you became within the ranks. Plato was often called at all hours of the day and night with questions and requests but he didn't mind. He felt as though he was part of the good fight. The money was not great – he'd double it instantly by moving into the private sector, but at Vauxhall Cross he was making a difference, even if he was legally bound to pretend he was nothing more than an analyst. This made his mum proud at least. Perhaps if he did get sacked he could go back to Brighton and live with her?

It was approaching seven forty in the evening before he managed to knock on Pamela Newman's door.

'Pamela, can I come in?' Plato was aware that his voice sounded croaky. 'There is something I need to tell you.'

Newman was reading a printout. 'Is it earth-shatteringly vital, Neill?'

Plato swallowed. 'Actually yes, it is.'

Newman waved him to sit, placed the paper back on her leather-topped desk, and looked at him over the top of her reading glasses. 'Go ahead.'

Plato didn't want to waste his words. 'I have indisputable proof that Ruslan Akulov did not plant nor set off either of the Camden bombs.'

'That's quite a big statement, Neill.'

'Yes it is.' Plato nodded, nervously. 'I know I'm correct.'

'Then please explain to me how you have arrived at this conclusion.'

Plato took a breath, cleared his throat, and explained, as calmly as possible, what he had discovered.

Newman removed her glasses, rubbed her eyes, leant back and stared at her ceiling before she managed to reply. 'Let me get this straight, Neill. You hacked into – on three occasions – secure databases of a sovereign nation?'

'Yes.' There was no way to sugar-coat it.

'What are you proposing we do, Neill?'

Plato was confused. 'Arrest me?'

202

'Have you left any trace at all that you broke into these systems?'

'No.'

'How certain are you of this?'

'One hundred per cent.'

'Then it didn't happen.'

'Pardon me?'

'I just did. Putting you on an immediate suspension and launching an official investigation into your actions, which may lead to possible criminal charges, would not be in anyone's best interests.'

Plato felt a wave of relief crash over him. 'Thank you.'

'Tell me, Neill, what do you propose we do regarding this discovery of yours?'

Plato answered with a renewed resolve, 'We need to find the person, or persons, responsible for this footage and take control of their technology before they can inflict any more damage.'

'I agree, but tell me, why was this technology used on the Camden bombing footage? Why was it so important to frame Ruslan Akulov?'

Plato shrugged. 'I don't know. It may very well be this is not the first time the technology has been used. This could in theory just be the first time it has been discovered. All we know for certain is that the smartphone footage is at least a year old, and that's a whole generation in the digital age.'

'If this is a year old …'

Plato nodded. 'Exactly, think how much more advanced it could be now with another twelve months of development.'

'Who is responsible for this? Have you any ideas?'

'There are a few names I could look at, people I think who may possibly be good enough to pull this off, but it would be pure conjecture.'

'Conject.'

'Henry Roi, Martin Sonderborg, George Eastman, Zaneta LaMos, and Justin Nash are the first that come to mind.'

'How do we narrow that down?'

'We would need to undertake surveillance on them, both actual and digital. I'm doubting even I could crack their systems.'

'Are any of these people British?'

'Justin Nash is, but I've got no idea if he lives in the UK.'

'I see. And again, you said Jack Tate believes another member of Akulov's unit may be the actual bomber?'

'Yes, Kirill Vetrov.'

'And do you believe he is?'

'Too soon to tell. I'm in the process of trying to get a match to anything showing him in the UK.'

'OK. Thanks, Neill. I know how hard you work for us, and I understand the courage it must have taken you to pursue this but, in the future, if you are contemplating any illegal activity, you must run it past whoever is responsible for the "sign-off" for that particular desk. Agreed?'

'Agreed,' Plato replied, sheepishly.

Newman glanced at the wall clock above Plato's head. 'Go home. The real bomber has been in the wind for four years. Twelve hours more will not make a difference.'

Fairbanks Heights, Texas, USA

Tate had their driver, a retired member of 3 Para, stop the executive van one lot over from the warehouse. Hunter stayed with the van whilst Tate and Akulov went to scout the building for any sign of a threat. Tate found it unnerving to be working with the Russian, but he recognised the man's skill set. Both men had suppressed 9mm handguns, Tate's was a Glock and Akulov carried a Beretta.

Akulov opened a door and went inside. Tate had instructed him to give a signal when it was clear to approach, but as soon as the Werewolf had disappeared from view, Tate moved tactically to the side of the building and waited. The building was huge and he guessed that old adage of everything being "bigger in

Texas" was true. He spotted another steel-plated door with a fisheye security lens. He backed away, hoping that if there was a guard on duty, he hadn't been seen. He did a circuit of the V structure and appeared on the other side. Akulov was leaning against the door, a disposable cup of vending machine coffee in his hand.

'Have you finished?' he asked, offering Tate a cup.

Tate shook his head. 'I need to see inside now.'

He moved past Akulov and noted the overhead lights were on, illuminating the space in stark, artificial light. He saw vehicles under covers on one side, a minivan and a prefabricated office structure. It reminded him of the warehouse at College Park Airport a year before, the last time he had, however fleetingly, been on the same side as Akulov.

The whirr of a winch, as Akulov opened the large roll-up doors, interrupted Tate's thoughts. 'My guests are in a cell at the back.'

'Cell?'

'The Mendez Cartel had it specially built.'

Tate followed Akulov past an empty office space. Akulov pulled open a door to reveal another metal door with bars. He held up the key for Tate. 'Here.'

'Thanks.' Tate peered through the bars at the two men inside. One was in a suit and lying on the floor. He looked to be asleep. The other was huge and sat with his back against the concrete wall. The huge man had both his wrists and ankles bound with numerous cable ties, and tape across his mouth. He pushed himself unsteadily to his feet. Tate unlocked the door and with his pistol in his right hand, used his left to pull back the tape.

'The Giant Bravo?' Tate said, as he took a step away.

Bravo looked down at Tate. His face was blank, then like the clouds moving and uncovering the sun, a huge smile appeared and he spoke in accented English. 'Yes. It is me.'

'I was a fan.' Tate's mind went back to the downtime between operations in Afghanistan where for entertainment he'd rekindled his enjoyment of American wrestling and had scoured the internet for classic matches. His searches eventually took him from the WWE to smaller, obscure circuits. Bravo had wrestled for an independent Mexican company before he seemingly disappeared, rumour had it just weeks before a potential try-out for a large US promotion. Bravo's hair was still jet black, and held back in a ponytail, and his physique looked bigger than ever, though the stubble on his chin had started to grey. 'You're the informer?'

'I am. I want out of the cartel in exchange for my information. I told the Russian this. I no longer wish to be a bad man.'

'And what about him?' Tate gestured to Vinyl. 'Is he going to ask for the same?'

'How do I know? Ask him when he wakes up.'

'Stay here.' Tate shut the door and moved back into the central space. His day had just taken an odd turn. He put his iPhone to his ear and told Hunter to come over and leave the van outside. Then he addressed Akulov. 'Do you know who that is?'

'Bravo? He's their surveillance guy, when he's not being an enforcer.'

'He's also the Giant Bravo.'

'So?'

'As in the wrestler? He's taller than the Big Show.'

Akulov shrugged. 'I grew out of TV in 1996.'

Hunter entered the room. Tate beckoned him over, opened the door and waited for his brother's reaction. If it was at all possible, Hunter had been a bigger wrestling fan than he. Hunter froze and an odd expression flashed across his face.

'El Gigante Bravo?'

'Sí,' the Giant replied, with a wide smile. 'It appears I am famous? You two gentlemen are from British Intelligence?'

'We are,' Hunter stated.

'How do I know this?'

'Here is my official British Embassy accreditation ID.' Hunter produced a plastic ID from his wallet and held it in front of Bravo's face.

'Very well. Now, gentlemen, can you please let me sit in one of the comfortable chairs in the office? We can discuss matters there in a much easier fashion.'

Tate shrugged. 'Why not.'

'Thank you.' The Giant stepped forward and the cable ties around his ankles snapped.

Giving him space, Tate and Hunter followed. Akulov was already inside.

'So—' Hunter started to say but didn't get the chance to finish his sentence as there was a sudden electronic trilling. It was coming from the mobile phone on the conference table.

'That's Detective Vinyl's phone,' Akulov stated.

'I don't believe it,' Tate, said. He looked at the screen, the number was withheld. The *Miami Vice* theme tune. Tate let it ring out to voicemail but a moment later it bleeped with a WhatsApp message. Tate picked the handset up and read out the message, '*Where RU?*'

'Who's calling?' Hunter asked.

Tate shrugged. 'It could be his boss, or his hairdresser. There's no name on the contact.'

'What is the number?' the Giant asked.

Tate read it out.

'It's Angel Mendez.'

'Reply to him,' Hunter said. 'Say: "I'm with Bravo." See what he says.'

'OK.' Tate tapped out the reply.

Almost immediately another message appeared. '*Vetrov called. Said you didn't pick up. You hiding from me?*'

Tate replied, '*Been busy.*'

'*BUSY! YOU BEEN BUSY! I got Feds crawling all over me! They just left Del Monte!*'

207

Tate frowned but before he could think of what this meant or how to reply the phone rang again.

'Let me speak to him,' Bravo suggested. 'If I warn him you can shoot me.'

Hunter nodded.

Tate answered the call but put it on speaker.

'Don Angel,' Bravo said, 'Vinyl is here with me and all is OK. Akulov is in the cell.'

'All is OK? Really? You wanna tell me why you got Vinyl's phone?'

'He's having a shit; it's his nerves.'

There was a pause and then Angel said, 'Where is Pedro?'

Tate saw Akulov glance over to the minivan parked to one side of the warehouse.

'He went home to his woman.'

'Now you listen to me good. I'm coming over to see that Russian *puto*, you hear that?'

'*Sí.*'

'OK. We'll be seeing you in one hour.'

The line went dead.

Tate looked at his brother and nodded. 'The man from Del Monte says "yes".'

Hunter rolled his eyes.

Bravo held up his hands. 'Now perhaps, you can untie me? Have I not won that privilege?'

Tate addressed Akulov. 'Remind me why this Angel bloke is so hot on finding you?'

'I killed his twin brother.'

'And you didn't tell us this before?' Hunter was astounded.

'Was it relevant?'

'You just lose count of who you kill, is that it? Oops there goes another.'

'They were trying to abduct two women,' Akulov said.

'He was not a good person,' Bravo stated. 'I think it was a reasonable course of action.'

Hunter looked at his brother. 'So we figure out a plan, we set a trap, and we wait for them to arrive?'

'Pretty much.'

'These men are soldiers,' Akulov said. 'Vetrov has been training them and Mendez will bring him. You will meet the man who murdered your parents very soon.'

Bravo's face became quizzical. 'Vetrov killed your parents?'

'He's a terrorist,' Hunter said, checking his watch.

'Angel trusts him, so did Caesar. I do not know why.' Bravo took a large breath and his chest became even more gargantuan. 'George Eastman is the person you are looking for. Eastman is the one who helped them frame you, who created the technology. But I have no idea how.'

'Where is Eastman?'

'A safe house in Montana.'

'The Mendez Cartel has Eastman?' Hunter furrowed his brow.

'Of course not. Blackline. Eastman is guarded by more Russians.'

Tate and Akulov exchanged glances. Akulov was the first to speak. 'How many men?'

'I don't know exactly.'

Tate was curious. 'Why Montana?'

'I'm not sure. All I know is Blackline have been ingenious. How do you hide in a digital world? You go analogue, you switch from high tech to no tech – you leave no trace.' Bravo smiled. 'They have no communication with the outside world, not even a cell phone. They are in total isolation, a total blackout.'

'How does Vetrov communicate with them?'

'In person – he goes to Montana.'

'How do you know this?'

'Remember, I designed and implemented the CCTV network. I also put bugs and tracking devices in their cars. But they are so stupid they did not see them. Ever.'

'So, Blackline is still operational and has the person responsible for the faking of the Camden bombing footage?'

'Yes.'

'Blackline is being run by Kirill Vetrov?'

'No.'

Hunter looked at Tate. 'Who then?'

'Its founder.'

'Oleniuk is dead,' Tate stated.

'Of course,' Hunter said, nodding. 'Chen Yan is running Blackline and this operation, isn't she?'

'Correct.' The Giant licked his lips. 'I know where she is; I can give her to you. I have taped conversations of Vetrov talking to her and mentioning Montana. She's in Texas.'

'Where?'

The Giant tapped his nose.

'The cartel is working with Blackline?' Tate asked.

'The cartel has no idea that Blackline exists. The cartel is working with Vetrov.'

'Why?'

'Money,' Hunter answered before the Giant could. 'Blackline needs money. One of its founders is dead and the other has been cut off from her finances.'

'That is true.' The Giant rubbed his hands on his face, as though attempting to wash away his tiredness. 'Vetrov figured out how to increase the cartel's profits.'

'How?' Tate frowned.

'Backhaul.'

'Like in trucking?' Hunter said.

'Exactly.' Bravo nodded. 'We were bringing our product into the US and returning on many occasions with empty trucks. Not anymore. Vetrov changed all that.'

'What were you backhauling?'

'Weapons.' Again Hunter answered before the Giant could. 'Correct?'

'Yes.' The Giant seemed surprised.

'What type?' Tate asked.

'The type that could be used to fight against the Guardia Nacional. Their formation represents a critical threat to the cartels, in not only Mexico, but also those beyond whose products and men must pass through Mexico.'

'These weapons were not bought in the US, were they?' Hunter asked, but by the expression on his face Tate knew his brother already had the answer.

'No.' Bravo looked as though he was enjoying himself. 'That would leave a trace. These weapons were stockpiled, completely unused and untraceable.'

Tate frowned again. 'Vetrov has contacts with US military personnel who are selling off oversupply or arms destined to be destroyed?'

'No. These were not just American weapons, were they?' Hunter said, jutting his chin at Akulov. 'But of course, you would know about them.'

Tate glanced at Akulov then back at Bravo. 'I think I understand, but I want you to confirm it for me, Bravo.'

'The weapons were in caches created by the Soviets, and later checked by the Russians in order to supply and arm their Spetsnaz raiding units if war was to break out. I thought it was an urban myth, but no. There was a large one near to the airport here, in Houston. It was like a treasure trove, an Aladdin's cave of armaments. I had never seen so much, and neither had the Mendez brothers.'

'Worth a few million.' Hunter smiled. 'Millions that would help fund Blackline.'

'The cartel's first payment was over two million American dollars directly to Vetrov. Chen Yan, I understand, has taken the vast majority of this.'

'These were our caches. Their location was known to my group and our commanding officer. He died in Syria,' Akulov stated, without emotion.

'And what type of weapons did these contain?'

211

'Everything to start a small war. The GRU and then the SVR were meticulous.'

'Vetrov is in this for the money.' Tate nodded. This was enough for him to know for the moment.

'I need you to tell me where Chen is.' Hunter's tone was firm. 'I also need the location of George Eastman.'

'As for me, I need immunity from prosecution and I need myself, and my mother and sister, to be put into witness protection.'

'That's something I can't do.'

'You can. I know how these things work. You speak with your boss in London, and you have a copy of the legal paperwork sent to my lawyer.'

Tate thought back to the lengths he had gone to ensuring the safe passage of Al Nayef to Australia. This situation surely warranted equal treatment, given what was at stake. 'Simon, call Newman.'

'Jack, I don't think that is an option.'

'I'll do it then.'

Hunter gave his brother a look. 'Fine. I'll talk to London.'

'I've got a question.' Akulov folded his arms. 'Why did Vetrov set me up?'

'Because he hates you?'

'Now that I can understand,' Hunter said, as he stood and walked out of the office.

They had to prepare for their guests. Tate checked his watch; they didn't have much time. 'What are we looking at, Bravo? How many men?'

'Two SUVs, one with Angel and one backup.' He nodded at Akulov. 'You have got him worried. So that's seven or eight men.'

'OK, they are expecting you, Ruslan,' Tate said. 'They don't know who the rest of us are.' He looked at Bravo. 'Can we trust you?'

Bravo shrugged and calmly moved his wrists apart, his muscles

212

rippled and the cable ties snapped. 'Does this answer your question?'

'Thanks.' A wry smile formed on Tate's lips. 'Ruslan, you've got the Beretta. Anything else?'

'A spare magazine.'

'OK, I've got my Glock.' Tate knew it wasn't enough.

Tate looked at his brother as he re-entered the room. 'What did London say?'

'London are going to speak to Washington. Washington will definitely want Chen Yan.'

The Giant frowned. 'So that is a yes?'

'It's a probably, but these things take time.' Hunter nodded.

'I understand, time is money,' the Giant replied.

'Unless I can give them something. Something that would show that you are acting in good faith.'

The Giant's brow furrowed. 'Such as?'

'Well,' Hunter started, 'you claim to know the location of both Chen Yan and George Eastman. If you can give me the location of Chen Yan, and we can verify it with the US authorities, then Her Majesty's Government will be more likely to believe you know the location of Eastman.'

'I see. Quid pro quo?'

'Exactly.'

'She's at 507 Ogden Trail, Sugar Land. It is just outside Houston.'

'You are certain of this?'

'Sí.'

'Then I need to speak to London again.'

'Please do so.'

Tate knew it made sense for Hunter to leave and take the big man with him, but he wasn't going to leave his brother alone with Bravo. They also needed Bravo to make the trap more convincing. 'Simon, stay in our ride over in the other lot until this is over.'

'Come on, we need all the backup we can get.' Hunter didn't move.

Bravo rose to his feet and pointed. 'There is a Kalashnikov hidden behind a panel over there in the corner.'

Tate tried not to show any shock. Anytime he wanted to, the Giant could have grabbed the rifle and gunned them down.

'We will only get to surprise them once.' Akulov retrieved his Beretta and held it in his hand. 'After that it will be a firefight.'

Tate gazed at the Giant. 'These cartel men, are they any good?'

'If it is his "Presidential Guard" they are acceptable. But he is not expecting a fight; he is planning Ruslan's slow death.'

'Here's my suggestion,' Hunter said. 'We open the up-and-over doors, to make the place look inviting. We leave Vinyl where he is. Bravo, you wait for them, inside the warehouse doors but visible to them. Act like normal.'

'I can do that,' Bravo replied.

'Akulov,' Hunter continued, 'you and Jack have perhaps four targets each. We need Vetrov alive, or at least breathing, but everyone else is expendable. Position yourselves in the two corners, behind whatever cover you can find, and create a kill zone in the centre of the space. As soon as the shooting starts, Bravo, you must get out of the way – or all bets are off.'

'Simon, you go now. Move. OK?' Tate said, placing his hand on his brother's shoulder.

Hunter nodded, not happy but perhaps relieved. 'Be safe, Jack.'

'Always.'

Hunter walked away looking dejected. Tate knew his brother's talents lay in planning not guns. Akulov checked Vinyl was secure.

Bravo took the Kalashnikov from its hiding place and handed it to Tate. 'I think you better have this.'

'Thank you, but I think Ruslan is better with a Kalashnikov than I am.'

Akulov accepted the weapon. 'This means you trust me, Jack?'

'It means I don't think you'll shoot me yet.'

214

Tate took out his phone and left the office. He dialled the UK. 'Neill? It's Jack. Listen, I need you to check a name for me. Does George Eastman mean anything to you?'

Houston, Texas, USA

Vetrov sat in the back of the lead car. Angel Mendez insisted on sitting up front. One cartel soldier drove whilst another sat next to Vetrov. A further four men were in the second SUV. Vetrov knew that he was by far the best driver, having received tactical driving training, but he never felt safe sitting with two armed men behind him. Hit a bump and he risked the fools putting a round in his back.

'This Tahoe is not as good as a Cadillac, but it will do for now,' Angel said, fiddling with buttons on the unfamiliar dashboard.

Vetrov said nothing. He would have much preferred a vehicle with ballistic plating, but they were travelling in Houston not Mexico. The two SUVs were different models and colours, driving a distance apart. Vetrov had insisted upon it, because an obvious two-car convoy drew attention. His mind drifted to the man they were about to meet, the man who had once been his brother in arms and the man he had set about destroying a year before. Akulov had been the best of them, but he had not been able to accept the realities of war, and that had made him a weak link. All weak links must be replaced before they snap and endanger the rest of the chain. Humanity was not a trait that was required in the Spetsnaz, and especially not in the Werewolves.

Using Akulov as the fall guy for the London bombing had been his idea. Neither owner of Blackline had known the true hatred he felt for the former Wolf 6, but accepted that using the face of an established assassin to test the effectiveness of the deep fake was logical in addition to freeing Vetrov to continue to operate for them. Although Vetrov would rather execute the man himself, he also found it fitting that an unhinged lunatic, such as Angel, would be the man to do it. There was honour in being bested and slain by a fellow warrior, but to be done away with by a maniacal midget was a highly dishonourable insult. Vetrov considered something else that had been bugging him for a while. 'Is he injured?' he said.

'What did you say?' Angel acted as though he hadn't heard the question.

'I said, is Akulov injured?'

'If not, he soon will be!'

Vetrov became quiet again as his mind tried to warn him once more. A team of five had been sent to take him, alive or dead, and Wolf 6 had defeated four of them, in the room, only for the fifth and smallest man to stop him with the help of crocodile-shoed Vinyl and deliver him to the Giant? It was not what he would have expected to hear, yet both Vinyl and the Giant himself had said that Akulov was with them. Surely there was nothing for him to worry about? Yet Vetrov had a feeling in his stomach and he had stayed alive for so long by listening to such feelings, by not taking chances and by thinking through his actions.

'It is a trap,' he said eventually.

'You what?'

'I said, Don Angel, that I believe this is a trap.'

'Sí, I know what you said but I am just attempting to process it, and why you said it, and shit.'

'How did he get past the four men in the hotel? You heard what Vinyl said before: he was in the van with Pedro and now Pedro is missing.'

'Vinyl and the Giant have both confirmed that they have him. You think they would lie to me?'

'I think that perhaps he has them.'

'What?'

'Akulov may have them.'

'The Giant and the cop? You think he's holding them both – one hand on each?'

216

'Yes I do.'

'Relax, man. You know what you are?'

'No, you tell me.'

'You're just worried about meeting this guy again because you think he may be better than you.'

'Yes, Don Angel, you are correct.'

'Of course I am. I'm always correct and don't you forget it. Look, I'll tell you what I'll do. Before I kill him. I'll let you give him a couple of slaps for old time's sake. All right?'

'Thank you, that is very generous.' Vetrov gritted his teeth.

'That's coz I'm a nice guy, a real people person.'

'Please, Don Angel, let the other vehicle go first. They can check the warehouse.'

'That's enough. You work for me or I work for you?'

Vetrov gave no reply, but clenched his fist on his lap.

The driver slowed the Tahoe as he pulled into the parking lot.

'He has the doors open for us,' Angel remarked, 'and there is the big *cabrón* himself.'

Vetrov saw Bravo standing just inside the door. He drew his Glock, a standard G17, and waited for the SUV to pass through the doors. Almost before the tyres had stopped moving, Angel opened his door and stepped down. Vetrov followed. He wasn't a babysitter but either these people listened to him or they didn't. He was way past repeating himself and besides a couple more consignments was all that they needed before they had enough capital. Perhaps he himself should take over the cartel; indeed, as far as he was aware none in this hemisphere had ever been run with real military precision.

Vetrov looked around and assessed the space. Nothing looked unusual or struck him as odd; they had been there numerous times before over the past six months, so why was he seeing ghosts now?

As per his instructions, the second SUV stayed outside and the men got out. Vetrov had ordered them to remain vigilant, but one instantly lit a cigarette whilst another pulled out a cell phone. The remaining two had their hands on the butts of their pistols. Vetrov would discipline them later.

'Where is the Russian *puta*, Bravo?' Mendez said peering up at the Giant.

'In the cell. I had to slap him about a bit.'

'Good, just make sure there is enough for us all!'

Vetrov noticed that the Giant was standing several steps to one side. He looked around as Angel started to march towards the back of the warehouse and the cell. Vetrov felt the hairs on the back of his neck stand on end. He swung his Glock up and trained it on the opposite corner. His nose sniffed the air. There was something there. 'Angel, STOP!'

'What the—?' Angel halted in his tracks and pulled his Glock 33.

Before Vetrov could say another word, a rough mechanical bark tore past his ears. He recognised a single 7.62mm round, fired from a Kalashnikov. Its retort boomed off the concrete floor and echoed around the corrugated steel walls. It hit the Mexican directly next to Vetrov and propelled him backwards. A cloud of red mist hung in the air for milliseconds and then dispersed. The scent of gunpowder and blood filled the air.

Vetrov was already moving. He had judged the direction of the shot, dropped to one knee and fired a pair of rounds towards the minivan parked near the left interior wall. He now tried to track away, backwards to the cover of the Tahoe, as a second round pinged off the concrete by his feet.

The remaining cartel man had started to shout and was running into trouble, into the direction of the fire. The stupid idiot had forgotten all the of the hours of training and was cut down by a duo of rounds after three steps. Rounds that came from a handgun located on the other side of the room. Vetrov spun and fell.

Two shooters, two directions; a kill zone. Vetrov saw a shape, in the corner, behind one of the cars. Now gunfire came from behind as the four men from outside ran in, guns up.

'Retreat!' Vetrov yelled, to Angel if to no one else.

But Angel was standing in the open, acting like he was invincible, screaming obscenities in Spanish, sending shots alternatively in each direction, holding his Glock with one hand and rocking with the retort of each magnum round he fired.

And then the Giant appeared in Vetrov's peripheral vision, ramming him into the Tahoe. First Vetrov's shoulders and then his head made contact, denting and deforming the metal and wrenching his spine. The Glock was torn from his grip by a hand twice the size of his and then a second hand closed around his throat.

It felt like the firefight has lasted minutes but in fact from the time the first round was fired to the time Vetrov felt his vision dim, had been forty seconds. And then the Giant jerked and his grip lessened. Vetrov brought both his hands up and attempted a bat strike to the Giant's ears but his arms would not reach. Instead he thrust them up at the man's exposed throat. The Giant coughed, stumbled away, letting go of him to grab his own neck. He coughed again and dropped to one knee.

Vetrov crouched against the vehicle as rounds zipped past him and he began to realise that neither he nor Angel were being targeted. And then the gunfire stopped and was replaced by a ringing in his ears and the wafting stench of gunpowder.

He saw Angel rush towards the open door of the Tahoe. A single shot rang out and Angel's legs were tugged from under him as though he'd slipped on a rug. He landed flat on his face. A figure advanced from out of the shadows, holding a handgun in a two-handed grip.

Vetrov saw his own Glock lying on the concrete, grabbed it and threw himself into the Tahoe. As he moved the Kalashnikov barked and a line of rounds whacked against the door, ripping through the thin metal and smashing the window. Vetrov put the heavy SUV into reverse and floored the gas. The SUV's V8 growled, and its tyres howled as it shot backwards out through the open doors, bumping over what could only have been dead bodies belonging to the men he had trained. His last view of the interior of the warehouse was two figures, one he recognised and one he did not firing rounds at the hood of the Tahoe.

His windshield crazed as he tugged at the wheel to bring the front of the Tahoe away from the threat. He floored the gas again and reversed into a sharp turn. His headrest exploded and the rear window blew out. Involuntarily ducking he turned to see another man aiming a pistol at him, but this one was silenced. A bullet grazed his left shoulder. As the Tahoe continued to move, Vetrov raised his Glock and snapped a quick-aim round at the gunman. The man collapsed from the headshot and Vetrov stamped on the gas pedal.

Next to Tate, Akulov let go of the Kalashnikov. It swung on its shoulder strap as he switched to the Beretta. The pair continued to aim rounds at the rear of the bulky Tahoe as it moved further out of range. The best they could do now was take out a tyre, but Tate doubted that would stop Vetrov from driving away. He cursed. He'd find Vetrov again.

Tate turned and advanced upon the prone figure of Angel Mendez. Blood was pouring from a hole in his left thigh. Tate hoped he hadn't nicked or severed the artery. Mendez had managed to roll onto his back and was now moving his arms. Bravo was back on his feet, blinking and rubbing his throat. He too had been shot, but unlike his former patron, the 9mm round had seemed to do nothing more than get lodged in his thick deltoid muscle. He walked towards Tate, blood streaming down his arm, then booted Angel Mendez in the side.

Tate glanced at Akulov, who stood next to him, the AK still slung by its carry strap across his chest.

Tate's iPhone rang. He pulled it out of his pocket and pressed it to his ear. A voice he didn't recognise with a Welsh accent said, 'Simon's been shot!'

Everything stopped, including all sound ... Tate started to walk out of the warehouse and then he ran across the parking lot, vaulted over low bushes and came to a stop. One figure crouched over another.

Their driver cradled Simon, his head resting against the man's white shirt, turning it crimson. 'Stay with me, boy!'

Tate fell to his knees. 'Simon! Si!'

Hunter's eyes were closed, his face was ashen, and the side of his head was slick with blood.

Chapter 16

Houston, Texas, USA

Vetrov was livid with anger, but he managed to control his actions and slowed the SUV down, cruising just below the speed limit. He took deep breaths. It had been an ambush but they had wanted both he and Angel Mendez alive. Even if he hadn't seen Akulov he would have known that no one else could be that precise with a Kalashnikov. How had the man managed to get Bravo to switch sides? It had been Akulov who had almost broken the man's skull and murdered his boss in front of him, a matter of days ago, and now the Giant was covering for him?

As far as he was concerned, his relationship with the Mendez Cartel was now over. Vetrov accepted that any thought he had of leading the cartel was pure fantasy. The Mexicans would never accept someone who was not of their blood as their leader. He now thought about the men he had way up north: his men. They were not Werewolves but they had once been Spetsnaz. He took a left and headed out to Sugar Land. Checking his mirrors to make sure that he didn't have a tail, he pulled his burner phone out of a zipped pocket in his jacket and typed in a number. It rang out to voicemail. He tried again and this time it would not connect – checking the screen he realised that he now had no signal. The Americans could put a man on the moon, but they couldn't ensure reliable cell coverage? He tapped out a single-word text message then popped the phone in his shirt pocket.

He concentrated on the road. His SUV was riddled with bullet holes and the last thing he needed was to get pulled over. He stopped at a set of lights and a long sedan, probably a Ford, pulled up behind him and then its lights and siren sounded. He waited for the lights to change, carried on up the road and then pulled over. He pushed his pistol under his thigh and realised that he had neither his licence nor registration documents for the Tahoe. One officer clambered out of the cruiser from the driver's side whilst the other got out of the passenger side. And then the one on the passenger's side started to move his hand towards his holster. It may have been a precautionary measure and strictly procedure – by the book – but Vetrov did not want to take any chances. Run or fight were his only two options, but if he fought these two there would be more and more. His cartel "get-out-of-jail-free card" was Vinyl, and where the hell had he been? Was he back at the warehouse with Akulov?

The two officers drew nearer and nearer and now he saw that the driver had noticed the dents and the bullet holes. Vetrov's left hand lowered the seat-back, and his right lowered the windows, unlatched his seatbelt then dropped to his leg and securely grasped the Glock. One officer was now level with his side window, whilst the other officer had reached the rear passenger's window on the opposite side.

Vetrov jerked back against the seat and twisted to his left. He brought the Glock up and fired a double tap directly into the chest of the driver, then he moved right and put two more rounds into the second officer. Both officers were down. Pulling himself upright, he floored the gas pedal, swung the steering right and bounced off the road and onto the sidewalk. He raised his seat as he nudged the Tahoe back onto the traffic lane. He needed to get away from the two cops he'd just shot, get out of the city, but most of all get in contact with Chen Yan. But first he had to ditch the Tahoe and find another set of wheels.

Vauxhall Cross, London, UK

Pamela Newman dropped the report onto her desk and shut her eyes. Although she lived for her job it generated so much damn paperwork, and paperwork was dull. She remembered way back when, as a more junior officer, she used to be out of the office running surveillance and counter-surveillance operations. She missed those days and she missed the thrill of sitting in a cold café in Berlin. What she didn't miss, however, was the cold itself. Berlin had been cold, Warsaw had been cold and Moscow had been even colder. It had been the cold war. She sipped her tea ruefully, to ward off a shiver. Her desk phone rang. 'Newman?'

'Pamela, it's Paul Page,' an excited voice said down the encrypted line. Page was the SIS Head of Station in Canberra and had been responsible for leading the debriefing of their latest asset – His Royal Highness Salman bin Mohammad Al Nayef.

'Paul, if you are personally calling me this must be important?'

'It is. It seems that Al Nayef may have been saving the best till last.'

'Go on.' Newman sat forward in her chair. 'What has he been holding back on exactly?'

'As well as validating the intelligence we had regarding his uncle, Faisal Al Nayef's support and links to certain extremist organisations, he has now given me detailed information on something we knew absolutely nothing about.'

'That's great progress.' Newman wished he'd cut to the chase. 'What's the issue?'

'The issue is according to Al Nayef his uncle has sanctioned a cyberattack on Qatar.'

'That's happened before; it's what allegedly started the last blockade.'

'This time, however, Al Nayef insists his uncle has contracted Blackline to carry out an attack using new deep fake technology.'

Newman tried to remain calm. 'But Blackline no longer exists.'

'Al Nayef says he was in a meeting with both Kirill Vetrov and Chen Yan where their cooperation was discussed and confirmed.'

Newman remained silent as she tried to understand the situation; meanwhile, the encrypted line whined and boomed.

'Pamela, are you still there?'

'Yes. I'm just thinking. When is the attack planned?'

'This Friday.'

'The holy day,' Newman said.

'Exactly.'

'How is this attack to take place?'

'Blackline will publish their deep fake footage. According to Al Nayef it will be flawless and the leaders of Qatar will be unable to prove it is not genuine.'

'What is on the footage?'

Page explained. Pamela closed her eyes, imagining both the footage and the uproar it would cause. 'One moment, Paul. How is Al Nayef sure that Blackline can deliver this footage?'

'Ah. He's seen another piece of footage they have produced.'

'What footage?' Pamela asked, but she already knew the answer.

'It's the found footage of the Camden bombing,' Page stated. 'Al Nayef says it's a deep fake and he knows this because he has seen both the real and doctored versions.'

'Where is Al Nayef now?'

'At a secure ASIS facility in Canberra.'

'Listen, Paul, you must ensure that he speaks to no one else. Sit outside his room yourself. Make sure that he does not share a syllable of this with ASIS until I say he can. And give me a full written report on what he has told you.'

'Will do.'

'Thank you, Paul.' Newman ended the call realising that she had little time to prevent what could be a new war from starting in the Middle East. She glanced up at her wall clock; it suddenly seemed to be ticking louder than before. And then her phone rang for the second time in ten minutes.

'Newman?'

'It's Jack.' Tate's voice sounded raspy. 'Simon's been shot …'

Sugar Land, Texas

Not since she was a child had Chen Yan felt so helpless. The attack she'd masterminded on the US a year before had failed and the details of her involvement had been swiftly shared, discussed and acted upon. Chen's entire fortune was now frozen, even her secret offshore accounts. She was now on a "most wanted list" among the likes of those accused of genocide.

Kirill Vetrov and the tiny team in Montana were all that remained of Blackline as facilities in Russia and China were seized and staff taken away. Chen now had just three million American dollars in cash to her name and was stuck in the United States. She had to recover what had been stolen from her and then continue to develop the deep fake program.

Her hair was a mess, and sweat dripped down her face onto the crude, concrete tiles. She moved faster and faster, practising her form, and her shape, as her butterfly knives sliced through the hot, Texan air, creating the quietest of hums as they did so. Like giant metallic wasps with deadly stings. As the child of a high-profile businessman, she had grown up being told she was a potential kidnap target. Her father had forced her to train in traditional Wing Chun Kuen, a form of self-defence requiring rapid arm movements and strong legs. As Chen had got older, she had augmented her moves with weapons, especially butterfly knives. In her mind it remained a graceful, flowing art form, until either of her knives found an attacker's flesh. She pushed herself harder, faster, attempting to seek the peace and balance her art had always given her.

Panting, she placed her knives on her patio table and grabbed her towel. She was wet with sweat but her knives were dry, and that would not do. They should be wet with the blood of those who had gone against her, those who had betrayed her!

The Saudis, who immediately after the failure of the last mission, had attempted to walk away from the deal. She started to shake; her wrath was all consuming. She had salvaged the contract or so she had thought but then the old man had refused to take her calls. Eventually he had reneged on the agreed one-hundred-million-dollar payment and made her agree to a much-reduced fee of thirty. Chen stared at her blades and imagined them slicing through the elderly man's scrawny neck, severing sinew and bone. She had been reduced to scrabbling for change in the dirt, and even this she would not receive until she delivered her final, completed digital package to the old prince.

Chen hated being beholden to anyone; however, receiving funds from Vetrov's arms sales to the Mendez Cartel was preferable to being enslaved to the Saudis. She would have her revenge when this was over. Chen noticed now her reflection in the blades. Her face was a mask of calm, and that was something she had not expected to see.

What Chen had also not expected to see was her cell phone lying, screen down in the grass next to the patio. She must have unknowingly knocked it from the table when she had grabbed her towel, or perhaps earlier still? She finished mopping her torso then reached down to pick it up. The cell phone was always on silent when she trained or meditated. Her brow furrowed.

There were three missed calls from Vetrov and a text message: 'RUN.'

She sensed something. Her breathing slowed and she listened intently. There was someone in her house; she was sure of it. She sprang away from the table, grabbed her knives and moved to the gazebo, crouching down but keeping her eyes on the house. She could see shadows inside, perhaps two men. She advanced towards the back door, twin knives longer than her forearms at the ready, prepared to defend herself to the death. She reached the top step. The door opened and a large, white man in a police officer's uniform came out.

She froze, knives poised to strike, and assessed his stance. His police-issue Glock was not drawn but his hand was over the top of the holster. His eyebrows rose and, as his right hand inched towards his firearm, his left hand came up in a placatory manner.

'Ma'am, please put down the knives! We mean you no harm; we just need you to answer a couple of questions.'

Yan didn't move, and didn't respond. Why hadn't he rung her bell, or knocked on her door? Why was he in her house? Weren't police officers supposed to knock and wait to be admitted? The man looked like a beat cop, the kind she had seen on the street, yet here he was on her property …

'Ma'am, I'm going to need you to drop the knives!'

Movement to her side now, in the garden. She readjusted her stance. A second policeman had flanked her and, pistol in hand, was advancing. He was louder and less polite than his partner. 'Houston PD! Drop your weapons now! Drop your weapons now and lie on the ground with your hands on your head!'

So, they had found her.

This was the end.

Surrender was not an option.

She nodded, let a smile form on her face, and then she moved, speedily, gracefully, ducking and turning, spinning and weaving until she found herself behind the first policeman, one blade at his neck and the other touching his protruding belly. 'Drop your weapon, or he dies.'

The second officer's voice became louder, more assertive. 'Drop it! Now!'

Yan heard a new noise. The front door. Heavy footsteps. Moving both arms, simultaneously, with grace and power, the right blade cut through the officer's throat and the left sliced through his stomach, and then she was turning and sprinting into the house, seeing two large, fit-looking men in suits moving hastily towards her along her wood-panelled hallway. These weren't policemen. Their weapons came up, she ducked, and wheeled and let fly with both her blades, turning them into heavy throwing knives.

The first man was hit in the chest and shoulder. He stumbled backwards, arms flailing, smacking the walls, but the second man was quicker, or better trained. He fired as Yan sprang into the air. She felt the heat of the round as it tugged at her blouse and then a white dagger of pain in her side, but she continued on and landed ready to deliver a combination of strikes. But then a heavy fist struck her squarely in the face. Small but sinewy, her head snapped backwards and she fell. Her back slammed into the wooden floor. Her vision started to lose colour and she found herself unable to keep her eyes open.

Undisclosed medical facility

The coffee was bitter, which matched Tate's mood, but drinking it gave him something to do. He sat in the hospital, dejected and broken, whilst his brother received emergency surgery for a gunshot wound to the head. Kirill Vetrov had killed his parents and may yet have murdered his brother too. Tate felt helpless; he was a fighter but there was no enemy he could attack to save his brother. Tate had never felt so scared, even when facing down the barrel of a loaded gun.

A door opened further along the corridor and a woman in a white doctor's coat headed in his direction. She had a serious expression on her face, which made Tate's insides twist and turn more than any physical trauma he had experienced. He stood when she was four paces away and prepared himself for the news.

'Mr Tate, your brother's surgery was successful. He is in a serious yet stable condition.' Her accent was precise, Washington perhaps, maybe brought to Texas as a specialist for her expertise. 'However, I have made the decision to put him in a medically induced coma.'

229

Tate felt two powerful, invisible hands tighten around his throat, whilst another pair pummelled and squeezed his chest. It took a quick mouthful of coffee to make his voice cooperate. 'What does that mean? Are you saying he's brain-damaged?'

The doctor wet her lips, before she spoke, as though she had expected to answer this exact question. 'The good news is that the bullet did not enter Simon's brain, rather it bounced along the side of it, like a stone skimming over waves, before it exited. Your brother has, however, suffered trauma to the right temporal lobe, which we operated on to remove any bone and bullet fragments and to ease the swelling.'

'That doesn't answer my question, doctor.' Tate tried to control his anger and remember the doctor was not responsible for his brother's injury.

'At this stage I cannot rule out that there may be temporary, perhaps even some permanent impairment; however, the majority of patients who suffer trauma to the brain make a full recovery.'

Tate's battlefield medical training didn't extend to brain surgery so he asked, 'What's the right temporal lobe do?'

The doctor smiled, now that she was on safer ground. 'It manages visual memory, including facial recognition, verbal memory – understanding language, and reading the reactions and emotions of others.'

Tate felt sick and was sure he was going to pass out. He thrust out his left hand against the wall to steady himself.

'Mr Tate, I think you should sit down. You may be in shock.'

Tate dropped to his seat.

'I understand this must be difficult. Would you like me to explain to you why I've put him into a medically induced coma?'

'Please.'

Tate nodded along, as she talked him through her reasons, but he couldn't take it in, and they both knew it. 'How long will you keep him under for?'

'I think a safe estimate would be one to two weeks. He's young, fit, and that helps.'

She stood. 'He's in a private room now. I'm sorry I can't let anyone, even his next of kin, see him at the moment. I suggest you get some rest yourself and come back tomorrow afternoon. You should be able to see him then.'

Tate managed to thank her, his voice low and hoarse. The success of his career had rested upon him taking lives in order to save others. Faced with a woman whose sole aim was to save life he felt insignificant, like a Neanderthal stabbing his fat fingers into the dirt to make cave paintings whilst she used the finest brushes, and pigments to create internationally acclaimed works of art.

'You really look like you need to rest, Mr Tate.'

'No rest for the wicked.'

She smiled curtly, turned back the way she had come and left. Tate waited a beat, finished his coffee, and threw the cup in the bin. As he walked towards the double doors they were opened and two men in dark suits nodded at him, fell in step – one in front and one behind him – and escorted him to an underground car park. A solitary dark Cadillac SUV was waiting for him. They climbed in and the SUV started to move.

The last few hours had been a blur and Tate could barely remember the details. Panicked calls to the British Embassy and Pamela Newman back at Vauxhall Cross had resulted in Simon being admitted to a specialist facility, with no questions asked. Whilst Tate had sat and waited for news of his brother's condition, Newman had attempted to sort out the fallout. She had instructed Tate the US authorities were not to be informed of the existence of the deep fake weapon, at least not until Neill Plato had got his hands on it. She had given them Chen Yan, traded her in fact on the condition that no questions were to be asked about what Tate was doing in the US.

This, however, left a large logistical problem. The team needed on-the-ground backup to help with the Giant and with tracking Vetrov. In the end it had been Akulov who had suggested a feasible option, although one that Newman had been against. Tate had argued that there was no other solution, so she had to agree and Akulov called in a favour.

Tate nodded in thanks to the two passengers already seated with him. Akulov was one and the other was heavy-set and sported a huge horseshoe moustache.

'I hear it is good news?' Miguel Becerra said, his moustache quivering.

Tate used the doctor's exact words: 'He's is in a serious yet stable condition.'

'That is … encouraging.'

'Update?' Tate said, changing the subject.

'We have not been tardy whilst you have been with your brother,' Miguel said. 'The Giant Bravo is in one of my organisation's safe houses. He is understandably not entirely happy; however, that is nothing compared to the mood of Angel Mendez who has a "room" along the hall. I am impressed by your boss, Jack. She has some serious "connections" in order to make the Americans look the other way regarding your activities. Oh and as for Detective Vinyl? Well, he works for me as well as the Mendez Cartel and has been compensated.'

Tate noticed there was now a smile behind the moustache. Tate didn't care if Vinyl also worked for Burger King. 'What about Vetrov? He's the only one who matters to me.'

Miguel nodded. 'You want him because he killed members of your family; this I understand. I want him because he killed my patron, my friend – Francisco Arellano.'

'Vetrov. He is in the wind,' Akulov said.

'Explain?'

It was Miguel who did so. 'From my contacts in local law enforcement I have learnt that a black Chevy Tahoe was stopped at a set of lights because the officers were suspicious of damage to its bodywork – bullet holes. The driver shot those two police officers dead. I have not seen the dashcam or bodycam footage, as I cannot be perceived to be getting that involved; however, from the description given to me it was him – Vetrov. He is now the subject of a state-wide manhunt for a straight-up double-cop killing. You know when you kill a cop, the gloves come off.'

'He's heading for Montana,' Akulov said.

'Obviously,' Tate replied, rubbing his face with his hands.

'I may know where.'

Tate looked up at the Russian. 'How?'

'There is another weapons cache in Montana. He could be going there.'

'You're just telling me this now?'

'I am. I am trying to help.'

Tate didn't have enough energy left to get angry. 'You think the team is hiding with a stockpile of weapons?'

'I do not know unless we go there. Montana is a huge territory.'

'If we go there and Vetrov is not there, we've lost too much time.'

'Jack, give me your phone. I'll type in the address.'

'Here.' He handed Akulov the handset and watched as he tapped on the screen. Once the Russian had returned it Tate sent the address over to Newman with a quick note of explanation. Tate closed his eyes.

The interior of the Cadillac became silent as Tate tried to think what to do. He had to get the address of the Montana team from the Giant. In any other situation an interagency effort would be made to locate Kirill Vetrov, which would include his name and face being added to the no-fly list; in this situation all Tate had to rely on was Plato and his access to the USA's vast network of surveillance cameras.

'The Giant was asking for you,' Miguel said, breaking the silence.

Tate nodded.

'He keeps insisting that he has a deal with you?'

'He has.'

'So, I shall hand over the Mendez brothers' lieutenant to you. As a man of my word, it is part of the debt of honour I owe to this man next to me.'

'Thank you,' Tate said.

'However, if it is information only you need from the Giant, then I have men who can extract it from him. I am sure even a giant would pose no problems for them.'

Tate didn't know what to say. Bravo and he had an agreement, but he needed the location. If Bravo did not give this to him, the mission was over, yet letting Miguel deal with Bravo was to sanction torture. It was crossing a line, but Tate saw no other choice. 'That is acceptable.'

Undisclosed location, Texas, USA

Tate didn't know where they were, only that the ranch house was large and empty. The stars shone above, uninhibited by any light pollution, providing the only light. He took in the panorama, the land flat in all directions and dark. The US was vast and in the past he had taken pleasure in being lost in it, but tonight its size was only a hindrance.

He wandered away from the still-ticking Suburban to make a phone call, while Miguel and his two men went inside with Akulov. He climbed over a low picket fence and walked into the scrub, all the while watching his feet for any of the local killer wildlife. It wasn't Camden; they had snakes, spiders and scorpions here. And armadillos; in fact, if his memory served him right nine-banded armadillos and a fifth of those, according to Simon, carried leprosy. In the dark he smiled and instantly felt a twinge of sadness. His brother needed to recover, and fully; otherwise what was the point?

He pulled out his secure iPhone, checked that he was out of

earshot and called his controller. Even though the line was encrypted they needed to be circumspect. 'Pamela, I'm about to see Luis Bravo.'

The voice at the other end sounded alert, even though it was either very late or very early in London depending on your persuasion. 'It's vital that you get the location. We need to prevent Blackline from launching its attack. Assure Bravo that the deal will be honoured.'

'And will it be?'

There was a pause, Tate didn't know if it was intentional or the line, before she replied. 'Yes. The Americans are very happy that they have Chen Yan. They know nothing about Bravo or what he had agreed to tell us. And this has given us leeway to get him out of the country.'

'The Arellano Cartel also want him.'

'It's your decision, Jack. We must get the location, and that is all.'

'What about the address Akulov gave us?'

'It looks like a deserted group of cabins. With the satellite resources available we couldn't see much of any use.'

Tate sighed, and watched a shooting star, or was it a comet or a meteor? He could never remember the difference. 'Has Neill found anything else out about Eastman?'

'No, apart from one thing. That's not his real name.'

'So what is?'

'Neill doesn't know, and if he doesn't, no one does.'

'Well that's great.'

'Jack, I have some new intel for you courtesy of Al Nayef.'

In the twilight Tate frowned. 'Go ahead.'

'Al Nayef has told us his uncle paid Blackline to carry out a cyberattack on Qatar. It's going to happen this Friday and it will use the deep fake weapon in an attempt to overthrow the emir.'

Had the found Camden footage been just a test for this much bigger, much more political attack? Tate was momentarily lost for words as he thought about the geopolitical consequences. 'Pamela, we can't let Vetrov get to Eastman otherwise they'll launch the attack and then vanish.'

'Jack, I agree but does Vetrov even know we're aware of Eastman's existence?'

'How would I know?' Tate snapped and instantly regretted it.

If Newman had noticed his short temper, she had chosen to ignore it. 'Either way, your mission now is to locate George Eastman, secure his technology and prevent the attack.'

'I know.' Tate was under no illusion which was more important not just to the SIS, but to the world as a whole. 'And I will.'

'Keep me updated.'

Call concluded, Tate vaulted back over the fence and raised his hand to knock on the front door of the house when it was opened by one of Miguel's men.

Tate said nothing and stepped across the threshold. Inside the house was illuminated like any other. It was the extra thick blackout blinds at each and every window that had prevented the light from spilling out.

'Don Miguel is this way, with your wrestler friend,' said the Mexican, dryly.

'Where is Angel Mendez?'

The cartel man's face contorted, as though he had a bad taste in his mouth. 'Do not worry about that *pinche estúpido*; he is being looked after in a special room for special guests.'

Tate followed the cartel soldier down a hallway, through a large living room and down some steps at the back. The man went first and knocked on a door at the bottom. 'It's me.'

It was opened by another cartel man and Tate entered. Tate was in a corridor that seemed to run the full length of the house. He noticed that, like the cell in the Mendez warehouse, the floor was poured concrete and pitched to the left. A drainage channel was cut, which led to a hole at the end. There was a smell of bleach. On the right, an equal distance apart, were four metal doors, again like those at the warehouse. Tate felt a cold hand along his spine. This was the cartel's private prison, or at least one of them. There was a low murmuring and mumbling from the far end, and the floor shone wet in the overpowering, overhead lights.

'Mr Jack!' a jovial voice called.

The man who had opened the door now moved in front of him and unlocked the second door along. Tate made a conscious effort to relax as he realised that about now everything could go wrong. He was in a cartel house with two cartel dons, an unknown number of armed men, a giant and a highly trained assassin, whose allegiance he couldn't one hundred per cent verify. If they made a move against him, he was either a prisoner or a dead prisoner.

'Come inside, please!' the voice of Miguel called again.

Tate entered the cell. The room was bare except for a metal table and a pair of chairs. Bravo sat on the chair facing the door. His size shrank the furniture to look like a child's tea-party set. Chains affixed to links on his wrists secured his arms, but he had enough space to make small movements. He nodded at Tate.

Miguel was standing by the door. He tapped Tate on the shoulder and left the room. 'He's all yours, for now.' The door closed behind him.

'How is your brother?' Bravo asked, concern etched on his face.

'Serious but stable. Thanks.' Tate jutted his chin at Bravo. 'How's your shoulder?'

Bravo self-consciously touched the dressing. 'A bit of damage but nothing that will not heal. It is good. Don Miguel has so far been honourable towards me, but I cannot trust the Arellano Cartel. They have been my sworn enemies for a decade. At any moment they may cut my throat, which is why you must get me out of here. What is happening with my deal? I have already given you Chen Yan's location.'

'Have you spoken to your lawyer?'

'*Sí*, I have. They gave me a phone and monitored me in case I tried to give him my location, but how can I? I have no idea of where I am! I told my lawyer I was at a place, not too far from the city and being taken care of. He has read the letter your embassy has sent and is happy with the deal, and informs me matters are progressing. But you know, I am worried for my mother and sister. Have they been collected?'

'Look, Luis, I've spoken to my boss again in London and to Don Miguel. You know things are in motion. Your deal is being honoured and your family will be collected and taken somewhere safe. It's time for you to honour your deal with me and give me the address. That's all I need.'

'Jack, I like you, but I like my mother and sister more. They are in Mexico; I am doing this for them.'

'Family is important. If I don't get there first, the man who shot my brother and murdered my parents will.'

'But your brother is safe. My family are not. No, I am sorry. I cannot give you what you are asking for until I have evidence that my family are safe. This is nothing personal. I believe that if it were up to you, you would honour any agreement, but I know this is the word of your boss, and your boss's boss and the American justice system.'

Tate battled against the guilt he felt inside, but he didn't know the Giant or what he had done for the cartel. Tate needed the location of the team in Montana; he had asked for it and Bravo had refused. He had one more trick to try. 'Lundeen Road, Eureka.'

The Giant seemed confused. 'What is that?'

'It's a place in Montana.'

'It is not somewhere I have heard of.'

Tate stared at the Giant's features and attempted to read them. Either he had the world's best poker face or the address really meant nothing to him. Tate stood. He was frustrated yet he couldn't blame the Giant for holding out. Tate was about to knock on the door when it opened. He tried not to let his relief show as he stepped back through and into the corridor.

Bravo called after him. 'Believe me, Jack, I'm sorry for this delay but I need to know my family are safe. How am I expected to sleep knowing that the cartel may still snatch them?'

Tate followed the man back up the steps and found Miguel and Akulov sitting in deep leather armchairs arranged in front of a stone fireplace. There was an empty third chair, a small table between them, and a bottle and glasses on that.

'Ah, Jack!'

Miguel had removed his dark jacket and Tate's eyes were drawn to a large flowering bloodstain on Miguel's shirt.

'Do not worry, it is the blood of Angel Mendez and not my own. Have a seat, Jack.' Miguel pointed at the bottle. 'Have some tequila too.'

'Sod it.' Tate bent down, poured himself a glass and took the empty chair.

Miguel raised his glass. 'To Simon!'

Akulov followed suit.

Tate nodded and emptied his glass. The liquor burned his throat. 'Thanks.'

'So let me guess, the Giant Bravo will not tell you what you want to know? Until his family are signed, sealed and delivered?' Miguel smiled at his own joke.

'Can you blame him?' Tate said, flatly.

'As a slightly older gentleman, let me tell you this, Jack. It is late and from the look of you, it has been one hell of a day. You are both my guests here. Mr Ruslan, or should I say Mr Russel' – Miguel paused and smiled at Akulov – 'is a man of his word and has honoured his contract to us, and as a friend of his you are of course a friend of mine. There are rooms for you both here. Take them and go to sleep. Tomorrow you'll wake up, and we'll all be done. You'll have your secret intel from Bravo, then

239

you can go wherever you need to. Ask me nicely and I'll lend you my Gulfstream.'

Tate wondered what business Akulov had with Miguel, but was too tired to think. 'OK.' Tate held up the bottle, Miguel held out his glass and Tate refilled it.

Texas, USA

Vetrov had lost Chen. He'd arrived at the end of her street to see a collection of official vehicles haphazardly parked on her drive and spilling out onto the road – two police cruisers, an ambulance, a dark panel transporter and, most tellingly of all, a coroner's van. An icy fist had clenched Vetrov's heart as he'd realised it was time to cut his losses. Chen, his lover and his employer, was either dead, or injured and in custody. Neither was any use to him. She knew the address of the team in Montana but Vetrov was confident she would not give it up. Did the authorities even know the team or he existed? Vetrov had no reason to believe they did. Nothing Chen said or did would help her; she was among the US's most wanted but he knew she would say nothing.

He'd gazed at the house for a moment longer, remembering her naked form beneath him. He bitterly remembered the several million dollars in cash hidden in the house, which would now be confiscated by the authorities, before turning back the way he had come in search of another taxi. He found one minutes later and ordered the driver to take him to an address on the eastern edge of the city.

Vetrov was on the move again. He didn't have a place he called his own, at least not in the US. He had a carry-on bag at Angel Mendez's and a few things left in the Mendez club in Matamoros but nothing that gave away his identity or that he couldn't buy again. His money was in several far-flung banks and he owned a flat in Moscow, another in Sochi and several dachas. If he could get out of the US he could disappear. And if he was frugal, he wouldn't need to work for a long time. Weeks before, he'd asked Detective Vinyl if the Houston police had anything on him and the detective had told him that, as far as the police were concerned, he was a no one. Just a face who had been seen with the Mendez brothers. Being in "vice", Vinyl said he'd know. Yet Vinyl had vanished and he'd thrown away his anonymity when he'd shot the pair of cops – if they'd managed to get decent enough footage of his face.

It wasn't just the cops he had to worry about, it was the cartel too. If they thought for one minute he'd given up Angel or been part of some sort of hostile takeover, they'd be out for his blood. The consequences of being a snitch and talking out against the cartel was death, in an appropriately agonising manner. Which was why he found it all the more difficult to believe that Bravo had done just that. A normal-sized human could change their appearance, name and location, but a mountain like Bravo? Now that was a tall order. Vetrov sneered; Bravo couldn't hide unless he went to a zoo. What was it that had made him turn on the cartel?

He had of course recognised Akulov, but not the other two – the one who had shot at him in the warehouse and the one he had shot as he'd made his escape. It had been the first time Vetrov had come face to face with Wolf 6 since the traitor had left the Russian Army. Blackline had employed them both for a failed mission the year before, but they had not met as Vetrov had been assigned to protect Chen whilst Akulov had been contracted to do what he was the best in the world at – hunting and killing his targets.

Vetrov shivered. He feared no man but Akulov. He had hoped that the doctored footage would be enough to get him locked up for life, or worse, but it had turned out very differently. However far or fast Vetrov ran, Wolf 6 would eventually find him. Their eventual meeting was a destiny he could not outrun. All he could do was control where and when it happened. His mind switched back to the warehouse. Who were the two men who had been with Akulov? One could handle a firearm and one could not, so one a field officer and the other, a desk officer? *Da*, that had to be it. They had to be DEA. Who else could or would make Bravo turn on the cartel, and who else could offer full-time witness protection – because that's what it would take – to keep the Giant and his family safe?

But his involvement with the Mexicans was over. Their little wars and squabbles meant nothing. They were debased criminals whose thiefdom would eventually implode, and once out of the US the Mendez name and money meant nothing. The issue was that he couldn't risk flying from any airport in Texas, but could he get on a flight in a different state? There was one place he could try, and he would, but even that was a day's driving away. He was under no illusions how far away Eureka was, and he knew he had to get there by air; the alternative was losing three days on surface routes.

There was of course nothing, except him, linking the cartel to Eureka. Akulov knew about Eureka, but not the other place. And he would be coming after him, of that there was no doubt. This gave Vetrov an opportunity to intercept him, but only if he got to Montana first. Akulov had not been acting alone in Houston, but who was helping him, and why were they? His mind went back to the DEA again. Did the DEA, or whoever they were who had been with Bravo, know who Akulov really was? Vetrov neither cared nor worried. Akulov would want to face him one on one, and no matter who he may or may not be working with, or what he had agreed to, nothing would save him.

So bypassing the airports of Houston and the surrounding area, Vetrov had taken a taxi to a hospital on the eastern outskirts of Houston. In the CCTV-neglected staff car park he'd then broken in to a beat-up Honda and continued his journey east away from Houston and towards the border with Louisiana. He knew that he had to get out of state fast before his description

242

was circulated and roadblocks were put in place. He had his training and he still had a handgun; if need be, he'd shoot his way through, but he hoped it wouldn't come to that.

And it didn't. As the needle hit red on the gas tank, Vetrov crossed into Louisiana and then carried on to the "Smokers Paradise Border Town Casino complex", which he found to be an overly fancy name for a gas station, strip mall, hotel and casino. In the fading light he parked the stolen Honda in the darkest place he could find, nose in, and then went in search of his next ride. He walked along the road, just outside the pool of vivid light thrown by the gas station and headed towards the building housing a 7 Eleven and a Subway restaurant.

The parking space nearest the road was taken by a silver Dodge Durango. Vetrov kept his head down and walked past the empty SUV. He casually checked for CCTV cameras, and saw one trained on the storefront but not the two individual parking slots at the side of the structure. All he now needed to do was to wait for the driver and anyone else who was riding in the SUV to return; if it was just the driver or the driver and a single passenger then he'd found his next ride. Taking on any larger number would be problematic.

Night was fast approaching and the shadows lengthening. Vetrov leant against the wall and pretended to be examining something in his hand. Headlights washed over him and he battled the urge to look up, some primeval instinct telling him it was a predator hunting him. The lights carried on and away. There was noise, a male voice talking animatedly, and it was getting louder. Vetrov looked sideways and saw an extremely thin man, dressed in dirty-looking ill-fitting shorts and a garish T-shirt, chatting on his cell phone. The phone was in his right hand and a paper takeout bag was in his left. He walked around the car, then used his scrawny cheek to clamp his phone to his shoulder as he reached into his pocket for the Dodge's key fob. He pulled it out but before he could press the "unlock" button, Vetrov was behind him – right hand twisting his head one way and left hand tugging his chin the other.

The bag of food dropped as did his large cell phone and his hands flailed, and then before he could cry for help, the thin man's neck snapped. It was a quick, clinical, tactical kill, as he had been trained to carry out. Vetrov looked around: no traffic and no eyewitnesses. No comeback for a few hours at least. He blipped the car unlocked, opened the rear passenger door and manhandled the dead driver inside. He followed him in and pushed him over the back seats and into the trunk. Lying flat in the darkness the body would be invisible. Vetrov then retrieved the cell phone and the food from the ground, shut the door and took the access road to rejoin the highway.

Five minutes later, after throwing the cell phone out of the window, he was munching on his free dinner. Driving into Louisiana took him away from the commercial airports that could get him to Montana. The nearest now was a three-hour drive to the east or a four-hour drive north, and something was telling him that if Akulov was working with the DEA he'd be on a "no-fly" list. Vetrov knew the safest course of action was to not even attempt to board a plane, but then the safest course of action was not always the best. So using the SUV's GPS, he plotted his course north. Fort Smith, Arkansas, was still an almost nine-hour drive away.

As the miles slipped by, Vetrov began to relax and calculate his planned route. Unlike the motherland, the United States had an infrastructure of roads, gas stations and hotels that jostled to service those who cared to crisscross it. At night, and sticking to the speed limit in a domestic, family SUV, he doubted he'd draw many glances from passing motorists or law enforcement officers.

Yet, safe as he was driving in the black of night, he realised that he did have to change his appearance just in case the presumed state-wide BOLO in Texas was escalated to a federal level. A change of appearance, however, meant a change of clothes, and that meant stopping either at a store that was still open at this time of night or finding some clothes elsewhere. Could he fit into the dead man's baggy, dirty-looking garments? He decided against it. Clean, presentable people became too nice or too normal to be suspected of anything and that's what he had to be.

He yawned and a crashing wave of exhaustion broke over him. A car horn sounded. His eyes snapped opened, lights flashed and he jerked the steering wheel away just in time as a pick-up truck passed him in the opposite direction. Vetrov swore, and thumped the wheel. His need for sleep had nearly claimed his life. He wound down all the SUV's windows and let the fresh, countryside night air envelop his face.

He stopped at the next gas station that was open and, keeping his head turned away from the camera, filled the tank. He glanced at the boot and noted that the body was not visible then went inside the station to pay. There was a rack of T-shirts promoting the local area, baseball caps, a few off-brand items of jeans and windcheaters. He didn't make eye contact with the guy at the till. Vetrov left the gas station with a full tank of fuel, a denim shirt, a navy-blue baseball cap, a matching windcheater and a bag full of chips, chocolate, water and Coke.

As soon as he was out of the lot he downed a can of Coke and immediately felt the sugar and caffeine combination start to work. He then started on the chocolate. He was now awake and alert again but without amphetamines – like they'd used in the field – he'd just crash again, and this time he wouldn't get lucky. An idea started to form in his mind and he tapped the address into the GPS. He needed to sleep and move at the same time, so he needed someone else to do the driving.

Two hours later, just before he entered the outskirts of Little Rock, he pulled off the main road and drove up a country lane. He opened the rear door and hauled the dead man out of the boot unceremoniously. He dragged him to the side of the road and walked several steps into the bushes before letting him fall to the ground, where the man instantly became buried in the thick undergrowth. He changed into his new clothes, swapping his tan-coloured shirt for the denim one and filled the pockets of his windbreaker with the rest of his food and drink. He then did a U-turn and headed into Little Rock. He parked the car within walking distance of the Greyhound bus station. Leaving the keys to the Dodge in the ignition, he left the SUV to be taken by whoever got to it first.

The bus arrived on time and he was one of only three passengers getting on. He let them on first and then deposited his bag from the gas station, which included his rubbish and his shirt, in a trash can next to the waiting area.

Vetrov showed the driver his ticket and made his way to the back of the bus. It was mostly empty, with passengers preferring to sit nearer the front. He took a seat on the back row in the corner and settled himself down for the two-and-a-half-hour trip. It was all the sleep he was going to allow himself and he hoped it was all he needed.

As the bus set off he looked at the backs of the heads of the other passengers. Americans were fools, and easily fooled with a smile and a clean set of clothes. And at the moment, that, and a few hundred dollars, was all he had, but as soon as he got to Montana he would have much much more. In under twenty-four hours he would give George the order to release her new Qatar footage. The Saudi had been adamant that it must not be released sooner than Friday or they would not pay a dime. Vetrov had to be patient for a day more, and that patience would be rewarded with millions. Enough to vanish, or to reform Blackline.

His mind jumped to Akulov and the shame it had caused him when the man had not stepped up as the real fight had begun in Syria. Yet gallingly without the rules and orders of the mighty Russian Army, Akulov had flourished and become the most feared Russian assassin in living memory. A fact that had always eaten away at him. They had been the Werewolves, they had been the best and he as their leader should have been the one to achieve recognition. But Akulov's elevated status on the circuit, and within the industry, overshadowed him. Akulov was the true MVP of the Werewolves, and that was the fact Vetrov hated most of all.

Vetrov was hungry, he was tired and he was angry but at least he was on the move. He was like a grain of sand carried along in the shallows by the current. It was known that he existed, that he was there but he could not be picked out from any of the other myriad of minute silica shifting in the surf. On the Greyhound bus, among the other passengers, all lost in their own worlds, he was that grain of sand.

He closed his eyes and pulled his windcheater up and his cap down and tried to blend into the dark interior of the bus. He was asleep within minutes.

Chapter 17

Undisclosed location, Texas, USA

Maybe it was the tequila, or perhaps just the build-up of fatigue, but Tate woke from a deep sleep at six a.m. A gnawing, pernicious feeling overwhelmed him. Extreme guilt. He'd had no dreams and no thoughts of Hunter or their situation had entered his subconscious. He checked his phone for messages. There was just one. It was from Newman: *'If you need me, I'm here.'*

Tate started to type a reply then deleted it. It was embarrassing.

He got out of bed and padded across the voluminous room to the bathroom. There was a full vanity kit provided for him but he was in no mood to shave so just showered. He dried and noted that the face that looked back at him in the mirror was tired and badly in need of a professional haircut. He dressed and there was a knock at the door. It was Akulov.

'Sleep well?'

'Yeah.'

'Miguel is eating breakfast. He told me to tell you if you do not wish to go hungry you should come now.'

'Are you taking orders from him now?'

'No. I am being polite.'

'What business did you have with Miguel?'

248

'He paid me to liquidate Angel Mendez.'

Tate shook his head. 'That was why you were really in Texas?'

'I was here to clear my name. The contract was agreed after I shot Caesar Mendez.'

'And he's paying you?'

'Do you work for free?'

'I certainly don't work for exposure. Bravo had told Miguel where the weapons are stashed that Vetrov sold to Angel. Miguel is so happy he is letting us use one of his Gulfstreams to fly to Montana.'

'Us?' Tate said.

'This is not just your fight.'

'Kirill Vetrov is mine.'

'He is. I merely wish to ask him a question.'

Akulov turned away and they carried on downstairs, through the terracotta-tiled kitchen and into a large patio area protected from the sun with a huge awning. There was a long table with three place settings. Miguel sat at one end and Akulov took the seat at the other. Tate was left with the setting facing out into the garden.

Miguel had his mouth full of eggs so acknowledged him with a nod and a shake of a fork. Tate poured himself a cup of wake-up juice and added a sizeable slug of cream.

'My mother makes the most wonderful *huevos rancheros*, but these eggs are not bad at all. Jack, you should really try them.'

Tate nodded. He wasn't one for forced morning conversations. He piled his plate with scrambled eggs and bacon from the serving plates in the middle.

'How have you slept, given the circumstances?'

'Well enough. Thank you,' Tate said, pointedly and started to calculate how much time he had lost in the race to get to Vetrov and Eastman.

'Ah, but of course!' Miguel reached his hand into his pocket and retrieved a piece of folded paper. He stood and extended his arm towards Tate. 'This is what you wanted. In the end it was not that difficult to obtain.'

Tate opened the note and read the address, written in a surprisingly delicate hand. It meant nothing to him but as soon as he'd got his scoff down his neck he'd check it and be off. 'Thank you.'

'My pleasure.'

Tate took a bagel.

'So look at us all here. Who would have thought it? The Mexican businessman, the British spy and the Russian assassin all working on the same side.'

Tate felt his phone vibrate. He excused himself and walked through the house to the front porch. It was Neill Plato. 'What's new?'

'Hi, Jack. Just an update really to say I've got no more on Eastman, I'm afraid, except for the fact that rumour has it he's a man from the east, hence the name.'

'Yep, that's helpful. Bravo's given me an address for Eastman, and it doesn't seem that far from the one Akulov gave me. I need you to pull up whatever you can find on it. OK?'

'Fire away.'

Tate dictated the address then asked, 'Anything on Vetrov?'

'Yes. Sorry. Facial recognition had a match to him taking a ferry from Liverpool Birkenhead to Belfast the day after the bombing.'

'No.' Tate sighed. He understood Plato had been working just as hard in London as he had in Texas so kept his tone calm. 'Neill, I meant now, contemporary hits in the US.'

'Oh. Sorry. No.'

'Thanks.' Tate ended the call.

Miguel joined him on the terrace. He had a mug of coffee in his hand. 'It's peaceful out here. That is why I selected this place – that and the underground prison.'

Both men gazed into the distance. Tate spotted a road, like a ribbon that showed the slight undulations in the seemingly flat and featureless Texan plane. It was deserted.

'Now that I have the address, I need to go. Can you have that Gulfstream on standby?'

'I can do more than that. Why don't we have a helo pick you up here and deposit you at the plane? That will save you over an hour.'

'Thanks.'

'You and Ruslan have been a great help. The Mendez brothers have been rats nipping at us and leaving their toxic shit all over our territory for over a decade, and now they are no more. So sincerely, thank you.'

'Does this make you the new Don of the Arellano Cartel?'

'It does. So if you ever need a friend in Mexico ...'

'Thanks.'

'I have one question for you,' Miguel said.

'Go ahead.'

'What is in Montana?'

'More Russians, but these ones are bad guys.'

'Aren't we all?' Miguel started to chuckle. He placed his mug on the wooden railing and retrieved his phone. Then started tapping out a message.

Tate continued to gaze out across the savannah, and now he noted a dust cloud in the distance on the road. A pick-up truck, one of the favoured modes of transport in Texas, appeared but then turned off the road. A quarter of a mile behind it, came a second one. 'Are you expecting anyone?'

'No, but that's a public road, quiet but public.'

'Don Miguel!' There was a shout from the side of the house. One of the men who'd arrived with Tate came running.

'What is it?'

'We've got a drone heading our way.' The man pointed at the road, in the direction both vehicles had been coming from.

Miguel's face creased with a frown. 'Who would be using a drone?'

Tate squinted, found the drone then looked again at the road. Now both trucks had vanished, perhaps driven off the road.

The second guard appeared, a pair of field glasses affixed to his eyes, but then he let them fall on their carry cord and yelled, 'Inside! Inside now!'

Tate saw a flash in the sky as he and Miguel ran for the door, followed by a thunderous explosion. Tate was thrown off the porch and onto the unforgiving desert tundra below. The world around Tate became black and white, as his vision started to grey out. He lay choking in the dust as a second explosion rocked him. He blinked and tried to breathe and his vision started to return to normal. He had no time to assess any injury he may have sustained. He scrambled to his feet to see Akulov hauling Miguel back inside what was left of the front of the house.

Tate felt his jaw fall open with shock. What kind of a drone-launched weapon could do this, short of military munition? And then it all came together in his head. Somehow the Mendez Cartel had found them and they were using the Werewolves' weapon cache.

Tate got to the porch steps and saw two cartel men, the ones who had travelled with him in the SUV. One was lying motionless and the other was trying to drag him into cover. As Tate's hearing began to return he thought he heard a whining, droning noise. A shadow flashed over him. It was a drone of a type he did not recognise, small enough to be launched from a vehicle but apparently large enough to carry munitions. He watched transfixed as it turned and headed back in the direction of the two pick-ups. Tate moved towards the duo, grabbed the injured man by the legs and helped the other carry him around the side of the house to the patio area. The injured man was coughing every couple of steps and blood trickled from his mouth onto his cream polo shirt. By the time they had reached the house the man had stopped coughing and his eyes had become dull.

'Shit,' the other guard yelled.

'There's nothing we can do for him,' Tate said.

Akulov appeared from the other entrance, now wearing a ballistic vest and holding a HK416 assault rifle in each hand. 'Tate, one for you. There are more magazines in the kitchen on the island.'

'What kind of shit have you dragged me into?' Miguel appeared behind Akulov, a crazed expression on his face and dressed in a ballistic vest. He was carrying a spare, which he tossed to Tate, then addressed his man. 'With me, to the front!'

They disappeared inside. Tate followed but only as far as the kitchen island where he saw a haphazard pile of magazines lying on the pristine worktop. He took two, thrusting them uncomfortably into the pockets of his cargo trousers.

There was a whistling from outside. Tate and Akulov went prone as what could have only been an RPG exploded short of the patio, kicking up a cloud of dirt and dust.

Akulov rose to his haunches. 'I'll go high. You go low.'

'Agreed!' Tate yelled. He advanced to the patio, the selector on the HK set to "burst". The dust from the RPG impact was still drifting in the otherwise still morning air. Tate worked his jaw to try to improve his hearing. He moved along the last bit of cover he had – the wall of the house – to the dwarf wall of the patio leading on to the garden. Immediately past this he could see the land at the rear of the property. There was a dust cloud and a vehicle bouncing across the open terrain towards him, one of the pick-ups. It had left the road to attempt a flanking manoeuvre. It was still out of the effective range of his short-barrelled HK416 A5-11 but getting closer. It slowed as a figure on the truck bed balanced a long tube on the top of the truck cab.

'Incoming!' Tate yelled and dived away from the patio to his right.

The RPG sailed high and exploded in the eaves of the house. The truck started to move again.

Loud retorts of unsilenced assault rifles now sounded, aimed at what or who Tate didn't know. Tate looked at the oncoming pick-up. As long as it was moving it was an unstable platform. Once the cartel men got out it would be a different story. Tate decided to take a larger gamble. He could open fire now but at that range the rounds from his HK would have less power. Controlling his breathing, he lined up the front on the distant truck and waited. It bounced towards him, rising and falling like a yacht riding the waves, up and down, peaks and troughs. Tate counted the seconds off, the black pick-up growing ever larger, drawing ever nearer.

He waited until he could finally make out a face behind the windscreen and estimated that the vehicle was now within the HK's effective firing range of three hundred and thirty yards. He took a breath, exhaled and squeezed the trigger.

Tate's controlled bursts emptied his magazine within seconds. The twenty 5.56mm rounds exploded towards the truck. The windshield crazed but the pick-up kept on coming. Tate dropped out the magazine and slammed a new one in. He waited, each second the vehicle drawing nearer, and he fired again. Steam started to pour from the bonnet. The truck turned to the left and now Tate emptied the rest of his second magazine into the side of the cab. Rounds snapped back at him now from the passenger in the front and the guy on the back who was holding on with one hand and waving a Kalashnikov with the other. None of their rounds were hitting Tate or even the house behind him. Not wanting to tempt fate, he dropped from his haunches onto his stomach, making himself an even smaller target as the truck came to a shuddering and juddering halt.

The passenger door opened and a guy almost fell out, clutching a rifle that had been too long for him to effectively bring to bear in the confined space. Tate saw the driver's head appear above the bonnet on the other side and then heavier calibre rounds of a Kalashnikov thundered towards him. Tate was a static target, but he was also low to the ground, and he hoped he was the better shot. He fired a three-round burst at the passenger, dropping him as he was still trying to swing his rifle up. Rounds hit the wall next to Tate, chipping the bricks.

Tate switched targets and fired a burst at the driver, who instantly ducked below the outline of the heavy bonnet. A head, then a shoulder and then a torso appeared from the truck bed. RPG man was on his feet with another RPG. Tate rolled to his right, pushed up and sprinted towards the corner of the house. There was a whoosh and a spurt of flame as the RPG rocketed towards his position. Seconds later an explosion sent Tate flying through the air. He hit the dirt and slid across the floor to the wall.

Tate got to his feet and leant against the side of the house. He sucked in a few deep breaths and waited for the ringing in his ears to die away. Then he dropped to his knee and spun back around the corner. RPG man was still standing on the truck bed, looking dazed but staring at the impact his rocket had made. Tate took aim, but before he pulled the trigger the man crumpled and fell backwards. Akulov on the roof had taken him out. Tate fired again at where the driver had been but saw that the last man had had a change of heart and was running away from the stationary truck. He got perhaps ten strides further away before a solitary round hit him in the back of the head and propelled him towards the ground.

Tate didn't know if the two men in the truck he'd shot were dead, but he knew they weren't returning rounds and that was all that mattered for the moment. He could hear shots from the front of the house and cautiously advanced around the side until he'd reached the second line of contact. He took the chance to change his magazine; it was his last. He'd not been economical, but when facing a larger force, dominating them with superior firepower was the only course of action.

There were two vehicles at the front; he had no idea where

the last one had appeared from. It was a white Cadillac Escalade, fifty yards away on the drive, shielded by the other pick-up. Tate pushed himself flat against the side of the house to assess the threat. A figure was leaning over the bonnet of the SUV with a long rifle. As Tate watched, he fired on the house. The heavy retort told Tate it was a 0.50-cal round, big enough to cut a man in two and penetrate a brick wall. In front of the Cadillac, and between the vehicles, two figures lay dead on the gravel in a pool of blood.

Tate took a long breath, calmed his breathing, acquired the shooter with the 0.50-cal and opened fire. Instantly the figure ducked and jerked as Tate's rounds missed and hit the hood.

The shooting had stopped. Tate didn't know how many men Miguel had at the house. He realised that his performance had been affected by his preoccupation with his brother, and he'd stopped being aware of his environment. Now was not the time to make mistakes.

Ahead the sniper behind the Cadillac had changed his target. He took another shot, but this time the heavy round roared towards Tate. He instinctively threw himself flat, knowing that to be even just clipped was life-ending. A chunk of brick was torn away from the wall of the house half a metre above his head. Return fire now came from the upper floors of the house, targeting the sniper.

On instinct, and without fully being aware he had done so, Tate sprinted out of cover diagonally towards the Cadillac, relying on their suppressive fire from the house to keep the heads down of any other shooters he'd not seen. He kept his HK up, ready to take on targets as and when they presented themselves. He heard rounds being fired but couldn't afford to think about them. Thirty yards, twenty, ten to go, and Tate realised that his course of action was perhaps not the best, as a line of dirt exploded in front of his feet. He increased his pace and, with tunnel vision, focused on the hood of the Cadillac. There was movement from behind the wheel arch, a figure hiding. Tate fired a burst as he ran. It was wild and hit the tyre and the dirt around but he'd just been trying to get the gunman to keep his head down.

He reached the hood and half ran, half skidded around the far side. A man wearing a red-checked shirt and blue jeans lay on his back, clutching a Barrett. He looked up at Tate, anger in his dark eyes and said in Spanish through bloodstained lips, '*Ya valí madre …*'

Images of Vetrov and what he'd done to his brother filled his mind. Tate delivered a burst to the guy's chest. Mind still burning with rage, Tate checked inside the SUV – it was empty – and then crabbed around to its rear. The sun blinded Tate for a moment, making him slow to spot two more shooters exchanging fire with the house, using the other vehicle for cover. He'd made a mistake; his mind had been elsewhere. Before Tate could react, one spun round and opened fire at him.

The round hit Tate square in the chest and pushed him backwards with what felt like the weight of a sledgehammer. Tate's HK flew from his hands as he hit the gravel. He lay on his back for several seconds stunned, winded, and unable to move. But then he heard two single shots and all the guns fell silent.

Seemingly miles away a voice shouted, 'Clear!'

Tate opened his mouth to speak but nothing came out. His eyes focused on the clouds floating above, and he managed to suck in a lungful of air. A shadow fell over him; it was panting heavily.

'Tate! Are you hit?'

It took a second for Tate to realise it was Akulov. 'Help me up!'

The Werewolf bent forward and grabbed Tate's arms and heaved. As Tate started to leave the ground, he gasped in pain.

'Kill or cure …' Tate muttered.

'What?' Akulov looked puzzled.

'Just pull.'

Tate got to his feet and leant against the Russian. 'You've been hit.'

Tate closed his eyes, then using his right hand felt the vest and found the deformed round. He purposefully inhaled as deeply as he could, to test his chest. It was bruised but there were no broken bones. 'Don't mess with the SAS!'

Tate took in the scene. Three more bodies lay in front of the pick-up; they'd come mob-handed.

'They tried to rush me,' Akulov said.

'Silly sods,' Tate replied.

Akulov started to laugh. 'I need to learn British slang.'

'Yeah,' Tate said. 'It's the bollocks.'

'Bollocks?' Akulov frowned.

'Never mind.'

Miguel emerged from the house. 'We need to check the bodies.'

'Understood,' Akulov shouted back.

Tate moved away from Akulov and walked to the Cadillac. He didn't need to check the Barrett guy for a pulse – he had no chest – and the two Akulov had taken out looked more like early Jackson Pollocks. On impulse, Tate had a quick look inside the Cadillac for phones or anything that linked the men back to whomever sent them. It was highly unlikely that they weren't cartel men, but he'd been wrong before. He saw a phone-sized boxy object and picked it up. For a moment he thought that it was a remote detonator but then he realised what it was. A tracker, but it wasn't receiving a signal. Tate popped it into his pocket, and decided he'd have a better look when he was inside the villa. He straightened himself up and now looked at the bodies lying on the drive. There was no need to feel any of the men near them for a pulse. 'We need to check the back.'

Both men started to walk towards the side of the house. Tate's chest hurt but the pain just told him he was still alive. They reached the back and continued on to the pick-up. The passenger of the pick-up was dead but RPG man was still breathing.

Whilst Akulov kept lookout in case any more men or vehicles approached, Tate painfully clambered up onto the truck bed and crouched down next to the injured man.

'Who sent you?'

The man's eyes fluttered and he turned his head. 'I … I don't … want to die …'

'But you wanted me to. Answer my questions and I'll get you some help. Who sent you?'

'M … Mendez … Mendez Cartel …'

'Why?' It was an obvious question, but he had to ask it.

The man's mouth opened but no words formed.

Tate stood and moved away. RPG man was beyond help, and besides five minutes earlier the guy had been trying to blow him up. Tate dropped down from the truck and winced. 'I think we're done here.'

They trooped back to the house, weapons up, aware that more cartel men could arrive at any time.

Tate retrieved the small black box from his pocket. 'I found this in the Cadillac.'

Akulov examined it.

'There's no signal.'

Akulov stopped walking. 'Bravo and Angel are underground in a concrete-walled bunker. That is why there's no signal now. The cartel must have tracked them here before they were taken to the cells. Perhaps they couldn't get their men here to attack before now?'

'Silly sods.' Tate let out a large sigh. If this was all a play then the address Bravo had given him for Eastman was probably made up too. And that meant Vetrov was in the wind. He no longer felt any guilt for what Miguel may or may not have done to extract the information.

They edged into and through the patio and kitchen. The body of the dead guard still lay on the tiles. Akulov bent down and closed his eyes. There were two gunshots. Loud, echoing 9mm rounds from a pistol. They boomed below the floor. Tate and Akulov exchanged glances and advanced down the steps, towards the cells and the direction of the shots. Akulov held up his fist at the top. They both listened – nothing. Akulov pointed to Tate and held up one finger then himself and held up two. Tate nodded, and took the lead.

At the bottom Tate pressed himself as flat as he could against the wall and then swung around and into the room, weapon up. Two of the cell doors were open. He advanced towards the second door, the first cell, trying to keep his footfall quiet but knowing that it was slapping against the concrete. Inside he saw the Giant Bravo still chained to the table but his head resting on it. Tate drew nearer and realised that the top of his head was bloody. Blood dripped onto the steel table and ran to the edges before seeping onto the floor.

The Giant raised his head slowly. His eyes were red and his face crimson, but Tate could see the white of his teeth as he opened his mouth. 'You lied to me!'

'Where did you hide the tracker, Bravo?'

'Tracker ... you think I am chipped like some sort of dog?'

There was a bleep from Tate's pocket. Using his left hand he pulled out the digital tracker. It showed the distance to its target as twenty foot; Bravo was less than a metre away. 'It's not you.'

The Giant pushed himself upright, the chains securing him to the desk tightened. 'Get me out of here.'

Tate turned away. Akulov was still in the doorway. His expression gave nothing away. He moved past Akulov and advanced to the far cell. They found Miguel standing over the broken, naked body of Angel Mendez. Mendez's eyes were open. He was still alive but there was a bloody wound in his left thigh.

Miguel looked up, as though he had merely been distracted from reading a newspaper. Once more his shirt was bloodstained. 'There was a tracking chip inside him, in his leg. Can you believe

260

it? I have removed it. Bravo told me on the provision that I did not kill him.'

'What will happen to him now?'

'Angel will of course die. Do not worry, Ruslan – you shall still be paid – and as for Bravo? That is still to be discussed. He now has no reason to run away, if we can come to acceptable terms.'

'I see.'

'Ah, but I almost forgot. I've received a text message. Your helicopter will be here in twenty minutes.'

Chapter 18

31,000 feet above Colorado

The Gulfstream G280 could be configured to handle up to ten passengers but on this flight there were just two: Tate and Akulov. Helicopters had arrived at the safe house. One had taken Miguel away to an undisclosed location whilst the other had ferried Tate and Akulov directly to the David Wayne Hooks Memorial Airport.

As far as Tate was aware George Eastman was at the address Miguel had given him. It was a place just outside the small town of Eureka in Montana. Plato was already trying to get as much intel as he could on the area, including satellite images, but there was still no way to verify the location extracted from the Giant Bravo.

'Eureka was chosen to have a weapons cache because it is only nine miles south of the US border with Canada. It is a convenient location for a team entering the US,' Akulov said, matter of fact. 'I believe Vetrov plans on escaping into Canada with Eastman.'

'That's obvious,' Tate said, tersely.

'I suggest we check the cache first. Vetrov may be heading there. He knows I am following him, and that is an obvious place for him to ambush me. He, however, does not know who you are and that we are collaborating.'

Tate knew it was again time to lay down the law. 'Vetrov may have framed you, but he killed my parents and shot my brother. When we find him, he's mine.'

Akulov nodded. 'I have already told you. All I want from him is an answer.'

'And what's the question?'

'Why did he choose to frame me?'

'He was your team leader?'

'He was once an outstanding soldier. He was an excellent operator, and he was my friend. War changes each of us in different ways, as you know. The fear, the horror and the suffering that we see, that we inflict on ourselves and on others, it distils who we are.'

'You mean it either makes or breaks us?'

'It broke Vetrov mentally, though perhaps break is not quite the correct word for him. It released something inside of him that was both deadly and inhumane. He lost all respect for any life that wasn't his own, that wasn't of his blood, wasn't Russian.'

'Are you talking about war crimes?'

'The entire war was a crime. We Russians were in Syria to prop up a corrupt regime. Conveniently for the Kremlin we could make-believe we were the good guys because we shot Islamic terrorists. The terrorists started out as ISIS and al-Qaeda but when the terrorists fled, or were killed, we then moved on to the groups who opposed the government.' Akulov looked out of the window, his fists now clenched. Tate thought he may be seeing ghosts. 'That was when I understood what the war had created, what it had done to Vetrov and the men around him. That was when I decided to leave those who I had been proud to call brothers. Once our Syria campaign was over, I gave in my letter of intention to resign. At that very moment, in the eyes of Vetrov I ceased being of the same blood. I became nothing. I became the enemy. I became a traitor.'

Tate understood the context. Special Forces operators were a specific breed of men, and when they became warped or snapped it never ended well. 'So you embarked upon the career of a freelance assassin.'

Akulov was silent again for a beat and Tate tried to read his face. 'Not all my work was private sector. The Kremlin would not let me leave until I had undertaken certain "tasks" for them. Once I was permitted to be so, I was selective. Did I assassinate people? Yes. Were these people innocent? No. As I have told you before, I have a code.'

Tate now stared out his own window. 'Whatever you say, Ruslan, whatever you may think, we are very different.'

'No, Jack, we are not. If you were born in Moscow you would have been on my team, and if I had been born in the green rolling hills of Surrey or Sussex or anywhere in the UK, then I would have been a member of your regiment.'

'Maybe.' Tate closed his eyes.

Eureka was at the other end of the country, over two thousand miles away from Houston, an entire continent in European terms. It would take approximately thirty hours of non-stop driving to get there. That would mean even if Vetrov had driven directly after the firefight at the warehouse, not stopped for food, comfort or sleep, he would still be in the car for at least another five hours. But he hadn't driven; he'd abandoned his vehicle in Texas after killing two police officers.

The fastest way to get to Eureka was by air. Before he'd boarded the chopper, Tate had been on a conference call with Newman and Plato. Now that they had an address for Eastman, Newman had agreed to send in a team to assist Tate, which would include Plato to secure and assess the technology; however, they would not be arriving until late the next day. Local talent was also unavailable to them at such short notice and given the classified nature of the threat. Her orders to Tate were succinct and unequivocal. Get to Eureka, carry out surveillance on the target and wait for the E Squadron team to arrive.

During the same call Plato had confirmed Akulov was fine to fly and was not yet on any watch list, but due to the double shooting of the police officers, Vetrov was now being treated like public enemy number one. He'd be pinged as soon as he stepped foot in any airport.

Tate thought about the task ahead. Vetrov couldn't fly, which meant that he'd either steal a car, hail a cab, take a Greyhound bus or catch a train. Amtrak didn't go to Eureka, and driving in a stolen car or a succession of taxis was both too problematic and too pedestrian. So that left either a mixture of trains and buses or just the bus.

So the assumption Tate made was that Vetrov was attempting to get to a place he knew by means he did not. Tate reckoned then it could be anything from, at worst, six hours to at best twelve hours until the lead Werewolf arrived. That is if he either wasn't stopped by the police or had decided to cut his losses and run. Regardless of Vetrov's intentions or mode of transport, Tate and Akulov would be arriving in another three and a half hours. Two more hours of flying time remained to get to Glacier Park International Airport, the nearest place to Eureka the Gulfstream could land without getting them potentially pinged, and then a fifty-four-mile drive from the airport to Eureka accounted for the rest.

Tate had been on Google Earth and Street View to get intel on the location and whilst both these tools got him near to the location, the blue Street View line stopped short of the actual address.

Tate sighed. The mission was a fastball. It had started that way and it would end that way – everything happening on the fly, without time to prepare or to plan. He was about to descend into a hostile environment with the help of only one other man, who up until a few years before had been on the same side as the men they were going to engage. Tate glanced over at Akulov, who as a seasoned operative had now closed his eyes and was taking the downtime to sleep. There was nothing either of them could do until they got to Eureka, but for Tate there was also no sleep.

He'd called the hospital to be told there was no change in his brother's condition. He'd had a creeping dread that Simon had worsened, even though the medical staff had said his condition had neither improved nor deteriorated. His guilt covered him like an invisible shroud, and it seemed to be trying to suffocate him. Simon shouldn't have been on an active mission; he was not a field operative but an intelligence officer. Tate knew the only way to break free of his remorse would be to capture and kill Vetrov.

But Vetrov was not the only wanted man. Akulov had assassinated two British diplomats.

International airspace

Neill Plato felt out of place and a little self-conscious. The plane was the smallest he'd been on, but it had been the longest flight he had ever taken. He didn't know much about planes; they weren't his cup of tea, nor were cars. The only type of transport that he really felt at home on was a train, or a cruise liner. Now that was style. To be able to sit back and watch the world pass by, or take a stroll on deck and do the same, that was travel as opposed to travelling. However, he had to admit that this jet was very comfy. There was seating arranged for fourteen, but he and the three-man E Squadron team were the sole passengers. The three soldiers were either snoozing or listening to music with their eyes closed.

Plato knew very little of the travel arrangements and had just been told to take whatever he needed to secure Eastman's software and hardware. Plato had grabbed his stuff, been driven to his flat by an SIS driver to collect his passport and an overnight bag, and then chauffeured out to an airfield he didn't recognise where the jet had been waiting. He wasn't, if he was honest with himself, at all nervous about the mission; he was only the "tech support" and who would want to target him? No, he was excited. He'd finally get a chance to meet George Eastman who, in some ways, may prove to be the biggest tech influencer of the decade. Sure Eastman hadn't been able to hack into the Qatari immigration database, like he had, but what Eastman had created was equal to any piece of fine art. Eastman had created digital life.

Plato finished his second cup of tea and realised that his mind had been wandering. He was tired, yet if he slept he'd not be able to fully enjoy the flight. He peered out of the porthole. They were over the sea. He wanted to see the US pass by below – the valleys, the mountains and everything in between. This trip wasn't by any stretch of the imagination a "jolly" but that wouldn't stop him jolly well enjoying it whilst he could.

He thought about Jack, and then of course he thought about Simon and he became angry with himself. Their lives were on the line and here he was behaving like a kid on his first flight to see Mickey Mouse. He closed his eyes and sighed as he started to assess whether he had everything he needed for the mission. It was a little late now, he reasoned, if he'd forgotten anything but at least if he knew now it would save him time on the ground. His time at SIS had seen him work with many outstanding operatives and Jake Tate was securely in his top two. Plato just hoped that he would not fail him, or his brother.

Glacier Park International Airport, Montana, USA

The smiling clerk at the Avis desk upgraded their standard SUV to a premium one. Tate took the keys without bothering to check the paperwork and walked into the parking lot. He blipped the fob and the lights of a vehicle flashed. Both men exchanged looks and Tate felt a sudden, stabbing sense of déjà vu.

'It would be useful if this too carried a full assault kit and was armoured,' Akulov noted.

Tate said nothing and climbed in behind the wheel. A year before, the men of Blackline had used the very same vehicles, and Akulov had been one of them. Tate tapped the screen on the sat nav, or GPS as the locals called it, and entered the address of the weapons cache Akulov had given him.

He then swiped at his iPhone, brought up satellite images of the place Plato had sent him. The road ran north-west to south-east, half a mile to the east of downtown Eureka. Partway down the road a wood obscured several buildings.

'The exact building is the one at the back,' Akulov confirmed. 'The cache extends under the building and the land. These places were built by Soviet engineers and are deep and in most cases remote enough that they haven't been spotted by the ground-penetrating radars of prospecting oil and gas companies. The buildings are occupied by several unrelated owners. The resident of that building is former GRU. He was given a healthy pension to become American and live out his retirement in Eureka.'

This made sense to Tate. Back in the Nineties IRA quarter-masters were responsible for weapons caches, but did not live with them for fear of detection. At that time the IRA and their associates were wanted men, but here in the US, Russia was not the enemy, allegedly. 'What's his name?'

'The Resident?'

'Yes.'

'We were never told. If access to the cache was required, we had to present him with a password, to authenticate who we were and then an operation code from Moscow to authenticate the mission.'

'Are you telling me these caches are active sites controlled by the Kremlin?'

'These were specific to several Spetsnaz units, and mine has been disbanded. I have no idea if the residents do or do not know of this. I imagine they continue to ignorantly guard an ageing stockpile of munitions.'

'How old are the weapons?'

'Some of the caches we inherited, others were created within the last decade for us. In some cases weapons were destroyed when new variants arrived. We may well find five-year-old weapons or something once kissed by Brezhnev. If Vetrov has visited this place, the man is either dead or has permanently vanished, and the weapons will have gone too.'

Rexford, Montana, USA

Vetrov looked out across the water. It was good to be back in Montana and it was especially good to have contacts who could get him past regional security and onto a private jet. The pilot at Fort Smith Regional was a small-time coke runner, and for an agreed discount on his next order and the promise that he wouldn't tell the Mendez Cartel about the money he'd been skimming from them, Vetrov had been flown discreetly north. The USA was the home of capitalism and he was glad that anything was still possible. Arriving at Glacier Park International Airport, Vetrov had used a credit card to hire a car. The card wasn't his but it matched ID he had, which did show his real face. It was a chance he knew but one he'd had to take.

The small hire car was now hidden in the garage of the cabin they were using as a base and Vetrov felt secure at least until morning. If Akulov had not appeared by then Vetrov knew he had to pull out and take Eastman to safety. Vetrov liked it here, by the river. It was peaceful and reminded him of home, except his home had never been this peaceful and the furnishings in the family apartment whilst being made from wood, were shoddy and ill-designed. It would be a shame to burn the place to the ground when they left, but as he saw it that was the only way now that he could disappear: he could die and then rise from the ashes anew, initially in Canada, and then who knew? And then after that he'd give Eastman another target, and another. Vetrov felt the giddiness of power surge through him once more. Free of Chen, he would become not only powerful but also wealthy, private-island wealthy.

There was a knock at the door behind him.

'Yes?' He turned, taking his eyes off the dark waters of the Tobacco River.

'George wants to talk to you.'

Vetrov's eyes narrowed. The man in front of him had been Baltic Spetsnaz but he doubted now that he would pass the medical. He looked the part: he was large, bearded and had a piercing stare, but he also had a stomach that pushed against his belt in an attempt to escape his shirt. 'George?'

'*Da.*'

Vetrov noted that the man had not called their hacker in residence "Eastman". This was another sign it was time for him and Eastman to go. 'Is there an issue with the project?'

'I do not believe so.'

'In that case instruct our colleague I am currently busy.'

'OK.' The man turned on his heels and left.

'Stop.'

The man turned back, a question on his face. 'Chief?'

'Has the Resident been reminded what is required of him?'

'*Da.* I told him myself.'

'Good. That is all.'

The six men here had served him and Blackline well, but when the Blackline money failed to hit their various offshore accounts in two weeks' time, he knew their loyalty would falter. However, they would not live to see that happen. Vetrov focused again on the water, hidden by the night but ever present, ever watchful. Tomorrow morning, when the operation had been completed and the footage delivered, he would take Eastman and kill everyone else; the men were no longer needed. Their corpses would burn with the house and the other excess equipment.

Lundeen Road, Eureka, Montana, USA

The drive from the airport to Eureka would have been spectacular in daylight, or even an hour earlier at sunset, but in the

270

pitch-blackness of northern Montana, even the mountains were hidden, seemingly behind a black, theatrical curtain. Tate killed the lights and let the heavy SUV roll silently down the incline awhile, before he hit the brakes and brought them to a halt. They were just up the road from the target buildings. Parked, with the lights off and not illuminated by any street lighting, the Tahoe sat like an ominous dark shadow against a darker background. Both their front windows were cracked open to listen for an approaching traffic, be it on foot or vehicular.

As they had travelled as regular passengers, albeit on a private jet, they were unarmed and as such vulnerable. It had been a trade-off between speed, stealth and deniability.

'Give me ten minutes. If I'm not back by then get out of here and call my boss.'

'Like we agreed,' Akulov said. 'Just remember you are Wolf 6.'

'Yeah.'

Tate made sure that the interior light was switched from "door" to "off" and exited the Tahoe. He crossed the deserted rural road and walked, tree side, down the hill. Newman had told Tate to get to Eureka and wait for the team to arrive, and he had agreed to this knowing full well that he would not. He had to get ahead of Vetrov; each and every minute he waited brought his adversary a mile closer to both him and George Eastman. In the drive from the airport, they had agreed Tate would be the one to make the first approach to the Resident. Until the firefight he had been an unknown to Vetrov and he hoped he had remained one to his men. And then there was the lurking doubt in Tate's mind. Could he really trust Akulov?

He reached the entrance to the property, a simple concrete access road leading to a rudimentary roundabout, with branches leading off to each individual property like some type of grey octopus. "Osminog". In the shadows Tate smiled – it was the Russian for octopus and somehow always tickled him and Simon. He instantly lost his smile and felt his resolve harden. Somewhere soon he would again find the man who had murdered their parents and had tried to kill his brother. Tate took a calming breath. He moved onto the grass and skirted the treeline before cutting across two lawns to bring him level with the start of the target building's territory.

He noted that although it was not late in the evening, none of the single-storey cabins had lights on. Neither inside nor out. It was as though the entire place was empty, like an abandoned film set for a WWII prisoner of war movie. Tate continued onwards and then a spotlight flicked on, flooding his vision with a penetrating white light. He backtracked into the shadows at the side of the cabin, blinking, as the front door opened.

A voice spoke. It was powerful but resigned and had a local accent. 'If you've come to rob me go ahead, but if you're here for any polite, social reason, stop hiding in the goddamn shrubbery.'

'That sounds fair to me,' Tate said, using an American accent that he hoped sounded half convincing. It was a stupid thing to do, but his only real course of action. Tate stepped into the light, raising his left hand to shield his eyes and instantly losing all element of concealment.

'Help you?' the man said, a tinge of fear now evident in his voice.

Tate could just make out his outline behind the light, but no detail, so he walked forward past its beam and stopped at the bottom of the steps. Blinking, he now saw the speaker was elderly, and dressed in sweatpants, a shirt and cardigan. Tate spoke the line Akulov had given him. 'I'm looking for my dog. I think he ran in here.'

Initially the man didn't reply, didn't move. The spotlight switched off, probably on a motion detector and timer set-up, Tate thought. 'This isn't a place for dogs. It's wolf country.'

Tate felt the soundless, night air gently move around him. There was a slight scent of wood – wet, barky. 'It's Werewolf country.'

'Then you'd better come inside, and shut the door behind you.' The old man turned and went deeper into the cabin.

Tate advanced up the stairs, all senses on alert. If this was the Resident then Vetrov either hadn't been here yet or hadn't made contact, or he had and it was a trap. Inside, the odour of polished wood overpowered that of the natural from outside and Tate found himself in an entrance hall. He moved through this to a central living area. The owner was now sitting in a wooden rocking chair and pointing to another. Tate scanned the room. He neither saw nor heard anyone else.

'Please take a seat.' The man had switched to Russian. The accent, unsurprisingly, was Moscow.

'I will, thank you,' Tate replied in the same, but his Russian was St Petersburg.

The Resident observed Tate for a moment before he spoke. 'So what is it you need from me?'

'Enough for a sole operator.'

'Just one man? So we are not invading yet? That is good. I have enjoyed living in this place and would not want to have to give it up.'

Tate didn't have time to hear the man reminisce. 'Am I the first who has come here?'

'What do you mean by that?' The Resident's face took on an uncertain expression. 'Since when?'

'You tell me?'

'Yes. You are the first. I had hoped that perhaps I had been forgotten about, but I am here to serve the motherland, whomever may now lead her.'

'I need to see the equipment.'

'Ah, I see it is urgent. Then I will need you to kindly provide me with your mission code.'

Tate knew this was where he'd hit a roadblock. 'Things have changed. This is a commercial venture.'

'What? Explain?'

'I do not have a mission code. What I do have is twenty thousand dollars, which is yours for a few pieces of kit I can't personally source, if you understand me.'

'A commercial venture?'

'Yes.'

'You have this in cash? Where, in your pocket?' The Resident sounded sceptical.

'In my car.'

The Resident leant forward in his seat. 'There was a time when perhaps I could have used my own strength and force to prevent you from just taking what you wanted. My days of fighting are over, much like the union it served. I can see that you are a man of honour. Which Werewolf were you?'

'I am Wolf 6.'

'Fine.' The Resident rose from his chair, with remarkable swiftness for a man of his age. 'You go and get your money, and we will have a deal. I shall wait here.'

Tate stood and walked back to the door, opened it and went down the steps. The Resident was very much alive, which meant that Vetrov, for whatever reason, had not been in contact. Tate wouldn't return with a single dollar; he'd return with Akulov.

Akulov still remembered the briefing when he and the others were informed by their commanding officer a decade before of the existence of the weapons caches. It was, the officer had beamed, a truly undetected weapon that they could weald against the United States. Akulov wondered what twelve men could do but supposed that they would just be a vanguard of sorts or perhaps a guerrilla unit sent to sow the seeds of havoc. Either way he was excited when the team had been sent to the US for several months to both perfect their accents and their knowledge of the customs and culture. Each team member had also been given a cache to inspect. This had not been his, neither had it been Vetrov's. So whose had it been, and what had happened to

274

him? Akulov wondered how many now of the twelve were left other than him and Kirill Vetrov …

He heard engines, the heavy growl of V8s. The sound seemed to be all around him and it was then he realised one was approaching up Lundeen Road towards him and one was coming down the road behind him. They were converging, and fast. He saw them both, one after the other, a second apart. Big, aggressive shadows in the night, and then the headlamps switched on. Flooding the entire area with harsh, hostile white light. There was nowhere for Akulov to go. If he got out of the Tahoe, he'd be either hunted or shot down. He had three options: ram the car in front of him, ram the one behind or break left or right and drive through a wire fence into the fields. If he could get away, he would draw the Russians, and it had to be the Russians, away from Tate and give him time to find George Eastman.

Akulov flicked the light setting to "off", switched on the ignition, took the handbrake off, floored the gas pedal and launched the Tahoe forward, tyres chirping …

The two assault vehicles were still tearing towards him, the one at the rear now arriving where he had been a moment before. The vehicle racing up the road was moving a little slower as it battled gravity. Akulov jerked the wheel to the left and the nose of the two SUVs missed each other by an inch. Akulov felt the front tyres hit the grass-covered bank at the side of the road as he bounced upwards in his seat and then the Tahoe crashed down the other side. Akulov braced himself and kept his foot on the gas pedal but the nose of the Tahoe hit the ground. Airbags exploded all around him and he was jerked first one way then the other.

Tate left cover and ran across the lawn, then darted towards the entrance to the road. He hugged the trees and moved nearer to the break in the foliage. Hearing more voices and muffled thuds, he poked his head out of cover and saw two dark shapes blocking the road, two SUVs slewed one above and one below where his should have been.

There were figures moving, the lights of the SUVs casting long shadows, their features rendered black by the harsh lighting. He saw several climbing up out of the field and they were dragging someone. Tate looked past them and could just make out, illuminated by the headlights, the rear of a vehicle protruding upwards from the grassy field. It had to be his hire car and it had to be Akulov they were dragging away. Tate watched helpless as they deposited him in the back of the rear SUV. Their doors slammed and both vehicles sped towards him. Tate scurried backwards as the convoy passed. And then Lundeen Road was silent and dark once again.

Tate moved back into the cover provided by the trees and waited. There was no more movement from the road or any of the cabins. Akulov had been snatched by the Russians. They'd arrived in two eight-seater SUVs. Akulov had been overpowered and Tate's presence would not have made the slightest bit of difference.

A tide of hopelessness started to rise around him, lapping at his feet. If Vetrov had already made it to his team then unless there was something Tate was missing, the Russian had surely already given the order to release the new footage and launch the cyberattack. He shook his head and clenched his fists. He wouldn't lose. This wasn't about the weapon or the world, this was about his brother and his dead parents.

Tate checked his Rolex and estimated that it was still at a minimum eight hours before the E Squadron team arrived. By that time Vetrov would have vanished, taken George Eastman with him and left Akulov, he imagined with several new holes in his head. Tate was on his own, which was nothing new, and he had to act.

He skirted the trees, taking even more care this time not to trip any sensors, until he was at the back of the complex and near to the end cabin. He could see just a single light illuminating the building he had been in minutes before, but nothing from any of the others. Tate darted to the nearest cabin and stopped by the side wall. Stock-still, he listened to the eerie silence of the compound. He moved around the edge, checked for a light or a sensor, saw none and went to the back door. He paused next to it, out of sight of anyone inside, and listened again.

He took a moment to try to comprehend what had happened. Had he and Akulov been pinged in their Tahoe and just Akulov targeted? No, that made no sense. Why just take one of them? Tate moved out of cover, peered through the door glass. He saw his own reflection caused by the moonlight, and realised the answer was looking him straight in the face. The snatch squad hadn't known there were two of them. The Resident was working for Vetrov. Tate thought back on their conversation, how the Resident had answered with long, rambling sentences – playing for time perhaps? And then when the Russians had appeared and seen a man in a vehicle, they had mistaken him for Tate. It made sense. Tate had pretended to be Akulov, and as they now had Akulov there was no reason to think that Tate existed.

Behind the Resident's cabin was a tall barn. In this type of place a motion detector would be constantly going off with the movement of the trees and the scourging of the local wildlife, which begged the question, why was one installed at the front of the Resident's property? Why was it so powerful? It seemed liked overkill. Tate made directly for the rear of the Resident's cabin. Across the dry grass his feet made no sound and left no trace, and then he stepped onto a concrete slab, the start of the patio, and another light snapped on. Tate hopped sideways into the shadow, and hid around the side of the cabin. Less than ten feet away he heard the sound of the back door open, and then the Resident came out onto the patio. He started muttering to himself. The man's phone rang and he answered it in Russian.

'I did exactly what you ordered me to do.' There was a pause and Tate heard the old man sigh. 'Now please, let me speak to my daughter.'

Tate moved out of hiding to see the Resident facing the barn. Without being seen he slipped into the cabin behind him and continued to listen from behind the open door.

'Have they hurt you?' The Resident's voice sounded softer but strained. There was a moment of silence, and then the man whimpered and ended the call. The Montana air became silent and then slow footsteps approached. The man shut the door and came face to face with Tate. His mouth fell open and he dropped his phone. It landed on the floor but was in a rubber case and bounced rather than broke.

'You looked surprised to see me,' Tate said flatly. The Resident didn't reply so Tate continued. 'They have your daughter, is that right?'

'Y ... yes they do.'

'Go back in the lounge, take a seat and tell me about it.'

The Resident shuffled into the lounge and retook the same seat he'd sat in earlier. 'Who are you?'

Tate remained standing. 'Who did you think I was?'

'Wolf 6.'

'And now?'

'I don't know. Perhaps this is a test? You are one of them sent to see if I'll talk?' Tears started to form in the older man's eyes and his shoulders slumped. 'Look, you have my daughter, what else do you want from me? Georgina is a sweet and intelligent girl with her whole life ahead of her.'

'How old is she?'

'Twenty-three.' The Resident puffed out his chest and raised his chin, a steely resolve appearing in his eyes he stood. 'If you have to kill someone, kill me. Take me and not her.'

'Sit down.'

'Make me!'

'Listen, Rambo, just sit down! I'm not Russian.' Tate switched back to English. 'I'm not American either. I'm here because four years ago Vetrov murdered my parents and two days ago he shot my brother.'

Frowning, the Resident sat. 'You are British?'

'Yes.'

'I see.' The Resident's eyes seemed now to be staring past Tate, seeing something else. The next word he said was the last Tate expected to hear: 'Camden.'

Tate sat, his legs leaden. All thoughts banished from his mind. 'My parents were murdered in the Camden bombing.'

'Then both my daughter and I are already dead.'

'Explain.' Tate's voice was terse.

The Resident sighed. 'I have been here for thirty years. I served the Soviet Union, and then Russia. I met a local woman, and we had a daughter. Her mother left me, and I was left with my daughter. She is gifted with computers. It is something that is beyond my comprehension but she can write code, defeat security measures, and yes she can manipulate images. It's what all the kids do with those face app things, but she wrote her own years before these existed. Living here with me she could not get a job. She has phobias, you understand? She gets distressed when anything changes, and she is scared of people. She became frustrated and then she lashed out, hacked the wrong people. The associates of those wrong people offered her a job.'

'Blackline?'

'*Da*. A man came to see me; I of course knew him by reputation, for even thirty years ago he had not escaped his own father's shadow. And he said there was a way that my daughter could escape mine – you see I was not supposed to have a child. This man's name was Maksim Oleniuk, the founder of Blackline.'

Anger flashed within Tate, and he wished it were possible to end Oleniuk's life a second time. 'So he offered her a job?'

'He did not offer, he ordered it be so. For five years my daughter has worked for his company, but for one year of that time she has been forced into hiding.'

Tate had a question: 'Where did she work?'

'Here. In my barn, which is not a barn.'

'And where does she work now?'

The Resident recited the address Bravo had given Miguel. Tate felt relief that the Giant had told the truth. The Resident continued, 'It is not far from here; it is where those men were taking the man they believed to be Wolf 6.'

'That was Wolf 6.'

The Resident's eyes narrowed. 'They have your friend, yet you are sitting here with me?'

'He's not my friend. He's an assassin. He killed two British diplomats. They were good men.'

'And who is not, in their own mind?'

'Tell me what you know about Camden?'

'My daughter was ordered to tamper with certain footage taken at the scene with an iPhone. This is the footage that was only given to the British authorities a year ago. It was to test out advances in her process.'

Tate was now finding it all but impossible to control his wrath. 'Oleniuk staged that bombing to assassinate my parents, and then later decided to also use it as an opportunity to test a new weapon?'

'Test is a good word. And that is what he did. He tested my daughter's process, her programming, her technology, and it passed. It was not detected. And it became a weapon.'

'And you know all this, how?'

'I spied on her. I am her father, and that is my job.'

Tate took a moment to calm himself. Then he said, 'You knew Vetrov was the real bomber?'

'I met him ten years ago when he came to check the cache. I had to hide my daughter of course. Then the next time I saw him was on that film.'

'Film?'

'On "the film".'

'When you saw the found footage on the news last year you knew it had been faked?'

'Of course, my daughter faked it. Something makes me believe that you already knew it was faked?'

Tate didn't answer the question. 'Did your daughter back up her work?'

'She made copies of everything, just in case …' His voice trailed off. 'Don't you see? She was forced to do this. If she hadn't done her best work, it would have been noticed and then both her and I would have been slaughtered.'

'Where are the copies?'

'I will give them to you for full immunity for my daughter and I, and safe passage.'

Tate took a deep, calming breath. He was not going down that route again. 'No. You give me the files and I will rescue your daughter. If you don't, I'll walk away and wait for my team to come, and they'll tear this place apart log by log until they find them. After that you'll get handed over to homeland security, and in the meantime your daughter will be either in Russia or dead. Your choice, Vlad.'

'My name is not Vladimir. My name is Yuri. What assurance can you give me that you will not kill me as soon as I hand over the files?'

'None.'

'You are not a good salesman.'

'I'm not selling.'

'OK, what choice do I have?'

Tate shrugged. 'None at all.'

'Thank you for your candour. Now listen to me. The men who

took Wolf 6 will be coming back to move the vehicle he crashed. This is a small community and a vehicle left by the side of the road will immediately be reported. They are going to place it in my barn.'

'When are they coming?'

'I would say within half an hour. Once they get back to their base of operations and then return with a tow truck.'

'They have one?'

'How do I know? But they can't call anyone, so they will do it themselves.'

A thought struck Tate, a question: 'Who lives in the other cabins?'

'No one now. Over the years, they were put up for sale and purchased by a Russian-owned shell company. We have the place completely to ourselves.'

'I need to see the copies of the files your daughter made.'

'I'll take you to them now. They are in the bunker.'

'With the weapons?'

'Yes, hidden under the noses of Blackline.' Yuri rose from his seat. 'Follow me.'

Tate let the Russian lead him to the back of the house and into the en-suite bathroom next to one of the bedrooms. Yuri got down on his hands and knees and used his shoulder to push the heavy-looking, freestanding bath out of the way. The plinth it was on moved too. Underneath there was a trapdoor. He pulled it up and automatically a light switched on, revealing a set of steps.

'Would you like to go first?'

'No.'

'Ha-ha, I understand.'

Yuri started to move down the steps. Tate let him reach the third then followed. He did not want to give the man the chance of raising an alarm or grabbing a weapon. It was still not decided in his mind if the Resident would rather let Tate help his daughter or just turn Tate in.

They reached the bottom. It was surprisingly high and Tate did not need to stoop. The subterranean space they had entered extended all the way under the barn. It was illuminated like a miniature aircraft hangar.

Yuri pointed at a bunch of boxes over to one side. 'Fortunately not everything has been taken by Vetrov's men. The older items have been overlooked.'

'How many men are there?'

'I do not know exactly. I have only ever seen four at a time. They have come here on several occasions during the course of this last year. Immediately after the EMP strike they came looking for electrical components. This bunker was well shielded from the EMP. The place they are holding my daughter is on the water. I own the place.'

'You own the site they're using?'

'I bought it to go fishing at the weekend. Its only ten miles from here. Secluded, waterfront, one road in and out.'

'Perfect for a Spetsnaz secret base?'

Yuri smiled. 'Yes, and now that is what it is being used for.'

'Any immediate neighbours?'

'No. Rexford has about fifty occupied houses, the rest are summer rentals or holiday homes. So I would expect some people are there now, drinking and being loud on the water. In Eureka you see, everyone knows you and your business; over there they are used to people coming and going especially if one is the daughter of the owner.'

Tate was puzzled. 'So your daughter is allowed out?'

'Not on her own.'

'Show me the files.'

Yuri walked to a packing crate in the corner. He prised it open, using his strong fingers to pull up loose nails, and removed part of the top. Inside were what looked like ammunition boxes for 7.62mm rounds. He carefully put two on the concrete floor then extracted a third. He handed it to Tate. 'Inside here is all you need. Some type of high-tech storage device. She told me off for calling it a floppy disc.'

'Thank you.'

Yuri nodded. 'You must understand that I have only ever served my country, but what they have forced my daughter and I to do serves no one but Blackline.'

Tate had no comment to make, so instead he said, 'Show me what type of firearms you have.'

Chapter 19

Rexford, Montana, USA

Akulov had an egg-sized lump on his forehead and wouldn't be winning any beauty competitions soon, but apart from that he was fine. No sooner had the Tahoe come to rest than Vetrov's men had dragged him out. There was nowhere to run or hide so he'd pretended to be hurt worse than he was and just let them manhandle him into their nearest vehicle. They'd punched him a few times to soften him up, squashed him into the rear footwell of the SUV, and driven away with their heavy feet pressing on him. Akulov lay there listening to the sound of the road, trying to work out which direction they were going and seeing if it tallied with the address they had.

The road they were travelling on was remarkably smooth but then the vehicle slowed to negotiate several turns before it came to a crunching halt. The barrel of a handgun was pushed into his cheek. He remained still, daring to move only his eyes.

'Get up slowly,' the man holding the gun said, in Russian. 'And then get out.'

Akulov unfolded himself, head throbbing. In a kidnap situation Akulov knew that the quicker the abductee escaped the better

285

their chance of survival became. But as he pulled himself up off the seat he felt his head start to hammer. He dragged himself out of the SUV and half stood, half leant against it. He didn't need to feign being disorientated. On the bright side, nothing was broken. He was bruised and cut, and otherwise still one hundred per cent operational apart from the throbbing in his head, which he knew was no way bad enough to be a concussion.

'Bring that inside,' a voice ordered.

In the pale light that spilled out of the cabin ahead, Akulov noted the men who had abducted him had not covered their faces, which was a bad sign. He knew what they looked like, and this had implications of its own. Two men, both larger than him and solid, grabbed him under the arms and half walked, half dragged him inside the house.

Akulov eyed the interior of the cabin. He saw an open-plan kitchen at one end with an island, a living room with large, soft seating and then three doors. One opened ahead of him and then the hands let go and he stumbled forward in the darkness. His legs hit something hard and cold and he tipped forward and fell onto a military-style cot.

He lay motionless for a while, one to keep up the pretence that his injury was more serious and two so that he could tune in with the sounds of the cabin. He sat up; the pain in his head had already lessened. He guessed Vetrov must have got to Montana already, and that meant he had someone with a plane. Akulov didn't really care how, it just mattered that the man was there. But where was Tate? Had they gone back for him, or did Vetrov's team not know that Tate was there?

Akulov stretched his upper body; his chest and shoulders were tight and his neck hurt. He felt as though he'd done more damage to himself than the car.

Akulov continued to listen to the sounds of the building around him. He heard water rushing nearby. He searched his memory and pictured the aerial photographs of the area. The

Tobacco River ran to the west of Eureka and there was another small town on the banks of that: Rexford.

The door opened and light flooded into the room. Three men entered, one holding a Beretta. He pointed it at him. The two other men grabbed his arms and frogmarched him out of the dark room, whilst the third followed several paces behind. They took him back through the main living area, and through the open patio doors. They pushed him out onto a terrace overlooking the river. There was a wooden table. At the table were two people: one was Vetrov the other was a young, dark-haired woman. Akulov was pushed into a chair.

The woman's eyes went wide as soon as she saw his face. Akulov ignored her; in fact he was hardly aware of her presence, as he finally locked eyes with Wolf 1 – Kirill Vetrov.

Akulov spoke. One word that summed up all he needed to know and all he had to ask. 'Why?'

Lundeen Road, Montana, USA

It was late, especially for a small town and especially for a back road in a small town, so the sound of the two engines drifting on the breeze told Tate to get ready. He stood stock-still in the trees and waited. The noise grew louder and he could now pick out the rumble of a V8 but also the throatier industrial snorting and grunting of a diesel engine.

Tate was in the treeline at the side of Lundeen Road. Yuri's place was behind him and the beached Tahoe was hidden behind the grass verge in the field in front. Courtesy of the cache, Tate was wearing a ballistic vest and armed with a brand-new twenty-year-old Makarov 9mm in a leg holster and an AK74SU, the short stock paratrooper edition of the modernised classic. Neither had been test fired or zeroed. This didn't worry Tate because the one thing the Russians did well was made things that went "bang".

Yellow headlights moved up the road. A couple of lengths behind these a pair of white, bright lights from an SUV followed, like a battleship following a pilot into port. The first vehicle was a dull blue tow truck that bore the livery of a garage. He didn't know if it was a local place but either way this could be problematic. Tate had to be certain that the men belonged to Vetrov and weren't just local tow guys on a job. The second vehicle growled past as the moon appeared from behind the clouds. It was a midnight blue Nissan Armada, large, powerful and empty apart from its driver. And this was good news for Tate.

He watched the truck manoeuvre so that its back was on the grass bank overlooking the beached black Tahoe. The driver jumped out, his solid frame and bushy beard fleetingly illuminated by the lights of the Nissan before they flicked off. The Armada's driver got out. Yuri had assured Tate there was once night vision equipment, but it had been taken by the Russians. This was both helpful and unhelpful to Tate at the same time. He would have liked to be wearing them now, but at least he knew the rest of Vetrov's men at their cabin had them.

The two men had torches and were doing their best to keep the beams pointed low and away from themselves. They were talking in whispers, the words urgent yet subdued. One man clambered up to operate the winch whilst the other went to affix the cable to the stricken Tahoe, but it was too dark for Tate to see any detail. Tate couldn't remember if he'd ticked the collision damage waiver on his insurance papers, but guessed now that it didn't matter. And then he heard a shout, and it was in Russian.

'Davai!' Go. One word with two syllables gave away their nationality, if not their identity.

Tate continued to watch as the winch started to whine. The truck jerked backwards and then the winch stopped. The man in the field reappeared and exchanged a few words. They both moved back to check on their work, vanishing from view.

This was Tate's chance to move. He came out of the woods and jogged towards the Nissan. He tried the rear door and found it open and darted inside. His luck held and he confirmed it was empty. He crawled over the back seats and into the cavernous boot.

He knew where they were taking the Tahoe, and he knew they'd be back. Tate heard the laboured growl of the tow truck as it moved forward and away from the grass. Yellow lights washed over the grey roof lining of the Armada as the truck turned. Once they had passed, Tate popped his head up and observed the Tahoe bounce back onto the road behind the truck. It was then unceremoniously dragged on its damaged suspension along the road, until the truck turned into the entrance of Yuri's place and both vehicles were lost from view.

Tate stayed stock-still. The boot of the Armada wasn't a bad place to be; at least it was dry and bug-free. After a while, he heard the truck start up again. Tate flattened himself to the floor, as he anticipated the Armada driver returning to the vehicle, his footfall lost on the tarmac.

Tate waited as the driver entered the car, started the engine and began to drive. The SUV picked up speed and then Tate rolled from his back onto his front. A sudden pain reminded him of his bruised sternum, and he decided he didn't want to be shot again. He slowly started to raise his head. He glimpsed over the gap between the headrests and confirmed that they were following the tow truck. Eventually the Armada came to a halt. Tate waited, in the boot, in the dark, the collapsible stock AK up and ready. A scratchy footfall, stones caught in the tread of a boot. Footsteps approached and then the passenger door opened and closed as the second man, the driver of the tow truck, entered the Armada. They moved off again.

'All OK?' the driver asked the passenger in Russian.

'Nothing to report,' the passenger replied.

'This is it then?'

'Like Vetrov ordered, we take care of our loose ends and we pull out in the morning.'

Vetrov. The name hit Tate like a punch to the throat. His mind drifted back to Simon and he felt his simmering anger start to boil. As he suspected, the man had somehow got here already and his team was planning to pull out. Tate realised that E Squadron would not be arriving on time; the cavalry would be late. It was down to him, every decision, life and death, everything. He had no time to observe, no time to plan. His only option was to use the element of surprise and attack. He'd hit hard and he'd hit quick.

The two men continued to talk in the front.

'This new place better have more action. If I'd wanted to only see men for weeks at a time, I'd have stayed with the 561st.'

In the darkness Tate's brow furrowed. That group was the GRU's Baltic Fleet Spetsnaz detachment, the unit Tate had attacked years ago in Ukraine. The same unit Oleniuk had been with when Tate had shot him for the first time. Tate didn't believe in coincidences; this was just further confirmation that Blackline were involved.

The passenger started to laugh. 'Maybe you should just screw George?'

'I have considered it many times, but she is afraid of her own shadow; seeing me naked will give her a heart attack.'

'It cannot be any worse than your face!'

Tate felt the Armada slow, make a wide turn and then the note of the engine changed a fraction as they started to encounter an incline. He consulted his mental map and assessed that they were now nearing Rexford. They'd pass Ponderosa Park, the larger houses of Rexford itself and then climb towards the narrower, more secluded tracks leading to the smaller cabins dotting the hillside. When they started to make sharp turns and descend steeply towards the river, he knew it would be time to introduce himself. He prepared, picturing exactly the order and direction of his movements. In his right pocket he had several sets of cable ties and in his left hand he held the Makarov. The AK was too big to wield, even in a large SUV.

And then the Armada slowed right down and made another turn. Tate knew from Yuri's explanation and from seeing satellite photographs that three more turns and a further fifty yards would get them to the cabin. Each turn was an almost switchback as the road lost height and dropped down the hill to the level of the river.

As the Nissan made the second turn, Tate pushed up over the back seats, then swung a huge, scything right elbow at and through the back of the passenger's head. The soldier jerked forward and then back, his head slumping sideways. Tate now pressed the barrel of the Russian pistol into the back of the driver's neck. 'Stop the car here and don't do anything stupid.'

The Armada juddered to a halt and the driver pushed the handbrake, and then moved the gearstick into neutral.

Tate reached into his pocket and dropped several cable ties over the man's shoulder. 'Tie your hands.'

The man's shoulders fell as he realised he wasn't getting out of this. And he obeyed.

'Now get out, slowly and lie on the ground.'

The driver hesitantly opened his door and Tate followed him out. Door lights illuminated the dry tarmac under their feet. Tate kept the Makarov trained on the driver until his face was touching the dirt. Tate peered inside the Armada and saw something that rang alarm bells in his head. A Beretta with a suppresser lay in the SUV's large door cubby. He reached for it, and his legs were swept out from under him.

Tate fell, half in and half out of the Nissan, his knees painfully hitting the road and his Makarov flying from his hand and landing with a thud somewhere unseen. The driver was on his feet. They made eye contact and in a sharp, practised move the man brought his hands down across his thighs and back. The cable ties snapped off. As Tate tried to move, a heavy boot made contact with his stomach with such force that it lifted him up and off the ground. Tate rolled back and away as the driver lurched forward, grabbing for the Beretta. He fired as Tate managed to scurry around the back of the Armada. The ping of the round hitting the road surface was lounder than the weapon's retort.

The driver followed Tate, thinking he had the upper hand. Feet scrabbling for grip, Tate moved further around the other side of the tall, wide SUV. Tate pulled the rear passenger door open in desperation just as the driver fired again. Tate then ducked through the interior, did the same with the front door, then threw himself to the right and into the undergrowth.

'There is nowhere to go!' the driver called and stepped around the side of the SUV, weapon raised, scanning for Tate.

From the bushes, Tate saw the man advance warily. His head jerked one way and then the next. On his stomach now, Tate knew there was no way he could overcome him. He started to slide backwards and then he felt his legs go light. He remembered the maps and the satellite photos and realised he was at the edge of the large bank. He started to slip backwards and then he fell. Arms flailing in front of him he dropped, down the bank, and through the trees. He slithered through the soil and then collapsed in a heap by the side of the road, the same road they had been on, but two bends further down, on the straight that led directly to the cabin. He shook his head and wiped mud and debris from his face. The Armada had to come this way if it was going to reach its base. Tate had no choice but to try and outrun it and hope that the Russian was still searching for him and that he didn't phone ahead. He jogged along the side of the road, each step taking him away from one gunman and potentially into the crosshairs of numerous others.

He heard the V8 start up, just as he caught sight of the cabin ahead. It was in darkness, save for a dim light that seemed to be seeping from a room at the back. Tate had no idea if there was any type of security in place by way of cameras or lights, but he had nowhere to run and was out of options. Staying to the very edge of the path, he made for another vehicle that was parked, its nose facing him: a black Ford Expedition. He hid behind it as the lights of the Armada rounded the bend.

The large Nissan came to a stop just feet away, and the driver climbed out and raced around the front of the vehicle to open the passenger door. He bent into the SUV and started to drag his injured colleague out. His back was turned and Tate was on his feet and running. He reached the driver's side and saw the Beretta once again lying in the cubby. This time he grabbed it, raised it and shot both men in the head, before they'd had a chance to react. The suppressed rounds sounded loud in the silence.

A light came on in the cabin. He saw two men hurrying to the door. A porch light came on and the door opened. Tate took a chance and shouted in his St Petersburg Russian, 'Quick help me! He's been shot!'

The two men didn't hesitate and jogged out of the house. Tate took a step left, concealed behind the Armada's open door and put a suppressed double tap into each man. They both fell, feet away from their comrades, their machine pistols rattling to the ground. Tate let himself drop into cover behind the Armada. He waited and when no further shouts came, he moved around to the other side of the SUV, and using the open passenger door and the two dead men for cover he advanced towards the two who had come from the house. He crouched down by the first, saw he was obviously dead and took his weapon. It was an HK MP5SD, a few years out of date now but still one of the best pieces of kit around and a weapon he was at ease with. He moved to the last man. His head was turning slowly from side to side as though he was watching a tennis match. Tate executed him.

'Our guest is highly ill-mannered, George.' Vetrov sneered.

George's voice was shaky. 'You're Ruslan Akulov, Wolf 6?'

'I am.' Akulov looked at the woman. She seemed edgy, nervous. 'You are George Eastman?'

George shuddered, and when she spoke her voice was little more than a whisper. 'I'm sorry. So, so sorry.'

'She has made you infamous, Wolf 6. The most feared Russian assassin of a generation shall forever be remembered as the terrorist who bombed a London market.'

'Is that why you did this? To take my legacy from me?'

'What else does a man have, but his name and what he leaves behind?'

'You couldn't bear the fact that I was better than you.'

'You were not!' Vetrov screamed.

Akulov said nothing.

Vetrov's eyes narrowed and his nostrils flared as he attempted to regain his cool. 'And so, Ruslan, you've come to kill me?'

'No.'

'And why should I believe that?' Vetrov stood, a pistol on a holster at his side. Vetrov drew it and pointed it at Akulov. He sensed the men behind him tense, but he remained still. 'You appear in Houston from nowhere, assassinate the head of a Mexican drug cartel and destroy my multimillion-dollar financing deal, just so, what, you can ask me why I framed you for a job that happened four years ago?'

'Yes.'

Vetrov shook his head. 'You are—'

There was a shout from the front of the house in Russian.

'Sir, shall we go?' the man behind Akulov asked.

'Go. Both of you. See what that fool wants.'

'Yes, sir.'

Vetrov looked back at Akulov and trained the Beretta on his head. 'Should I end this now, Wolf 6? Should I just kill you so I can cross another one of our twelve names out?'

'Is that what you want, to be the last Werewolf?'

'I do not want to be the last. I want to be the best!' Vetrov moved the gun away. 'I'm working on something large, something that would help reshape everything.'

'You were working to start a war?'

'To end wars! Don't you see? We can make people – politicians, generals and dictators – do and say what we want and when we want without being detected. We and only we can do this and that is total power. Think of the possibilities? This is what we were working on.'

'But then the money ran out?' Akulov said.

'Yes.' Vetrov looked down. 'Blackline lost all its funding and then our clients also refused to pay. But we have one last contract in play, one last attack that will start the restoration of our fortunes. Tomorrow morning, George will send the doctored footage to our Saudi client and tomorrow the sun will rise on a new war in the Middle East.'

HK up, Tate slipped and slid through the grass to the left of the cabin. No more men had appeared, which meant the others were waiting for him inside. Vetrov, George and Akulov were still unaccounted for. He slithered down a steep incline and found himself next to a veranda. Shouts came from inside and he recognised one of the two voices, Akulov. A man appeared on the veranda within touching distance of Tate. They both swung their identical HKs at each other and fired. Tate couldn't feel where he was hit but the force made him tumble down the side of the bank and into the water.

It was August but the chill of the Montana water took his breath away. Water filled his mouth and he slipped below the surface. But then his feet hit rocks and he kicked off, breaking the surface and gasping in air. Tate's HK was gone and so was a lot of his strength. His chest was on fire and his lungs felt constricted. But the ballistic vest had held. He knew he couldn't be seen from above; he was a black shape in black waters. He drifted past the house, saw a terrace above him, and a man with a gun pointing at Akulov. Tate let himself drift to the shore and found himself bobbing in between several boats.

There was more shouting outside in Russian. Vetrov frowned. His two men still hadn't returned. '*Dima*, Vadim!'

There was a banging of feet. Another man appeared, neither of the two he had called. His face was smeared with blood and he was holding his side. 'They're dead, they're all dead. But I got him. He fell in the water.'

Vetrov glared at Akulov and raised the Beretta. 'Wolf 6. Tell me, who is that outside?'

Akulov had nothing to lose. 'That's the man who came to kill you.'

George started to sob. Vetrov grabbed her by the arm and addressed the new man. 'Keep your eyes on him. If he moves, shoot him.'

'Yes, sir.'

Vetrov frogmarched George Eastman back into the house.

'He's deserted you,' Akulov said to the man guarding him. 'Walk away now and you can live.'

'I've got orders.'

'This isn't your war.'

'He's my boss. He pays me.'

'His money has run out.'

'What?'

'Listen to me.' Akulov slowly stood. 'He has lost it all. He cannot pay you.'

The Russian snorted. 'We are Blackline!'

'I was Blackline, last year with the EMP.'

'You know about that?'

'I was in Maine and then I was in Washington.'

'I was here,' the man said. 'We did nothing and saw nothing. We were babysitting.'

'I was with Maksim Oleniuk in Washington. Where was Vetrov?'

'I don't know.'

'So he was not with his men?'

The man looked down. 'No he wasn't I—'

Akulov shot forwards, grabbed the gun, turned his shoulder and twisted, throwing Vetrov's man to the floor. He held the gun on him then shot him in the leg. 'Do not run away.'

Akulov rushed into the house as the soldier lay on the decking writhing in pain. The house was quiet, empty, the only sound a metallic banging from below. Akulov saw steps leading down and took them. A door at the bottom was open and banging against its metal lock. He burst through the door to find himself out in the open, beside a jetty. Vetrov and George were at the other end.

The two Werewolves faced each other. Vetrov held George in front of himself like a shield. Akulov's anger rose again. The man was not fit to be a Werewolf and never had been. Each held a Beretta trained on the other.

'Let George go,' Akulov said. 'And I'll let you go.'

'Put down your gun, Wolf 6, and you can walk away.'

'You've lost everything; why lose your life too? I cannot let you take her.'

'You won't stop me. If George dies, the deep fake program dies with her; it is in her head!' He sneered. 'Now I understand. It's your code. You won't kill a Werewolf, not even me.'

'Let her go.'

Vetrov's Beretta started to move up, towards George's head.

Akulov dropped his Beretta.

In the light cast by the house, Akulov saw Vetrov sneer again ... and then a shape rose like a demon out of the water from behind Vetrov, and violently grabbed his legs. Vetrov fell sideways into the water and George fell onto the wooden decking of the jetty.

Tate stood up in the knee-high water, holding Vetrov by the collar with his left hand and punched him in the face with his right. Vetrov stumbled backwards and Tate dived on top of him. In the shallows, Vetrov's back slammed against the pebbles on the bottom as Tate pummelled his face with his fists. Vetrov tried to defend himself and managed to buck and push Tate sideways. He grabbed a rock and tried to slam it against Tate's head, but Tate brought his shoulders up and twisted away. Tate rose to his feet, but the Russian twisted his foot and Tate crashed to the ground. Winded, Tate felt himself drifting into the deeper water, his chest aching, the water getting colder and sucking away the pain. He realised it was actually stealing his strength.

With a monumental effort, his ballistic vest now weighing a ton, Tate stood and waded back towards the Russian who was stumbling onto the shore just past the jetty.

'Vetrov!' Tate yelled, finger pointing.

The Russian slowly turned to face him but backed away onto dry land.

Tate continued to move forward. They squared off on the sand.

'What do you want from me?' Vetrov asked.

'Everything,' Tate replied.

'Who are you?'

'You murdered my parents in Camden, you shot my brother in Houston and now I'm here to finish you.'

Vetrov smiled.

Tate lunged forward, the jacket making him slow. Vetrov stepped aside and swung a fist at Tate's head. Tate blocked it and moved into the arm and drove it down. Vetrov fell to his knees and Tate delivered a straight kick to his head. Vetrov sprawled backwards against the sand. Tate took a step back, panting, and undid the ballistic vest. He slid out of it, immediately feeling lighter but wincing at the hot needles of pain that enveloped his lungs. He staggered. Vetrov sprang at him, his shoulder striking him in the stomach and driving him back to the ground. Tate tasted blood. Vetrov straddled him and launched several quick blows to his head and face. Tate got his arms up, but the second and third blow got through. Tate's vision started to grey out and his arms began to fall away from his face. Vetrov drew back his fist for one last, huge, killing blow.

As if in slow motion Tate saw the fist moving towards him, in and out of focus. He jerked his head to the side and the fist hit nothing but sand. Tate's left elbow jerked upwards and struck the side of Vetrov's head. The Russian wobbled. Tate now struck with his right elbow. The Russian's jaw cracked. Tate pushed away from Vetrov and got to his hands and knees as the Russian fell face down into the sand. Tate rested for a few second and then got to his feet, grabbed the Russian by the collar and dragged him towards the water.

'Jack! Jack, it's over!'

Tate paused to look up at Akulov standing on the jetty above and shook his head slowly. Then he carried on towards the water. He waded out until the water was above his knees and pushed Vetrov's head below the surface. The Russian came round and frantically tried to fight back. But Tate's hands tightened around the man's neck. The struggling began to slow as his limbs weakened. After a few moments, the water grew still again. Tate rolled him over and watched Vetrov's eyes become lifeless, as he killed him with his bare hands.

Epilogue

Three months later

Vauxhall Cross, London, UK

The room was cramped for two people and too warm, but Plato didn't mind at all. He watched, enthralled by George as she again went through her latest piece of code. Plato munched on a fig roll and nodded. For the last three months George and Plato had been engaged in what could only be described as a "code battle". George would create a new algorithm and Plato would then interrogate it with one of his own. It was an ongoing process of both improving her deep fake creation and strengthening Plato's programs designed to spot it. Each day she spent six hours with him, before being taken back to a classified SIS facility.

Plato knew it was immature, unprofessional, but he felt like this had been the best three months of his life. He found himself thinking about her when they weren't together and gazing at her when they were. It was irrational, but it was both her work and her that he had fallen for. Plato knew, however, that whatever he felt for George had to remain locked up, like she was when they weren't together.

'Do you have any more fig rolls?' she asked.

'Right.' Plato got to his feet, and half stumbled across the room to grab another packet. He was still clumsy around George but at least he was no longer tongue-tied. In fact, he realised, George was the only woman he'd ever really been able to talk to.

There was a knock at the door. Plato saw George flinch, like she always did. 'Come in.'

'Hi, Neill, George.'

'Hello,' George said, tersely.

Plato's smile widened when he saw both Jack Tate and Simon Hunter standing outside. 'How are you?' he asked.

'Fine thanks, just a little tired.'

'I think he was talking to me, Jack,' Hunter said. 'Better each day, Neill, thanks.'

'Good. What can I do you for?' Plato asked.

'Have you got anything new on Akulov?'

'Sorry, Simon. Nothing. It's as though he's completely disappeared off the face of the earth.'

'I see. Please keep looking. We need to find him.'

'Will do.'

The doors of the lift closed. 'Why on earth did you let the bastard go?'

Tate cut his brother a look but made no reply as they rode the lift down to the ground floor of Vauxhall Cross. This was not the time and certainly not the place for Simon to accuse him of anything.

'He should be in prison or six feet under,' Hunter continued.

'We've been through this.'

'And we bloody well will again, Jack.'

It was a touchy subject for both men. Tate had looked the other way whilst Akulov had simply taken the Armada and driven into Canada. Hunter was incredulous that the man

301

responsible for the assassination of two British diplomats was at large. Tate knew it was wrong, that his actions went against everything he stood for, but the man had saved his life. Letting Ruslan Akulov go had felt like the right thing to do then, and it still did now.

'How do you really feel?' Tate asked.

'Er normal, oh wait. Let me think.'

Tate placed his hand on his brother's shoulder. 'Go on. You can tell me, Simon.'

'I feel exactly like someone who was shot in the head three months ago.'

It had taken a week and a half for the doctor to be happy enough to bring Hunter out of the medically induced coma, and then another three and half before he was released to home care. Now all outward signs of the injury had vanished, but Tate still worried that Hunter was not yet himself. He seemed a little blunter and a little more irritable, whilst Hunter, he knew, was fed up with being asked how he felt.

They reached the ground floor, scanned their passes to leave and exited onto the street. Both put on dark sunglasses. Hunter's were on medical advice whilst Tate wasn't a fan of squinting.

'Do the Americans know yet? About George and her technology?' Hunter asked. He'd been out of the loop and today was his first visit back to SIS headquarters.

'No,' Tate confirmed.

The deep fake attack the Saudis had ordered on the emir of their neighbouring Gulf State had not gone ahead. According to Plato the video footage was more than faultless. George had also confessed to creating a second piece of footage that showed a perfect deep fake of His Royal Highness Faisal bin Salam Al Nayef ordering the attack and then ranting against the US President. If either of these pieces had been released, a rift would have been created that could have taken perhaps a generation or more to mend. In terms of geopolitics George

Eastman's deep fake program was the equivalent of a nuclear bomb, and Tate was happy that he had stopped it. He just wished the technology had been lost and not taken by the Secret Intelligence Service because he could never trust a video ever again.

A car pulled up in front of them. Both men got in and it pulled away from the kerb.

'Where are we going?' Hunter asked.

'A trip down memory lane.'

'Where?'

'We're going somewhere to have a drink in your honour.'

Hunter sighed. 'You know I can't stomach surprises.'

Tate tapped his nose and went silent for the remainder of the journey across central London, whilst Hunter scrolled through his mountain of emails on his reactivated work iPhone and muttered mild obscenities.

The car slowed, and Tate looked around. 'We're here.'

Tate got out of one side and Hunter got out of the other. Hunter looked at the street sign on the wall in front of them: Pratt Street, NW1.

'You chose this place because of the name, didn't you?' Hunter said.

'What's so funny about "Tony's"?' Tate said, with a straight face, pointing at the name of the café next to the street sign.

'I meant the name of the street, you pratt!'

'How dare you. I'm outraged!'

Hunter smirked and sat at an empty table outside the restaurant. 'Buy me a coffee then.'

It was autumn but the sun was out and the sky was blue, and Tate felt good. They waited to be served. Tate sighed and looked around. 'Did you ever think we'd be doing this, Simon?'

Hunter was confused. 'Doing what?'

'The pair of us – you and me – sitting on steel chairs and luxuriating in Pratt Street, Camden?'

'Yeah, that's exactly what I told the careers adviser at school I wanted to do when I grew up.' Hunter smiled. 'You know it's good to be back.'

'I hear you, brutha!'

Halifax, Nova Scotia

Ruslan Akulov pulled up at the address he had been given by the priest at the local church. It was the same church the man had worshipped at and the same place where a stone had now been laid to remember him when all hope of his return had finally dried up.

The Canadian, Kevin Belanger, now existed in memory only, his sun-bleached remains long forgotten in the rubble of a compound in Syria.

Akulov stepped out of the car he had rented with a new fake identity. As he walked up the path to the front door of the neat-looking, granite-fronted house in Fergusons Cove he knew he had to be Ruslan Akulov. He knew he had to tell Pat and Jane Belanger what had happened to their son and he knew he had to beg for their forgiveness.

Gulls whirled overhead and shrieked like avenging angels warning those inside that evil was approaching, and deep down Akulov knew this was true. Speaking with Belanger's parents would not bring him any peace or redemption, but he sincerely hoped it would help them. Their son was dead and he could have prevented that from happening. Whether they decided to report him to the Canadian authorities or whatever they wanted to do, his fate was in their hands. The course of action they chose was acceptable to him. Ruslan Akulov was tired of running away.

***

If you loved *Total Blackout*, don't miss the new blockbuster thriller from Alex Shaw!

TRAITORS

You never know who you can trust ...

A traitor who can't be caught.

French Intelligence officer Sophie Racine is tasked with travelling into the heart of a warzone in Ukraine. Her mission is to assassinate Sasha Vasilev, a Russian mole who took the French secret service apart piece by piece and gave their secrets to the Kremlin.

A prisoner who can't be killed.

Ex-SAS trooper and MI6 Officer Aidan Snow is also in Ukraine. Sent by British Intelligence, he must extract Mohammed Iqbal, an innocent citizen caught up in the conflict in rebel-controlled Donetsk.

A war that can't be won.

As Snow and Racine find themselves drawn deeper into the crisis, their missions collide with devastating consequences. Outgunned and outnumbered, their only hope is to fight their way through and out of Donetsk before Russia closes its new iron curtain.

Perfect for fans of Chris Ryan, James Deegan and Vince Flynn, this is an explosive action thriller you won't be able to put down.

Acknowledgements

Writing is often a solitary process, which is why I am so grateful to those around me who have by turns inspired and supported my journey.

My biggest inspiration has been my wife Galia, for without her I would not have been able to carry on. I'd also be unable to write without my two sons, Alexander and Jonathan, and writing something that they one day will read and hopefully enjoy spurs me on.

I need to thank my editor at HQ, Finn Cotton, and my agents, Justin Nash and Kate Nash, for believing in my work and wanting to champion me and publish it.

I'd like to thank my friends both inside and outside of the book world for putting up with me rabbiting on about my next book, my next idea, and for being vocal supporters. This is a long list but includes: Neill J Furr, Liam Saville, Paul Page, Chris Salter, Steph Edger, Paul Grzegorzek, Alan McDermott, Charlie Flowers, Jacky Gramosi Collins, Louise Mangos, Rachel Amphlett and Karen Campbell.

Lastly I must thank you, the reader; if it were not for you I'd simply be talking to myself!

Dear Reader,

We hope you enjoyed reading this book. If you did, we'd be so appreciative if you left a review. It really helps us and the author to bring more books like this to you.

Here at HQ Digital we are dedicated to publishing fiction that will keep you turning the pages into the early hours. Don't want to miss a thing? To find out more about our books, promotions, discover exclusive content and enter competitions you can keep in touch in the following ways:

JOIN OUR COMMUNITY:
Sign up to our new email newsletter: hyperurl.co/hqnewsletter
Read our new blog www.hqstories.co.uk
: https://twitter.com/HQStories
: www.facebook.com/HQStories

BUDDING WRITER?
We're also looking for authors to join the HQ Digital family!
Find out more here:
https://www.hqstories.co.uk/want-to-write-for-us/
Thanks for reading, from the HQ Digital team

ONE PLACE. MANY STORIES

If you enjoyed *Total Fallout*,
then why not try another gripping
thriller from HQ Digital?